'A haunting illustration of how, at th[e] _____
normal life became impossible for m[any] _____
Kashmir home . . . Waheed's talent lies _____
detail he brings to descriptions of everyday liv[es] _____
meshing of domestic intimacy with political events is done
deftly, with integrity. Like his great-grandfather's gold painting,
Waheed's work will undoubtedly endure'

FINANCIAL TIMES

—

'A harrowing tale of love in a time of conflict and change . . . The
language in this book is lyrical, indeed at times it seems to be poetry
masquerading as prose. *The Book of Gold Leaves* is the sort of
book one can read and re-read – and then read again'

NEWS ON SUNDAY

—

'A romance set against the backdrop of unrest in the Kashmiri
valley in the 1990s, Waheed's second novel explores the reasons
behind young men taking to bloodshed'

SCROLL INDIA, 'BOOKS OF THE YEAR'

—

'What keeps you reading is the story. Waheed relies on family
dynamics to drive the action . . . it's ultimately how the novel
accounts for the moral toll of war'

SUNDAY TELEGRAPH

—

'Poetic and political with a warm sensuousness. As beautifully written
as the paintings on papier mâché that one of its central characters
executes, this love story leaves the reader both wretched and transformed'

HINDUSTAN TIMES, 'BOOKS OF THE YEAR'

—

'Like the gold leaves of the book's title, Waheed's prose is like
pixie dust, sprinkled all over a city of heartbreak and despair. It is a
city that has found in Waheed, the great-grandson of a much-admired
pap[ier] _____ [s]veep'

BOROUGH OF POOLE

551074490 Z

Mirza Waheed was born and brought up in Kashmir. His debut novel, *The Collaborator*, was an international bestseller, a finalist for the *Guardian* First Book Award and the Shakti Bhatt Prize, and longlisted for the Desmond Elliott Prize. His latest novel, *The Book of Gold Leaves*, was published in 2014 to critical acclaim, and longlisted for the 2015 Folio Prize.

The Book of Gold Leaves

MIRZA WAHEED

PENGUIN BOOKS

PENGUIN BOOKS

UK | USA | Canada | Ireland | Australia
India | New Zealand | South Africa

Penguin Books is part of the Penguin Random House group of companies
whose addresses can be found at global.penguinrandomhouse.com.

First published by Viking 2014
Published in Penguin Books 2015

001

Copyright © Mirza Waheed, 2014

The moral right of the author has been asserted

Set in 10.8/13.18 pt Dante MT Std
Typeset by Jouve (UK), Milton Keynes
Printed in Great Britain by Clays Ltd, St Ives plc

A CIP catalogue record for this book is available from the British Library

ISBN: 978-0-241-97082-9

www.greenpenguin.co.uk

To Mirza Nisar Ali (Chacha) who gave me
my comics, books, politics and dreams

When I witness ups and downs, banks and demarcations,
I lose my temper
I seek oneness and equality, for that
I run and foam and fret;
Hence is it that, water though I am,
I have fallen on the burning coals of the mulberry-woods.

Abdul Ahad Azad

We know their dream; enough
To know they dreamed and are dead;
And what if excess of love
Bewildered them till they died?

. . .

Wherever green is worn,
Are changed, changed utterly:
A terrible beauty is born.

'Easter, 1916', W. B. Yeats

PART ONE

Shadows by the River

Faiz

The light-bulb in the room is of low voltage. A pale, sad light – they cannot afford high-voltage lamps for each of the eighteen rooms – is, has been for more than a year, his sole companion as he paints deer, lions, cypresses, tall rose bushes, chinar leaves, Mughal princes on hunting trips with their high elephants, on the pencil boxes that Mustafa Peer, the handicrafts middleman, wants finished and delivered in a month. Five hundred boxes in thirty days. Eight rupees per piece. The slender boxes will go to a buyer in Delhi who will then ship them to an art & crafts dealer in Calgary in Canada, 9.99 dollars apiece at Christmas. Faiz, smoking his Four Square tens in halves, melts his fingers into each figure. He could simply buy his own lamps but he has come to love this peculiar pastel glow. Also, he does not want his to be the only room with bright light.

Faiz shares what his little sister Farhat calls the financial burden of this large family – three sisters, three brothers, eldest brother Mir Zafar Ali's wife and three children, all of whom are older than Faiz, and his mother, Mouj – through his handicrafts work, and on most days, derives satisfaction and meaning from this role. He was never really forced into it: various attempts to keep him at school failed, as he preferred to run to the nearby swamp of Dembh to play marbles, which soon turned to card games, and then to only slightly serious gambling. He was good at it, and often used the winnings to watch Bombay sagas at the Shiraz Cinema in Khanyar, walking distance from their home in Khanqah where they have always lived, since the beginning, from the time their ancestors the Shahmiris, it is said, owned exactly forty-four houses in the area but lost them gradually by paying for weddings of poor girls. Such was the dread that the government middle school filled in a young Faiz, its building, its dark classrooms, its memorably coarse jute mat, and its oppressive teachers, that at least on three occasions he buried his books in the marshy soil of Dembh, each time claiming he had lost his schoolbag while playing cricket after school. Mir Zafar Ali, silenced by the grief it caused him to see his father's wish that the youngest of the brothers get the highest education, and his own dreams – he had, after all, named Faiz after the great Pakistani revolutionary poet Faiz Ahmed Faiz – buried in the swamp, emerged heartbroken and quietly angry after a week's consternation in the house. It is often said in the neighbourhood that the older brother, the sole breadwinner at the time, had no choice but to send Faiz to the Gulfarosh Handicrafts Workshop, owned and run by the legendary papier-mâché artist and venerated orator of elegies, Sadat Beigh Shirazi. Yes, the same master-craftsman whose art adorns the ceilings of all the major shrines and some of the oldest houses of Kashmir, whose three-letter signature no one could copy even as they copied his art, and whose masterpiece, a flower vase that he'd spent seven years painting with 22-carat gold dust, had so charmed the houseboat-loving American diplomat J. K. Galbraith that he had insisted Shirazi come to America as a guest of the State Department and paint a wall in the Oval Office. What Shirazi had said in response is still a matter of pride for all papier-mâché artisans of the Valley. 'Respected sir, I warm my paint over the little coals of a kangri. You won't be able to keep or afford one in your White House.'

In a more generous version of the story behind Faiz's difficult and short-lived education, it is said that Mir Zafar recognized the artistic talent of his youngest brother quite early and did the right thing by not forcing the boy to go to school, so that he could hone his talent and start making a living as an artist soon, rather than wait for ever for a lowly government job. Zafar Saéb has never spoken about the matter, so we do not know what really happened.

What we do know is that a year after Faiz had started at Gulfarosh Handicrafts, Mir Zafar Ali took a substantial loan from Shirazi against Faiz's future output as a papier-mâché artist.

Faiz spent ten years at the workshop, graduating from an apprentice to junior master and, eventually, the lead artist among Shirazi's disciples – and, it must be noted, the fastest hand in the land. Faiz can unleash a thousand nightingales from his brush in a single night of work. And yet he has never thought of himself as a bonded painter-slave.

His gaze fixed on the orange and green paint on his nails, Faiz thinks of freedom today. Of air.

When he was ten, he used to go to the ghat for daily swims, lancing through the quick brown waters of the Jhelum to be among the first to emerge at the opposite bank. (He always swam alone, away from the row of racing boys.) Before going home, he would dry himself on the riverside balcony of the Shrine by the ghat. He would make sure he entered through the tall deodar gates at dusk, so that he did not invite too much notice. Mir Zafar, of course, always knew and would often find himself torn between allowing his little brother his playtime and disciplining the boy's reckless spirit.

Faiz's mother, bent under her day-long work in the house, among them cooking for twelve mouths, would often set aside, and sometimes still does, a large bowl of rice and red beans – and the biggest piece of meat on Saturdays – for her son's never-satisfied appetite.

But never before in her forty years of running the Mir kitchen has she faced such paucity of means as now. Seeing her youngest bring home money fills her with pride but also with a vague sense of regret. When she had come into the Mir household as a sixteen-year-old bride, second wife to the grand Mir Mohammed Ali, the sole heir to the house and its riches, both material and spiritual, and fabled artist-trader of Shahtoosh paisleys and fine silk saris, she had, for obvious reasons, taken for granted a lifetime of affluence. Now, in her grey years, she spends most of her time in a kitchen where the only sign of affluence is the enormous vault of copper- and silverware that is opened on festivals or if the Mirs have a revered moulana over to recite from the Qur'ān.

The house still presents a stately aspect, especially on full-moon nights and during the first ten days of Muharram, and the older neighbours still send an emissary before visiting. The Mirs of Khanqah are known throughout Downtown, and young men in the neighbourhood still fall silent when Mir Zafar, or a woman from the house, walks by.

Faiz scratches the paint from his nails, not all of it, though, as he sometimes feels different, less himself, if he does not see his hands flecked with the colours he has worked with during the day, and tries to decide whether he should go to the mosque or to the shrine first. He turns on the radio to listen to All India Radio's Urdu Service, which plays the best music for evenings such as these, the finest ghazals he can find on any radio station. He turns to his creations, the floor full of them, finished, semi-finished and just-begun pieces spread all around him. The half-done pencil boxes present hills and jungles in formation, and animals in chase with no quarry in sight. A tiger sparkles golden here, and a deer cranes its neck against the blue of the sky. A lion reclines, its eyes red with passion, and the end of its tail a fine blond goblet, Faiz's signature style and a would-be master's sign, Rangrez the old paint-seller says. Only one box is fully finished and varnished. Faiz did it at the beginning as a sample for Peer, who wants all the boxes to look exactly like this one. That is always the specification, Faiz knows, and that is why he always keeps the master artifact in front of him, but he can never quite bring himself to produce exact replicas, even though he is capable of it. He will always add a little something to each piece, a tiny nightingale that peeks out of a corner bush, a gazelle darting across a border, a kingfisher's reflection in a turquoise pool, a Persian couplet intertwined with a forest vine. The only time he does not do it is

6

when, towards the end of a job, he starts to worry he has been away too long from his secret personal work-in-progress, *Falaknuma*, the biggest canvas he has ever embarked upon, his life's work.

His eyes stop on a small screen he had finished just before the pencil boxes arrived. It's a copy of the painting Mustafa Peer had allowed him to trace with pencil in his presence, taking the original back with him when Faiz was done. In the centre of the screen, the Persian poet Omar Khayyám, leaning against ornate cushions on a narrow boat, is holding a papier-mâché cup into which a woman with the most beautiful hair Faiz has ever seen is pouring wine from a long, curved flask. The flow of the wine, by design it seems, reflects the woman's tresses. The river the boat is floating along – there is no boatman – is a pale blue, revealing dark weeds, water plants and golden fish. Tall grasses grow on either side of the river and the world outside is not visible except for the blue-black sky that has no moon but a multitude of stars. Faiz remembers painting each of them with great care, washing his brush for every new star.

He turns back to the centre of the screen and remembers the cup. Was the painting on the cup a miniature replica of the main painting – Khayyám is again holding a cup as the woman with the dark hair pours wine into it – in the original too?

The evening is beginning to slip into night. Faiz switches off the radio and heads out.

Roohi

Roohi is prostrate before her God. Caressing the aged velvet of the prayer mat with her forehead, eyes, and finally her lips, she begs Khoda Saéb to make her one wish come true, for the boy of her dreams to come and take her away. Roohi wants a love story.

In the dream, which she has at night and during the day, she sees him sitting in the courtyard of the shrine opposite her house. From her balcony room every day, she prays to the shrine's golden spire, which looks as if it is adorned with the hoops of a huge earring. After the evening namaz, as dusk gathers over the fourteenth-century building, her eyes search the stone-paved courtyard, then gaze at the smoky skies over her city.

Even when she wakes up at night and considers her recurring dream, her eyes often turn in the direction of the shrine. The thought of being in the kitchen in the morning, listening to Mummy's orders and the little gibes about the shameful way she displays her looks, only briefly muzzled by the listeners'-choice programme on the kitchen radio, fills her with rage. I am not like that.

At school, too, it was the same story. You are so pretty, you are so lucky, you are so different, everyone looks at you. You must really like to be with the boys . . .

Roohi has certainly always been aware of the effect she has on boys or, for that matter, on anyone who happens to see her in the street. Old men, mothers with children in tow, street vendors often found scratching their groins or backsides, gangs of cheeky urchins, students from the prestigious Gandhi College, potbellied beat policemen in their curry-stained uniforms – or lately, the leering moustachioed soldiers manning the sixteen bunkers on the road from home to her former school – and, of course, those indisputable kings and queens of the street, the cross-dressing matchmakers of Srinagar, famous especially in Downtown, who too often allow themselves the licence of a public remark, and promise her a luxurious life as the wife of a 'prince', whom they are bound to find for her. Roohi has never minded the attention, but . . . she is not like that. She lived in her own world, in the dreams she saw and recreated in her room on the top floor.

In the autumn of that year, when the stunted chinars in the courtyard of the shrine once again defied the Shrine Board's pruning men with a flaming chiaroscuro, Roohi turned twenty. She began to pray longer, harder, in a tone so tender that it would surely move her Khoda Saëb to fulfil what she has desired for so long, as though wishing with fresh pain would deliver her saviour out of the ether.

Roohi's departure from the Women's College – no, not *the* Women's College of Red Square, that famed vanguard of girls' education in her land, but the modest Women's College of Downtown – followed by two quiet years at the local university, was perhaps the main catalyst for her restlessness. 'MA is more than enough for you,' it was said and repeated over the next few weeks, until one day she said to herself: So be it. I can read what I want to.

She now spends her days doing housework, mostly to keep her mother happy, and thinking about her life and place in the world. She makes sure she wakes up soon after Mummy does, tries to do everything she can to help in the kitchen, takes a nap in the afternoon, like everyone else does in this congested heart of Srinagar, listens to the radio from three to four every day, reads whatever she can find – *Shama*, *Filmfare*, the *Daily Aftab* and photocopies of Akhtar Mohiuddin's stories, this last being her favourite bedtime reading – whenever she can find the time to slip into her room, then starts the evening shift in the kitchen. This way, Roohi believes, Mummy will remain calm, if not entirely happy about her only daughter's unwavering refusal to entertain any talk of marriage.

On the day after her birthday, Roohi finds herself looking at the little mountain of greens she has just chopped and cleaned, and wondering what her twenty-first year will bring, when her mother enters the kitchen.

'Naseem is coming tomorrow. She will have lunch here – let's just cook enough now . . . Is it done? And where's your father? He went to buy meat soon after lunch. He must be at it again, discussing politics with his useless friends, as if the resolution of Masla-e-Kashmir solely depends on this idle lot's roadside gossip.'

'Mummy, he did say he might take time as he has to go to the DC's office to enquire about that part-time job. You have already forgotten, haven't you?'

'And how long should that take? It's not as if he's meeting the DC himself, or are they making him the deputy commissioner?'

Roohi stays silent, gently nudging the wicker basket full of greens towards her mother.

'I don't know if this is enough. Is God going to reveal to me how much meat he is going to bring home? But who listens to me?'

Roohi brings down the pressure cooker from the top shelf, gives it a quick wash, places it by the side of the Superflame gas stove, and in her mind calls out to her father. Papa. It has worked on occasion, enough to keep Roohi's faith in the system. But today there's no indication that her father is listening. And Papa, much-loved man of gossip in the neighbourhood – in fact the centre of most shop-front conclaves in his mohalla – is indeed going over the intricacies of Delhi's decision to appoint a loyalist politician as India's minister of home affairs. While Nabbè Galdar, the oldest and richest shopkeeper in the area, believes nothing will come of it, Ali Clay Pujj, the toothless butcher, suspects it's a deep 'internal' conspiracy to hoodwink the 'Unity Nations' into thinking people have been given power. 'If only our own hens weren't so vile . . .' he laments, while chopping yesterday's lamb shank for Kabir Ahmed Khan, Roohi's papa. Ali Clay slips in enough bone to make 800 grams of meat weigh a full kilo. No one ever objects to this.

The crows, the night-vigil keepers of the Great Sufi's seat, have surrounded the shrine. It is what they do at dusk, when they know the humans have left and it is theirs again. They are everywhere, on the roof, in the balconies, on the timber verandas that have for ages been the seats of both venerable saints and venal caretakers, on the large weathered cobblestone platforms and the pavements, in the water tank meant for the ablutions, on the austere marble cupola that presides over the entry gates as if it were a worshipper's skullcap, by the side of the wrought-iron donation boxes, and a strong few have occupied the bronze and gold spire that completes the sacred building. God's own earring adorned with black petals.

The light that accumulates amid this bird festival, this Kaawē-yeniwol, is a darkening orange, the river sending up its brown lustre too, and the few devotees that remain in the courtyard watch this magic gathering in absolute silence. Roohi watches it too, as she does every evening, even if only for a few stolen minutes, then goes back to her rituals in that smoky kitchen. As she leaves her room today, a dark figure, dressed in a pheran, his face dimly lit by the cigarette he's just put to his lips, quietly finds his place by the central chinar tree, amid the crows.

The Kitchen

In the kitchen-cum-dining room downstairs, dinner is nearly finished. Faiz sits down silently by Mir Zafar Ali who shifts to allow his hardworking brother more room. Mother has covered Faiz's heaped plate of rice and the bowl of today's dish – radish and greens – with the spare end of the floor covering. There is also yogurt for everyone in the large copper bowl. Faiz stands up to go to the sink to wash his hands. Mir Zafar eyes him briefly. Sajad, Mir Zafar's elder son, balding, and the man with the biggest paunch in the Mir household, owing to his sedentary lifestyle both in and outside the house, switches on the TV and sits back, waiting for a second helping.

'You just can't do without it, can you? How many times do I have to say this? No TV when we eat, and there's nothing meaningful on it anyway. But, oh, no, you must be missing *Chitrahar*. I am so sorry. It is, of course, extremely important for you while you eat. After all, where else can you find these half-naked women dancing their vulgar dances, and how can you digest your food without taking a proper look?'

'Abba, please, these are just songs. Everyone watches them – why must we alone be made to suffer? I'm not dancing with them, am I? I'm just watching.'

'Oh, shall I get someone to teach you how to dance, then, son? That's what Raghunath Koul's daughter apparently does, doesn't she? Why don't we just send you to her? But, no, she can't teach you *this* stuff, she only does Bharatnatyam et cetera, classic dance. You wouldn't know.'

'Why can't we ever eat in peace, Abba? It's just TV – you bought it for us, remember? And it's classical dance, by the way.'

'Yes, I bought it so that I could watch the news and some

Pakistani dramas, not this insane tamasha. Look at Faiz, he never watches all this. You should learn something from him.'

Faiz's reverie is broken. Thankfully, he hears the last part and since this conversation is almost de rigueur at dinnertime, he knows what to say before Sajad can clap and scream, 'He does, he does, just not when you're around.'

'I like cricket. I'm glad it doesn't come at this time, otherwise Sajad and I might have fights over it.' Faiz wants the conversation to end, or shift, so he can have a brief chat with Mir Zafar Ali about his painting. All he wants is one day a week devoted exclusively to it, and he wants his big brother's blessings.

He grabs his chance as Mir Zafar Ali wipes his hands with his old towel and leaves the kitchen for his after-dinner smoke. Faiz prepares the chillum for him, filling it with a thick ring of tobacco first, then chiselling a fine pit in the centre for the coals. Lighting the coals with his own matches, he begins his pitch.

'In my last week at Gulfarosh, Shirazi Saëb once said if I ever painted a large piece he'd be interested in taking a look . . .'

'That's very kind of him. He is a good man, from a good family, you see. But aren't you busy with Mustafa Peer's work?'

'Oh, yes, yes, Peer's work keeps coming, thank God, but it's all small stuff, Abba, nothing really major, nothing, hmm, that you could call art . . . I have been thinking about this idea for a very large painting. It will take time, I know, as I can't work on it more than one day a week. But it will be my best work, I know that. I already have a name for it. *Falaknuma*.'

'Very good, Faizå, very good. And the name is nice, too. Like the sky. So what is the problem?'

'There is no problem. I just wanted to tell you before making a proper start.'

'You have told me now, so start whenever you want to. Why didn't you tell me before?'

'Er, I wasn't sure, and then there was too much work.'

As he climbs up the stairs to his room, he goes over his plans.

Already some of Peer's work is pending. But he has to start now. He has thought enough.

The earth and the world contained in it, in all its detail and glory, in all its life and light, reflected in a saucer-shaped sky, is how Faiz has imagined *Falaknuma*. A large round canvas, much larger than the one-thousand-rupees-apiece papier-mâché shields he has seen all his life. He was commissioned to paint twelve such shields a few years ago at a time of high demand from Japanese parents and B-grade martial-arts filmmakers in Bangkok. It was always the same motifs, the same scenes, the same spears, lions and fat princes, even the same six colours. He could have painted layers and layers on it, an entire world, if he had wanted to, if he had been able to expand the canvas.

Falaknuma, however, could be the centrepiece of a ceiling, or adorn a wall in a large hall. And Shirazi could in reality fetch him enough money for it, which would allow him to change direction and move from small papier-mâché objects to large paintings, even murals or ceilings, like they used to have in the old days, as opposed to breaking his backbone poring over a thousand jewellery boxes or Easter eggs, making a million blades of grass, the right hand an automaton going up and down, up and down . . . As it is, his deer have started of late to appear slightly deformed, hurried and skeletal, not fleshed out enough, the habit of the finger threatening to break the intimate cord between the brush and the painter's eye. If he finds a larger canvas, his search for depth, grandeur, will keep him busy and happy, and hopefully not poor.

You never know, he nods, some rich dealer may ask him to do a number of large paintings and he may then be able to work as the old masters did, improve his craft, even demand his price, his name having travelled far and wide in the world of art and handicrafts. Even the government buys art sometimes, he has been told. He must start soon, now.

For practice, Faiz has stashed away three replicas of the large round shield he intends to paint. He will first draw the schema of his world on the cardboard that he has covered with fine tracing paper, perfect it on a second, and move on to the third only if necessary.

As the light in the room turns pale, he starts with the centre, drawing the shape of a lake he has seen in his dreams. Soon he changes his mind and turns it into an oval shape floating diagonally across the centre of the shield. He puts two dots inside the lake. Green and blue. Then another with pencil for the third shade that he wants to use here. He must persuade Rangrez the paint-seller to give him the magic pigment.

He lights another cigarette, then draws a long, gently curving line from the lake to the edge of the circle. This will be his river, running along the circumference. He is not sure how he will depict the return of the river to the lake, but makes a note of it at the end of the river's path, where the beginning meets the end. Between the lake and the river, Faiz marks his sky, as reflected in the lake, by drawing faint clouds. Something dramatic will happen here, in the fashion of the sixteenth-century patron saint of naqashi, or papier-mâché art, Ustad Kamangar, who worked in the court of Yusuf Shah Chak, painting royal chronicles in his later life. This, of course, Faiz has only heard of; he has never seen Ustad Kamangar's work, because none of it survives, or so he thinks. He does not know, and perhaps should not know, that a panel from the Chaks' palace by the Chenab river survived the pillaging Mughal soldiers in the autumn of 1598 when Yaqub the Balladeer was waging a guerrilla war against the imperial forces. Centuries later, the panel somehow found a home in the only Museum of History in Faiz's land, but a minister for culture in the 1960s, a man simply known as the Contractor Sahib, had taken it home, for reasons of preservation, and never remembered to return it. Now, even if Faiz finds out about its survival, it's unlikely he'll ever visit it at its present address: a stately home in England where it looks over a banqueting hall open to the public for two months of the British summer.

Faiz picks a matchstick, dips it in red paint and starts marking the expanse of his city. Soon, clusters of red spots begin to assume a pattern. It starts narrow, then expands, and finally dissipates as it touches the river at the rim. He now draws two moons, more or less of the same size. This, he knows, is the tricky part, especially since he does not want to conjure a hall-of-mirrors effect. As he finishes a few more touches – a settlement of animals on the fringes of the city, with two roads linking it to where the people live; an infinitely long line of sparrows flying away from the oval lake; and finally, many lights, each constellation signalled by a drop of different colour – Faiz is determined to finish the piece by the end of the year.

The Meeting

It is already a stressful day. Mummy's two sisters have come to visit. Married to two brothers, they often come together. The younger aunt, Shameem, chatters on. The elder one, Naseem, loves Roohi.

'What is she going to do with another degree – become a director? And who gets a job without a big sufarish or bribe nowadays? Do you know how much Mahdé Shah, the Matric-Fail education minister, charges for a teacher's job – do you have any idea?'

Mummy looks on in anticipation.

'Five lakhs. How are you going to raise that kind of money, Behanjee? I'd thought she was over this PhD nonsense – that's what you told me the last time. And even if you did manage somehow, why not just spend it on her wedding? I simply don't understand this PhD after MPhil after MA after BA madness.'

Naseem Aunty, the softest-spoken person Roohi knows, doesn't say much, just bites her lip a couple of times in front of her two sisters. The middle child yet again caught between the ferocity of her younger sister and the bitter sadness of the eldest, she remembers and smiles. She has brought her MPhil political science notes with her, in spite of knowing academic research has been a non-starter for her favourite niece, and is looking for a moment alone with Roohi. In her day, in the glorious seventies, she used to be called Heema Maali, the Downtown name for Bollywood's dream girl at the time. Roohi resembles Naseem more than she resembles her mother.

Naseem's beauty and independence had earned her a reputation, all of it, of course, we must remember, spun by spurned suitors and unsuccessful matchmakers during her time at the Women's College of Red Square. But people feared her as well. She was a keen debater at college and had once asked a famous minister, a certain Mr Abdullah, to take his hands off her shoulders after he had presented her with the first prize: 'Minister Sahib, you may not know this, but the sweat from your hands is making my dupatta wet. And sweat smells sometimes, especially that of politicians. Not your fault though, sir.' That day, a brief but loud cheer, including six forceful claps from a proud college principal, had reverberated through the august Iqbal Memorial Auditorium. It is rumoured that the minister's wife had hit him so hard on his head with her old disused iron shovel that evening that he had passed out and regained consciousness only after she consigned to flames an entire tin of rue near his nose. After that he had never participated in a public ceremony involving women, and once he had gone bald, and it started showing, old satirists who still have their secret conclaves on either side of Zaine Kadal nicknamed him the Minister of the Rising Crescent. It is also believed that he spent a fortune, his earnings from the sale of construction materials meant for eleven thousand toilets for the poor that were never built, on bad hair transplants in Dubai but just could not make the imprint of the shovel go away. A scratchy pitted half-moon remains permanently etched on his scalp.

Now Naseem is a quiet mother of three boys in a well-to-do and well-regarded business household of Downtown. A homemaker not discontent with her life. What still disconcerts her is the unfairness meted out every so often, ever so casually, to the women around her, especially younger girls, particularly promising girls from the extended family. And Roohi's looks and manner make her especially dear to her, for she reminds Naseem of her own promise.

Contrary to her mother's belief, Roohi knows everything that is going on in the house. In fact, she doesn't even need to hear the whole exchange among the sisters. She climbs up the narrow mat-covered stairs to her third-floor room. Her refuge, her skyward escape, and the depository of her stories and desires from the time she was three. She hides everything in the tall cupboard she inherited from her grandfather when he died. The cupboard with twenty layers of lacquer, painted over sixty years of its existence, on its doors. What does it contain?

Scribbles from childhood, often ending with 'I'm very happy' or 'I'm very sad today'. Teenage declarations of true love for an unknown boy.

Couplets written in crayon, red and blue ballpoint and, finally, black felt pen, from Parveen Shakir, the Pakistani romantic poet who died young, which perhaps makes Roohi more drawn to her than she might have been, had the melancholy poet not been killed in a car accident on a bright dusty day in Islamabad in 1994.

Urdu magazines, some literary, some melodramatic, with covers either bearing cryptic typography or kitschy film-poster designs.

Photocopies of that tormented writer Akhtar Mohiuddin's short stories. Also Ibne Safi's detective novels. She used to love the hero, Imran, and his fiery assistant, Juliana Fitzwater. She had decided to be like Juliana but had given up the idea six months later as she didn't want to grow up to be someone's assistant.

Sixteen hairbands. The most expensive cost fifty rupees. It has small mirrors embedded in its *faux*-pearl body. Roohi used to wear it on every Eid, until her mother and brother – she has a younger brother who's increasingly started to act as a big brother – both said she wasn't a little girl any more: she shouldn't invite everyone's attention in the Shrine Square on the morning of Eid, when children would form groups to play, run around and spend their Eid money amid the happy crowds emerging after the prayers.

A toy makeup kit she received as a gift at Naseem Aunty's wedding years ago. It now conceals the burgundy lipstick her mother dislikes.

★

As she skims through the notes Naseem has slipped under the door, she notices a handwritten paragraph visible through a page in the middle. Quickly flipping the page, she recognizes the writing.

My dear Roohi,

I know how you feel. When I was your age, I had the same feelings, the same wounds. I tried my best to follow my heart, but it was a different time, life was hard and the world too mighty, so in the end I had to do exactly as my family wished. I'd already won my big battle by going to the university, doing an MA, and didn't have it in me to fight another war. I was lucky to get married to your Maasu. As you know, he is a good man, kind-hearted and a dutiful father.

You are a woman now, Roohi, and inclined more, if I may say so, towards the matters of the heart. Keep your mind alert but do what pleases your soul. Be who you want to be. You know I am there for you and you will always have my support in whatever you do.

Yours and yours alone,
Naseem Aunty

Roohi thinks of burning it, but then, suddenly alert to the filmy melodrama of the thought, slips it under her clothes in the cupboard.

She spreads her mat gently, squats at its lower end, her knees touching the base of the two pillars of the minaret that points to Mecca, and waits for the azan from the mosque at the right-hand edge of the shrine compound, away from the river.

Her personal prayer, which she lets rise from her palms after concluding her business with God, is always the same, following which she inevitably turns her gaze towards the courtyard. Today she starts from the left, where the iron fencing of the ancient graveyard at the back is visible through the side lane at this end of the shrine. In her childhood, Roohi used to be afraid of walking along the lane, of its stone walls and cobbled floor, dark and mysterious with age, yet something made her do it often, her last steps out of it always hurrying into a sprint. The Graveyard of the Wild Roses is closed for business. Its tombstones, inscribed with verses from the Qur'ān and Persian poetry, are the last pieces of Central Asian stonework in the land. It won't take any more guests to unsettle that order.

The Window

Roohi lets her hair fall long at the window and closes her eyes as the breeze from the river comes through the gaps in the glass.

This is another thing of which Mummy and her neighbours disapprove. Why doesn't she cover her head? Why must she comb her hair by the window? We say this because if she carries on she is bound to attract the evil eye at some point. Why must she show herself to every stranger walking by? She shouldn't do it, and you should do something about it. I have told her so many times, but children, these days, you know how headstrong they are – my father would have dragged me down by my hair if I'd dared to do so, even slapped me a few times, but, you see, you can't hit a grown-up daughter, can you? At least I can't. She's my only daughter, after all.

It is early evening. Roohi is content to have warded off yet another marriage proposal – the sixth in all since her college and university life ended – brought by the younger aunt. The Jhelum is racing down by the ghat, its journey marked by swallows in pursuit; they will run along to the next bridge or the one after it, then disappear for the night. Many have their tiny nests inside the vast labyrinthine woodwork that supports the old bridges.

Lights are born along the two banks, hundreds of tasselled, stained-glass and embroidered windows pouring charms and warm shadows of Srinagar's oldest residents into the water. Men of houseboats, intimate friends of the river and the city's forgotten heroes, sit on their jetties while the women, far more heroic, some believe, than the men, as they keep order inside the boathouse and defend their patch on the river, pump life into their kerosene stoves. Down on the Zainė Kadal Bridge, hawkers, keen to go home without any of their wares, shout out their last-minute sales pitches before curfew time.

Fatigued fishermen are pulling their boats upstream to get to their homes on time, or are resting by the steps of the ghat, their oars wedged between the rock faces of the bank, like outstretched arms.

This river made the city, and the city has tried to unmake it over the centuries. While it brings the heavenly waters of the emerald Verinag spring from the hem of the Pir Panjal Mountains, the city thwarts its dreams, pouring refuse, bad wishes and dark stories into it. Of late, it has also started carrying the dead, many tales of cruelty drowning in its onward rush, and with them, the dark deeds of the oppressor, too. It has moved mountains, yes, it has bestowed life on the enslaved tiller through the ages, yes, and it has brought romance to this old city, too, but the city has proved to be an unfaithful lover. This city's rulers, its little tyrants, have tried to blacken its face, suppressed its soul and poured rock into its heart and yet, even after so many insults to its pride, the river lives on. The city tamed the river, gone are the days when it could put the fear of the deluge into the hearts of the townsfolk; people say it will take whatever you throw into it. But people are wrong. The river can break barriers of lead when it is angry.

This river is witnessing the decay of the city – there never was a more fitting revenge. It is just that people are blind. While you are busy burying your filth in it, while little tyrants plunder the mystic arcs of its bridges, while the occupier lays siege to it, the river has tender things to attend to – it has a love story to write.

Faiz has finished the first coat of base-varnish on the pencil boxes. He has laid a caravan of light-red coffins on the floor. He smiles. He smells of glue. His fingers relax, and that constant furrowing of the brow begins to ease. He collects the bits of excess onion-skin paper he uses to smooth the rough corners, these shreds of translucence he always feels sad to throw away, and dumps them in a plastic bag, along with a heap of cigarette butts. In the echoing hallway, he gropes for the keys on the clay shelf built into the wall, locks his world and goes downstairs.

Every time Faiz finishes a layer of work on the current consignment, as Mustafa Peer calls it, he goes for a long bath, sometimes spending an hour in the bathroom. Today is that day. This is the only time he looks after himself well, sees himself in the mirror, shaves with care, applies oil to his hair, and often, if it is a Friday or Saturday, goes to Red Square with his best friends, Majeed and Showket. The visit to Red Square is just that – a visit. Of late, however, the weekly or fortnightly strolls in the city centre have become rarer. These days, the city goes dark early.

To the shrine, then, he must go. His childhood echoes from every stone and wall, the ghat his old playground, and the balcony overlooking the river his first refuge from the world.

As he goes down the steps, something makes him change course and, instead of going to his favourite seat by the chinar, he heads straight towards the large stone platforms in front of the shrine. He stops at the centre, gazes at the three floors of the building, wondering what it must be like to sit on one of those dark verandas, and what lies beyond those portals. He also wonders, as he would in his childhood, what it is like inside the always-locked, all-wood annexe at the back of the building. There is a basement, too, he has heard, where no one can go. It is said that nothing has changed in the underground part of the shrine for centuries.

A breeze from the river lifts eastward, coils round the shrine, making the lights flicker in its many halls; the crows momentarily recede, halting their evening congress. It now sweeps across the cobblestones and the cold blue-grey pathways between the platforms, hurries on to the steps, then rises towards the street outside, gathering speed as it does so. Faiz closes his eyes, smelling the river and some memory on the air. He wants to rise with it too, float away, but instead turns around to check how far the chinar leaves, swirling in the breeze, will go. He watches them fly up to the arch above the gates. Some drop down, as though exhausted, while others go further up, up, into the roofs of the houses opposite the shrine, mixing with the human world until, finally, they disappear from sight.

Mad Hearts

In the last moments of her namaz, Roohi's mind is racing ahead of her. She sits on the prayer mat, her hands pressing against her breast. How will the night pass? What does she remember of the man who was watching her through the parade of chinar leaves?

'Shukur Khodayas kun. I thank you, God, for peering into my soul. What shall I do now? Shall I wait for him to come this way again? Shall I wait to confirm again what my eyes saw? Was it real?'

She cannot let the moment die. It was not a dream. A letter will have to be written, a message will have to be delivered, a meeting in secret will have to be arranged. Was it *him*?

Faiz has been looking at his copy of the Omar Khayyám painting. The poet, the wine, the river and the sky recede into the background. The long black hair remains. Surely, it's a coincidence, a clever trick of time. He had only wanted to go to the shrine for a walk, but then again, he hadn't been there for more than five years. He had wanted some air, to go back to the old river, but why now? Who was that girl? What was she like?

Like no other.

He has seen many girls, of course, although he has never really had the courage to try to be with one, apart from the occasional, and innocuous, roadside flirtations with the college girls passing through his neighbourhood when he was sixteen or seventeen. He did it because everyone did.

She smiled at him, didn't she? Or did he imagine it? He is not sure now and the questions surround him in his world of colour. He tries to look at the pieces he's been working on or the occasional reject he has kept for himself; he tries to repair an odd lopsided lion or a disproportionately large-headed kingfisher; he tries to add a few quick roses to a vase. He tries to see the object in front of him, but he finds himself looking at the woman with the black hair again.

'Faizå, Faizå . . . Your rice is getting cold – come down now.' As she does every evening, Mouj steps outside the main door to the house and shouts up to her youngest son working away on the third floor. Faiz never makes her wait, unless he is about to finish a piece. Today he finds himself unable to move.

When Mouj has called a few times, Faiz finally gets up, having half made up his mind to ask around about the girl in the narrow house in front of the shrine's gates. As he shuts the door behind him, he thinks he sees the woman in the screen again, looking at him. Just a trick of the light and too much work, for God's sake.

The Letter

On the fourth day after seeing Faiz, Roohi makes a connection. By way of a chain of cousins, their friends and the friends' sisters at her former school – the Government Girls' High School of Bohir Kadal, housed in that most intricate and elegant building of a hundred and one windows – Roohi finds Faiz's doe-eyed youngest sister Farhat.

While Faiz had been still contemplating the meaning of the painting and the image of the girl with the long hair in the window, as he worried about finishing Mustafa Peer's pencil-box order, Roohi, even though nerve-racked, decided to do something about it. She followed the boy in the pheran all the way to his home the next evening; he had not been able to see her from his seat by the chinar but she had seen him. From behind the curtains in her room, he had looked gentle, a bit lost perhaps, with a sad face she knew at once she wanted to see for the rest of her life.

Why didn't she show her face? Why did she quietly follow at a distance? Should she not have made sure he saw her again? Should she not have gone to the shrine and walked past him, possibly even smiled at him? Should she perhaps have let her hair down once more? The truth is that Roohi, in spite of all her bravery, was in pain. All these years of waiting at her window, her secret has been her secret. Except Naseem Aunty, who has always had some idea of Roohi's restless heart, she has never really allowed anyone into her dream world. It was only natural that Roohi wanted to relive that first moment, to savour its particular and acute delight, to make sure it was real. Was he like the boy from her dreams?

He had really been there, all by himself, smoking a cigarette.

After his second visit to the shrine, she had thought hard about what to do next and, as though her legs knew where she must go, she had followed him home, to the great Mir Manzil, and that was where she had discovered, with a faint twinge, Oh, so he is a son of *this* family. One of the Mirs, *the* Mirs. That he is a Shia. It wouldn't be an entirely honest account of what happened that evening if it wasn't made clear that her discovery did make her pause, that the thought did cross her mind, that images of an irate Mummy did fly into her head, that she did think about how furious, even violent, her brother Rumi might be, that she did contemplate how tormented Papa would be, for he loved her more than anyone ... But, then, these are matters of the heart, and in this case a young heart, which has waited for this moment all its life. Roohi may perhaps have spent half an evening contemplating this, during the walk back from Faiz's Shia neighbourhood at the other end of the main road that leads to her home, but that was all. She did not have a choice. Later, she reproached her mind for trying to get in the way, for having even considered the 'problem'.

Soon after, during some discreet enquiries about the Mirs, she found out that the youngest girl from the Mir house went to the same school as she had done a few years earlier. And a couple of distant- and near-cousin connections later, Roohi, mildly surprised at her own resourcefulness, and luck, of course, had been shown the girl. Farhat. Faiz's sister.

When you leave the somewhat dilapidated but still stately Mir Manzil, you first have to walk a narrow lane, then across a small square marked by an elegant brick mosque on the left and an ancient house on the right – long abandoned by the wealthiest family in Shamswari – to emerge at the centre of the Shia area in this part of the town. The door to the small Shia mosque, and the graveyard at its front, is at the middle of the narrow lane. The muezzins of this mosque and those of the brick Sunni one have fought many a pitched battle, most often at Fajr and Isha, to sound the most earnest and sonorous, but this has never been a source of any real friction between the two. The road then forks into two, one going left to the educational area near the waterway – comprising a dark polytechnic, whose main purpose, it is said at the shops, is to provide endless opportunities for embezzlement to its supervisors and section officers, often in the guise of dozens of fictitious employees drawing monthly salaries; the MP School for Boys whose glory days are over but is still venerated; and the prestigious Gandhi Memorial College – and the other linking to the main traffic artery, packed with minibuses so tiny that they are also known as Kebab Matadors.

On her way to school, Farhat walks around a hundred metres on the main road before turning right into the street that goes past the shrine, then onto the square where her school is. Forty years earlier, there was a fresh-water canal here that came all the way from the Dal Lake and, along with the cool breezes for the city's residents, brought with it vegetables, flowers, fish, charcoal, straw mats and firewood from the vegetable gardens flanking the lake, which would then be sold at a small ghat by the wooden bridge. This canal, a gift bestowed on the city by Sultan Sikander's spirited son Zain-ul-Abidin, is a tarmac road now, dark and shiny, pouring endless streams of buses, cars and scooters into the once bustling marketplace by the water. The school is just a few steps from here, its six storeys of latticed windows visible to all, although lately threatened by bright billboards advertising colourful sweaters, as worn by an ageing Bollywood star, and too-white vests and briefs, and the six bunkers that have come up in the square in the last six months.

Roohi walks behind Farhat for ten minutes until they have gone past the shopkeepers who have known her since she was a little girl with pigtails. The street climbs up briefly, narrows down as the shopkeepers' encroachments eat away, inch by inch, at the pedestrian path, and then descends into the square. There are dye merchants and dyers here, dealers in wedding materials, garlands and decorations, purveyors of laces and silk curtains, wholesale dealers in dried fruits, jaggery and sweets, and spice merchants too, seated in front of hill stations of red, yellow, orange and brown; there are also the city's headscarf shops, a thousand shades draping the shop fronts, the shopkeepers often hidden away behind these waterfalls of colour, only the steps into the shops visible. Both Roohi and Farhat have bought dupattas and knitting yarn and scarves here and dreamt of their wedding clothes. It is here that Roohi finds her chance.

She puts a hand on Farhat's bulky schoolbag. 'It must be very heavy. Do they teach so much at school these days? I used to go there, too.'

Farhat looks at the hand and the dazzling face above her. 'Oh, today is our laboratory class. I have brought my lab notebooks with me, that's why. Salam alaikum.'

'Walaikum salam. I wanted to give you this. It is for your brother. Give it to him when no one's around, will you, for my sake? Please.'

'Oh, oh, I mean yes, I will, I will . . .'

Farhat does not want to move, wants to know more about this girl, but is anxious she might be late for school. She turns, puzzled, pleased, to have been approached by this wonderfully dressed girl, and starts walking away. A minute later, she is back, running.

'Which brother and what's your name?'

'The youngest. He will tell you.' Roohi smiles, puts her hand on Farhat's shoulder, says thank you and turns to leave.

It is only at her door that Roohi regains some sense of what she has done. What will he think of me?

Farhat somehow knows the letter is precious. She has waited all evening, through dinner and the long clear-up in the kitchen with her mother, Mouj. She has gone up three times to check her bag, the lab notebook and the letter pressed inside it. She has smelt it, detecting a faint whiff of Itr, the fragrance having found its way from Roohi's clothes to the only letter pad she owns.

Soon, as Mouj puts away the last copper plate, each with a name etched on it in dotted calligraphy, Farhat runs up to Faiz's room where he is taking the last drags on his final cigarette of the day. Amid the smoke and the dim light of his room, he sees his sister enter with a plain white envelope in her hands.

'I met this beautiful girl near the school, she looks like lightning, and she gave me this. For you. Who is she, Faizå, who is she?'

Faiz pauses, his hand unsteady as it accepts the letter from the girl in the window.

There is a small problem. While he knows he can read Urdu, albeit with some effort, he is not sure if he should entirely trust his semi-literate eyes. The long black hair appears in his mind. Opening the envelope with his scratch knife, which he uses to peel off excess onion-skin or a redundant vein of paint from his pieces, he feels exhausted with excitement. Farhat smiles. She wants him to hurry. He cannot.

In the end, lighting another cigarette, he slowly pushes the open envelope to his beloved sister, who doesn't say a word at this and starts reading.

Salam alaikum,

You may not know me, but I have known you for a very long time. I saw you at the shrine on Saturday evening. We should meet. Can we meet? We must meet. I will wait for you this Saturday, soon after Sham Namaz, near the graveyard behind the shrine. I'm sure you will come.

God bless,
Roohi

Roohi. Roohi.

Faiz cannot sleep. He has looked at the screen again, wondering, turning, thinking. The thought of coincidences hasn't gone away. But the letter is clearly a most extraordinary thing. A girl, *the girl* in the window, wants to meet him. He has watched enough films on Doordarshan, and at the Khayyám and Shiraz cinemas, to know what the letter means, and yet he cannot decide what it really means to him. At the thought of meeting the girl, he feels an unmistakable churning in his heart, a pulse like never before and, perhaps, the seed of a life-changing moment too, but he can't fully grasp it. For a long time, he has hardly thought of his own self; his failure to be like everyone else and not to have climbed the neat school, college, government-job ladder, has always been on his mind and kept him hidden away in his world of paint. For a long time, Faiz has remained content with his immediately meaningful work, with the instant gratifications his brush brings him every hour of the day. It brings in money, it makes him valued in the house even though no one, apart from his big brother and his mother, acknowledges it in as many words.

Faiz's engagement with the external world has always remained limited to the trips to Rangrez's paint shop near the old Fateh Kadal Bridge and, of course, his visits to Red Square with his friends Showket and Majeed, where they marvel at the sight of fashionable modern girls and the new Maruti cars driven by the city's rich men. The weekly or sometimes twice-a-week trip to the paint shop is a necessity that Faiz loves. Near that bent wooden old bridge, which on some purple evenings appears as though an old dervish is hunched over the Jhelum, are small wooden shops, fronted by glass or cloth; some even have old hand-embroidered silk saris as sunshades. In the midst of G. M. Master Tailors & Drapers (Estab. 1953), Hridaynath Bhat Chemists & Druggists, owned and run by Pandit Hridaynath of the white turban fame – he has dispensed viscous cough syrups and Septran for the entire Mir clan for half a century, the doses meticulously marked by little towers of paper diamonds joined end to end – and Wani General Store & Kiryana Merchants (Sole Distributors and Retailers of Hamdard Unani Medicine) is Rangrez's paint shop, an establishment nearly as old as the art of naqashi itself and a place where Faiz feels at perfect ease every time he visits. There are thousands of little bottles on its shelves, some empty and some filled with paint that has turned to concrete. There are pouches here that contain pigments from the last century, and handmade brushes that Rangrez refuses to sell except to a select few clients, Faiz being one of them because he is Mir Mohammed Ali's son. (There are also two rare brushes, with just a single hair to them, which the old man has promised himself he will leave to this young man.) There are little hills of pigment on the floor, each on its brass plate or a piece of old Dhaka muslin. On a bright day, when Faiz sits by Rangrez's seat, they look like mountain ranges of different colours, blue, purple, lavender, crimson, silver, blood, orange, green, and he often imagines going into them, wandering around each summit with his brush. What is his most prized purchase from Rangrez? Gold, gold dust or, more specifically, gold foil pasted onto leaves of a book that is called just that – the gold book – which he uses to embellish his pieces just before applying the final coats of lacquer.

And what of Faiz's contact with women? It has consisted of very little beyond this: evening gossip with the extended family's girls by the lone walnut tree in the family courtyard, a pastime that has made him a lifelong confidant and a willing accomplice in their little adventures – a stolen visit to the cinema, a cigarette each handed over to the older second cousins Shakeela and Daisy, as well as to his own sister Shahida, and accompanying his niece Mehbooba, Mir Zafar's eldest daughter and considerably older than Faiz, on her clandestine dates with her Sunni boyfriend, Waheed, until a couple of years ago. He has, of course, always looked at women, especially the extraordinary girls who come out of the nearby college, and often imagined what it might be like. His physical contact with the female form, though, has remained strictly limited to accidental brushes against women's bodies in a jam-packed minibus during his trips to Red Square, and then, too, he has always pulled himself away, except perhaps three times when the feel of a soft thigh through a crêpe burqa or a particularly tight college uniform has had the better of his genteel spirit. It must, however, be said that, notwithstanding the momentary lapse of reason, Faiz always felt strange after these encounters: shame, guilt and fear of the unknown.

But this is different, Faiz knows, as he turns in his bed for the hundredth time. He breaks into a smile as he looks at the screen again, the georgette headscarf he had draped over it having skidded off in the night breeze.

Shadows by the River

Roohi does not wear her best clothes for the rendezvous. Her magnificently embroidered green salwar-kameez remains where it is, and the bright red Kashmir silk one she wore to a few weddings last year would be a bit excessive, too, she decides. The black cotton salwar-kameez, the one with the soft grey paisley patterns on its borders, tells her something, perhaps because it is the only one drooping from a hanger or perhaps because Naseem Aunty once told her that its dupatta, with its petite lotus plants threaded in a light silver, makes her look beautiful. Roohi is not sure if she should take out her best lipstick, the burgundy that her mother loathes. In the end, she applies a light coat, just a hint of the colour.

Farhat is sweating from the effort she is making to iron Faiz's dark-brown trousers. The ironing is always done on a blanket covered with a clean sheet. He had wanted to wear his jeans – since that's what he sees most college boys wearing in the city centre – but his younger sister rejected the idea, laughing gently at him. The off-white shirt that he hasn't worn since Mehbooba's wedding last year – she didn't marry her sacrificing Sunni boyfriend, the matter wasn't even raised, such was the dread that Mir Zafar Ali instilled in her and still does in everyone in the whole Mir clan – will go very well with these trousers. Faiz wants to wear the second-hand leather golf-cap he purchased last month at the Sunday Market. He feels it makes him look trendy.

'No, no, she will think you have a bald patch or some kind of scabies of the scalp. I just wish you went to a better barber, though, brother.'

Faiz gives in to everything that Farhat decrees. He also gives her a twenty-rupee note.

He is there at least twenty minutes early. She is watching his shadow.

Smiles, words, brushes of the hair, circling of a foot, twiddling of a thumb, coiling and uncoiling of a dupatta end, and a heavy stillness in the heart.

Roohi wants to touch his face. He wants to see the hair.

The sun's beams, broken by the columns and grilles of the balcony by the ghat, cross through them, the silver on the black dupatta shining and sending patterns on to Faiz's face.

They just sit there, backs leaning against the paling of the balcony. Now they look at the river flowing below, now at each other. Roohi picks up a handful of dust, lets it slip through her fingers, then gathers it again. Faiz hesitates for a bit and takes out a cigarette. Lights begin to appear in the water. Shadows cast by the shrine, the trees and the tall houses with palanquin balconies on either side of the complex meet each other in the Jhelum, sometimes stirring, sometimes holding hands silently. Roohi watches it all.

Faiz speaks. 'Same time next week?'

'Same time next week.'

'Can I shake your hand?'

'Yes.' She laughs.

Of Love and Letters

'I used to spend a lot of time here in my childhood. We used to play hide-and-seek and I would often hide in the graveyard.'

'Oh, it was like my own playground too. We used to play hop-scotch in the courtyard. You know, I was the leader of our group. In the evening, I would buy roasted peanuts and eat them on the steps of the ghat. I threw so many shells into the river. They would sail away like tiny houseboats.'

'I used to see girls playing hopscotch,' Faiz says, meeting her eyes.

'I remember the hide-and-seek games, too. I would sometimes join in uninvited. The other girls didn't, except my best friend Shahnaz. She's married now.'

'I would go home well after dark.' Faiz looks at the darkening sky.

'I wished I was allowed to play in the dark, but I always looked at the courtyard from my window. That room, *my* room, was my grandfather's. He died soon after I passed my matric exams. I can't tell you how happy he was.'

'I never saw my grandfather. My father looked like a grandfather.'

'I was my grandfather's favourite. He gave me a rupee every Friday when I was little and a hundred when I passed matric.'

'My brother has been like a father to me, to everyone in our family. He is much older than I am.'

'My father dotes on me. He is very fond of me. My mother too, although she is a little too strict sometimes. She is always worried about a suitable match for me – you know how it is with girls.'

'No one is worried about my marriage. There are two sisters

ahead of me and then there are Abba's own children who are also older than me. How old are you?'

'Twenty.'

'I am twenty-one . . . You have been to college and university. What is it like?'

'The best years of my life. I miss it. My friends, my group, my teachers, strolls in the market, even the stress of the exams, everything. I wish . . .'

'I didn't even finish school. But I have been earning for a long time.'

'Will you show me your work some day? I love papier-mâché art. I want to see you doing it. I used to draw at school and I still have my drawing book from Eighth. There are things in it no one has seen. I can show you.'

'What did you draw? Did you paint? Papier-mâché is different.'

'Hmm . . . nothing worth showing, actually. Just some scenes I remembered from storybooks and films, some people talking, like you and me, you'll see.'

'When?'

'I can bring it with me when you invite me home. I can't come uninvited. I can look at your papier-mâché and you will see my childhood art, ha-ha. Won't you?'

'Hmm . . . I will think about it. I mean I will think of something, you know how it is. I can ask Farhat if she can do something.'

'I love her.'

'She's very dear to me. Do you have any brothers or sisters?'

'I have one brother, Rumi. He is two years younger than me and his real name is Rameez but few people call him that. Even his friends call him by his pet name. Grandfather called him Rumi when he was born.'

'What does he do?'

'Nothing actually . . . He finished class twelve but didn't want to go to college, says he wants to go into business, although no one knows what kind of business. He is a bit spoilt, being the only son, you see, but he's good at heart.'

'One day, I will set up my own workshop and export business. I like to paint, I love papier-mâché too, but it's tiring and you can lose your eyesight if you paint pill boxes all your life.'

'You shouldn't say that.'

'What?'

'About your eyes.'

'Your eyes are beautiful. Farhat said looking at your face was like being struck by lightning.'

'What did you do with my letter? I hope you have kept it safe somewhere.'

'It's locked in my trunk. Inside the book of gold leaves. I have the keys here.'

'Oh, no, what if it spoils your gold? It must be expensive.'

'I will buy more from Rangrez.'

'What do you do with the gold? How do you paint with it? I have never understood, actually. What we used to get in the watercolour tubes was fake gold paint. Synthetic.'

'It's simple. I peel off a foil with my fingers, mix it with glue and water and bring it to a boil. That's it. I don't even think about it, the thickness of the liquid is always right.'

'Don't they sell gold paint like other paints? Wouldn't it be easier?'

'Yes, but I like to prepare my own from the leaves. And, these days, some dealers mix metal dust with the gold pigment. Rangrez will never do it but you never know what the suppliers send him. Have you seen his shop?'

'Isn't it near Fateh Kadal? I used to buy crayons and watercolour bottles from him when I was at school, but I don't remember much. Isn't he an old man with a very old, tattered Karakul hat?'

'Best shop in the world. He has some pigments that are two hundred years old, paint that never fades. Some people say he even has rare pigments that change colour every few years. He doesn't sell them any more. I hope he gives me a pouch some day.'

'I'm sure he knows some secret verse or something that makes the paint so. Otherwise it's not possible. There is no way.'

'Anything is possible here. In the ceiling of our hall of mourning, there is a papier-mâché panel that has always changed colour. Abba says its background was green when he was little and now it is blue. You can see for yourself if you –'

'Yes, that might be true but your hall of mourning, too, must have been blessed with sacred verses or something when your house was built, mustn't it? The old holy men, who were really pious, had great powers, especially Shia pirs, isn't that true? That's what I've heard at least. Mummy sometimes goes to a Shia holy man in a village near Budgam. He lives on a hilltop. I don't remember his full name, Mummy just calls him Syed Saéb. You have so many.'

'There are Sunni pirs too, maybe not as powerful as ours are, but there definitely are many.'

'Yes, there are. We both have pirs on our side.'

'Do you really believe in them?'

'It depends. Sometimes the amulet works and sometimes it doesn't. Mummy got me one for my final-year exams and I passed in the first division, actually. I had prepared hard, of course. If you ask me what I think rationally, no, I don't believe in them. But if carrying a verse from the holy Qur'ān around my neck for a few days makes my mother happy, then I believe in them. Do you believe in them?'

'I don't know. I always wear this around my neck. My father had it made by the senior Agha Saéb when I was born. He died when I was three. I always keep it with me. Abba doesn't like this kind of stuff, spiritual cures et cetera, it's all a hoax, he says, which is probably true. But it's all I have of my father. The case is to protect it from water. It's silver.'

'We will go to both a Sunni and Shia pir, ha-ha.'

'Have you always had such long hair?'

40

'Yes, it's my natural purdah, but I let it loose sometimes. Why do you want to know?'

'Did you have two long plaits when you were young?'

'Yes. Yes.'

'Can I touch it?'

The School

There is a winding queue extending from the main gate of the school all the way to the dyers' lane. A long white wall with a chain of schoolbags at the middle, which sways this way and that. Sometimes green-ribboned plaits swing in the air as a head turns swiftly. Farhat closes one eye and thinks of it as a caterpillar. Boys from the neighbourhood – as indeed teenage Casanovas from all over Downtown – who come to try their luck every morning and evening, and sometimes even during the recess, are busy flirting, eye to eye, with some of the girls. A bold few venture forth briefly with quick declarations of true and undying love and withdraw as soon as one of the teachers guarding the students threatens to intervene. 'Hey, madam! She is my cousin,' can be heard every two minutes or so through the chuckles. A few fruit vendors have suspended business, their weighing scales turned upside down, to gawk at this most unexpected spectacle, and the minibus conductors linger even longer at the bus stop, but today their passengers are not piqued. Girls who are already inside the school building hang out of the windows and wave to their friends or to the brave whistlers among the boys on the road below. A class-six girl is tearfully arguing with Meena Madam, the religious-studies teacher, about her dupatta, which, she rightly insists, had slid off because the girl behind her had pulled at it. The teacher relents and allows her to step out of the queue briefly to spend her pocket money at the Gulshan Pan House, whose signboard shows Amitabh Bachchan and Rekha, both blindingly pink-cheeked and larger than life. *Do Bhai Painters*, it says in thin paint at the bottom, the *i* a long curved brush. Meena Madam accepts a toffee as a gesture of peace and glares at the big girl behind the now-calm class-six student. A senior girl, the monitor of class ten, who was among the first few to enter the school building, has hung a hastily sketched poster in a large window: 'We want? Azadi, freedom,' it says, in dripping, shining blue ink.

Farhat wishes the most beautiful girl in the world with the most beautiful handwriting would come and talk to her for a bit. She lives nearby – she must pass through here a lot, Farhat thinks, looking around. Roohi is indeed in the area, at this very moment, but in a different market lane, the one that belongs exclusively to the yarn merchants, where she is looking at multi-coloured castles of knitting wool just arrived from India's wool town, Ludhiana, and is wondering what colour to pick for the gloves she wants to knit for Faiz.

The last time there was a queue outside the school was when the minister for education, the same man who charges a flat rate of five lakhs for recruitment to a junior assistant, trainee teacher or peon post, and who has very recently opened his own educational institute, comprising an English-medium school, a polytechnic, a BEd college and a nursing academy, by filling a wetland at the western edge of the city, came to make an inspection. Then the waiting had just lasted ten or fifteen minutes, primarily because the queue had extended into the assembly ground at the back where the girls needed to be seated for the minister's speech, but today it's already been half an hour and the queue is moving as if there were no classes.

Sometimes, if the queue bends enough to present a clear view of the gate, Farhat thinks she can make out Nazir Sir, the games teacher and general administration busybody, sitting in a chair behind a table. But that can't be. And are there men behind him? Who are these people?

By noon, the hold-up at the gate seems to have been resolved and the queue starts moving. Nazir Sir is indeed making notes in a ledger and waving the girls in one by one. Farhat feels something has changed. As she finally gets closer to the porch whose cobblestone steps once went down into the Nallah Mar canal, she sees it.

There are six uniformed men standing behind Nazir Sir and, behind them, an officer sitting on the red sofa from Principal Shanta Madam's office. Farhat steps up, says, 'Salam alaikum,' and waits in front of the table. There is pressure from behind, the queue having now gained an elastic momentum. Nazir Sir asks for her full name, her father's name, her class and section.

'Mir Farhat. Tenth B, sir. Late Mir Mohammed Ali, sir.'

'From today you will sit with your friends from Tenth A and C, and all of you will sit in Section C on the top floor. Understood?'

Farhat looks at the military men and their short black guns. 'Sir, what about our class timetable? We have different timetables.'

'Don't worry about that now. New timetables will be on the notice board soon. You can go now. Straight to the top floor, not your old classroom. Understood?'

'Yes, sir.'

The officer on the sofa smiles. He seems nice. As she climbs up, thinking of the new seating arrangement and which of her friends she would prefer to sit with, the class-ten monitor comes out of a door and hands her a lab chart rolled into a slender tube. 'Take it with you and unfurl it from the window facing the street.'

Farhat reaches Section C and sees all the furniture is gone, except the chair and table meant for the teacher. Instead, there are rows and rows of red jute matting laid out in parallel lines. She forgets about the chart, sits in the middle row and stares at the blank blackboard.

'May lightning strike them. Why have they come to your school, plague upon them?' Mouj says, while piling up rice on each plate.

'It's only for the time being, Mouji, don't worry, and we don't know the details yet,' Abba raises his voice before touching his first mouthful, which is sprinkled over with a few drops of the day's dish, whatever is for dinner in addition to the rice. It's a habit from his father's days, who did it all his life, a few drops of gravy poured delicately at the base of the white knoll of rice.

'Shanta Ma'am said we must not engage with the military-wallas. She said it's normal these days and they will be gone in a few weeks.'

Mouj mumbles curses under her breath. These are not the harsh words of a bitter woman but heartfelt pleas to God, who must surely do something about such things. Sitting down to eat from her high, ornate copper bowl, she once again calls for a plague on almost everyone in the ruling classes, from that devious and dead maharaja to the Lion who betrayed all to the current Downtown MLA and all the way to the President of India. Even the weather, which sometimes causes too much mud in the front yard, is their fault.

Faiz wants to know if Farhat is happy going to school in this situation. 'It's fine. I'm not the only one. They keep to themselves and we do the same. And, if you ask me, I quite like it in the combined class.'

They are gathered in the girls' room on the third floor. It is the second biggest and the brightest room in the house, always has been, the only one with two high-voltage lamps and massive bay windows that look over the grassless backyard and Master Dinanath's red-brick house behind it. There is no wall in the yard. This is Downtown Srinagar. The master's daughters, Bimla and Kamla Handoo, are childhood friends of Feroza and Shahida, although recently they haven't been spending too much time together in the daytime, as the neighbour's girls are at their college while the slightly older Mir girls, having finished their degrees, lead lives of leisure, making up irrefutable reasons to reject suitors who are sent up every once in a while. The evening window-to-window chats still continue.

'You girls should mix laxative in the military-walla's water. They wouldn't want to stay after that. And if they do, do it again, a pill from each of you would mean more than six hundred pills of Dulcolax in the water tank. Do it when the school breaks for the weekend on Saturday.' Feroza lands a hard slap on Faiz's thigh as she begins to check Farhat's English essay, 'Advantages and Disadvantages of Science'.

'What have the poor soldiers done to you? It's not their fault. They're just doing their duty,' Shahida, the eldest sister, says.

'What do you mean it's not their fault? They just shouldn't come here,' Faiz protests.

'It's not up to them, Faizâ. What are you saying? Their officers decide these things, the government does. They are just poor sepoys, someone's son, someone's brother, like you . . . They just follow orders.'

'Okay, their *officers* shouldn't do this. *They* shouldn't send them here. Happy? This is not a chicken-and-egg situation, my dear sister. They wouldn't have taught you this at college, but remember one thing, the soldiers came first! The boys took to arms later.'

'Oh, please, don't start now, you two. It's such an elegant building. Those brutes will ruin it – they won't care what happens to it, I'm telling you.' Feroza closes the notebook and throws it at Farhat, who makes a face. 'It's very good, little one, don't worry. You need to change the conclusion, though. And you may need to add a few more lines about the advantages, please.' Farhat opens the notebook, smiles at the large-headed cartoon her sister has drawn of her on the inside cover, and slips it into her bag.

'Look, as Shanta Ma'am says, it's a temporary thing. It's only been three days, the girls have been fine, so let's not get ahead of ourselves and needlessly worry Mouj and Abba. That's all I'm trying to say.'

'Okay, but, Farree, you must tell us immediately if anything happens. In fact, tell us first and then we can decide if matters need to go to the high court. Besides, you won't know how to tell him. Faizâ, do you have a little something for your best sister? Come on.'

'If Abba finds out, he'll break your legs.' Faiz pushes his Four Squares towards Feroza who, having moved into the large bay window, lights up with a flourish and mimics Parveen Babi by leaning

46

across a round cushion, blowing smoke into the curtains and letting the cigarette dangle loose in her fingers.

'I hope you don't burn the house down some day,' Shahida says, as she prepares her and her smoker sister's bed.

Roohi stops for two minutes by the gate to Mir Manzil. Its iron chain is massive, black and forbidding. But it's looped back to a peg on the doorpost. On top of the doorframe is a calligraphed verse from the Qur'ān. The carving looks ancient: *Nasr`u min'Allah wa Fat'han Qareeb*. 'Help from Allah and victory is near.'

Roohi knows what it means and it makes her smile. She enters.

She is supposed to ask for Farhat. If asked, she is to say she's come to teach her trigonometry. No one in the Mir family was good at it and no one really knows anything about it. But even Roohi doesn't know much. She prays she doesn't see Mir Zafar Ali today, even if she has to meet him some day.

Mouj has just filled up the kangris, one for everyone in the house, with charcoal and sawdust, and is struggling to get the precise slow burn going in the braziers. It's the beginning of winter so the sawdust isn't crisp enough yet, and the moisture in it produces gusts of pungent blue-black smoke. A nimbus of blue light and smoke surrounds her as she crouches like a mystic performing a secret rite. As she finishes, blowing tearfully into the last two uncooperative braziers, she sees someone approach. It is the time of day when dusk will, any moment now, turn suddenly into the black of the night. The light from the now aglow kangris throws red into the evening, lighting up Mouj's wet face, and it is this light Roohi steps into and says, 'Salam alaikum.'

Faiz's mother sees a white face, like that of an angel, she would tell her daughters later. 'If only she was Shia.'

'Walaikum. Whom do you want to meet, dear? Where have you come from?'

'I – I'm looking for Farhat. Hmm . . . I'm her . . . new tutor.'

'Farhat. Someone's here for you. Farhat! Farree, have you gone deaf? She will come down soon. May this TV burn some day. Come in, come in, dear.'

Farhat, contrary to her mother's charge, which is often true, is not watching TV today. She has been waiting by Faiz's window for a while and has watched every moment of Roohi's encounter with Mouj with a certain delight.

She's at the door now, breathing heavily, having descended three flights of those giant stairs in thirty seconds.

'Roohi Madam, salam alaikum.'

'Walaikum. Is this a good time, or should I have come earlier?'

'It's fine, madam.' Farhat smiles.

Faiz is doing the watching now from the top, having quickly eased into Farhat's position. There's a continuous trickle in his heart.

Farhat has chosen the girls' room to be her study for the duration, because there is a dressing room at the back, partitioned from the main hall by Wuroosi woodwork. Roohi, sitting between the two bay windows, tries to focus on the trigonometry textbook. Farhat can't see a thing on the pages. Roohi slowly turns a page, then another and another, then she can't any more.

Farhat leaves the room, walks down the stairs quietly, peeps into the kitchen where her mother is busy at the oven. She goes across to the drawing room, again partitioned into two chambers by a Shahmiri arch. The partition comes down at night when Mir Zafar Ali goes to sleep in the inner chamber. He is seated by his desk, copying verses from a poetry manuscript in his elegant calligraphy for the printing press he works for in his spare time.

No one else is at home. Farhat has chosen the evening carefully. Only the sisters know and they are in the boys' room opposite the girls' room. Shahida has tied her dupatta around Feroza's ankle. Farhat has allowed them a peep through the inch-wide slit created in the shut door by temporarily removing an egg-sized knot in the wood panel. 'If you don't listen to me, I will tell Abba you smoke.'

Farhat had played her ace when persuading her elder sisters not to appear before Roohi. She doesn't do it too often. Roohi knew someone was watching her the moment she stepped into the hallway.

'Faiza, go. Don't take too long. I will be on the stairs.'

Faiz enters the room, shutting the door behind him carefully, and sits in front of Roohi. He looks at her red feet, the almonds stitched into the bottom of her salwar, and the faint pink nail polish reflecting the patterns on the ceiling. She looks at his combed hair, clean-shaven face and the few hairs rising up towards his Adam's apple.

'I painted this a few weeks ago. It just needs a final coat of varnish before it goes back. I have been stalling, wanted you to see it.'

Roohi looks at the Omar Khayyám screen leaning against Faiz's knees. She has never seen anything like it. She marvels at how real and blue the water is. Like Faiz, she focuses on the cup on the painting into which the girl with the long hair is pouring wine or kehwa. She breathes in at the sight of the sails on the boat. She is amazed he can do it. She loves it.

Roohi has brought the gloves. Chocolate brown, she had chosen in the end. Now, she feels a little hesitant. How does she say it? What if he doesn't like them? She lets the polythene bag slip out of her purse. It lodges in her lap. 'It's for you.'

Faiz colours too, lifts the flap of the plastic bag, then takes out one glove with his index finger and thumb. 'Oh, you won't believe this but I have never worn gloves in my life. I always have two pockets in my pheran.'

'Will you at least try them?'

'Oh, yes, yes, that's not what I meant. Where did you get them?'

'I knitted them.'

He touches the gloves now, as if he has only just seen them, which in a way is true. He feels the soft new wool. Faiz knows what he is about to do is something you might see in films, but he also knows it is the only way he can express what he feels, so he hurriedly, awkwardly, touches Roohi's hands, runs his fingers over them, accidentally lifts the sleeve on her wrist, recedes, and lets his palm rest on the fingers of her right hand.

Roohi doesn't really know the exact moment when she turns her hand upside down but she's holding his tight now. Faiz presses her hand and laughs.

'You should wear the gloves.'

He puts them on and cups her face in the wool. He laughs again.

Kabir Ahmed Khan, Roohi's father, has not felt so upbeat since he retired from government service last year. The meeting at the DC's office seems to have gone well. He is to help the commissioner's office in a new census they want to conduct in the city's downtown areas. This is the first piece of administrative work that the new commissioner wants to undertake. Having worked all his life in the now-comatose Census Department, Khan Saêb, as he is popularly known in the area, feels confident he will be able to prepare lists of all the families in Block Eight, which comprises twenty-six localities in and around Bohir Kadal. The all-important PA to the commissioner came down himself to meet him, and handed him the new census charts. He could easily have sent a clerk or an orderly with the papers, Khan Saêb thinks.

'They are straight from the DC's office. You can take them home but please do keep them in a safe place. We are not advertising these assignments. Only trusted former government employees have been contacted and you are one of them. Let me know when you can complete them. Only then will the Commissioner Saêb decide.'

Khan Saêb did not tell the thin, chain-smoking, middle-aged PA, always dressed in a sweater and tie, that this is easy work for him. That the area he has been entrusted with was *his* area, that he was born in Khanqah-i-Mualla, went to the local high school and, soon after his MCom, started work as a junior assistant, retiring from the same department as assistant director after thirty-eight years of honest and unblemished service. Khan Saéb did not tell the PA that it was highly probable he had walked through every lane and by-lane in his area and perhaps knew every general store in the neighbourhood and beyond. That, back in the day, he used to operate through his informal network of shopkeepers, tailors, chemists, ration ghats and barber shops. That he had had tea at almost every mohalla president's home in the four major censuses that had taken place during his long service. Khan certainly did not tell him his little secret. That copies of all the final census documents he had helped prepare are tucked away in a large cupboard in his daughter's room on the top floor of his house.

Pleased with himself, Khan sits down for evening tea with his wife and daughter. 'Where is Rumi?'

'You ask that almost every day, Papa. When does he ever sit at home during the day?' Roohi cuts open a bun for her father and applies butter on the soft insides.

'It's all right, he's still young, must be playing cricket down at the school ground,' Mummy says.

'I may get that part-time assignment from the DC's office I was talking about.' Minutes ago, he had told himself that he would not talk about the job until it has been confirmed.

'Remember your promise, Papajee,' Roohi says, in a state of calm bliss these days, and pours tea from the thermos.

'I haven't forgotten, but it will take time, dear. It is not confirmed yet. May take a week or two.'

'I don't know anything about your promises, but we must repair the chimney before the winter comes. I don't want to see icicles stretch down to the oven.'

'Yes, yes, everything will be fine, madam. Why do you worry so much?'

'Someone has to.'

Roohi looks at her parents, puts an arm around her mother and smiles. 'The tea is delicious today. Have another cup, Mummy.'

The Principal

When Farhat goes to school on Monday after a day and a half's break, the building has been transformed. All the windows, except the two small ones at the top, have vanished.

Windows of intricate patterned work, with ginger and green and blue stained-glass rhomboids behind the lattice, windows with a thousand handmade brass latches and hooks, windows that have looked out at the town for more than eight decades have gone, except the fitted glass pieces in the domed crowns, and the occasional panel that must have refused to fold inwards and which is now hanging out, abandoned.

All the windows on the first three floors have turned into square sandbag embankments with dark slits in the centre. Only birds can see through those holes, Farhat thinks. There are sandbags hanging everywhere on the façade, hundreds of them, grey and pale and bulging. They remind Farhat of floods. They remind her of piles of rice sacks at the ration depot on the bank of the river she used to visit with her eldest brother when she was a child. They also remind her of where she is, of what is happening in her city, of what is being done to her city. Until now, Farhat has veered between two states of mind: it won't reach here, her, her school, her home, it's a boys' thing, she and her friends have nothing to do with it, and even if it does come here, we won't really be affected, it's what makes the news at night. Or: it's beginning to happen in many places now, brave Kalashnikov-bearing boys, entire neighbourhoods staging demonstrations, defying and chasing away whole armies, families providing food and shelter to the brave ones – when will we get to see something, when will we get to chant the freedom song, when will I actually see a mujahid? She has been unsure, she has been confused, she's fifteen.

But this is certainly not how she had imagined it. My school?

She enters with fearful steps. There is a military-walla at the gate, a huge demon in the door, behind another sandbag castle, and he has a gun. Of course he will have a gun. He looks at her and asks her to stop. Farhat takes a deep breath and decides to be brave. I don't know what has happened, I don't know anything, maybe it's just routine, maybe we now have to learn to deal with these things, these men.

'What's your name?' The sentry smiles. Farhat relaxes.

'Mir Farhat. Class ten. Father's name, late Mir Mohammed Ali.'

'Good, you can go. Oh, one minute, let me check your bag. Don't worry, it's nothing, something we have to do. You understand, don't you?'

'Er, yes, yes, sir. Here, take it.'

'What's this? Kaashmiri apple, aha.' He turns it round in his hand. 'Good girl, go.'

In the classroom, Farhat is relieved to see most of her friends already seated on the coarse red mats, as indeed are most other students of the combined mega-class of matric students. Some girls are 'on leave', as their parents have refused to send them to the school.

'One day they will put us all in these sacks and send us home for good,' Rehana jokes. 'Then there will be no more maths classes.'

Nazli wonders how they managed to fill all these sandbags so quickly. Did they dig up the Hari Parbat Hill?

Masarat Jabeen Qadri, Farhat's closest friend and the most studious girl in class ten, says, 'They must have gone down to the river and looted it.'

'You are all wrong.' Beenish Ali stands up. 'They have everything under the sun in their cantonment. What is a little clay?'

'Maybe for our safety. The school will be safe now. No one will set fire to it, will they?' Farhat, desperate to sound brave and wise.

53

'Have you gone mad, Farree? Are you fine with being leered at by these dirty men? This was a girls' school until two weeks ago, now it's a barracks. Don't you get it?' Beenish fingers a hole in her white dupatta.

'Oh, come on. They won't dare to. We are in the middle of the city, Beenu. Besides, didn't Shanta Ma'am say it's only for a little while? And the sentry at the gate was nice enough, wasn't he?'

'Oh, that's what they always say – only for a little while, temporary! It's all Shanta Ma'am's fault. If she had refused in the first place, we wouldn't be all cramped together like this. My buttocks are itching from this mat. I wish someone had burnt the school down. She should have said no, but why would she care? Her own relatives are in the Convent, aren't they?' Beenish goes pink and shoves her ruler into her bag.

'What if it wasn't up to her? How do you know for certain she was asked?' Masarat Jabeen comes to Farhat's defence but perhaps also because she cannot help her bright contrarian self.

Nazli, the oldest of the group, stands up and addresses her friends in the manner of a teacher. 'Look, we all know this is not nice. I don't like these people here – may hellfire descend on them soon. But there is nothing we can do. Shanta Ma'am has been like a mother to all of us. Let's not forget that. I am absolutely sure if there's anything she can do, she will do it.'

'I agree,' Farhat says. She has become wiser in the last two weeks than all of this year. 'We should talk to Ma'am and see what she says.'

'Yes, we should, and also ask her what we are supposed to do if the mujahids attack the school, and why shouldn't they? This is a siege, I swear upon Allah.' Rehana, who has listened quietly to the exchange, ends the conversation and raises her eyebrows at everyone.

They all sit silently now, waiting for the first class of the day, for their English teacher Sara Didi – she has forbidden the use of 'Ma'am' in her class – who will start explaining the extract from

Maugham's *Of Human Bondage* in the English anthology they've been studying this term.

Shanta Koul, renowned educationist Professor Madan Koul's eldest daughter, is looking at a part of the old red sofa in her office. The other part is now in the main laboratory, which for a short time – the exact phrase used in the conversation – will serve as the makeshift office of the officer in charge of the soldiers in the school. Shanta Koul has been at the school for fifteen years, teaching history, geography, moral science and English. She was made principal four years ago. Her father, himself the principal of the Gandhi College in his post-retirement life, wasn't entirely happy with her for taking on this new role. She should have spent a few more years in active teaching, he had felt. 'Nothing can stop me teaching classes when I'm the headmistress,' she had responded. She smiles drily now, remembering her father's sombre face. In the last two weeks she has spent most of her working hours talking to soldiers.

Nevertheless, she feels she has managed this unforeseen development, as she refers to it, rather well, especially since she was able to extract a promise, in writing, from the visiting army officers that they would leave as soon as they find 'accommodation' more suited to their needs and, in any case, before the six-monthly exams, when she will need all the classrooms, including the laboratory.

Shanta stands up now, adjusting the three pins on the front of her green and purple rough-silk sari, and gazes out of the large window that looks over the assembly courtyard. As always, she admires the evergreen hedges lining the wall at the back. She has heard it said that Sajida Ahmed, one of the earliest educationists of the Valley along with Begum Z. Ali and Mehmooda Shah, planted these hedges in the school when it became a high school in the sixties, and feels a particular pride in having looked after them well. She looks at the newly constructed junior wing towards the left of the yard, running from the main building all the way to the back. 'We shouldn't cut those three hedges. We could stop a few feet from the wall.' She remembers the argument she then had with her deputy headmaster, Syed Afaq Bukhari, or Syed Sir, as he was known in the school. 'We can always plant more on the other side, Shanta Jee, I want the little girls to have more space, their own space. You can do the planting yourself. We will even erect a small plaque with your name on it. "Planted by a Legend",' he had joked, trying to end the discussion on a cheerful note. She misses him sorely now, sometimes with a tear in her eye. She remembers his clipped greying beard. The three Waterman fountain pens, blue, black and red, in the top pocket of his blue blazer. Syed Sir was killed in firing by the border security force outside his home in Raazè Kadal, as he was returning home with bread from the local baker. His youngest, Aasiya Bukhari, is in class seven A now, in the classroom directly under her office. No, above her, in the combined class seven these days. She sighs.

Shanta's gaze stops at a group of senior girls standing near the junior wing. They are in a loose huddle, sort of hiding by one another's sides and talking in whispers. One of them begins to go forward but then hurries back to the group.

'You go, you go.'

'Why should I? You go first.'

Then she sees two soldiers sitting in the sun, smoking, near the steps to the bathrooms, their rifles hanging loose from their arms as if they were broken branches of a tree.

Shanta picks up her bag and headmistress's cane and storms out of the room. Then she comes back and leaves the cane behind.

The Officer

Major Sumit Kumar is looking at a vast chart spread on the dissecting table. Around him are chairs piled high on each other, towers of steel legs and arms. Charts of human anatomy hang on the walls, life processes in masterfully drawn, all-colour posters.

1. Circulatory System
2. Respiratory System
3. Digestive System
4. Nervous System
5. Skeletal System
6. Muscular System . . .

Clots of dust have begun to cloud a heart here, a lung there, a spinal cord in the far corner, a brain on the front wall. He remembers these diagrams well. His boarding school near Dehradun had them too, bigger, better. He never really disliked biology but his heart was in physics and chemistry, subjects he excelled at and which helped him to get into the National Defence Academy a couple of years after high school.

Kumar lights up a Gold Flake and decides to come back later to the chart in front of him. The task seems daunting but it is doable, and he has all the support he needs. He takes a long drag and looks out of the window into the courtyard below.

Principal Koul is talking to two of his men, pointing towards the toilets at the back. She is waving her index finger as though delivering a lecture. What an elegant woman, with her impeccably polished low-heel brown shoes, the bag over her arm, the sari perfectly tucked in at the waist. Reminds him of his mother back home in Delhi, always in a sari and never without polished shoes and makeup.

The soldiers seem to be protesting, albeit gently. He does not like it and yet he does not want to intervene. He can't hear everything but:

'We were only smoking, Madamjee.'

'But can't you see the girls were . . . ? Do not ever forget this is a school. Is that understood?'

They mutter something and leave, slinging their rifles over their shoulders as a farmer would carry his plough at dusk. Kumar sees they have tucked their trousers into their boots. He likes it. Among the very first things he'd said on taking charge a few weeks ago was, 'I don't want to see your uniforms crumpled, ever. And trousers inside the boots, always. Always ready, do you follow?'

'Yes, sir.'

'Yes, sir.'

Principal Koul is now having a word with the girls, who are listening in rapt attention in a cluster around her. As she leaves, the girls hurry into the washrooms, a couple waiting outside. Kumar is pleased with the outcome and goes back to his boat-sized chart.

He is at the centre of it, in the school. In front of the building is the Bohir Kadal crossroads, the north and south of the main road and the two streets criss-crossing it from east and west, one of which goes into old Malaroutt, connecting Bohir Kadal to that other, older, centre of the city, Nowhatta, and the other into the Zaině Kadal area on the banks of the Jhelum. The chart shows a little shrine on the Malaroutt street. It's called Rahgeer Saěb, a quiet little green hut in the middle of the street with a padlocked donation box at the front. Kumar does not know anything about it. The chart also shows the Jamia Masjid in Nowhatta, the oldest and the grandest mosque in this scenic land, which of course, he knows about, even the fact that it was erected by Sultan Sikander at the end of the fourteenth century. Opposite the school, behind the square and the bus stop, the street goes towards Zaině Kadal, the fourth bridge on the Jhelum, marked by a hash sign on the chart. Then there are two more lanes: the dyers' lane goes towards the famous shrine of Khanqah-i-Mualla;

the lane diametrically opposite the school leads onto Maharaj Gunj, the ancient trading district where a million smells – of spices, perfumes, bales of garlic with their stems intact, copper, Unani medicine and minarets of wet tobacco, of silk and cotton and wool, hardware and paint even, and of Srinagar's famous wedding decorations packed in cradle-like wicker baskets draped in gold and silver lace – waft up into the city's air and sometimes even imbue the Jhelum's waters, it is said, with their inebriating fragrance.

At the mouth of each street and lane, there is or will be a bunker. At the other end of each street and lane, there is or will be a bunker. Three sandbags and a line-drawn machine-gun mark the bunkers on Kumar's chart. In total, his grid will cover twenty-six localities, starting from the school to Nowhatta at one end, Raazė Kadal towards the north, Khanqah and the MP School area towards the south-east, Naid Kadal and Khanyar police station on the east, and up to Fateh Kadal in the south-west. Fifty-two main bunkers and twenty-six small checkpoints in all. It's doable.

And yet the picture daunts him and the thought of six similar grids covering the entire city makes him somewhat uneasy. On paper, it all looks clinical, meticulous; the city, its natural defences of water and waterways already choked, will in no time be theirs again and he will have fulfilled his role. Most of the bunkers are up, the light machine-guns are mounted, the ordnance chain is foolproof, and he has personally selected the men in charge of each bunker and planned the daily supply and patrol route from the school. He's also made sure that there is a bunker and a mobile unit near the entry points of each waterway in his grid – in fact, surveillance of the waterways was his idea, and, once again impressed by his logistical brilliance, his superiors decided to implement it in the other grids, too. Delhi and the local HQ from which his instructions arrive via Signal, he has been told, are both pleased with his plan.

At night, Kumar will sleep in a string cot with two double mattresses on it. His men will sleep in the large rooms below him, rooms that were classes ten, nine, eight and seven, Sections A, B and

C of each, until last week. Rooms that have for ages listened to the whispers of the older girls, the laughter of the younger ones, the proud recitations of poetry by the brightest girls, the sombre readings from the Qur'ān in the religious studies class, the grumbling drone of a bored, waiting-for-retirement-day teacher, the sweet, proud lectures by the headmistress after yet another illustrious set of results for the school.

He feels secure enough in the narrow storeroom of the lab that serves as his bedroom, although these damn things stare at him for far too long when he goes to bed. Dissection boxes, an array of coloured-pencil cartons, timer clocks, these eerie suspended scales, an old-fashioned Bell microscope that has a particularly acute downward gaze, and scores of jars and test-tubes, some broken and some containing residues of old experiments. Yesterday he used an old lab chart to cover up the glistening plastic replicas of the human brain on the shelf in front of his bed. In the dimness of the light, they had seemed to throb, almost come alive.

Kumar folds the grid of his territory after imagining the route the machine will take. He is not entirely sure of the purpose of this exercise but he must follow orders. The directive about the machine came suddenly yesterday. It will sweep sensitive areas, the signal man wrote, before all foot patrols. The officer in him is curious to see the new invention, what it can do, but a part of him is not entirely confident. This sort of stuff only works in sci-fi films, he thinks. For a moment, he imagines himself as Mel Gibson driving the machine in some *Mad Max* film. The directive read that only two machines will be deployed at first, one in Srinagar and one in that other troublesome town, Sopore. More if needed.

He wants to see it, drive it, but he also dreads what it might do. He thinks of the girls he saw earlier.

Of Promises

Their meetings are furtive, whispered, and in the dark mostly. Either under the decaying wood-inlay ceiling of the balcony by the river, or in that dark basement, the secret path to which Roohi has known since her childhood but has never entered, except when she'd hidden there ten years ago during a game of hide-and-seek. She had soon felt scared when she realized no one would ever find her there.

Roohi escapes from home on the pretext of offering her evening namaz, which she sometimes does, in the women's section of the shrine, Faiz by making sure he stands in the last row at the mosque so he can slip out as soon as the mandatory prayers are over. He doesn't stay for the post-namaz verbose supplications that the Iran-returned young imam, Abid Shah, offers mostly for his own dead relatives but also for Kashmir and the larger Muslim world sometimes, or for the cricket and political chit-chat that ensues in the seductively warm hamam of the mosque.

On entering the shrine premises, he doesn't look or wait for Roohi. He goes past the graveyard and onto the balcony, taken in by the murmurs of the river in the dark. He knows the exact moment when Roohi appears by a particular tightening of the body he feels at the first smell of her scent.

Today is Thursday, Shab-e-Jummah, the evening before Friday. Sad supplicants pray tearfully in the shrine, as they sing of unconditional love for Allah and his Prophet:

> You were, you are, you will be, our only saviour
> O, beloved of Khoda, you're the beloved of His subjects too

Old men rest their backs against the wood panelling inside the main hall and wipe off half-dry tears. The panels are painted so intricately, in that high genre of zaiwyul naqashi, that even the oldest masters find it daunting to reproduce them. Persian miniatures sit amid wide royal vistas. Verses from the Qur'ān enclose moments of beauty as though to prevent violation. And then there is that colour of magic, Seher, a sharp fusion of crimson and orange, whose delicate chemistry was known to Mir Mohammed Ali but, alas, he didn't have time to whisper it to his youngest, or perhaps the son was too young to understand the language of colour. It is among the pigments Faiz covets at Rangrez's. At this hour, when the people of the city and the long-travelling devotees from the country sit in the warm, perspiration-filled air inside the shrine, the colour actually begins to glow, almost with a pulse.

A somewhat similar papier-mâché prayer hall in a mosque in Mashhad in Iran was covered by a polystyrene coat to preserve it but the colours have since dimmed, 'turned off their light', as the young Persian poet Sabeel sang on seeing it. The other, in a forlorn hilltop shrine in northern Tajikistan, is still fine, fresh and thriving – the secret way, as we all know, is sometimes the only way to survive in a world filled with noise – and is in the hands of the Family of Forty Poets, all women and each named after the patron saint's disciples. The men of this most rarefied of Sufi lines work the orchards below the hill. Seven orchards – apricots, pomegranates, almonds, walnuts, plums, pears and, most importantly, the delicate Seher plant – circle the hill. A different group of men work in each orchard and, depending on what fruit is in season, the men not tilling run the household while the women compose verse and assess each other's work before submitting it, with varying degrees of trepidation and self-belief, to the *grande dame* of poetry, author of fourteen collections and head of the order, Hafa Khatoun. It is the root of the plant that is the source of the paint used in the papier-mâché art in this shrine, in the suppressed one in Mashhad and, of course, in the one we have momentarily left behind. Roohi and Faiz's shrine was last painted with the colour at the turn of the twentieth century, when sheepskin pouches carrying pigments were still travelling from Tajikistan to artists' workshops in this part of the world. When Kashmir, Kashgar, Samarkand, Tashkent, Bukhara, Baghdad, Khorasan and Shiraz were tied by both verse and colour. When schools of artists from the central mountains created workshops in the heart of Srinagar and made its shrines sing.

The hall is stuffed with men and the stained-glass panes bear little rivers of condensation. As the old lean back and contemplate their own past and their children's future, the young fill the room with chants that echo through the chambers, reaching the women in their quarters on either side of the main congregation; they join in with a stirring rendition of their own, more urgent and musical than that of the men, the cumulative ache and the specific effect of a thousand souls in harmony, wafting out into the smoke-filled evening air of this hallowed neighbourhood. The crows stay still – always, it has to be put on record – at this most affecting hour at the shrine. People in the houses on the opposite bank often turn off their radios and TVs at this time, many joining in the chorus from across the river, marking their presence by not only partaking in the recitations but also switching on every single light in the rooms, kitchens and verandas of their riverside homes. It's a magical hour, when the devotee, the peasant and the landlord, the saint and the Omniscient all seem intimately bound together. An hour that has defined this neighbourhood through the ages. It's a time when everyone is free and people know that no one can take away their liberty. It is said that the people of this ancient part will not blink if it comes to giving up their lives to protect this hour; the defence of the shrine is not a matter of discourse for them, it is who they are. It is said that they remember their soul-histories so well that not even mass murder will turn them into people they are not; it is also said that there are those who want to impose their shallow tales on this hour of freedom, those who want these people to stop their old chant and sing another song from another country, but these are people who don't know what love can do.

Faiz has things on his mind. Roohi has Faiz on her mind.

'What will we do when someone finds out?'

'Don't your sisters already know?'

'Yes, but I'm not talking about them.'

'Who are you talking about, then?'

'The elders. My people. Your people. What will they say?'

'They might want to kill me. But will you let them do that?'

'I won't know what to do.'

She offers her hand. Faiz puts it between his palms. They both look towards the back door of the shrine. Above it are very small lights, scores of them, which glow and quiver like candles. 'It's the special filament that makes them flicker so,' Faiz mumbles, and looks at Roohi. She doesn't say she knows.

Below the lamps is the arched door, an entire surah carved into the dome. Chalk white on blue, it seems the script is flying off the door, then reappearing from the start as though being written by itself. Faiz presses Roohi closer to him, his hand clenching her shoulder.

'I don't think you should worry about my family yet. They don't know anything.'

'One day they will, and I don't know what will happen after that.'

'What will yours say?'

'Hmm . . . My mother is the gentlest woman in the world but then again she's old, old-fashioned. Abba has seen a bit of the world and he is fond of me, so I don't think he will have too much of a problem. But I don't know about my other brother, about Abba's children, about the extended family, and then there is the rest of the neighbourhood, the town . . .'

'Papa dotes on me. Mummy loves me a lot, too, even though she won't show it much. I wonder why the whole town has to worry about these things.'

64

'What is the first thing you want to do after getting married?' He's surprised at his courage.

Roohi just looks at him, keeps on looking at him. With only the slightest movement of her lips. She presses on her thigh through the pocket of her pheran, the fingernails sinking into the flesh. She doesn't say anything.

'Hmm, I would like to go to Nishat–Shalimar, on a shikara,' Faiz says, instantly thinking of boat-rides on the misty lake, of couples reclining against florid cushions. Roohi thinks of sparkling honeymooners from India, of aching, sentimental songs enacted on their black-and-white TV by Shammi Kapoor and Dharmendra and Shashi Kapoor, and that face of utter magic, Sharmila Tagore. Faiz wants to hold hands. He has never been on a shikara ride or any other kind of journey into the lake since the long water picnics of his childhood ceased, when the city decided to cull its inland waterways and fill them with rubble. In those days abundant with water, boats and watermelons, fish and lotuses on the boats, the lake and the city were one. He remembers the architecture of land on water, water on land, and the large boat loaded with the whole Mir clan and their samovars of tea, enormous copper pans filled with rice and fish-and-greens, towering lunch boxes with lamb stews, his mother's delicate walnut dip and the poppyseed-coated bread from Mir Kandur the family baker. They would anchor at the Dembh waterway, soon start nibbling at their picnic, then drift on through the willow-covered blue-green liquid pathways to the lake and on to the Mughal gardens in the palm of the Zabarwan hills. It all ended the moment a loony minister, Sheikh Samandar, decided a road was development and water was not. Some Sheikh of the Sea.

Roohi, on the other hand, has not only been on the lake – it is the river she hasn't sailed on – but also visited almost all of the tourist spots, the ones bordering the city and the pieces of paradise in the mountains, too. She has composed many a sad poem looking at the city from the ramparts of the bookish Mughal prince Dara Shikoh's library, the Abode of the Fairies, Pari Mahal, in the belly of the mountain. She has imagined lying under the ageless chinars in the Nishat Garden, always stopping short of etching 'Roohi +' into the supple bark of the maples, and sighed at numerous sunsets by the Shalimar. Roohi has entrusted many a prayer to the dream-green Sar at Harwan, the reservoir blinking only to talk to the pines at its edge. She has also been on every school picnic since class three – often the first girl to board the SRTC bus at dawn. At Wular, she beheld for the first time what a sea might look like, the vastness of the lake that takes in the Jhelum, *her Jhelum*, then lets it go to Pakistan, filling her with love and pride for her land. In Gulmarg, when she was twelve and had just started reading books beyond the scope of the school curriculum – poetry that made her blush but also gave her secret pleasures – she was the only girl to enter the near-deserted St Mary's Church in the middle of the flower meadow. The Manasbal Lake, that little marvel, which had not yet been trampled over by tourist hordes, had made her sing aloud. Meena Madam, the doyenne of deenyaat, had taken Roohi aside and said, 'It would be such a blessing if you recited in class as well.' Roohi agreed, and from then on always said the closing prayer at the end of Meena's religious-studies class. And she still remembers the music of the Lidder river of Pahalgam, which had filled her heart with a storm of her own. *When will I come here with him?* she had wondered, but had soon cheered up as her friends started a water fight by the banks of the stream. Roohi, self-conscious about her new black bra, had made sure she spread her dupatta over her shoulders and chest.

'Yes, we will go in a shikara. In the moonlight.'

'I will row the boat with the shikara man. I like its sound.'

'Will you not sit with me on the cushions, then?'

'Oh, oh, of course I will. I didn't think of – I want to, I do.'

'We will also go up to Pari Mahal and make our wishes there. The city looks quiet, at complete peace, from there. And the sunset is like God's own hour.'

'We will also drink from the water of Chashm-e-Shahi. Have you been there? Abba says people come from all over the world to collect water from the royal spring. Even rich people.'

'No. Is it like Aab-e-Zamzam?'

'No, that is the water the Hajis bring from the well in Mecca.'

'And we will spend a few days in Gulmarg in the snow. I have never seen it in the snow. The school picnics only happened in the summer, you see. Only private schools take their students camping-shamping.'

'Of course, of course. I'll take you to Gulmarg in the snow, I promise, Roohi.'

'Say that again.'

'I promise.'

'Not that.'

'Oh.'

'We can also go to Pahalgam, if you like.'

'Hmm . . . Isn't it supposed to be too crowded now? Majélal, my friend, says there are more shops than there are horses in the villages.'

'So what? It's still Pahalgam and I love it. The water is just incredible.'

Roohi stops at the thought of being with him by herself. She wonders if he'll throw water over her. She wonders if she can throw water over him.

Thus, they dream and dream. Together and alone. A tightening of the chest their shared language. They meet and talk, the evening prayer their pretext and sanctuary, the shrine their witness and refuge.

While the area is beginning to smell of exhaust from the Leyland trucks ferrying the soldiers in and out – mostly in, you could say – while the boys are learning to assemble shining new guns down in the high-walled backyard of the MP School, and play with grenade pins in their mouth, while the bunkers come up like warts in all of Khanqah, their machine-guns watching everyone and their shadow like an evil jinn, and while susurrations bearing words such as 'action' and 'encounter' are beginning to fill the evenings, Faiz and Roohi embrace in the darkness of the shrine's basement. Some evenings they feel guilty but do not speak of it to each other. There is still a white sheet lying in the alcove where some old manuscripts and handwritten copies of the Qur'ān, a great sufi's original treatises on Sunnah, theology, social reformation and his thoughts on high Sufism, are kept safe in sealed trunks, and where all the old rugs from the main hall are rolled and wrapped in muslin.

On the sheet there are three books from which Roohi reads to Faiz every evening: an abridged version of *Shirin-Farhad*; an anthology of poems, including her favourite Parveen Shakir; and, of course, the three stories of Akhtar Mohiuddin she has had photocopied from the now proscribed and nearly extinct journal *New Nation*. Faiz likes the verses from *Shirin-Farhad* but feels a strange pull on hearing Roohi read from Akhtar.

As they speak on this sixth Friday evening, a young boy runs furiously into the educational area, grabs another boy by his collar and punches him in the stomach. 'If you even contemplate sullying my sister's name again, I will skin you alive. I'm sparing you today as you are from our mohalla. Remember that!'

The boy who has been hit turns, and when he thinks he is at a safe distance from his assailant, mutters, 'Control your sister before it's too late.' Rumi, Roohi's brother, hears him but does not turn back.

'It's the night-time prayer, I must go now.' Faiz refuses to let go of Roohi's hand. She pulls a couple of times, then lets it be. Love has made her lazy, a bit like Faiz. They sit close to each other, breathing in each other's warmth.

She knows Mummy will be on the verge of stepping out to wait for her in the street. She feels guilty, remembering her mother's creased, anxious face. She also knows Papa will pretend not to care and will carry on watching *Doordarshan News* – 'All a pack of lies,' he will say at the end of the bulletin – as he keeps an ear out for the door or at least his wife's remonstrations with her daughter.

She knows it's another opportunity for her brother to provoke her mother. 'No other girl in the neighbourhood stays out at this time. Many don't even come out during the day. Mummy, why don't you say anything?'

She also knows of her mother's defence of her. 'She offers the namaz at least, Rumya, you just stay out to waste time.'

Nevertheless, it is at the thought of her brother, or owing to some foresight, that she abruptly gets up, puts her hands on Faiz's limp shoulders and says, 'I have to leave now. You see, I do want to meet you again, and again, until the day we don't have to meet like this.'

Faiz stands up too.

Rumi stops in front of the house as he sees his mother pacing by the door. Angry, he runs in the direction of the shrine.

Faiz pulls Roohi towards him and holds her.

Rumi leaps down the stairs to the shrine, three steps for one.

Roohi slips her fingers into Faiz's hair and pushes him away.

Rumi stops near the donation box, gazing up towards the women's halls, his eyes darting left and right. With no sign of his sister, he decides to wait by the steps that lead to the main hall.

Under those ancient stones, his sister suddenly begins to cry as an inexplicable feeling comes over her. It has struck her with such clarity and force. She doesn't want to let go. Faiz remains silent.

*

Rumi thinks he has heard some noise but there is no one in or near the shrine; the halogen lights that the government's Shrine Board put up last year cast a bright moth-scraped light all around.

Roohi emerges into a cellar by the women's hall – one that is in the direct line of vision from her own room – and ascends the steps into the hall. She goes up to the windows and looks down upon her brother, who is sitting on top of the green donation box. He is not looking up but straight towards the main gate of the shrine, where a shadow has just hurriedly ascended the steps and vanished.

Sister, Brother

'Tell me something, Farree, where does Faiz go in the evening? I know he tells you everything.' Mir Zafar plays a little tune with the toothpick, a to-and-fro strum against the base of the penholder on his desk. He lets go of it just when it's at breaking point.

'He goes to the shrine, Abba. He said he likes to sit by the river. I like it too, but I can't go.'

'No, you can't. These are not good times, what with policemen and soldiers everywhere. They had even come to the printing press, Haqqani Saéb was saying. So they haven't left your school yet?'

'No, Abba, but we have become a bit used to it, and they mind their own business. The sentry at the gate doesn't check my bag any more. He is like a giant, he is so tall, his name is Rathi. Calls me Kaashmiri Apple, ha-ha. Shall I make your bed now?'

'Yes, my dear.'

Farhat lifts the lid to the vast wooden trunk built into the window bay. It contains mattresses, quilts and pillows for the ground-floor sleepers, including her eldest brother. Tiny pouches of naphthalene sit in the four corners. Mir Zafar changes them himself every spring. Farhat likes the smell of this wood, its colour now a beaten, polished light brown, decades of wear having rounded off every edge. When she was a little girl, she used to slip twenty-five-paisa coins through the slits in the door of the trunk so she could be lowered in to retrieve them. When she was slightly older, she once hid in it after her sisters had refused to take her to their friend's sister's wedding. She had sobbed and sobbed, overwhelmed by the immense weight of self-pity – had I had a father, he would have ordered them to take me along – and then fallen asleep on her father's Indian velvet pillows, one of the few remaining articles from their past. Mir Zafar

Ali still uses them and Farhat loves looking after them, the cotton covers over the velvet always spotless.

Farhat does the bed methodically, meticulously, tucking in the ends of the quilt under the mattress with the base folded under. Mir Zafar also likes his torch, rosary (all the way from Karbala), glass flask of water and a copy of *Tafsir-al-Mizan*, by his side on a mat on the floor, even though he has not looked up 'Interpretations of the Qur'ān' in more than a year now. He has read it once, and is disappointed that the young imam at their mosque does not know anything about scholarly work or if he reads any books at all.

Since it's the weekend, Farhat sits by the laid-out bedding, waiting for her weekly pocket money. Mir Zafar sometimes deliberately delays it, just a little, to watch his baby sister's expectant, reddening face.

He takes out a crisp ten-rupee note and raises it towards Farhat with two fingers; she swiftly slips it into her pocket and smiles.

'Is Faiz paying for your new tutor, Farree? Is she any good?'

'Oh, she's wonderful, Abba.'

'Did Faiz arrange for her to come to teach you?'

'No, no, he didn't. I did. A friend at school said she's a master at trigonometry and, you know, it's my only weak subject. So I asked her if she could teach me. I was ready to go to her home, but she said she prefers visiting her students, so I said it was all right, please do come. They live nearby, very close to the shrine.'

'That's good, Farree. I need to know who's coming to our house, don't I? Someone should have asked me first, wouldn't you think?'

'Yes, Abba. I thought you knew . . .'

'As I said, it's fine now. But Faiz knows her?'

'Yes.'

'Good. Go to bed now. It's very late. And here.' Mir Zafar takes out a five-rupee note and puts it into her hand. Farhat wonders what the extra pocket money means.

⋆

The sparks fly out in quick half-arcs and die. The sounds echo briefly. The wisteria leaves at the top recoil briefly, as though from a bad smell. The thickness of the wall, the dense creepers on the other side that have risen up to the top, the rows of willows and poplars on the waterside and many strips of a jute sack wrapped around the barrel of the Kalashnikov, all the way up to its muzzle, smother the otherwise unmistakable noise. Scars, as though dark tears on the white wall, appear on the old limestone plaster.

Rumi has completed three weeks of his training and when it's his turn he takes it with some boredom. The initial thrill is now replaced by waiting for the real thing, although a part of him is scared of the prospect. And he has been distracted of late. Who was that man at the shrine? Is Roohi really going out with a Shia boy?

'Come on, what's taking you so long? The man is a giant, Rumi, shoot for God's sake.' The trainer, known to Rumi and the other boys as Panther, is waiting for it to get fully dark so he can finish for the day and take the group's only rifle to the hideout. Rumi wakes up and lets the rifle go. The bullets hit the large sketch of a body on the wall. The charcoal lines are smudged in places by the white residue from the holes. He is still not officially a member of the New Salvation Front (NSF), even though he has known Panther and the others for more than two months now. All he has understood so far is that they are to provide backup for the main groups in the area, create small distractions now and then so the big boys can do the real thing. A part of him is pleased he is not in a major group, another part envious of the Pakistan-trained men.

College Street

Professor Madan Koul, principal of the Gandhi College, steadies his double-decked lime-white turban and leaves his office. Every day, as he leaves college, he looks at the row of large portraits of the six former principals, all from his family. Sometimes he feels guilty that the college hasn't had a single Muslim principal, even though he has known many highly educated Muslims and is friends with some; at other times, which is often, he doesn't, family pride taking precedence over everything. His father Captain Shambhujee Koul, the only member of the family to serve in the State Forces and then the Indian Army, was the only one who hadn't worked in education, or he might have, or not, Madan sometimes suspects, had he not been killed in the 1948 war between India and Pakistan. Professor Madan is proud of his lineage, high Brahmin, educationists and social workers, learned folk, and doesn't particularly like to talk about his late father. It is his uncle, Neel Chacha as he used to be known to the children, whom he often remembers and invokes during moments of doubt. Neel Chacha was known for his frontline campaign on land reform, during which he voluntarily gave up almost all of his land holdings, an action so noble that Professor Madan could not but follow suit later. He had given up his share of the family lands soon after his return from Government College, Lahore, a decision that to this day is remembered among the Muslim tiller clans in the rice bowl of Sumbal, who for generations had broken their backs tilling for the Kouls. He now looks at the uncle in sepia and mutters his favourite couplet, a daily and satisfying ritual before he emerges from the vine-draped brick and timber building.

In the street outside are huddles of boys, some tucking in their shirts, some wiping their shoes against the backs of their trousers, and some upturning their collars. The last batches, the seniors, have been leaving in chatty columns of four, five, six, just ahead of the principal. Near the shops, Nab Galdar's ancient general store and Bashir Gour, the milkman, a couple of boys start chanting the film song 'Aane se Uske Aaye Bahar', as they do every day, at the sight of Sameena Geelani, final year BSc (botany and zoology), the tallest and brightest of the Gandhi College girls. The singing boys are at least four years younger, and at least a foot and a half shorter, than her. She does not mind being compared to the spring. Even Professor Madan does not mind the singing.

Ragini Kachroo, who is mistakenly known as 'the voluptuous one' among the boys in the street, all because she wore a body-hugging trouser suit on her first day at college, blushes at the thought of a risqué phrase that may be flung her way. But she, too, is not uncomfortable, as she knows it's essentially all innocuous and her principal is not far behind. Raajė, the archetypical angst-ridden, tragic but occasionally humorous unemployed post-graduate, is seated on the top step of the milkman's shop. She knows. He has conducted a burning one-sided love affair with Ragini ever since she appeared at this very shop front looking for change on a particularly lovely rainy morning two years ago. Raajė hasn't been quite himself since 'lightning struck him from a clear sky', as he prefers to remember that day. He has composed two long narrative poems for Ragini, *Rainy Day 1* and *Rainy Day 2*, but has not presented them to her, fearing his oblique English composition may extinguish any ray of love that may yet kindle in her heart. As the object of his unexpressed and hence comprehensively unrequited love approaches, he lets out a loud sigh and says, 'We too have shed blood, madam. What about us?', then stands up and runs home with a berserk heart demanding him to stop. Sameena Geelani bursts into laughter first, Ragini's other classmates join in immediately and the boys from the romance vigil squad readily participate, while Faiz, our Faiz, who has been sharing a secret of his own with his friends, Showket and Majeed, by the general store, suspects he is the only one to have understood the reference to blood and martyrdom in Raajė's desperate but cryptic declaration of love, and guffaws. It is at this moment that the lanky figure of Principal Madan, the sight of whose starched turban and walking stick usually brings about a silence full of awe, appears in front of Faiz.

'I know you, lad. I know your family, your brother, and I knew your good father. If only you'd gone to college, what wouldn't have been possible? You are an artist – aren't you? What are you doing here with these idlers, bothering my girls?'

'Sir, Madan Sir, I was just, I was just talking . . .'

'Why have my girls run away, then? What did you say to them?' Professor Madan chooses not to notice Sameena and Ragini, who in fact have not run away and are at the bend of the road waiting to see the spectacle of Professor Madan reproaching the now-sweating and mumbling Casanovas.

'Sir, God forbid that I ever say anything to, er, your girls. I didn't, I swear.'

'I saw everything, Faizȧ. I'm old, not blind.'

'Sir, please ask around. You know me.'

That is a fact. Madan has long been fond of the prodigious artist-son of the Mirs, a family he has known of for nearly fifty years if not socialized with.

'I will never do such a thing, and if you ask me, nothing bad happened here, just our Raajė being poetic as usual, sir, you know how he is.'

'Oh, yes, I know him, another failed lover. What can I say, son? I have conveyed to his father and uncle that they should send him to me. He could help in the lab while we find a more suitable job for him. Why hanker after government jobs so much? I don't understand. You tell me, why?' What Madan doesn't know is that Raajė finds his advice, and manner with the boys, condescending and disdainful sometimes, is annoyed by it often, but doesn't confront him because of his old age.

'Yes, sir, it's pointless,' Majeed chips in, having recently completed two years as a junior assistant in the Civil Secretariat.

'You stay quiet, Majêlal. I know your father, too. And you should all go home now. Why waste time on the road like this? Go.' Principal Madan lets the stick swing by his legs. It's past four thirty, and soon it will be time for the first of the evening army patrols. He really wants the boys off the street now.

'Oh, yes, I have to go to Rangrez's, sir. I will walk with you, at least till halfway – can I?'

The professor and Faiz walk back towards the lane that goes past the Mir house, winding all the way to Fateh Kadal, the third bridge on the Jhelum, and then to the main traffic road that leads to Nagar, where the Kouls have lived perhaps since modern-day Srinagar came into being.

'You should participate in these handicrafts exhibitions that the government organizes in Delhi. I can put in a word with the director of handicrafts.'

'Sir, the clerks ask for ten, fifteen, sometimes twenty thousand, for a permit. Besides, I want to be free, sir. These people can't discriminate between fine papier-mâché naqashi and quick-fix Christmas balls with paint daubed on them. And I want to set up something of my own, here, at my home.'

Professor Madan remembers Faiz's father, his crisp Dhaka cotton turban, the trademark round-neck pheran, grey lambswool in winter, terry-cotton in summer, his white trimmed beard, and wonders what Faiz will be like as a grown man.

'Sir, I did not say anything to the girls, I swear.'

'I know.'

'Oh, I have to go now, sir, before Rangrez closes his shop.'

'Take care, son.'

PART TWO

Echoes

The Godmother

Slicing gently through the marshy stillness of the Namchabal water-way is a straw-laden boat. In it are three men, all silent. The youngest is at the back, the eldest in the middle, their local contact and boat-man at the front. They have the temple in their sights now, a simple one-room affair, almost entirely hidden away behind reeds and willows grown wild. It has stood on this little island for almost three hundred years, almost exactly as it was born, the swamp and the restricted access by boat forbidding delusions of grandeur and keeping modernity, and expansion, at bay. It has to be said, also, that most Hindus from the area and beyond prefer it this way. Devotees come every Tuesday, spend an hour or so on the small patch of grass at the front and in direct line of vision of the deity, then quietly leave. Recently, it has been visited by other pilgrims too, men from foreign parts, just to check if all is well, they say, if it might need protection, a small bunker, perhaps, and, if not, daily visits at least. The long-serving caretaker, Pandit Bishambarnath Zadoo, had smiled and said, 'Thank you for your concern, but I and He are just fine. There is no need to worry.' A bunker on the opposite road is marked on Major Sumit Kumar's grid but it has not gone up yet.

The men disembark under the trees behind the temple and quietly move into a mossy clearing in the middle of the willows. From here, they can easily slip out and have the road leading to Fateh Kadal Bridge in full view. It is the eldest of the group who, after making sure his two companions are well hidden, steps out and crouches in a little jungle of reeds at this edge of the island. He can see the road, the street that crosses it at the far end and the auto-rickshaws, cars and minibuses hurrying along it. He can also make out the blurred outline of the two bunkers in the distance, standing guard just before the bridge begins, as though sentries of the river.

It's a bright afternoon. Sparrows, mynah birds, pigeons and two white-chested kingfishers have taken over the courtyard of the temple where the Pandit has just spread barley and oats and bits of bread left over from his spartan breakfast. It has been like this for hundreds of years, the courtyard always brimming with food, the birds never disappointed. The sun darts through the trees, leaping across the patch of ground, warming the birds, lighting up the deity. The Pandit smiles from his seat just behind the doorway. There is a small safe attached to the wooden platform where he has sat and slept for forty-five years. He was entrusted with care of the temple in 1946, when the men with the bunkers hadn't arrived, when there was no India and no Pakistan, he remembers, when there was only Kashmir, and his uncles and their friends had launched their movement against the cruel king. He was twenty and was made to pack overnight and park himself at the temple when it was taken over by local Hindus, the Temple Committee, to prevent it from being sucked up into the Maharaja's Temple Trust.

Zahid Shah goes back to his two companions and nods. He unfolds the map of the grid they discussed in the meeting last week. A somewhat reduced photocopy of the grid Sumit Kumar has in his school office, it does not have any handwritten notes or marks on it. Everything, he's been told repeatedly, has to be committed to memory but do keep a copy just in case.

It is time. They sit down for a smoke and once again check their arms. The youngest unties the bit of rope he'd used to anchor the boat. Then, slowly, he slips his large weapon back under a loose plank. They have made sure the bottom of the boat is covered with three layers of polythene. A few willows have come up through the water near the shore. He is unsure if they were there first and the water gradually encroached on the island or if someone actually planted them in the water. Their leaves, chiselled and fine, kiss the water. He sees some fish underneath, their quicksilver not unlike the willow leaves above, although he has heard the water here is dirty, unfriendly, the contamination from the city beginning to kill the river life. This used to be a fresh-water pool, a reservoir created by the abundance of the lake, which fed the Nallah Mar canal that traipsed through the city. In fact, this is what remains of the canal, a strangulated cripple of that waterway, a sickly reminder of what will, over a generation or two, become a legend, a story the young may or may not believe.

They row along the island's rim for a while, slowly, slowly, the boat as if reluctant to leave water for land. They disembark at the edge of the new road that has come up just behind the compound of the MP School. This road, too, was built on water, filling yet another artery of the city.

After showing themselves briefly on the main road – not that they always care, in fact it's all right if people see them so they can get away or slip back into their homes, or if nothing else, it gives the younger ones a kick – they slither into the narrow cobbled lanes of Namchabal. In about ten minutes, they are back on the road where it joins the traffic artery near the new Fateh Kadal Bridge. The old bridge, yet another marvel on the river, with its ancient shops that used to sell gold, muslin and brocade from Bukhara, spices and potions from Lahore and Amritsar, is too old to carry traffic. Until a few years ago, it was the main link from this part of the city to the part where the big hospital is, or from where you could go to the central police station. It was one of the city's most glorious landmarks, albeit one with a dark history. In the time of the bad king particularly, they used to have a pole and hook on the bridge on which to hang the bodies of executed men driven to killing cows to feed their starving children.

Now, it is the southern end of the Girls' School Grid. Beyond here starts the Maisuma Grid, an assignment about which Kumar is alternately relieved and disappointed – he wasn't chosen to take charge of this most fearsome bastion of resistance in the city.

The two bunkers come into view now. Zahid Shah uses his hands to communicate with his boys. The bunker on the right is the bigger one, the main node of the grid here, Zahid knows. They are to target the bigger one. That is the message they want to send. You cannot have siestas inside your safety nests. You are not welcome here, never were.

The three men emerge out of the narrowest lane, Zahid at the back, the other man in the middle, and the younger one, who carries the new RPG, at the front. The co-ordinates are all preset, the calculations set to the last decimal. He just has to make sure the bunker is at the centre of the lower arc of the scope. He has practised hard, even on moving targets during his training in Pakistan. He is confident it will be a hit.

The time is set – between five thirty and six p.m. It is five forty-five now; they didn't have any difficulty in navigating the swampy waters near the island, as someone had suggested they might in the meeting. He fires.

The rocket jets out of the launcher, leaving the smell of matchsticks in the young man's nostrils. He is happy he's manoeuvred the thrust exactly the way he was trained – by bending his back a little without moving his feet, letting the blowback of the launcher pass into his body.

The rocket sails over the road, over the nests of electric wire, past the small crossing before the bridge starts and is now on its downward curve, on target to hit the bunker.

The breeze from the river is deceptive at this time of the day. It swirls upward in small channels near the bridges, forming wind tunnels that envelop the road above as soon as it escapes the intricate architecture of the bridge. The rocket only grazes the tin roof of the bunker, carrying a part with it, and, its speed impeded, curves downward into the river and hits the opposite bank, sending sand and slivers of stone into the courtyards of the houses overlooking the riverbank. The water quickly swallows the rest of the debris.

The men in the bunker have a machine-gun. A shining new IOF Tiruchirappalli piece. The machine-gunner knows what he has to do. He is always ready. He lets the tripod go into a free swing and pulls the trigger. First into the lane from where the rocket came, or seemed to have come, then right and left, then everywhere. He doesn't stop on seeing the school minibus. He doesn't even spare the sky.

Faiz hears a thump and thinks he might have heard a low buzz through the air, too, just before the bang. Then he listens to the rat-a-tat of the LMG and his heart stops. Instinctively, he and Rangrez duck, although inside the shop they are fully out of the range of the bunker.

Rangrez will not let Faiz leave.

He must.

His reading interrupted, Principal Koul is pacing in his study. He cannot believe his ears. Since when did machine-gun fire become a part of the city's ambience? He opens the door gently to check on his daughter. Shanta hasn't heard a thing. As usual she is cooking to the sound of music coming from her cassette player. Professor Koul is annoyed with the boys who, he thinks, brought guns into this peaceable land. He doesn't like them much.

The birds have stopped the racket they'd started soon after the rocket blew a cloud of concrete dust into the air. They have not stayed to compete with the rat-a-tat of the machine-gun. The magnetic hiss of the bullets in the air and their ricochets give way to hesitant, then increasingly desperate shouts. The machine-gun man is trembling. He knows he could have stopped. An old man steps out from behind a short tin door, bending his head under the 'Bismillah'ir Rahman' written in silver-coloured rivets on the doorframe. The imam of the all-stone Masjid-ul-Fateh, startled from his late afternoon nap, steps out too. He is holding a Qur'ān on his head, its wide green covers flapping on his shoulders like a banner. He looks like a Messiah, an image that emboldens Faiz, who has convinced Rangrez, against his hands-folded advice, that they should come out to check. They all converge towards the mini-bus – the old man, the imam, the painter and the paint-seller – inching towards the vehicle while keeping an eye on the bunker at the mouth of the bridge. A distinct grunt of vehicles can be heard. The sun is preparing to set amid the city's many spires and at least twelve Downtown azans, and a lucid light is filtering into the streets.

The minibus stirs and groans as its front tyres try in vain to rise out of the drain. It has stopped right in the middle of the street, its nose bent towards a door that has just been double-locked from inside, and the body parked near-horizontally on the road. The driver, managing to unfasten his door, is struggling to step out. The old man reaches him first and lowers his shoulder to give him support as he tries to avoid the drain. Faiz begins to run towards them when Rangrez calls under his breath, 'Don't run, don't run.' Faiz slows down. The imam lets out a cry so sharp and loud that the few birds that had stayed behind or those that had come back, begin to flap away again. Faiz asks Rangrez to help the old man, and he him-self moves towards the imam, who is bent over trying to unlock the main door of the minibus. He has now tied the Qur'ān around his neck, the holy book resting, its covers spread-eagled, on his broad chest.

Faiz manages to slide open the small window nearest to the door and tries to reach the handle from inside. He hasn't looked yet, he doesn't want to. Then he wants to. Then doesn't. The imam signals he should move the handle up the moment he waves so that they can both pull at the door at the same moment. As the imam pulls and Faiz keeps the spring handle high, a trickle appears at the base of the door. It slithers out, begins to form a small pool, but then curves back towards the drain. Still, he doesn't want to look. The imam takes a breath, whispering prayers at life-and-death speed, waves to Faiz suggesting he, too, wait for a moment. Then they pull at once and the door swings open.

He doesn't remember the children. He hardly looked at their faces. He doesn't remember their clothes or their bodies. He had tried to imagine they were all sleeping but the uniforms would not let him. He doesn't remember what happened to the driver or if the conductor, who had emerged from under one of the seats, was injured. He does not remember what happened to the old man after he fainted, or when the imam stopped sobbing. All he remembers is Faatė. Fatima, his godmother and beloved matriarch of the Modern Kindergarten and Primary School of Habba Kadal, was losing her breath when she looked at him. He remembers the red bloom on the gold-embroidered neck of her chocolate-brown pheran. He remembers Faatė had always worn embroidered pherans, the design around the neck like a large heart. Unable to decide what to do, he had embraced her and she had slowly wrapped her arms around him. He remembers carrying her small body in his arms and finding himself in Rangrez's shop. He remembers pouring three sips of water into her mouth from Rangrez's mug. He had also put Rangrez's cushion under her head. Fatima had taken her house keys out of her pheran pocket and handed them to him. Rangrez had closed the shutters of his shop and sat down to rub the old woman's soles. He remembers the small hills of paint powder on the shop floor, some now crumbled around Fatima, some bordered by rings of red as though in preparation for a new colour. He remembers her feet and the bright indigo at the heels.

Where is Roohi? He wants to hold her and tell her everything. But they cannot meet, as Khanqah, the whole city, is under a round-the-clock curfew now. All movement proscribed. All meetings banned. All life besieged. A deathly calm has spread everywhere, as soldiers circle the area from all sides. They are near the houses and at the mouths of the lanes, at the waterfronts and on the bridges, on the empty roads and inside their many bunkers, in the school at Bohir Kadal, and at the temple in the water in Namchabal, by the ghats of the Jhelum and outside the gates to the shrine. Roohi watches from her balcony, prays, thinks and prays.

On the branches of the chinars, the crows maintain a stark vigil as dusk gathers its ancient mysteries over the shrine. It is all silent, except a lone muezzin, who moans from an invisible mosque somewhere. Roohi sighs. There are no chants rising today. A dim light emanates from the main hall of the shrine. The only other light in the compound is that of the two clay lamps burning at Goddess Kali's feet in the mulberry-tree temple behind the shrine, just by the ghat. Two beams of gold ripple across the river but do not make it to the opposite bank. Roohi ends her namaz with a prayer, for Faiz and the shrine. Oh, Khodaya, may the darkness not last long.

They cannot meet.

Faiz paints, cries when no one is around, and prays. Again and again, he finds himself dipping into his indigo pot, even though he should be using crimson and pink for this flower, each of its six petals requiring a crimson base that slowly diffuses into a mellow pink towards the periphery. He will have to repaint the tall vases again, he knows, but for now, he just cannot stop. He keeps the Khayyám painting on the side, Mustafa Peer having agreed to let him keep the replica screen for some more time, as long as he promises to deliver this new order, six 8 × 16-inch flower vases – base and top rims to be embossed in silver – in a month. He paints with pursed lips, with an intensity he thought he had left behind at the Gulfarosh Handicrafts Workshop, when, under the exacting tutelage of Sadat Beigh Shirazi, he would compete with three of his peers to be the best. He turns to the woman in the screen after completing each flower, filling in yellow stamens at the pith, dark granules in the hollow centre of each and, finally, marking gradations of tone by lightening or darkening his strokes. Still, this flower is not supposed to be indigo. He knows.

He cannot remember everything. He cannot sleep. And there is that hole in the golden heart, which he wishes would disappear now, which he wishes he could forget.

The Zaal

'Grid commandants are to deploy with immediate effect.' The new missive from the signal man is brief. 'The situation cannot be allowed to slip out of control.'

Major Sumit Kumar knows he cannot delay it any further. This last week, he has not slept well. The images in his bedroom are now questions. He thinks of the children and the old woman but has no answers. A sense of something besides regret has made him sit up at night. Sadness, perhaps, anger, but not quite. He is increasingly thinking of home, of Delhi, and more and more his thoughts of home include his grandfather Pandit Somsharan Gupta, freedom-fighter and renowned Indologist who, early in Sumit's childhood, had insisted Sumit come with him on his personal pilgrimage to Sabarmati, to the Gandhi Ashram, so he could relive those moments when he, along with thousands of other young men, had joined Gandhi at Dandi. Sumit remembers the photo gallery of the Salt March; he remembers Dada's face when he had asked him what people put in their food when Gandhi had gone on the salt strike. He also remembers his grandfather's answer: 'Salt was hardly a sacrifice, my dear. In those days, we were ready to shed blood on every word the Mahatma uttered, but the great soul didn't want blood.'

Sumit remembers the long, epic train journey to Gujarat and back, and Dada's list of dos and don'ts for the journey.

The gigantic Leyland truck, a twelve-wheeled beast in new camouflage drapes, customized for local colour by some quirky army tailor – chinar leaves in overlapping Amazonian clusters – begins its journey from the north wing of the newly extended cantonment on the southern outskirts of the city. The cantonment, a vast township of mostly identical apartment blocks and pale villas, as though transplanted from a former socialist experiment, runs parallel to the highway that connects the Valley to India, and to the Jhelum, which enters the city soon after escaping the military district. This is also a part of the town with the chief minister and the governor's mock-Tudor residences as well as a former prince's palace, which was the Paradise Hotel until two summers ago, but is now used as a detention, torture and processing centre called Paradise One.

The truck emerges from the cantonment and smooths its ride on the impeccable road that people will refer to as the Collaborator Avenue. Whether it's sheer coincidence or the cunning of the politicians of the past, the truck will begin to enter Downtown near Dalgate and eventually carry on to the Nallah Mar Road, the same road that was once a canal, which carried lotuses for the city's people. Now it must carry this truck, and the new 'vehicle' within, meant for Major Kumar's grid.

But who is the first person to see the truck with the vehicle inside it? It should have been Kumar, and he has planned it to be that way: departs cantonment at 7 a.m.; arrives at Girls' School at 7.30 a.m.; but it isn't, as Shanta Madam has decided to come very early today so that she can have a word with the officer. 'I meant to ask if you have heard from your seniors. I ask because the exams are approaching and I do need the space . . .'

Shanta smiles at the sheer size of the truck, its arrogant length hiding the school gate as well as what used to be classrooms on either side. She almost marvels at such an impressively built vehicle. And since it says Ashok Leyland® on its nose it is surely Made in India – an achievement indeed, her father might have said. But Shanta has no idea of the contents of the metal beast that has parked itself in front of her world; she doesn't know the purpose of the visitor, and just accepts the supposed goodness of a government enterprise. It must be something that these people need. There are so many of them here – and at this her brow does shrink, her face darken – that they must need many supplies. In a way it's good that they do this so early in the morning, quite considerate of the major, she thinks. Shanta goes around the vehicle and enters her school. The sentry at the gates has started saluting her, a gesture Shanta has decided, with some discomfort, to take in her stride rather than ask Kumar to tell his men that she doesn't really like to be addressed in military style.

She enters her study and is soon engrossed in a complicated examination timetable.

Kumar walks down the staircase with a curiosity he has not felt since his training at the NDA and during his year-long stint at a newly formed armoured brigade. Discreetly, silently, he enters the truck and sits in the driver's seat for nearly an hour. He would stay longer if it wasn't getting close to the beginning of the school day.

To Rahim Razor it appears like a municipal vehicle. A grey, flat opaque body is usually reserved for garbage-collection vehicles or the exteriors of bulldozers, except that the snout of this vehicle is something he has never seen before. He is to make sure no one comes near it and, of course, he himself must never mention it to anyone. Rahim Razor remembers his glory days, when he was district president of two ruling parties, a time when he had many vehicles at his disposal, including three blue Tempos that belonged to the City Municipal Corporation. These days, he is content with the protection that the part-time informant's job with the military provides. He knows not to be too curious.

It's the hour in the bazaar when shopkeepers are beginning to lift their shutters in preparation for the evening shoppers. School-children returning home will buy toffees or sachets of chickpeas or chewing gum, which will customarily find its way to the sole of irate elders' slippers; some will also buy new exercise books while a few will buy a single Wills Navy Cut cigarette and slip into a side lane. Mothers will come out with wicker baskets and five-rupee notes to take home freshly baked bread; a few will also replenish the odd spice jar. Chilli powder, turmeric and salt, mostly. A few government servants returning home on time from work will pick up a half-kilo of mutton from Ali Clay the butcher. The all-important assistant Nannè Saèb at the Dar-ul-Shifa Clinic is already on a pencil vigil in front of the plywood door to the doctor's cabin inside the shop, his notebook brimming with patients' names, the circled ones those with priority appointments, endorsed by Dr Teng himself. The legendary gastroenterologist has been in constant demand for over forty years now, a specialist who has on occasion been spotted by the local children, smiling while passing the main graveyard in the Kalashpora area on his way to the clinic. He has just finished construction of four identical villas overlooking the Nishat Garden, one for each of his four children.

Groups of boys are beginning to form circles by the shops or at the small crossings where the narrow lanes open out onto the main street. The auto-rickshaw stand is a music gathering, drivers in twos or threes playing their favourite cassettes while waiting for the next customer inside their vehicles. The smoke from their filterless cigarettes appears to drift out of the ends of the large stickers at the back and front of the rickshaws, which simply declare 'Love is God' or 'Love is Pain'. A steady stream of walkers is beginning to fill the road, as is the evening rush of the minibuses. This is the third day since the daytime curfew was lifted. It seems people have already forgotten Fateh Kadal and the school bus. It seems that people are willing to move on, even though the irises on the graves haven't yet faded. It also seems that the people of Khanqah might believe that what happened near the bridge was an accident, an aberration – it simply cannot have been a matter of policy, and it most certainly wasn't deliberate, some elders have repeated at every gathering in the mosques since the first day of the relaxation of the curfew. We cannot let anger determine what we do. They have promised an inquiry.

It would only seem so. For the young, while listening patiently to the old, are beginning to make up their own minds, and the conversation has shifted decidedly from the mosque – where they must defer to the elders – to the street-corners. And it is these congregations we are looking at now. Cigarettes are smoked with a certain vehemence. Hands are waved. Fists raised. From time to time someone whispers, 'Keep it down, keep it down.'

Schoolchildren and lazy gossipers are walking up and down the street. The shutters are all up now. The baker has just released a blast of dense smoke into the street. The thud of the butcher's arched cleaver on the walnut-wood block can be heard too. Conductors, hanging by a thread at the open doors of the minibuses, whistle as they gather speed after a hasty pick-and-drop at the stop by the auto-rickshaw stand. A taunt is hurled at the idle auto-rickshaw-wallas. 'Does this thing not fly?' The assistant at Dar-ul-Shifa starts yelling out the names of the patients, with the pleasure known to men who have absolute power over the names on a chart. Mir Zafar Ali makes his approach towards the shop as he, too, has an appointment with Dr Teng. The burning in his heart, he suspects and earnestly hopes, is something to do with his stomach. Teng will know in fifteen seconds and write his standard Vita Pepsin plus ranitidine prescription in five, in a scrawl that only the assistant and the in-house chemist can read.

Faiz is at home but not in his room. He is downstairs in the backyard, spreading his vases on an old bed sheet. The coat of lacquer needs to dry quickly. Bleary-eyed and exhausted from not having slept since Fateh Kadal, he leans back against the stone plinth of Master Dinanath's house. The stones have stood here for a hundred and fifteen years. They are weathered to a soft, quiet green and are cool at this time of day. For decades, women from the Mir house, as indeed generations of chefs who have cooked here for weddings and Muharram nights, have rested their backs against this wall. And since the backyard is narrow, hemmed in by the two tall houses, it doesn't get much sun, making it an oasis in the summer and a

94

garden of ice for most of the winter. It is also a refuge for the children, providing hiding places for hide-and-seek or a cover for their fifty-paisa gambling games that must be undertaken away from the eyes of Mir Zafar Ali. Light from the houses makes possible night-time conversations among the girls. It is safe and away from older ears. Often, an old carpet or rug covers a portion of the yard. This is where Faiz is seated now, looking at his work. He must wait for them to dry. If he leaves the yard, a passing stray dog or cat may leave their imprint. As it is, he is late with them, having had to redo all the indigo ones. He sits there, listening to faint echoes of songs playing on the girls' radio three storeys up, and the sounds of Mouj cooking the evening meal in the kitchen a few yards away. Where the kitchen is now, there was once a stable. The dark hallway with heavy cedar doors at either end had stood there until Faiz was six. Round iron hooks meant for tying the horses are still buried somewhere in the plastered walls.

Faiz can also make out muffled sounds from Master Dinanath's house but can't decipher what is being said. Faaté, Fatima, would have been home, too, at this time, cooking in her spotless kitchen while listening to folk ballads on the radio. Faiz remembers this from his childhood when, at the insistence of Mouj, Mir Zafar Ali had sent him to her for a couple of hours every evening so he could read his primers under her care. It is another matter that Faaté was not exactly the best tutor in the land as she had soon taken to feeding Faiz from the meals she cooked for herself, often from her favourite, meatballs in onion gravy. She didn't have children of her own. Only her embroidered pheran now remains, upstairs in Faiz's trunk, surrounded by his pigments and brushes, alongside Roohi's letter and the gloves she knitted for him. He had found it crumpled in a corner of her living room. He had hesitantly entered the room, not sure if he really wanted to see her after they had given her her last bath. He had tried to ignore the ruined cloth on the floor but just couldn't leave it there. He had rolled it into a small bundle and carried it home after the burial.

Roohi is calm today, as meeting Faiz on Thursday seems more and more likely. The curfew is no longer an impediment. The shrine, too, restored to its peopled state, is back to normal, and her evening vigil on the balcony is no more an anxious affair. Every day of the siege, she had stood behind the curtains and prayed for Faiz, for them, for everyone. At first, she was content with not meeting him. On the penultimate day of the curfew, she began to panic: what if something happens to him? What if they take him away too? What if he never comes back? I must meet him, see him one last time. In the end, she drove these thoughts away by sitting with her parents every evening of the siege.

Today the late-afternoon buzz from the bazaar gives her faith, the blaring horns of the minibuses and the trumpet drone of the speeding auto-rickshaws in the near distance, pleasure.

Last night, helping Papa sort out his old census papers presented Roohi with what she thought was a good omen. In the documents, she came across the Mirs of Khanqah. Alongside names, ages and professions of family members and children – Faiz featured in the latter – a note said, 'Prominent old family, respected in this part of Downtown.' Roohi smiled as her father circled all the men, including children who must have grown up to be men now. Khan Saéb's papers are from the 1980 census when Faiz was eleven years old and already apprenticed as a junior papier-mâché artist.

Since there was nothing to do during the days of curfew, and there certainly were no shop-front discussions to chair, Papa has made progress with the assignment from the DC's office, having, as he knew from the beginning, not much to do to collate information from his meticulously preserved personal archives. In essence, all he has had to do is mark the number of boys and men in each family and make a list of School/College-going, Unemployed and Employed youth in each of the twenty-six neighbourhoods he has been assigned. All he needs to do now is cross-check to see if any new families have moved into his domain – an unlikely prospect as people tend to move out of the old city to vast brick mansions that look like badly made cakes in the suburbs; or if an extended family has branched off into two or more new families with young men in them. The last time he met the DC's secretary he was finally told about the specific purpose of the exercise: the Chief Minister's Employment and Income Generation Scheme for Downtown Srinagar (CMEIGSDS). Directly funded by the central government.

This evening, they are seated around the dastarkhwan on the kitchen floor. Roohi has charge of the large tea thermos, and has just poured Papa his third cup. Mummy drinks two. The kitchen is washed in the white light from the mercury lamps, which Naseem Aunty's husband brought by the dozen all the way from Calcutta last year.

'I think it's a noble cause. Some of these loafers should start earning an income, help their families, rather than bother girls on the street. Such a good initiative, I say.'

'Why not do something about your own son, too?'

'I can't do him any favours, madam. Besides, my job is to prepare a report, not distribute jobs. I will, of course, enlist him under Unemployed and Undecided, ha-ha!'

'What kind of father makes fun of his son? Thank God he is not here.'

'What kind of a son thinks studying until class twelve is enough to start his own business? And, well, he is never here and he is undecided, isn't he?'

As Mir Zafar Ali begins to climb the three steps to the chemist's shop, having escaped the vulgar din of these auto-rickshaw-wallas, he hears a low, smooth hum, the mosquito buzz of racing cars on TV. The auto-wallas, who know of Mir Zafar's disapproval of their choice of music and their proclivity for staring at passing men and women, also turn to hear the noise. A couple even get up from the comfy back seats of their rickshaws. The three groups of boys, one at this end, where the lane from Faiz's area joins the bazaar on the main road, the other assembled in front of Qadir Waen's oil and spice store in the centre of the street, the third by the snacks stall at the curve that leads to the shrine, continue their gossip undisturbed. Their conversations are full of laughter and liberty after more than a week of confinement in their homes.

Mir Zafar Ali is peering into the long narrow road that goes through Kalashpora – one of the oldest parts of the city, its earth a calm relay of stupas and temples and mosques and shrines buried in layers over the ages – and opens out on the Nallah Mar Road, trying to make sense of the approaching noise and the cloud of dust that seems to be rushing towards him. He staggers on the steps, falls back, but steadies himself on the road again. His hand is still on the handle of the chemist's door. Many Kalashpora residents seem to be coming out onto the street behind the beast of dust that is galloping away, sucking in the very air. There are cries but then there is also silence. It is all too quick.

In comes the vehicle, then. Grey, its nose hound-shaped. Mir Zafar Ali realizes it has taken the cloud of dust, this motor, less than a minute to speed through Kalashpora and get to just a few feet from him, and that's when he sees something, a quick blur, emerge from the wings, sweep off two people and disappear. No sign again of the two men. He is lucky to have witnessed a full swoop near him as it has allowed him to stumble back on to the steps and firmly pull at the handle, although his hands are trembling. He sees it more clearly now: a green net, shaped like a garden-swing with a dark rubber exterior, opens out from the body of the vehicle, swings down in the same motion and traps his leg in it. Mir Zafar Ali is dragged for forty feet or so, during which he understands that he may have actually escaped this trap. The machine relaxes its jaw-like grip and makes a fresh swoop near the auto-wallas. As he lies on the road, his elbows burning from the graze, his trousers torn at the buttocks and his Haji skullcap lying like a deflated ball near a shop front, he sees the vehicle swallow Seythhá, the best-known and his highly trusted auto-walla, with another driver. Now it's the turn of the Khanqah residents to scream and stare with dry mouths, as the truck speeds on after another partly successful swoop near the group of boys in the centre of the bazaar. Mir Zafar Ali does not scream. He puts his face down on the warm tarmac of the road and closes his eyes as the long, dark truck disappears around the bend that leads to the shrine.

Devotees waiting for the evening prayer by the shrine gates, the three lazy policemen on duty, who don't even carry their batons any more, Mannė Dar, who was until now busy perfecting batter for his fried-fish stall, seven class-eight girls from Farhat's school on their way to their maths tuition with Shafi Tension, three cows peaceably sharing watermelon leftovers dumped near Roohi's house and, of course, the legendary Mahraazė, the Persian-conversant dervish, who may or may not wear trousers but always has a colourful bridegroom's garland, complete with a string of ancient five-rupee Gandhi notes, around his neck – all watch Major Sumit Kumar's vehicle race past, leaving a whirlwind of dust, straw and paper behind it. No one speaks.

The auto-rickshaw-wallas, whom Mir Zafar Ali has always kept at arm's length, these heartbroken charming men full of songs for every occasion, these stalwarts who, in their puny vehicles, keep the city alive in times of chaos and peace, these chain-smoking boys who sometimes prefer to be called by the names emblazoned on the backs of their black auto-rickshaws – Dilbar Ashiq or Shayar Majboor or Nameless Poet – these are the people who come to the rescue of Faiz's eldest brother.

Faiz wakes up, startled, from his nap. In the twilight that has since spread in the backyard, he sees four men coming towards the house, carrying what looks like a mattress. The men see him too, just as they begin to proceed towards the front door. They turn now, deciding to bring Mir Zafar Ali to his younger brother instead as he has just uttered his name. Faizå. Faizå.

Mir Zafar Ali raises a hand, asking him not to panic. Faiz clears the papier-mâché pieces from the sheet and signals to the group to lay him down there. Fida, Qayoum, Sher Ali and Muza sit down soon after putting the back seat of Qayoum's rickshaw on the sheet. They are unable to speak. They sit hunched, their hands on their knees. Faiz holds his brother's hands. The sisters, having seen their brother lying in the backyard, make a run from the top floor. Doors slide, windows burst open, stairs creak, the TV is switched off, cooking is abandoned, prayers are halted. The Mir family comes together and forms a protective circle around Mir Zafar, as though there is an enemy knocking at the gates. Farhat sits at his feet, trying hard not to cry.

It is Feroza who decides to take control.

'We can't keep Abba here like this, Faizå. Come on, let's move him inside. Farree, get up, get up, go inside and prepare his bed.'

'Mouji, heat some water, quick, go, go. I will clean his wounds. I will clean his wounds. Shahida, go inside and find the iodine and cotton wool. Faizå, go, run to Dr Muztar, he must be home. And, Farree, open the drawing room; Mouji, put on some tea for these people. Qayoum Saèb, do come inside, rest for a while.'

Unable to comprehend much, except that Mir Zafar seems injured – in some accident, in a fall, did someone do this to him, who could have possibly hit him? – everyone follows Feroza's instructions as if they had been waiting for them. Faiz takes a long look at his brother, presses his hands and stands up to leave, but just then Mir Zafar coughs and turns his head to one side, his nose suddenly leaving streaks of red on his chest and the mattress. Faiz pauses, his jaw trembling, and clutches at Mir Zafar's hand.

Farhat breaks down. Shahida holds her. Mouj, already in the kitchen, looks out of the window. The auto-wallas all stand up, staring at each other. Sher Ali tries to light a cigarette but fails, his hands shaking.

'It's just a nosebleed, for God's sake. Faizå, will you go or just stand here doing nothing? Let's go, let's go in, for God's sake. Don't make a scene here. He is fine.'

By the time they are inside and Mir Zafar is transferred from the rickshaw seat to his own mattress, he is unconscious. For all her courage, Feroza's hands shake as she cleans the blood from his nose. And as she does this, she sees his elbows are scarred, flakes of skin curled up into helixes. As she folds his torn sleeves and begins to clean his wounds, she sees that his trousers near his buttocks are red too. Turning him on his side, she also sees two swollen red patches on the back of his head. They look like plums. As her hands tremble and a certain dizziness begins to take her over, Farhat and Shahida press on her shoulders. Muza, the oldest of the local auto-rickshaw drivers, whispers something to the others. As they all nod in agreement, he slowly takes the cotton wool and iodine from Feroza and sets to work on Mir Zafar's waistcoat. He expects the women to leave as he undresses him. They do not.

'We must look at all his injuries in case he needs to be taken to the hospital. But don't worry, don't worry, he will be fine.' Farhat begins to sob again.

'What happened?' Shahida asks Sher Ali, whom she has known from her college days when he used to take her to the examination centre during her finals or to Master Shafi Tension's lessons at the Elite Academy before that.

'There was a raid on the street. They . . . took away people. There were no police. There was no army. It was strange. I don't know what it was. I can't describe it.'

'A raid? For what? What are you saying?'

'Er . . . we didn't see it clearly. There was some new kind of military truck, very big, very fast, and very strange. I don't know how to describe it. Qayouma?'

'We have never seen it before. They have sent some new kind of truck that drives very fast and grabs people. It is like a net that arrests people on the street. No, not arrests, it captures them. Sort of swallows them. It's a Zaal.'

'What are you saying? You're not –'

'We're telling you the truth, behanjee. Ask anyone on the street. It drove so fast that no one could take a proper look but I definitely saw it grabbing people off the street and . . . that's how Mir Saéb was hurt. They tried to take him away.'

'They tried to take him away? Who? Why? What has he done? Are you sure? Have they gone completely mad?'

'Yes, yes. I mean, the vehicle tried to trap him but he escaped after being tangled in the thing for a little while. He was lucky, behanjee, he was lucky.' Sher Ali sits down with his head in his hands.

'They – it – took Seythhå. You know him?'

'Oh, no, what do you mean? Where did they take him? Yes, yes, we know him. He is our neighbour. Why did they take him?'

How does Qayoum describe the vehicle? Does he say it's a trap or a mobile prison? Does he say there is a contraption attached to it, which he may or may not have fully seen, that sweeps people off the ground and deposits them into the vehicle?

Qayoum feels short of breath and starts pacing up and down the length of the backyard. Then he turns his back to them and hides his face.

Grief, Joy

That evening, Mir Zafar Ali's living room is packed with visitors. Neighbours, near and distant relatives, friends.

'You're a lucky man. You're a lucky man.'

It is also revealed that six boys, *only six*, were taken away by the Zaal. Over the cups of thick salt tea that only Mouj can prepare, men argue about the shape and size of the Zaal – yes, the name has spread across the city as though a crazed bear had descended upon the plains – and whether more such demons are roaming the city.

'Are you saying one is not enough?'

Mir Zafar is on his bed, a blanket over his knees and two large cushions behind his back. The family's oldest heirloom, a tall copper hookah with silver ringlets around its stem, is seated next to him. One of the first things he said, after regaining consciousness while retired Dr Muztar administered a diamorphine injection plus a small syringe of cortisone for his many inflammations, was 'Faizå, go and put some tobacco in the hookah.' Mir Zafar wants to talk about what happened, even if his words are slurred, the zeal of a first-hand witness spurring him on. His face grows dark only at the mention of how they trapped Seythhå. He keeps saying he is grateful to Khoda Saéb that he wasn't taken away. He keeps saying better him than Faiz or any of his sons. He talks about the cloud of dust. He jokes that he owes his life to Dr Teng, who is usually an emissary of death for people of his age. He tries to reassure the gathering that the boys who have been taken away will be back soon. 'They have done nothing wrong and it will soon be clear to whoever it was.' He approves of the name Zaal. Yes, it is a Zaal. A dangerous, perfect trap.

As he begins to give in to the effects of the drugs in his body, Mir

Zafar asks Farhat to sit next to him. He knows her crying face so well. She sits with her hot teacup in her hands.

Outside, the evening is a dark purple. A few orange beams from Dinanath's house have laid bridges to the Mir house over which Shahida is narrating the day's incidents to Bimla. Both have looked at Faiz's papier-mâché vases, knocked over in the yard below. Shahida thinks about how furious Faiz would be if she'd even accidentally done this. Master Dinanath himself is in the Mirs' living room, not saying much, a thousand cares of his own afflicting his mind.

While there is great relief, one may even say joy, in the Mir household, there is mourning in Seythhá's house, only six houses away. Seythhá's mother has refused to leave her threshold since her son disappeared. Feroza sits behind her with a few neighbours on the cold stone-paved hallway. They can all hear Seythhá's mother repeating to herself, 'I am sure he will be back soon.' She is not crying. 'They will let him go. He hasn't done anything. They may have already set him free. The government is not blind.'

It is another matter that her husband, who runs a power lathe behind the house, carving wood for window-frames, banisters, cricket bats and poor man's cricket balls, has spoken twice to their distant relative, D. S. P. Reyaz Khan of Barzulla in the upper city, about his son's bizarre disappearance, and has been told that the police have no knowledge of any such incident in any part of the city having taken place or the existence of this vehicle.

Mouj comes in and once again puts her hand on Mir Zafar's head. She wants to tell Farhat that her tutor is here and she should take her up and explain what has happened. 'Maybe take her to Faiz's room. It is quiet and away from all the comings and goings here.' Mouj, of course, knows why Roohi is here this evening. She knew the moment she saw her face and promptly put a hand on her shoulder and said, 'All's well now, daughter, all's well, thanks to the Almighty.'

Roohi is a picture of frailty when Farhat and Faiz, who have thrown all caution to the wind, run out of the living room to see her. Together they climb the stairs in silence.

'I will be in the big room,' Farhat says, as Faiz and Roohi enter his room. Immediately then Roohi embraces Faiz. Faiz holds her too. Not a word is said for a few minutes.

'I heard a son of the Mirs was among those taken away.'

'Oh, no. They did try to trap him but, thank God, he escaped. It's all those amulets Mouj keeps in the house.' He tries to laugh.

'Faiz, I thought it was you. All the others were young men. Don't you understand? I couldn't breathe. I came to your door earlier but then went back.'

'It's all fine now, isn't it? I'm here, in front of you. Here.' Faiz kisses her forehead and sits her down. She cries, then smiles. He keeps his face close to hers. The last azans of the day resound, Sunni and Shia mixed, the tuneful and the shrill, the plain and the beautiful, competing for Allah's audience.

'Roohi, I wanted to tell you something. I don't sleep any more. I lie awake all night, thinking of Faatė all the time. She is there somewhere, in her house, you know.'

'What are you talking about? What do you mean you don't sleep at all? Faizå, what happened?'

'I just can't sleep. Every time I close my eyes, I think of her. They killed her, you know, they killed her. Did you know she was my godmother? She used to feed me, put me to sleep. I used to sleep by her side in her kitchen. I remember it was this cool, peaceful place. I would feel drowsy soon after eating and she would just pull me towards her and tuck me in under a blanket.'

'Poor woman. She died through no fault of hers. She was very good with children. Everyone says so. And she must be in Heaven now, Faiz, you must remember that.'

'They killed her.'

'I know, but what can we do? You should take a sleeping pill for a few nights. Do that.'

'I already have. Nothing helps. My work is beginning to suffer and now poor Abba . . .'

'Yes, thank God. You should make an offering, shouldn't you?'

'You know what makes me angry? It's that no one's responsible, as though she died a natural death. Is this a natural death? What kind of a life is this? No one has said a word about her, as if she didn't exist, as if her life meant nothing. I guess that's what happens when you don't have any family. No one cares apart from a few prayers in the mosque.'

Roohi is in two minds. She can't decide whether letting him talk about Fatima helps him. It's near dark now. The city's nights are not what they used to be. People now leave the streets and the shrine to the dogs at night, no one comes out, as if their ownership, their claim, their bond with the place is severed at sunset, the city and its lovers sundered as soon as the soldier from the plains begins his nocturnal vigil. There are no lights. The area's garrulous poets and satirists, who have for centuries held their evening conclaves on the banks of the Jhelum and defied the city's ghosts, stay indoors now, not just when it's dark but during the day as well, coming out only when it's essential, to buy bread and milk. It is said the ink in their pens has dried up.

The Unforeseen

Faiz lies there each night, inside his old bedding, which still smells of the turpentine that Farhat accidentally spilt on it while cleaning his room last year, sometimes chewing at the edges of the quilt and staring at the ceiling or the piles of unfinished objects around him; he smokes every hour or so, admonishes himself for it, then smokes again. At some point he wonders if cough syrup might help, and he tries that too, drinking half a bottle at first, then all of it in one go, then a bottle every other night, and it begins to work, knocking him out for a couple of hours each evening. Then it's the same story all over again. His head begins to hurt now, his eyes itch almost all the time; in the morning he doesn't come down until everyone has had breakfast and left, and when his mother asks him why he hasn't shaved and if he has been working too hard of late, he says, 'It has to be done, Mouji, it has to be done.' Mustafa Peer has commissioned new work and he can't refuse the money, can he? Mouj, dear old trusting Mouj, feels that old pride again, how noble, selfless and giving her youngest boy is, how sincere and gentle his thoughts, and how blessed she is in him, what peace he brings her. She does not know that her youngest boy is on the verge of some kind of a breakdown, in the borderland between sanity and insanity, or that, increasingly, his mind is filled with thoughts of escape, of flight, of running away and freeing himself. He cannot take it any more. How has it come to this? At times he is unable to lift his mood even with thoughts of Roohi, the air both inside and outside stifling him.

Three days after Roohi's last visit, he goes up to the top floor, climbing stairs that he climbs only once or twice a year, and sits in the empty but always numinous hall of mourning, staring at the bejewelled copy of the Qur'ān that his great-great-grandfather had brought from Mecca in the last century. Soon he finds himself feeling the half-folded black banner that covers the breadth of the wall during Muharram and on which, he remembers, he had painted large silver letters when he was sixteen. Still he cannot rest and goes further up, up another flight of stairs, and emerges at the opening in the corrugated-tin roof where there is a narrow wooden platform for pigeons from which his nephew, Mir Zafar's younger son Shabbir, used to fly his pigeons and kites, and from where he now looks towards the heavens and at the city's tin-roofed vistas under a free sky and, further out, at the poplars by the Namchabal waterway and behind them, in the distance, the unceasing outline of the Zabarwan hills, which circle the lake as a girdle, beyond which the horizon touches other worlds, extends infinitely, or so he imagines, and it is here that he sees his flight and imagines himself hopping from one low peak to another, then higher into the mountains beyond Zabarwan, thence forward and higher, until he disappears into the blue light.

Coming down the stairs, Faiz sits on the last step, his trousers covered with dust. He goes still at the thought of Roohi. But he cannot sleep. If everyone decides to remain in their own small worlds, how will it end? Who will end it? Then again, how will he make a difference? But what about Fatima? Who will stand up for her? She has no one. People have already moved on; there's hardly a mention of her. With this Zaal thing prowling around, I may not last long here anyway. I might as well put myself to some use. I will be back soon and Roohi will surely wait for me.

'Aye Parwardigar, I beseech you to keep my Faiz safe. For the sake of Sheikh-ul-Alam, for the sake of Dastgeer Saêb and Makhdoum Saêb, I beg you to keep him safe. He is troubled by the dark shadows, I ask you to lift these ominous clouds from our life. His is a tender heart. May he not wilt in this strange and fierce storm, I beseech you, quell this storm before it quells him. He is angry now, and he has reason to be, but may not this anger bring more misery to him.

He may not see things clearly, but you can see everything. I ask you to calm him down in case he does something that I cannot undo. Aye Parwardigar, cast away these aliens from here, so Faiz can breathe, so I can be at peace, so we can be us again.'

She prays for their future, for her brother, father and mother, for Faiz's gentle brother, his mother and sweet Farhat, for Roohi and Faiz, for their future together, as husband and wife. At this, she smiles and goes down to join her mother and father for dinner.

Faiz goes down too, to the main door of the house, studies it for a moment, opens it slowly, and leaves.

Another Sleepless Mind

Major Sumit Kumar is struggling to make sense of the points in the inquiry:

(a) *Why did Grid Command not have the road from the waterfront to Fateh Kadal patrolled?*

(b) *Why was there no bunker blocking the narrow lanes?*

(c) *Why was Grid Commandant unable to retaliate?*

(d) *What has been done to apprehend the culprits?*

(e) *What measures have been taken to prevent such an attack in future?*

We cannot allow the situation to get out of control.

Weighed down, not just by these seemingly simple questions but also by the close deadline, Kumar curses the signal man. He is tired and wonders if he can really submit the report in a week's time. He knows what's been happening in his area, in his grid – Rahim Razor, nicknamed for his spectacular success as a pickpocket in his youth, has assured him that his information is authentic, straight from the ground, that the loyalty of the old party cadre is unquestionable and they are, of course, well rewarded – *Thank you, sir, thank you, sir* – so he must act, and he must do so based on the precise information he has given him. After all, we risk our lives, too, sir.

Yet a niggling shadow of guilt is not far from Kumar's mind. In the seclusion of his cell, in the darkness of the storeroom, behind the shut steel door, he allows himself to feel shame for being relieved that there are no questions about the dead children of Fateh Kadal, or about that old woman. What was her name? But these things happen. In any case, he hasn't done anything himself. But what might Dada have said if he was alive?

I suppose I should concentrate on things at hand, he decides. First, I must somehow finish the damned report and, next, I must write to HQ about Shanta Madam's concerns. It is, after all, a perfectly legitimate request. She has nothing to do with all of this, she is one of us, after all, and it is only fair that her exam goes ahead without any hiccups. Such a nice woman – what must she think of me now that I haven't vacated her classrooms? Perhaps she understands that my hands are tied. Yes, she must surely understand. The orders have to come all the way from the cantonment and may even have to go to Delhi for approval, which, as she must well understand, takes time. Oh, the bureaucracy in our country, it will be the undoing of this great nation, Dada used to say. 'We have replaced the British with people who are just the same when it comes to official work, only lazier. Paperwork and more paperwork. No actual work.' Dada could be simplistic at times, Kumar smiles, but this is not as simple as it may seem. As he prepares to go to bed, he has an idea. He will explain it to Principal Shanta Koul first thing tomorrow. Thank God, the school is open again. Schools must stay open.

Echoes

Mahraazė is furious with the Telefunken. Every time he puts in the cassette to check if it will record, the machine starts eating up the reel. He has another tape in his pocket, newer, but he is determined to record over the old wedding songs he loves. 'This rubbish, this shitty fake thing, I knew this would happen. Yaara, you should never ever forgive Sheikh Abdullah, Indira Gandhi, Ayub Khan and that Reagan chap.' His curses are often followed by conversations with God whom he addresses as 'Mate' at night. Since it's a matter of utmost and urgent importance, he decides to wake up Akbar Shah, the caretaker, who will curse him, as a matter of habit, for waking him up yet again but will eventually do everything that Mahraazė wants done.

It has worked this way for nearly fifteen years, since the day Akbar found him lying on the ghat by the shrine with the same tape recorder around his neck. He still remembers the pain as Mahraazė went for his balls after he'd woken him up. 'I'll leave those walnuts alone if you give me a cup of salt tea and two breads. What do you say?' Mahraazė had said, as Akbar tried to drive away visions of his crushed balls in the quirky dervish's hands.

'May you burn in hell, you crazy man. Do you know what time it is?' Akbar shifts away from the Telefunken in his face.

'It's not as if you have to go back to your wife in bed, Akbar Pad-shah! Come on, for the sake of the Prophet, take a look at this tape and fix it.'

'But why now? Why not tomorrow?'

'It has to be done right now, you fat, stinky Moulvi Saėb. You know it has to be done now. I can't wait.'

Akbar takes the blue Telefunken from him, unspools the coils of brown silk stuck in its entrails, brings some mustard oil from his kitchen and applies it to the head of the player with the tip of his shirtsleeve. 'It is completely rusted now, Mahraazė, you should give it to Gul Kabbadi while it can still fetch you twenty rupees in the scrap market.'

'I will do it the day your mother buys me a new one. You talk too much, Akbar the Great. She should marry me immediately – what's the delay? – so that I can rightfully spank my son and teach him manners.' He pulls Akbar's cheek and heads off into the dark. Akbar rubs his cheek and goes back to bed.

It is just before dawn and the crows are beginning to stir. The river, drawing in light that is about to be born, has turned a faint red.

Sumit Kumar, groaning for some sleep in his dark bedroom, makes up his mind. I will let the bosses who send the missives do what they want to do, but I will have no part in it. My conscience cannot allow it. I will never be able to sleep if I did it. The boys taken away by the Zaal, as it's known in the city, are still inside the vehicle. He feels satisfied, too, that he has managed to persuade his superiors that only those who could reveal something will be sent away; the others will have to be set free.

Only Faiz and Shahida have known, understood, that Mir Zafar Ali has not really been well since the day of the attack. They have heard him talk in his sleep, asking everyone to flee. On the third day after his escape, he had asked Faiz to bring him his calligraphy tool set so he could start on the new transcription for Gousia Printers & Publishers of Khanyar, and resume his part-time work as calligrapher. All these years it has augmented his meagre income from his day job as record-keeper at the Department of Land Records. He has always expressed gratitude to God and to his old friend Haqqani Saëb of Khanyar, for that delicate fatherless creature, Farhat, who would have suffered if he didn't have the second job.

He had brought home the new Urdu-to-English school primer in which he has to draw Urdu letters in the Firozi font – the English part, even though he once again expressed his interest in doing it too, will go to another scribe. At first, he didn't tell anyone he could not keep his hand steady over the drawing board, assuming it would get better as he went on, but when the bamboo reed dropped from his hand, he sent for Faiz.

'Please rub my hand, I think it's still weak. Does it happen with you sometimes?'

'No. I get tired if I'm at it for long, but then it's fine the next day. I'm sure it's nothing, Abba, let me see.'

Faiz notices the discoloration, the paleness of the fingers, but doesn't think much of it. He presses his brother's hand gently. 'It's probably cold, Abba, why don't you warm it over the kangri, give it some rest and try again tomorrow?'

'Yes, that might help. It's nothing probably, just a bit of weakness.'

'Yes, yes, get some sleep.'

Mahraazė is shouting like one of the fruit-sellers in the street, in the tone used by tireless merchants of second-hand clothes at the Sunday Market, who often come up with inventive, and sometimes borderline risqué, slogans to attract customers. A small crowd is forming around him, mostly schoolchildren and idle sales assistants. He issues a warning to those assembled.

'This is not child's play, my dears, not child's play. Go and get your parents and grandparents, their parents too, if possible.'

He has polished the Telefunken for the show and places it carefully on the road in front of him. 'What are you waiting for? Go and get your mummy, daddy, unclejee and auntyjee, go. Tell them the groom has good news.' A few children and men, sensing he's up to something different this time, not his usual sermon on plain living and a life of zero expectations, actually run to bring more people. And some of them clearly remember it was Mahraazė who had dared to run after the Zaal when it took away the boys. Having seen the vehicle whiz past, he had unleashed a long poem of expletives, in a metre reminiscent of the lyric-poetry form, shruk – he'd peaked as he rhymed 'Aala' with the Kashmiri word for 'pimp'. No one, neither those who want to be free nor those who have always loved Pakistan – not even those few who would rather be with Hindustan – minded his words, as he ended with a mighty expletive hurled in the direction of the vehicle. It is not without reason when people say of Mahraazė that only the mad have presence of mind in this land.

'Ladies and gentlemen,' he resumes his speech, 'this is a song you have never heard before and may never hear again. I have spent long hours of the night in bringing it to you. You can sit down if you want to or, if you prefer, please do keep standing, but you must observe utter silence when I start because, as I said, this is not child's play. Come one and come all, listen to what Mahraazė has brought for you.'

With the elan of a veteran street performer, he takes out the tape from his side pocket and raises it in the air. 'This, my dears, is what you have all been waiting for. Is that not true? This is the word, the news, the proof, the thing you don't want to hear but also the thing that's been in your hearts all along. Come one and come all. Hurry up, you lazy pests.' He addresses the people looking at him from the nearby windows. 'O Heema Maali, how long will you stay on your balcony, my dear? Come down. So what if the hero is not here today? I know everything. Come, come, listen to me today, my princess.'

Roohi, not having fully heard what Mahraazė has said to her – the balcony is three storeys up and at least a hundred metres from where he has set up shop – wraps herself in a long shawl and comes down. Mummy is at the door. She hesitates for a moment, then makes way for her daughter.

There are now at least three rings of people around him. Something about his voice and the intensity of his flailing arms has brought them. The last time Mahraazė had drawn such a large crowd was three years ago, when he had begun his parallel Eid sermon as soon as the fattest imam in this part of Downtown had started his. In a rambling lecture on the wastefulness of Eid celebrations and the growing ostentation among the poor, Mahraazė had challenged the cleric to a face-off in the square. 'In the presence of my most beloved Khoda Saėb, I will prove to you that you are wrong and the only thing that stops you preaching austerity is personal gain and kebabs. How else did you become so fat, Imam Saėb? Look at me!' he had thundered, and when he lifted his cloak, revealing his trouserless legs, the sermon had come to an abrupt end. It hadn't needed the cleric's fearsome sidekicks or the staff of the shrine to remove him. Some people in the crowd remember the day and are slightly nervous at the thought of witnessing his flagrant nakedness once again.

Then it begins, first with the croak of the worn-out cassette player struggling to read the tape, then a sudden loud harmonium tune, a prelude to the famous wedding song 'Aakho Shahr-e-Sheerazo'. People have listened to this before, the young perhaps all their lives on the radio and many older people on the same cassette player since Mahraazė appeared on that starless night at the ghat fifteen years ago.

They all begin to stir, disappointed.

'Patience. Allah has advised patience, don't you know, you heathen brutes?'

The song abruptly fades into silence, then a mechanical susurration, then what sounds like Mahraazė talking to himself, advising patience to his 'hasty mind', and then they hear a couple of shouts. Stern slightly muffled warnings, it seems. Then the tape seems to move closer. There's the sound of his clothes brushing against something. Mahraazė's voice comes again, a quick prayer to his old mate in the heavens. 'I am in your hands now. Kindly save my arse from these dogs.' Sniggers from the young in the crowd invite a fierce look from the fakir.

He sits down by the cassette player. 'Get ready now, hold your breath, and be brave.' All give their full attention now, eyes fixed on the Telefunken and its grave owner and operator. As the approaching dusk casts cold shadows over the group, the houses lapping over the shrine gate, the scene begins to resemble a Muharram gathering, an elegy about to rise into the sky. Everyone is silent. The tape plays smoothly.

Someone's crying in the distance.

Then they hear whacks, thuds, slaps, thuds, cracks, the sounds all rolling into one another, each flurry followed by the same stern voice. Then they hear some more whimpering. A spell descends on Mahraazė's congregation. People begin to murmur, then they don't. Mahraazė raises his hand. 'There's more, there's more. I have captured many voices, my unwise dears, voices that you may or may not hear in your dreams. I have seized them with my own hands and locked them here. You had better listen now.'

Roohi and a few of her neighbours come closer, pushing their way in. It must be said that Roohi has an additional reason for coming. How can she not hope to see Faiz in the crowd? But he isn't here today. He is somewhere else, in the shower room of his mosque, trying to overcome the effects of the Corex bottle he had gulped down after lunch. The news of Mahraazė's tamasha – his shrine-side rants have often been called by that name – hasn't yet reached Mir Manzil, although a few men from Faiz's neighbourhood, including Raajė, always a fan of Mahraazė's sometimes poetic outbursts, and Majeed, one of Faiz's best friends, are in the first circle around the cassette player.

The sobs on it are slightly louder now, enough to make each cry a recognizable voice, if one were to try. Some words, too, begin to ring in the darkening, leaden air.

Then a scream, hollow and dry. Then stillness again, all eyes glued to the old Telefunken as though it might suddenly open. Then these verses from an ancient wedding song, accompanied by Sarangi and Santoor:

'In some dreams, do come to me now
For spring is here with the irises now.'

The chorus of the song, louder and clearer than Mahraazė's captured voices, echoes in the street, and passers-by, who cannot afford to stop as they'd rather get home before the night curfew begins, wonder why the people of this area are listening to wedding songs in the road. As they leave, some of them start humming the old tune, popular among newlyweds in the meadowlands of the Valley, nodding their heads.

And so it continues, the wedding songs making abrupt intervals in the long, slow recording of voices from Farhat's school. No one in the crowd knows how he managed to get so close to the premises and the temporary detention centre within to be able to record, or *seize*, as he calls it, these voices. Perhaps he just crept close to the wall of the class-ten laboratory that the army was using as a provisional interrogation centre at night and put his tape recorder on the windowsill. Or maybe he had entered the school during the day, pretending to be a mad beggar, and managed to hide all day behind the canteen, only to emerge at night and fulfil his mission. Someone in the crowd remembers the underground passage into the school, dating back to the time when there was no road by its front steps but the Nallah Mar canal. Mahraazė has, of course, never offered an explanation, his response to challenges from foolish teenagers often consisting of a single sentence: 'You go and try it, brave heart!'

In the days after Mahraazė's performance, the residents of Khanqah visit the shrine not to pay their respects, not to cry their hearts out in the post-namaz recitations of old hymns, not to touch for the hundredth time the votive threads they have tied for a suitable and successful match for their daughter, or that government job for the son, the success of the studious teenager in the entrance exam, the safe return of the pedlar father, son, husband from India, the ultimate blessing of a journey to Mecca, offspring, preferably a son, for the long-waiting couple . . . but to listen, and listen again, to the voices on Mahraazė's German machine. For a note of recognition amid all the muffled moaning and crying, for the peculiar way the son shouts, or the unique drawl when the brother says, 'Hai Khodaya,' or even the way someone's voice breaks during a charged argument at home because, no matter how muffled the voices are, no matter how mixed up Mahraazė's medley of torment is, no matter how far away they sound and seem, even though they are only a kilometre distant, locked away in what was once the prestigious girls' school, the mothers, the sisters and the brothers of Khanqah can pick out the voices they have known all their lives. They deduce from the voices that their boys are alive, or were alive at the time of the recording, and all express relief and gratitude to Mahraazė, who is ecstatic when he sees a glimmer of recognition on someone's face or hears that peculiar sigh of relief.

Pleas are made in that vestibule of faith once again, the rapture of the intonations bringing the interiors to a febrile state, and the river that night is carrying the names Aqeel, Shafeeq, Jafar, Rayees (Seythhå, the Mirs' favourite auto-rickshaw-walla's real name), Qaiser and Umar, along its dark waves and drowning them in peace.

But what is to be done now that they know? A demonstration in the square in front of the school, a march to the building, a memorandum to the United Nations office or to the corpulent former chief minister, who's obsessively partial to photo-opportunities with B-grade Bollywood starlets and who has not set foot in the city for more than two years, or at least to the city's new commissioner, or perhaps letters to the newspapers, invitations to the city's many media men?

'But have you forgotten Fateh Kadal? Have you forgotten what they did to that woman – what was her name, Fatima?'

These are the concerns of the old, of the parents and the uncles. These are the themes of the early-morning bakery conversations, the topics of discussion for elderly minds at dinnertime. For the young, the boys and girls, it is a moment of indubitable clarity. They want to take things into their own hands. Many of them believe that it is better to vanish in a struggle against the enemy than to disappear in some shady rumour-like interrogation cell. In their late-night gatherings at the mosque or in the by-lanes, they find themselves in clear opposition to the Zaal. How can that machine roam so freely, pounce upon us as if we were cattle in its path?

It is this air that Faiz, our Faiz, Roohi's Faiz, breathes as he gets ready. It means parting with Roohi, a separation that he, and she, only two weeks ago had thought inconceivable. But it won't be for too long. I will be back. Will you wait for me? I will. I will return in the spring and then we can be free.

Roohi, in her solitude, in her contemplation of Faiz's words, in her private hour, in that singular personal mood that comes over her in this most intimate pigeonhole, her balcony, listens to the chants of her people, her neighbourhood friends, their parents and extended families, who are all inside the shrine tonight, and smiles. Then sighs. Farida Khanum is singing a melancholy ghazal on *Taameel-e-Irshad*, her favourite programme on All India Radio:

'Mujh se bichhr ke Yusuf-e-bekarwan hai tuu
Mujh ko to khair dard mila, tujh ko kya mila
Ek but mujhe bhi gosha-e-dil mein pada mila
Waa-iz ko wahm hai ussi ko khuda mila.'

'After we separated, you are as Yusuf lost from the caravan.
I have been condemned to eternal sorrow – tell me, what did *you* gain?
. . .
In a corner of my soul, I discovered someone worthy of worship.
The cleric lives with the illusion that only he can find God.'

PART THREE

In Another Country

Ilaqa-e-Ghair

In the snow he thinks of her. He walks and walks. You might think he has the mission on his mind and that the frostbite, licking at his toes, makes him more determined – but he cannot help dreaming of Roohi, amid the wasting stars on this cold and clear night in the dark Himalayas.

As their destination, the first camp for the boys on this side of the mountains, draws closer, Faiz believes the happy day will come when he returns himself to her.

There are many like him here, under a low concrete ceiling, cramped together in a large hall, whose walls are rough brick and bark. As they feel warm for the first time in three nights, the smell of unbathed men rises up. Faiz thinks of the warm hamam in his mosque and the way steam collects in the corners of the green-varnished ceiling. As a child, he used to collect the beads of condensation in a ceramic bowl and take it home. One of the older boys had told him it was the cleanest water you could find. He feels thirsty and his eyes search for a container that might contain drinking water. He doesn't know who to ask as the handlers haven't returned after depositing him here. There is nothing to do but wait. He longs for a bed. Also some hot rice with onion and meatball gravy, two glasses of the lassi Mouj makes, some tea at night, a cigarette with Feroza in the girls' room, then to bed with his radio, his head under the quilt, faint echoes of the city's dogs and the crickets nearby eventually putting him to sleep. But he wasn't getting any sleep, none at all, he remembers. It was unbearable.

Should he have met Roohi one last time? Should he have explained everything to her? Should he not at least have tried? She would have understood – she's educated, after all. Why didn't he do it, then?

What if she's angry with him, and what if she doesn't love him any more because of what he has done? What *has* he done? Surely she wouldn't blame him for doing what is certainly the right thing to do and something everyone is doing? And he might not have survived at all. She would definitely understand *that*. What would she be doing now? Perhaps having supper with her parents. Might they be discussing him? Surely everyone must know by now. He wonders what they think of him. When he goes back, he'll visit them at the first opportunity, have a long conversation with her father and mother, talk about Roohi and him. He'll be very deferential, only make requests, politely and humbly. They are, after all, better off than his family; her father is more educated than anyone in his house, so he must show extra respect, Faiz decides. He is unsure if he should carry his gun with him when he sees them. It might be seen as a threat, interpreted in all sorts of wrong ways, an outcome he already dreads. He doesn't want to come across as intimidating, but then again who will he be if he does not carry his arms? Can he possibly go there as a normal person? Even if he does go without his gear, without anything representing his new life, won't they know who he is now? Will they still treat him as normal? But Roohi will explain everything to them. Yes, of course, she will.

They're moving again. The tarpaulin-covered truck is almost comfortable, with a seat for everyone. There is a warm air of camaraderie in the cabin. As they go over bumps or cruise over a smooth stretch, a conversation starts. Laughter too. Someone lights a cigarette, and Faiz immediately grabs the Wills Navy Cut pack he had brought for the trip, instead of his usual Four Squares, and lights one. He feels less hesitant. It's already getting better. He is yet to talk to anyone in the group. The two boys with whom he left were assigned at the last minute to a group crossing two days after him. God knows where they are now. What does it matter? He's here now, with all these boys and, after all, they're from his place – some may even be neighbours he has never had the chance to meet before.

'Do you know where we're going?' he asks the man he has heard addressed as Engineer, who is seated opposite him. The truck sways a bit too precariously for the first time since they left Muzaffarabad.

'I don't know. Balakote, Ilaqa-e-Ghair, Afghanistan – does it matter, my friend? We are here now and we know what for.'

Faiz takes a long drag on his cigarette in an attempt to look relaxed. 'You're right, my friend, you're right. What does it matter where they take us? We're here for a single purpose, right?'

Engineer looks at him. 'Give me a cigarette.'

'Sure. Here – here. Take two, take three.'

'Where are you from?'

'Khanqah.'

'Oho, so is it true? Was there really a car that trapped people?'

'Not a car, it was a big van, like a truck. I saw it. Did it not come to your area? You're lucky, then. Where are you from?'

'Lal Bazaar. Do you know where Mirza Bagh is? We live behind it. No, the Zaal thing never came there. We would have burnt it.'

'Well, we wanted to burn it, too, my friend, but it wasn't that easy. You haven't seen it. Nothing can happen to it. It's like an iron cage on wheels. *Nothing* can happen to it.'

'We would have surrounded it and set fire to it, no matter what. If I'd been you, I would have asked a hundred boys to be ready with rocks, and as soon as it appeared in our area, we would have unleashed a rain of stones on it, blocking its way, then torched it and dispatched it straight to Hell!'

'And what if they'd opened fire on your hundred boys, sir?'

'So what? We all have to die one day, don't we?'

'It's not that simple. You don't know what it did. I'm not afraid of dying, but there are many things to do in life. You have to think of family, friends, other people . . .'

'Why are you here, then?'

'For the same reason you are. I couldn't take it any more. It was too hard. They're too cruel. They shouldn't be in our homes. Are you really an engineer?'

'What do you think?'

'I don't know. I'm just an artist.'

'Well, I am, sort of. I finished my degree at the Regional Engineering College the year before last. My parents wanted me to join ITI as they had some vacancies for fresh telecom engineers, but I had other plans. This is my fourth trip here.'

'Why did you come?'

'Because I wanted to. Everyone's fighting, I thought the more the better. They are so many, thousands and thousands. Didn't you know?'

'Of course I know.'

'As a matter of fact, I didn't need to come here. I became friends with some senior commanders who used to stay at our hostel. They told me I could join any day I wanted to. You see, I know a bit about how these things, bombs, guns, launchers, et cetera, work, but I wanted to see the real thing, experience the training they've undergone.'

'You can make a bomb? You mean a bomb you can throw at a bunker?'

The truck is moving gently now, as though going down a slope. A faint smell of jasmine enters the stuffy air under the tarpaulin and makes Faiz smile. He remembers the peculiar strong fragrance of the cellar under the shrine, where packs of incense sticks, perhaps forgotten from some previous age, had crumbled to a brittle powder in their sacks. There were also bags of dried rose petals hanging on the wall, overlooking the folded carpets he and Roohi had once sat beside. She had wanted to bring one down and spread the petals around them. He had been scared, as it might have been a desecration – some holy man might have left them there as an offering. She had said, 'They're just flowers, Faiz, unused because the devotees brought too many.'

He had said, 'No matter what, they must be there for a purpose and we shouldn't touch them.'

She had said, 'Maybe you're right. They belong to the shrine so we shouldn't disturb them. As it is, no one's allowed inside the basement. We should be grateful for what we have.'

At that he had touched her hair. She had shaken her head and moved a little away.

'Yes, but I don't throw them just like that. You'll understand it all. Be patient.' Engineer lowers his voice: 'This is proper training, Artist Saéb . . . I know some people who have been to Afghanistan, who have spent a long time in Afghanistan!'

'Oh – is that really special? I mean, does it matter where you train?'

'Huh. Do you have any idea what happens in Afghanistan? You can learn how to shoot down a plane there.'

'But there are no planes to shoot down in Srinagar.'

'Oho.'

'I mean, what is the point of learning how to shoot down a plane when there is no plane?'

'Listen, Mr Artist. At school, they taught me Urdu, Hindi, English, geography, history et cetera, but I became an engineer. Do I need Urdu now? No.'

'Oh – I understand, well, a little. Still, all I want to do is finish off those evil bunkers in our area. Maybe a few more after that. Then we'll see. All I know is, what they're doing is wrong. That's all.'

'That's good, Artist Saéb. Stay with me.'

'Yes, I will. I don't know anyone here. Will you tell me now where they're taking us? I'm just curious. We're in Pakistan, after all.'

'I really don't know, trust me. I guess some big camp, away from town. Muzaffarabad, as you saw, is a town, and they wouldn't do it there, even though the people were very friendly.'

'We were in Muzaffarabad? I didn't know. I was in that brick hall for three days. It stank. Came out only a few times to pee, you know.'

'Well, had you met me earlier, I would have shown you around. It's a nice town, I went outside the city to where there's a river, very pretty, the Neelum, maybe, I wasn't sure. Of course, nothing compared to Srinagar. You can't find that anywhere in the world, can you? I live near the lake, my friend.'

Faiz thinks of the family picnics on the lake. There were so many of them in that large boat. It was like a government bus on water. He remembers his reflection as he bent to scoop water with his hands. The nectar of Paradise, Mir Zafar Ali had said at the time.

The truck has come to a stop and they can hear voices outside. People are arguing about breakfast. 'How many times have I said I want omelette-paratha? Now run and get some eggs from your mother. Tea and katlam? Do I look like a fucking flatbread-eating sisterfucker?'

The encampment is larger than anything Faiz has ever seen. It seems spread over miles. There are low brick buildings here and there, some separated by small dunes. Faiz can see an elegant white mosque away from the houses. It has a courtyard whose walls are pomegranate trees. He is pleased to see them. He knows the smell and the weft of the branches, just as he has painted them over the years and seen them in the backyard of their other neighbours, the Hakims. He used to jump the wall to fetch a cricket ball and spend a long time inside the grove, pretending not to have found it. The air is warmer here, Faiz realizes, but not too hot. It's still early morning and the heat may get more intense as the day progresses.

'You will stay with me. Will you?' Speaking in Urdu, Engineer startles him.

'Oh, it's you. I was a little frightened.'

'Frightened? Why? Are you sure you want to do this, my friend? Although it's too late now to change your mind.'

'Not at all, sir. It's not as if I am doing something unpleasant. It's my duty, too.'

'Good answer. You're learning fast. Listen, stay with me. I know a few people here and I can contact home if we need to.'

'But who are you? You haven't even told me your name.'

'They call me Engineer, you know that. I'll tell you more at some point. Don't worry. I like to believe I'm a good man. I usually don't throw myself at people, but you seem nice.'

'Well, I like to believe I'm a good man, too. Nice to meet you, Engineer Saéb.'

The camp staff arrive. There are six of them, led, it seems, by a nicely dressed middle-aged man. Green polo shirt, brown cords, sunglasses that Faiz has only seen in Hindi films, longish hair combed sideways. The others are clad in clean well-ironed salwar suits, Khan Dresses, as Faiz knows them. Two are also carrying Kalashnikovs. Faiz doesn't even notice when the boys arrange themselves, including him and Engineer, in straight rows.

'My name is Kamal. Kamal Mustafa. You all must be exhausted, these people here will show you to your rooms. Take some rest, bathe, eat, sleep. I will talk to you tomorrow. Don't worry about anything. If you need anything, Safdar and Hashim will be over there, in that room by the mosque. You can shout for them any time you want. I'm happy to see you. See you tomorrow. Khuda Hafiz.'

The man who calls himself Kamal then drives away in a large blue Toyota pickup. One of the armed men goes with him in the passenger seat. There is a lot of dust in the air and the singing of larks on the trees behind the flat houses.

At the morning drill, all Faiz can see are backs. He is waiting for the moment when someone will turn his head towards him. But they do not, as each body moves left and right, back and forward, bends and straightens, in imitation of the leader at the front whose face, too, he cannot see. It annoys him. He is momentarily distracted by the rhythmic flapping of the pyjamas in the wind, as though a column of human flags is blowing together. A sleeve tries to break free, a hem attempts to fly away, a collar rises up from a shoulder.

*

Of the main training courses – physical fitness (jumping, crawling, climbing, and basic hand-to-hand combat involving wrestling and an unknown variant of kung fu), weapons and ammunition (AK47 assembly, cleaning, refilling magazines with speed, marksmanship practised on a heap of sandbags, semi-automatic pistols, RPGs, launchers) – Mir Faiz Ali finds himself in the last, the bomb-making workshop, essentially a large backroom with materials scattered on the floor and two low tables that look as though they were stolen from a primary school. Faiz finds it hard to believe he is here, sitting on the floor on jute matting that is the exact colour and texture of the matting at his childhood school.

It is in many ways a place of unceasing tedium. Faiz already begins to sense the seeds of the same tension that he used to feel when he went to school, and wonders about recess timings here. It doesn't help that the days are arid and warm, thirst being a frequent concern – at first he finds himself hesitant about asking for water too often.

Other than the colourful courtyard of what seems to be the kitchen complex, the camp is pretty spartan. The courtyard, as though designed by children, has bunting all around the low wooden fence, disused light-bulbs painted in bright colours hanging from wires strung across the centre, alongside old magazine covers featuring cricketers, whose sun-glassed glossy faces shine in the sun. An afternoon stillness seems to last all day. There are no women here, apart from the wives of the cooks, who run the camp kitchen. But even in the kitchen, the women do not exist, only the shadows of their dupattas visible in blurred flashes now and then. Towards the evening, the air gets cooler, and that is when some of the boys gather to chat or play volleyball. He likes the smell of burning flour from the rotis that the cooks must make twice a day. The smell mixes with that of lavender from the thickets around the dunes, the breeze from the mountains carrying it across the camp.

While Faiz eats everything that is on offer at mealtime, dal, four rotis, slivers of raw onion, a large piece of meat or chicken, he is disappointed when he realizes it is not a rice day. He counts the days to the weekend when he hopes it will appear in the insufficiently camouflaged dining hall behind the kitchen. In the five days they have been here, Faiz has decided that the breakfast is fuller than what is eaten back home. He loves the thick oily paratha and the constantly boiling sweet tea that never runs out, although very soon he will crave his mother's salt tea. The cigarette after breakfast, as he paces in front of the courtyard, has already become the best smoke of the day, a view that his new friend shares with Faiz. They still have the Wills Navy Cuts from India.

Only the first few days seem truly exciting: the introductions to the arms and the equipment, the making of a bomb. Perhaps it's because there's something artistic to it, perhaps because of the relative risk involved. The latter is exacting too. It requires you to dedicate long hours to the precise mixing of materials and hooking wires in the correct order. Faiz learns that neither of the romantic explosives, RDX and TNT, are used in everyday bomb-making. It is mostly phosphorus and gunpowder, and in some cases nitroglycerine. The expensive materials, he's told, are for the specialists. You may never make a bomb yourself, you just need to understand the basic technique in case there is an unexpected need.

Faiz sits there, knees folded from habit, and glances over the materials lying around. There are polythene bags of gunpowder, and nails of many sizes, blue, red and yellow wires that he knows from the old coils in their storeroom at home, soldering torches, heaps of some brown powder he doesn't recognize, screws, adhesive tape and fluid, small electrical objects that he guesses must be detonators, and a tin of red paint with two brushes beside it. Faiz is surprised by, and only later, at night, uneasy about, the gruesome intimacy he shares with the explosive materials. They are just lying around, like flour or lentils, and he cannot bring himself to be sufficiently shocked by their potential danger.

The wiry thin-bearded man at work now, dressed in a faded tight

T-shirt from the 1987 Cricket World Cup, looks like a chorus member from some copycat Sufi-fusion music video. He has great heavy shoulders on an otherwise lean frame and thick, calloused hands. Two earrings hang from each ear. Faiz wonders what a bomb-maker should look like: spectacled, bearded, intense, silent? This man is some of these things. An old Noor Jehan film song – 'Mainu Nehr Waale Pul Te . . .' – plays on the stereo as he slices off the plastic coating from the red wire, revealing shiny copper bristles that he quickly ties into bow-tie-shaped knots. Every five minutes or so he drinks water from a sick-looking plastic bottle by his side.

A stack of soapboxes catches Faiz's eye as he once again tries to take in his new surroundings. 'Those are small car bombs, my speciality,' Pintoo, the bomb-maker, informs him.

Outside, a fight breaks out between cockerels and Faiz is tempted to look. He glances at the man for a sign that he is allowed to do so, doesn't find any but stands up anyway.

Two middle-aged men clutching strings tied to the legs of two giant cocks are exchanging mock war cries while the birds tear at each other. Faiz feels sympathy for the taller, leaner of the two fighters as the shorter, more aggressive one attacks. Behind each man a group of children is cheering their respective fighter.

'Do you live here?' Faiz says, in his softest voice.

'Yes, yes, we live here. Where else?' The victor sizes up Faiz.

'Someone has to cook for all of you. We do everything, and they help with the small jobs,' the older man, the master of the now whimpering vanquished cockerel, says, gesturing towards the children.

Faiz goes over to the children and asks their names.

'We have to go now, bhai, and you shouldn't be talking to us anyway.'

The bomb-maker is standing at the door, watching Faiz, the departing fight masters and their flock of cheerleaders.

'Take your time. We're nearly done for the day.'

'What do I do now?'

'Do you play volleyball?'

'Yes. I used to play every evening at the college. I can serve deadly stuff.'

'You went to college?'

'Not really. It's near my home and has a good ground. We used to play against the students' team and beat the crap out of them every time.'

The Orchard

There is a large green and white flag on the top of a dune. On some Fridays, flower petals are spread in circles around the flagpole. Faiz feels drawn to it, to the now risen now fallen banner, to the secluded elevation of the dune. Today, his third week in the camp already – he is a deft assembler of the AK47 rifle and a keen student of the craft of bomb-making – Faiz comes closer to the dune. As he walks, he suddenly remembers that some of the boys here expect him to be a poet but he has yet to recite anything for them, as the only verses he knows are Kashmiri na'at and nauha, which he doubts anyone will understand. For a couple of years in his teens, Faiz was the only boy in the entire neighbourhood who recited both Durood Sharif on the sidelines of the very festive Urs at the Dastgir Saèb shrine and elegies at his home or in processions during Muharram.

This dune is unlike any other in this place, which is neither plain nor mountain – a land between lands. As he gets close to the middle of the mound, he notices for the first time traces of a footpath, so faint it seems as if the people who walked here never came back. Already, he can see the full outline and expanse of the camp. Again, he is taken home, where he's watching *Mughal-e-Azam* with his sisters – Prince Salim commanding an encampment of rebels against his father Emperor Akbar. At first he smiles, remembering Shahida joking that this king is too fat to fight, not the slim, elegant Akbar of Faiz's papier-mâché boxes – how can they show him as one of Hindustan's greatest kings? As he turns his eye towards the high flagpole, he thinks of Salim's love for the royal maid Anarkali, a love so intense and consuming that he had gone to war against his own father and the greatest Mughal in history.

Round limestones, arranged around the flag, like the boundary of a country park, mark the small flat top of the dune. Inside this miniature stone-framed courtyard, he sees the delicate yellow residue of what he recognizes as marigolds, a few shrivelled raisins that look as though they were the eyes of kingfishers, some rose stalks and the curled, brittle remnants of the roses. The pole, as he'd guessed, is a tall piece of bamboo with white paint flaking off in many places. The rope is weathered, discoloured by the wind and rain. Because of the folds in the flag, he cannot read its full inscription and wonders if he might have been able to read it, guessing the parts hidden in the folds, had he been to college.

He takes a long look at the camp and spots his quarters, a shabby but solid brick, mud and sand structure, the kitchen compound with its little land of colour in full show at this time of day, the bomb workshop at the back, the white mosque at the edge, the training grounds where groups are seated now in the shadows of the mounds that serve both as target practice during the sessions and as sunshades during recess. It is only now that Faiz realizes that the training grounds are lower than the rest of the encampment.

As he takes a last look at the flag and the children's enclosure around it, he remembers Muharram must be drawing close, when flags, more ornate and sacred than this, he believes, will appear on the roads back home, heralding groups of mourners in their annual processions. As a child, Mir Zafar Ali had had one specially made for him and he had carried it almost every day from the first to the tenth of Muharram when those long days of mourning would culminate with the procession that marks the martyrdom of Imam Hussain. He had carried his flag, his small child's banner, with him all the time, he remembers, even sleeping beside it at night. Many aunts had tied two- or five-rupee notes into the knots on the black silk dupatta cloth draped around it. Mir Zafar Ali had looked at him often then, pleased by his brother's enthusiasm for being a flag-bearer, however ceremonially, of the faith. For many years, Faiz had felt guilty for having taken two five-rupee offerings from those silken folds and spent them at the Shiraz Cinema once Muharram was over.

As he decides to climb down, he looks in the opposite direction, beyond the flag, away from the camp. There is something of his old neighbours' dark pomegranate orchard about it – as a child he had been forbidden to go there but he would, in search of the ball that Shahida often hit over the wall.

He cannot help himself and heads over to the grove. Once inside, the temperature drops. There is hardly any sun here. The earth is cool, the leaves heavy with moisture; someone has been watering this place. A fine fragrance makes itself known. It is blissful, the scent here, and it reminds him of Rangrez the paint-seller. How strange, he thinks, that the old man should come to mind in this place. He moves on.

As he sits down by an old pomegranate tree, the sun disappears altogether. The evening azan rings from behind the hill. There is no dust here, he notices. He cannot see any walls or a fence, just the trees and their dark shadows. He loves the smell, the cool, and wonders why they didn't set up the camp here, or make it like this.

There are flowers in the distance, not too far, so he stands up to be near them. He hasn't seen flowers since leaving home. The azan is over but he is in no hurry. Among the things he has come to like here is that no one asks anyone to pray or wonders why they didn't show their face in the mosque or why they were late for prayers. Gulzar Dar, their immediate neighbour and string vest-clad care-taker of the mosque and chief fund-collector during Muharram at home, is such a pain in the arse, he thinks. How many times have I changed course, even turned back, on seeing him approach? God, he must get paid to harass people in the name of namaz. And it's not as if I didn't pray. No one harasses me here, even though the place is supposed to train us for jihad.

The flowers come into view and glow in a wave. He recognizes them instantly for he has painted millions of them. Daffodils.

There is a thick row in front of him, a congregation of stalks and petals. As he sits down to touch them, they sway and lean back in the breeze. There is a beat to these flowers, Faiz thinks. Briefly, he looks back and thinks he can see the white and green flag in the sky through the trees, and is reassured to know he hasn't walked too far, although it feels as though he has been out for a long time.

Over the top of the crowd of daffodils, he sees what appears to him as the first sight of brown earth in this dark-green island. He walks through, careful not to tread on the plants, and finds himself in the centre of a private graveyard. Simple, austere graves are scattered about and look as though they're from a previous age. The daffodils started here, he now realizes, and took over. Each grave is bordered with daffodils, like the lush gardens he painted on the coaster sets last year. He had stretched the petals so they could wrap around the edges of the box and the coasters inside. Where must they be now? he wonders. Some rich house in Delhi or Bombay, or even some place in Amriika, perhaps.

Back at the camp Faiz remembers the scent in the pomegranate grove. It is of the Seher pigment. He remembers the dry paint, the crimson and orange pigment that he has seen and felt at Rangrez's shop, a magical colour he covets, and hopes to include in his painting at some point. He feels sorrow at this thought.

Faiz goes to his quarters and, on a large square of brown paper that he has fashioned from envelopes, draws what he has seen and then some more – hard sheets of water crushing the flowers, stems sailing in the swirls, like the remnants of destroyed boats. He also sketches a thick-stemmed rose bush with hundreds of blooms gleaming in the fierce rain. He remembers.

Faiz throws an arm around Seythhå, the man his older sister once loved, and takes him away from the group of drivers at the auto-rickshaw stand, lighting two cigarettes at once.

'How long have we known each other, Seythhå?'

'I have known you since I was a child, Master.'

'You remember the cricket ball I spruced up with layers of red paint and lacquer?'

'Great days, Master, great days. But then you stopped playing with us.'

'You know why, Seythhå. I started working before any of you did, didn't I?'

'Yes, yes, that is true.'

'And we're still friends, aren't we?'

'What kind of talk is that? Of course we are.'

'I need your help with something. It's important. I'm asking you in complete confidence. No one should ever know.'

It is a known fact that the young help the young with the logistics of love. And Seythhå was, perhaps still is, secretly in love with Shahida, even though he had no choice, he had thought then, but to treat the girl from the Mirs as a sister, at least in public. But once he started doing that, there was no going back, the small conflict tormenting him each time he drove her to her lessons. Little did he know that Shahida, too, had nursed a tenderness for him since they were thirteen . . . There were a couple of seasons when, looking at his face in the mirror from the back seat, she felt she might be in love with him, but the boy would always call her 'Sister' and did not seem to think of her in that way, although having grown up since, she does wonder if it might just have been a matter of making her intent more obvious. But then she had grown up, looked at Mir Zafar Ali's face one evening in the depressing light of poor winter electricity, contemplating how he might react to the idea, and never spoke of it. Men react differently upon hearing their daughters or sisters are in love, particularly if the girl has given her heart to a boy from another world. Older men find it difficult, nearly impossible, to think much of a woman's heartbreak, even if they themselves have known a broken heart.

It is a Friday. Most streets are deserted at this midday hour, and a speeding auto-rickshaw is worming its way through the great Boulevard Road that circles the lake like a silver bracelet. In the back seat of Seythhâ's rickshaw, Faiz and Roohi hold hands, press shoulder against shoulder, the warmth of their bodies both soothing and suffocating as they sit next to each other but not too close. They are both anxious on this, their first outing together, in the safest yet the most dangerous mode of transport: it will be futile to attempt an excuse, should they be seen by a relative or, worse, caught by the city's newest vigilantes. These days, it is said, both kinds of armed men, the uniformed and the non-uniformed, patrol the city's many gardens of Eden, also roads, lanes and dimly lit, darkly curtained restaurants in the hunt for young couples. Some are sent home after a severe tongue-lashing, or a quick transfer of cash and valuables, and others are gently invited to murky police stations, where phone calls to a moneyed father or uncle are made.

'I've always seen these people on shikaras, you know, tourist couples. They wear clothes that we don't wear any more, then take photographs in the Nishat Bagh. I like the clothes very much. I've seen a lot of it on TV. Remember Shammi Kapoor and Sharmila Tagore?'

Roohi nearly cries at what Faiz has just said. He has never been on a shikara ride on the lake! What do the great Mirs of Khanqah do to their children? 'Faiz, I will take you to all our lakes and rivers. I will float on the Jhelum with you by my side, and we will see what lies beyond the shrine. We will go as far as the river courses, through the heart of our country. I am sure, no, I *know*, that the river, and the fields and the forests, will give us shelter, create havens for our children and us in the years to come. Then we will come here again, on shikara picnics to the Shalimar and the Nishat. I also want to spend one night in that red palace you see there – can you see it? It's Pari Mahal. Once upon a time, it was home to thousands of magical books, and it is said angels used to guard it, protecting both the texts and their readers, but now there are no books in it. There is still love left in this land, so what if this lake is blighted and the Jhelum stifled? One day they will heal. One day I will plant so many willows around the Dal's magic rings that no one can cut through to its heart with their dirty hands. You must think I consider the lake my own –' she smiles at herself '– and the rivers and mountains, too. Well, aren't they yours as well, Faizâ?'

Faiz keeps looking at her, smiling. He realizes he can now hold her hand without feeling self-conscious, without looking down too many times.

I dreamt of you by the banks of the Lidder once, when they drenched me in ice from that raging stream. I knew then and I know now there's no one else. I knew you would come.

In her heart, she prays to the lake. A gift preyed upon by all, violated over the years by ruler and ruled alike. Still, it is tranquil, like an ageing seer, trying every spring to purify itself of the poison that men have hidden in its green folds.

There they are now. On this festive sofa on water, the bright curtains of the boat flying high in salute to the breeze from the Zabarwan hills. The young boatman eyes them suspiciously at first, then rows silently as Faiz finds his Downtown voice and commands him to take them all the way to Nishat Garden, the Mughal emperor's magnificent endowment to the lake and the people of the city. Some call it a folly, others a paean to beauty and love, and a few just a garden with old chinars and fountains.

There is silence on the blue-green waters today. In the distance some kingfishers have died in peace. Their tiny bodies, locked in moist feathers, glide gently towards the cool shade of the island locality known only as Yirĕwann, the Forest of the Willows.

Far away, a couple, boat people who, too, have been waging their own quiet battle against the threat of extinction, are plucking lotus stems from the belly of the lake, the man dipping his long lance into the water and twisting it around the stems, the woman gently depositing the ivory into a pool inside the boat. They will make wreaths of the stems, each tied with a fresh hay ribbon, and ferry them in the morning to Hazratbal, the marble moon by the western shore of the lake that holds the Prophet's hair in a glass jar, and sell out by the time the sun shines on the white shrine in this part of the city and the biggest in the land.

Faiz and Roohi sleep against each other. The boy is happy and rows ever so gently. Someone in the houseboat *Queen of Sheba*, moored for ninety-one years in the same spot, plays Gulrez, 'Whether he listens or not . . .'

It all seems such a long time ago now, although it was only a few months earlier, at the end of the autumn. It's the distance that makes it seem so far away – although, in fact, he reconsiders, they are just across those mountains. She must be in bed, too. What is she thinking now? Does she remember our trip on the lake? Of course she remembers. She had taken lotuses from it, two, and kept them both.

Last night, he had gone straight to bed after dinner and his now customary cigarette stroll with Engineer. He had briefly told his more-educated friend about his walk up the hill and into the daffodil haven, then the strange tiny graveyard beyond it.

'Oh, my friend, I'm sorry I didn't tell you before.'

'What?'

'About that hill.'

'Yes, I went to the top. I wonder why they put the flag there. Its base looks like a small grave. Have you seen it?'

'It is a grave.'

'What?'

'He's called the flag bearer. Apparently he founded this camp and was injured in action in Sopore, but the story is that he didn't want to die there so he walked back across the mountains, bleeding, and dropped dead near that dune. A feud arose between two factions here, one arguing for a proper mausoleum for the man and the other calling for a simple grave. The authorities settled it in the end by coming up with a compromise. They had the flag bearer reburied on top of the dune, creating a natural mausoleum for the pro-shrine group, while keeping the grave itself a simple affair, to satisfy the other faction. Personally, I don't believe in all this, shrines, saints et cetera. Allah and the Qur'ān are all there is and all you need. They call me a Wahhabi, Mr Short Pants, ha-ha, but it doesn't matter. To each his own, isn't it? I – *we* – have more important things to attend to than worry about petty sectarian shit . . . And I have a group to run when I get home, bhai.'

'I don't even know what Wahhabi means, sir.'

'I don't either, ha-ha.'

'One more thing, boss. Are you saying since one person, this flag bearer, was buried here, they made a small graveyard behind the dune? Is that right?'

'What small graveyard? There is no graveyard here.'

'Er . . . Forget it. It's nothing probably, some old orchard grown wild.'

They stand up together as the sun lights their room. It is time for drill, followed by working the guns, then a bit of wrestling. There is no shooting practice for him today as they are rationing the ammunition until new supplies arrive.

At Home

Roohi's game of fates with the walnuts is not going well. She has broken five so far and none of them has opened evenly at the centre. If the shell breaks into two equal halves at the first blow, then Faiz is well and will be home soon. If not, then she doesn't know. At the seventh, she tells herself it will be the last and she should not try her luck so hard. It's a silly superstition in any case. She places the walnut on the windowsill, waits for it to settle after its little dance, and brings down her fist in one swift motion.

Roohi has not looked so hard at her inner life, and the delicate privacy within it, for a long time. She has to steel herself, she believes, for the outside world; to be able to do things on the outside, she must keep her inner life closed.

There was only a week or so when she thought she might have to contemplate life without Faiz. Her anger with him arose not so much out of disapproval for his decision, but because he had not consulted her, or even told her, beforehand. And there had been only a couple of occasions, as Mummy brought up the marriage question at dinnertime, when she wondered if he might be the kind of man who thinks it's normal not to talk to women when making life-changing decisions, especially when making life-changing decisions. Or perhaps he knew he would not be able to go through with it if he did.

Today – a month after the Mirs, Roohi and all of Khanqah learnt about the disappearance of the famous papier-mâché artist and some worried he, too, may have been taken by the Zaal and thrown in the palace that is now a torture hall although his voice wasn't found on the tape from the school – Farhat and Roohi meet by the riverside. It is late afternoon, an hour of complete inactivity in the area before sunset and evening prayers, and they are sitting under the ancient, drooping wooden ceiling that, only a few weeks ago, had sheltered Faiz and Roohi, listening to each other. As the Jhelum's clay-brown silk carries straw mats, flowers, rubbish from riverside hospitals and mosques, torsos or body parts of those dismembered in some detention cell upstream, Roohi wipes Farhat's tears.

'Many never come back, Roohi Di, I know that. I am not a child.'

'Who said you are a child?'

'Almost everyone at home, except Mouj and Abba.'

Abba, Mir Zafar Ali, has more or less convinced everyone that the octogenarian healer, Hakeem Usman of Rainawari – a veteran from undivided Kashmir, who spent time in Muzaffarabad and Lahore when a grand cleric travelled there in 1947, and whose three sons spent time in jail in the late sixties for being part of an underground movement – has arranged for Faiz's safe passage from Pakistan.

'But I am not sure if that's true, and even if it is, if it's possible. I think Abba has made it all up, this story of Hakeem Usman, to make us feel better, so that we don't worry too much about Faiz. Abba is a wise man and he knows how to tell a good story,' Farhat says.

Roohi doesn't really hear the last part of Farhat's report. She just holds Farhat's shoulder and rubs her arm, her mind trying to piece together a coherent narrative of the old healer with connections in Pakistan and, more crucially, the wherewithal to deliver a man safely home in these precarious times. Only last week Roohi found herself running to the newspaper vendor with a blackened paper, thinking their copy was a printing mistake, and asking the man for a replacement. 'They are all like that, my daughter,' old Bukhari Saëb, father of Syed Sir, Shanta Koul's deceased deputy, said, point-ing to the stack of unsold and returned papers. He explained to her that it was a statement of protest by the editors at being asked repeatedly by the government's media watchdog to keep down the death-toll figures.

What Farhat and Roohi do not know, but may soon find out, is that the old healer has a grandson who goes by the name of

Engineer and has just written his first letter to his grandfather, the epistle bearing the postmark of a small neighbouring country, delivered via circuitous secret airmail. The old man, after reading the letter once and showing it briefly to his daughter, Engineer's mother, shredded it into tiny pieces and burnt them as fuel for his chillum.

'Farree, wake up, wake up, you have to go home now.'

Farhat is embarrassed at having gone to sleep on Roohi's shoulder. 'Actually, I had a lot of homework, so I've been staying up late to catch up. Our six-monthly exam is quite close now. But you know how it's been with us.'

'I know.'

'We're all in it now, Roohi Di, there is no escape. Sometimes I think it's good he went. Who knows? He may not have been with us anyway, considering what happened in the raids. They took everyone. At least he went of his own accord and we know where he is, roughly.'

'Yes, roughly.'

'Do you know what Mouj says?'

'What?'

'She says she's glad Faiz wasn't home when the raids happened, but at times she feels guilty for being the only mother in the neighbourhood with none of her sons in custody or dead. I think Faiz's departure has affected her badly, even though she knows he's alive.'

'Farree, it's really getting late now. It *is* late now. We must go home.'

'She doesn't speak a lot with Abba now. She thinks he pushed Faiz away by the way he kept telling him, "Save yourself, save yourself," after his escape from that demon truck. I hope someone sets fire to it one day, and to the people who run it.'

'What?'

'Abba said that a few times to Faiz. "Run for your life, Faizâ, run." But he'd say that to everyone who came to visit. Even to me. You know how he's been since that day. Sometimes he wakes up screaming at night, panting, Faiz told me. Faiz slept in Abba's room in case he needed something at night, in case something happened to him. Didn't he tell you?'

'No, Farree, he didn't, but then we hardly met after that day. My mother was scared they might take women, too, and Faiz wasn't allowed to go out often, you know. I'm sure he didn't want to make your mother or brother too anxious. Then he left. So, no, he didn't talk to me, Farree. He couldn't.'

The walnut cracks open.

A Father's Mind

Khan Saëb is pacing back and forth in the narrow hallway downstairs, blowing smoke from his nostrils as he waits for his wife and
daughter to come back from their shopping trip. Rumi refused to go
with them, but would join them at the cloth merchant's later. He is
determined to stop his mother buying him dark checks for his winter kameez-pyjama suit. Roohi, too, has decided to buy something
different this year, not her usual dark maroon or green. Khan Saëb
is content for his wife to choose both the fabric and the colour for
him. With every drag on the cigarette, Four Square, the same brand
as Faiz, Roohi will remember this for the rest of her life. Having
smoked two already and lighting up a third, he's turned the hallway
into a tunnel of smoke. Today, what his wife will say about this is
the least of his worries, although he has told himself many times,
since yesterday, that he need not worry for he has played no part in
the raids. But a dark whisper refuses to go away. He wants to be
near his wife and daughter, but today of all days, they are late, as
Roohi's mother has got involved in a long exchange with an old
friend at Bombay Garments & Fabrics.

'Where are they? They should be here by now.'

What if some people assume I had something to do with it –
that I was part of the plan? Khan goes over and over the same
question.

But wait. What did I do? I didn't do anything. I merely compiled
a list of families in my ward, based on a survey that was already
there. Please do remember that, please do.

He can feel the smoke, the smell of tobacco, washing over his face.

They will think he is some kind of informer – it *is* a matter of fact
that the army swooped on almost all of the families whose names

he had entered in his updated census report – and make a poster of him. 'Kabir Khan is a traitor.'

Where are they? What's taking them so long?

The truth of the matter is that he has not done anything wrong; all he did was check his old sources and compile a list. Perhaps he should not get too anxious – paranoid is what Roohi would say. After all, who knows about the list? Only Roohi and his wife are aware that he was asked by the commissioner's office to prepare it – and, yes, they know it was for an employment generation programme for the youth of Downtown – besides the commissioner's secretary, of course. That wise and kind man knows and he won't tell anyone. Why would he? After all, he is the one who assigned me and knows about it all. Or perhaps, like me, he did not. Oh, God.

Khan paces from the front door to the back of the house, as some of the smoke escapes through the slits in the plywood ceiling of the hallway. It has absolutely nothing to do with him, he says to himself again, and he should not draw attention to himself by talking about it. Neither among his friends nor with his family. And even if something was to happen, everyone would stand by me. 'I am a well-respected man, although not so much at home – where are they?' he mutters to himself. 'I have at least earned that much respect in the area,' he says, as he thinks of Nabbé Galdar, Ali Clay the butcher, Bashir the milkman and others.

Khan is saddened at the loss of company, not just because he is a central figure in the neighbourhood, and is admired, even loved, in the streets, but because early on he had chosen his friends among the shopkeepers he grew up with, and not the educated officers in the area. Those middle-class men had in any case shunned Khan because, unlike them, he had not amassed wealth by dipping his hand in the till at his work. When he was ostracized by these rich men fond of embezzlement, he hadn't felt slighted but was rather relieved.

*

Roohi enters the kitchen late at night, sits at her father's side and, pressing his legs, says, 'Don't worry too much about it, Papa. You didn't do anything wrong.'

He looks at her, his face dark again, holds her hand and gives a sigh so deep and childlike that Roohi cannot do anything but leave the room and run to her attic.

Faiz, look what has happened here. Please come back soon.

No, no, don't come back now. They are taking the boys away. Please do not come back now. Did you hear me? Do not come here.

Wide-awake in her sanctuary she makes a decision. She will go to Mir Manzil soon and find out everything about this Hakeem Usman of Rainawari and if he really has contacts, and influence, on the other side.

The Officer's Problem

Sumit Kumar has decided that the best way to rehearse what he wants to say to Principal Koul is to write it down. This way, he told himself last night, as he read Shanta Koul's letter for the fourth time, he will not be lost for words or fumble in her presence. He should be informal, personal – there is nothing in the book that can help him here, he thinks. Besides, she is so, so nice and reminds him of his mother, especially her sartorial manner, her beautiful saris and the way she wears them.

What might have been a warm and comforting relationship with a cultured native, the encounter a perfect anecdote in an officer's dinner-party repertoire, enhanced and added to over the years – 'I still receive letters from her,' he might have said, years later – has most certainly been marred by this unfortunate situation, Kumar thinks. He begins to draft his response and, as he does so, reminds himself that he must destroy the paper immediately after the meeting. But he finds himself stuck at the very first sentence.

I am sorry? I regret? Apologize? I wish we had met in more, how do I put this, normal circumstances?

What might Dada have said? Would Dada ever have found himself in a situation like this?

Dear [Principal Koul], Shanta Ma'am, I am very close to my mother . . .

It is a hot afternoon, so hot that Kumar wonders if the creeping destruction of this once glorious city has anything to do with the unusual change in its climate. Whatever happened to the cool, soulful Kashmir weather that had brought the Mughals here and made them declare the Valley an earthly Paradise, as though it solely existed for imperial pleasure? he wonders. Of course, it only meant they had sought and found a haven from the punishing heat of the Indian plains they had made their home. The Summer Capital is perhaps the oldest royal euphemism for a place whose weather gains the approval of a spoilt prince. He smiles at this without a hint of irony.

He considers a sharp beam of sunlight that has warmed a part of the polished concrete floor and wonders if this is what one fundamentally lives for while on earth: build and plunder, desecrate and repair. He drinks water from what was once a beaker in the class-nine chemistry lab, and looks out into the dusty school courtyard.

Shanta Koul and the late Syed Afaq Bukhari's evergreen hedges are defiant in the sun but there is a certain weariness about their leaves. Dust has begun to coat them. Quite a few students have stopped appearing for class. He didn't notice at first, but then he realized he hadn't seen some familiar faces for days.

There was the slender girl who won the painting competition but refused to accept the 101-rupees cash prize, without saying why, and hurried off the stage quietly, her ears blood red.

There was the little girl he had often spotted at the tap in the courtyard, her white canvas shoes sometimes dark with water.

There was the pretty, red-cheeked girl from class ten whom everyone always called by her full name: Mir Farhat.

And there was the quietly angry head girl, Shireen Shah, who once slipped a photocopy of her essay 'Not All Uniforms are Welcome in Schools' under his door, with the sweetest note attached: 'Please don't take this personally, sir. You are an educated officer, I hope you like it.'

He smokes, against his earlier decision not to go to the meeting with Shanta Ma'am reeking of tobacco.

As Principal Shanta Koul approaches his office, he stands up, already burdened and possibly close to minor heartbreak for she is dressed in that impeccable sari again, very light purple with a saffron border, three crisp folds neatly tied into her waist, as though it were paper craft. Shanta puts her bag on his desk, on *her* desk, and smiles at him.

'Major Saéb, won't you offer me a cold drink? All right, all right, please get me a glass of cold water.'

'Oh, I am so, so sorry. Please give me a minute.' He picks up his walkie-talkie and mouths instructions into it. 'Two bottles of Gold Spot, ice separately, remember that, and two glasses.'

'Thank you. So . . . how have you been? I hear things outside are not very good. Too many raids, I think, too many raids on people's homes. I hope you will spare us.'

'Oh, no, no. I didn't have anything to do with them, ma'am, trust me. You know me.'

'Yes, I know you. You live in my school.'

'I was coming to that, er . . . I read your letter . . . You write very well, ma'am.'

Principal Koul smiles and feels bad about it.

'My mother . . . I'm so sorry . . . I've written to Headquarters twice, trust me, and spoken to my boss a couple of times.' Kumar says what he thinks she'd like to hear.

Shanta Ma'am knows and decides she shouldn't dislike him for it. 'What a fine young man they have ruined,' she mutters to herself.

'I didn't hear that, ma'am?'

'That's all right. I was talking to myself. What now, Sumit?'

'I don't know what to say, really, ma'am. All I can say is I'm sorry I couldn't live up to the promise they, we, made. Trust me, I didn't want to occupy your school for such a long time. I feel equally bad about the girls –'

'No, you don't,' Shanta cuts him short. 'You don't know my girls and will never know them, or me.'

'I said I'm sorry. Please forgive me.'

'I forgave you the day you entered my office.'

'So why the . . . ?'

'You see, I don't think you quite understand. My letter wasn't meant solely for you. It's for your bosses, their bosses, and so on . . . If I were you, I would even take it to your parliament in Delhi. You see, I have run the oldest school for girls in this place. Did you know I gave up a senior lecturer's job at the university to do this? I could have been a professor by now, even head of department.'

'I understand, ma'am.'

'No, you don't. Have you ever heard of a man called Afaq Bukhari, *Syed* Afaq Bukhari?'

'Sorry. No.'

'He was the deputy headmaster here. He had a PhD. I don't. You see those evergreen hedges in the courtyard? They are as old as the school and were planted by the great Begum Z. Ali herself. Syed Sir and I fought over them. Do you know why? Because he wanted to build a new wing for the younger girls, which meant sacrificing a few of the bushes. I didn't want to. I was wrong. We did need space for the little girls. He was right. Do you know where he is now?' Shanta's voice betrays a low timbre of sadness.

'No.'

'He is dead. He is dead. He was killed in the crossfire between you people and the militants. In fact, he was killed by one of you.'

'I was not aware of it, Shanta Ma'am.'

'I know. Why would you be? You see, you can't have much interest in the people here and I can understand that. It's not part of your upbringing, your imagination, your story. Please don't misunderstand me, but have you ever considered going back?'

'I can't do that until my posting is over.'

'Go back, Sumit. No one wants you here. I definitely don't and I hope you understand why.'

'But I have a job to do, ma'am.'

'You are sitting in my chair, major.'

Major Sumit Kumar feels both shame and anger. A part of him wants to leave this room immediately and never come back but a darker voice says he could easily have this woman thrown out, even barred from the building. Well, he could have her arrested. He colours and clenches his teeth. He badly needs a smoke.

'Shanta Ma'am, as I said, I wish it was in my hands. I'm sorry, I can't do anything. Please forgive me.'

'Oh, you want me to leave, do you?'

Just then a soldier with the biggest rifle Shanta has ever seen enters the room with a tray. Two bottles of Gold Spot have stamped thin rings of vapour on it. A steel bowl has a heap of crushed ice in it. The glasses look dirty.

'Please have some, ma'am. It is quite hot, these days. I didn't expect high temperatures here. Please . . .' Kumar says, as the soldier takes his leave with a silent salute.

Principal Koul peers at the orange drink in front of her.

Remembrance

Mir Zafar Ali has not given up on his right hand. He has it massaged with olive oil every morning in the hope that one day it will spring back to life. By the looks of it, the hand seems perfectly well. It seems exactly like his healthy left hand. But it's the fingers, they simply refuse to move. Haqqani Saéb, proprietor of Gousia Printers & Publishers, has been patient but has hinted he might have to ask another calligrapher to take over from Mir Zafar who is beginning to get anxious about the potential dip in income. The publication of the firebrand poet Majzoob Qadri's narrative poem *Kalhana's Kismet* has already been delayed by more than three months. Mir Zafar had read the poem twice, was struck by its stunning invention, and had started transcribing it in his old-fashioned style, when the accident happened. He hasn't copied a single verse since.

He is still hopeful that the hand will not let him down. This week he has been able to make the gentlest of movements with his fingers. A little murmur among the five friends, he calls it. Wahab Wattangour, the local masseur and specialist fixer of broken bones, the garrulous peddler of tall tales, mostly chronicles of his miracles in the high art of mending multiple fractures, has assured him that the rare oil from Mecca – which is actually just garden variety Spanish virgin olive oil one of his customers brought back from Hajj nearly a decade ago – has magical properties and his hand will soon feel even better than before. Mir Zafar did not correct him.

As he tries to pick up the pencil Farhat has sharpened for him, he remembers the painting Faiz had talked so passionately about. He would give anything to hear Faiz talk about it again, to see if he has done any work on it. He could possibly go to Faiz's room and look for it but has resisted the temptation so far. It could be a bad omen. He would rather wait for Faiz to return from Pakistan, safe and sound, and then see *Falaknuma*. His mind wanders back to the night Faiz and he had talked as they settled into bed. It was the third night after his escape from the Zaal, when Faiz had started sleeping in his brother's room.

'Come, come, you must be tired, Faizå. Sleep now.'

'I'm fine, Abba. Are you feeling any better?'

'I'll live. It's you I'm worried about . . .'

'Why, what's wrong with me? I'm fine. Nothing will happen to me.'

'Faizå, do you have any idea what would have happened if it was you and not me on the road?'

'But it wasn't.'

'They wouldn't have let you go. They would have come back for you.'

'Why would they do that? I have nothing to do with anything, Abba.'

'The boys they took away had nothing to do with anything, either. And even if some of them were involved, this is no way to find out. Hunted like cattle. Snared like chickens. Caged as if they were mad dogs. Even Hari Singh's reign was better than this. I could have been one of them, Faizå . . . I'm scared for you, my dear. Anything may happen here now.'

'Hmm . . . But things will change – it can't continue like this. You worry too much,' Faiz had lied unconvincingly.

'Listen, I want to say something to you. Listen carefully.'

Faiz had looked at the half-lit face of his brother, his form that of an aged man as he leant against three cushions. A feral pack of dogs that gathered every night in the neighbour's dark pomegranate garden had broken into a shrill dirge. The house sparrows protested meekly, aware they could make no effective intervention at this hour.

'You should leave home, Faizå. You need to run.'

'What? What are you talking about, Abba?' Faiz had said, in

genuine surprise, even though the thought had occurred to him, too, quite a few times since Fatima's death.

'I have thought about this. You need to run.'

'Why just me? What about Sajad, Shabbir?'

'They are older and government employees. Shabbir has a paunch and is balding, too. They won't be interested in him.'

'What are you talking about, Abba?'

'Just listen to me.'

'But where will I go? Why?'

'Anywhere. Don't you see the state I'm in? My hand feels as if it isn't there!'

'Anywhere?'

'Yes, anywhere.'

Mir Zafar Ali's reverie is broken by a knock on the outer door to the large drawing room, of which his bedroom is a part. The knock is tentative – someone he has not met before.

He drops the pencil, tries to move the tips of his fingers again, and looks through the inside door into the hallway. He leaves his snug seat on the mattress, hops over the knee-high partition into the drawing-room space, and through the windows spies a young woman standing on the threshold. A strikingly beautiful young woman. It's got to be Roohi.

He opens the door, the slide of the heavy walnut-wood panels fraught with a hundred moments. Why is she here? Didn't her parents bar her from even coming to the area?

'Salam alaikum.'

'Walaikum salam.'

They stand looking at each other in the bright sunlight that has suddenly burst into the room, her hair glorious, shining. She has a light-green chiffon dupatta partly covering her head, her curls draped over her neck and shoulders.

Quite suddenly, Mir Zafar is filled with a profound sadness for her and Faiz, the world's cruelty somehow manifest in the countenance of this young woman in front of him. He will remember his first glimpse of her for a long, long time. He will cry about it every Muharram when people mourn the death of Imam Hussain, his tears soon lending themselves to the tragedies in his own life, this, the story of his brother and his only love, being the most lovely and intimate of all.

Roohi, beginning to feel the weight of the silence between them, speaks first. 'I'm sorry I've landed here like this, but I didn't have a choice.'

'Come in, come in . . .'

She follows him quietly, sighing at the realization that the moment when Faiz's elder brother would present her with something on seeing her for the first time may already have vanished. This is not how I wanted to meet you, Abba, she says to herself. As she sits down, she envisages herself, for the briefest of moments, sitting in this very room as a bride, with all of Faiz's family seated around her bridal seat. It is still possible. Of course, it is certainly possible. 'Everything God does has a purpose,' she murmurs.

'Farree, Farree!' Mir Zafar calls, hoping she might come quickly and make this visitor comfortable. 'She will be here soon. Would you like some tea?'

'No, no . . . I just had some at home.'

'Oh, and how is everyone at home?' Mir Zafar has never seen her parents.

'They are well . . . I'm sorry I came like this. I wanted to . . .' Roohi wants somehow to come to the point of her visit before Farhat appears. It might be awkward, even hard for her, if they find out she tells me everything, Roohi thinks.

'It's all right, dear, really, it's fine. It will all be fine, trust us.'

'How?'

'Sorry?'

'I am sorry. You were saying it will all be fine?'

'What else, my dear? We can't despair, lose hope, and there are things one can do.'

'Yes?'

'I'm just saying let's wait, let's be patient. You see, I'm an old man. I've seen a lot over my long service, I know people . . .'

'Have you been in touch with Faiz?'

'No. That's not possible and, I'm sure you know, dangerous. As it is, I barely escaped from the claws of that ghastly vehicle. But . . .' Mir Zafar looks intently at Roohi, her features, the mix of pain and fire in her eyes, her clasped hands, and decides, in that brief moment, that he likes her very much.

'Your parents will be very cross with you if they find out you came here. Go home, don't worry. Farhat will find you if I have something to tell you, which might be soon.'

Roohi stays silent, but finds her gaze fixed on Mir Zafar's hand. He gradually slips it inside the sleeve of his pheran. Roohi colours.

'My parents will not be cross with me for coming here,' she says at last, not particularly addressing Faiz's brother but as a statement of fact.

'Farhat, Farree, where the hell are you?'

'I'm here, I'm here.' Farhat enters the room, having listened to some of the conversation from behind the curtain. Before Roohi can say anything to her, Faiz's mother enters too. She's carrying a samovar – hardly anyone uses them these days, unless it's a special day – and a basket full of fresh homemade rice-flour bread. Of course, Roohi doesn't know, and Farhat and Faiz have never had occasion to tell her this, that in this house, under Mouj's regime, tea served in a thermos flask is frowned upon, and the bread from the local baker – the Mirs still have privileged access to what was once their own baker in better, more affluent times – is brought in only when Mouj is away or, at best, as supplement to the bread she makes. These are domestic rituals from a previous age, mostly decided and demanded by men, without any consideration as to what they might mean for the women.

Mouj quickly responds to Roohi's greetings, presses one hand to the floor to balance herself, and starts pouring tea into four cups.

Farhat beams with pride and wants to tell her mother and brother that she has known the most beautiful girl she has ever met for a long time. Her spirits are soon dampened, though, not only for the obvious reason but also because Feroza and Shahida are not here to witness this.

'I made these especially for you,' Mouj says, lifting the cloth cover from the stack of breads in the basket. Sesame, flour and warmth spread in the air. 'Now, let her drink her tea in peace.' She gives Mir Zafar and Farhat a look and drinks from her own cup. Brother and sister smile.

As she walks home, the echoes of various azans amid flights of birds filling the dusk with urgency, Roohi cannot stop her hand sliding into her side pocket. Her fingers feel for the small velvet pouch that Faiz's mother had slipped into it when she left. Dark blue with a silver knot at the top. She trembles with happiness, sadness. Inside it she finds large gold earrings with a small ruby studded at the centre.

It will be months before Farhat finds a chance to tell her, against her mother's wishes, that the earrings were Mouj's own, her last legacy from their wealthy days. Her husband, Mir Mohammed Ali, had had them made in Bombay in 1956 and shipped to Kashmir via special courier.

Mir Zafar's words come back to her late at night. 'Farhat will find you if I have something to tell you, which might be soon.'

Come soon, Farhat. Please.

A Friend in the Wilderness

The man known as Kamal Mustafa is furious. He and Faiz are seated in the courtyard of the kitchen, the sun's light changing to blue, green and orange through the flags that flap above them. Faiz finds himself distracted by the colours but knows too well he has to appear serious before this man who, he knows now, is the boss. He also knows he should not feel angry with the bomb-maker for reporting him.

'I'm sure you know whose name you share?'

'Yes, sir, I know, a famous poet.'

'Yes, the great Faiz Ahmed Faiz, Pakistan's greatest poet, some say.'

'I haven't read anything by him, sir, only heard my brother recite his poetry from time to time.'

'Do you know what we did with him?'

'No, sir.' Faiz suddenly realizes he is not really afraid of this man.

'Well, we threw him into jail. The fucker wrote too much poetry. Did you hear that? We put even the great Faiz in jail. Do you know why?'

Faiz decides not to say anything.

'Let me educate you, then. For treason, for conspiracy, for being critical of the good name of our nation.'

'Sir, I —'

'So, my dear friend, let me say this to you. Do what you are asked to do. Everyone you see here is from some far-off place, away from home, but they are here for a purpose. And remember one thing. We did not force you to come here, did we?'

'No, sir.'

'I have been told you are some kind of artist, so I can understand you may feel the urge to paint, draw or whatever it is you do. Occasionally it is all right – and do not tell anyone I said that! – but you cannot spend your training time and our resources on your art. Do you understand?'

'Yes, sir.'

'Good. I am not against art, or music, as some people are. We have plenty of artists and singers in our country, too, but they don't have to do what you are here for. Isn't that right?'

A quickening breeze sends the bunting aflutter and the slivers of colour shimmy on the ground. The dust Faiz has come to associate with the camp begins to rise too, spreading a dry, pleasant smell in the clay courtyard.

'Sir, with due respect, I know why I'm here. I know it very well. I just want to say I do not spend all the time painting. I've only drawn here, and just one piece. I don't have my paints here, sir. There are no colours here. You can see what I have drawn if you want to, sir. It's a scene from here, actually. Would you like to?'

'Not now. Some other day. Listen, just do what you're supposed to do. I don't like it when people say Kamal hasn't trained his men well. Do you understand?'

'Yes, sir, I do. It won't happen again.' Faiz bites his upper lip.

'Good. You can go now.'

'Khuda Hafiz, sir.' Faiz stands up immediately to leave.

'One last thing. Don't take the painting, drawing, whatever, with you when you go back. Remember that.'

Faiz, already at the edge of the courtyard, turns and nods.

He spends the rest of the day in silence. It helps that all he has to do in the workshop today is paint layers of some thick tea-coloured glue on the soapboxes he has been told will be used for car bombs. The room is filled with painted boxes, everywhere, like a pile of toys in a spoilt boy's room. His hands shake once, maybe twice, but then an unthinking rhythm sets in and he sticks liquid glue all day, furiously, again and again, until there is no glue or soap-box left. Faiz and Pintoo the bomb-maker do not speak all day.

The evening brings two pleasant things. There is rice and mutton korma for dinner, and Engineer seems in a happy mood, chatting and patting people on the back as he does a round of the mess hall. Faiz wishes he were like him.

After dinner, Faiz discreetly rubs his belly in satisfaction, and they saunter out with a bunch of boys from home and settle down at the base of the big dune. There is a camaraderie between them, an unsaid closing of ranks. Among them is a boy from Kupwara, who sings in the most affecting voice, making Faiz and everyone else nostalgic for home. The evening gives way to a cool night. Stars appear overhead, like silver studs on a black dupatta. In the blue glow of the night, Faiz looks at the white and green flag. It is still. Gradually, the other boys begin to leave for their rooms, until only Engineer and the Artist are left.

'Don't worry about what Kamal Sir said. Don't worry about it at all.'

'How did you know? Oh, yes, you know everything, right?'

'Look, it's normal here. You actually escaped with a mild warn-ing. I know people who've come back crying. And you may not know this, but Kamal Sir is a proper officer in the army. You were lucky – I've been told he can be ruthless when he has to be. Trust me. I know.'

'But I didn't do anything wrong. For God's sake, why doesn't any-one understand that all I did was draw something on a piece of paper that had been thrown away?'

'Yes, I know. The thing is they don't like boys who appear less than serious, or the ones who don't wake up early enough for the morning drills, like me.'

'But they don't say anything to you. Have you bribed the trainers or Kamal Sir himself?'

'Well, well, let's just say I may know a few people who know the people running this place. Okay, the truth is my grandfather knows some people.'

'I knew it. I knew you had family influence here.'

'All right, all right. Here, look at this.' Engineer takes a brown envelope from his pocket and waves it in front of Faiz's eyes. The envelope shines in the starlight.

'Take it, touch it, feel it. It's a letter. A letter from home.'

Faiz just looks at it, trying to keep calm. He doesn't recognize the postmark. It's not the Three Lions mark of Indian Post & Telegraph that he has seen all his life. His most cherished memory of letters is from when he was eight or nine. Mir Zafar Ali had gone to Calcutta to try his luck at the handicrafts trade, attempting to revive the family's old contacts and fortunes. He would send a letter home every week or so until he returned six months later, failed, humiliated and so heartbroken by homesickness that he didn't leave his room for an entire week. In those days, postmen still came to the door on their Hercules bicycles, rang the bell three times, dropped letters, even had a cup of tea sometimes, particularly if they were bearers of money orders. Faiz used to sit in a corner, waiting for the sentence meant for him to be read aloud. He would marvel at, what seemed to him then, the stunning feat his brother achieved every week by writing a three-page letter in beautiful handwriting. He remembers the exaggerated long arcs of his own name – فیض. He remembers those long-gone letter-reading occasions as the Mir family's secret evenings of happiness. Now Faiz cannot but think of his brother's lifeless hand, as Engineer puts the letter back in his pocket.

'I would have thought you'd be happy for me. What's with the drawn face? Come on . . .'

'Oh, no, I'm really pleased. This is a miracle, a letter from your home. Congratulations!' Faiz holds back a sigh.

'Hmm . . . I won't torment you further. Let's go and listen to some music. It's too dark in any case to stay out here. We'll talk inside.'

'You are joking, aren't you? How will we listen to music?'

'Don't you trust me? I told you we're friends. Did you think I was joking?' Engineer, Hakeem Usman's grandson, speaks in a serious, deliberate voice, and puts his hand on Faiz's.

'I didn't mean it like that. Just didn't think it was possible that there'd be a music system here, and if it was possible, that it would be only for special people. That's all.'

'Let's just say that from now on you, too, are special. Now get rid of that sullen face. In fact, leave it in that workshop of yours tomorrow.'

Panther

Rumi sits with his head down as the chief commander of the New Salvation Front, Moulvi Panther or Commander Panther, reads from a prepared statement at the gathering of the executive committee of the newly formed militant group. There are three other boys in the room.

'I say this with utmost regret that our own people may have helped in this. How else could they have raided every single home and all of them in a single night? It is a shame, it is a tragedy, it is a crime. It has happened in our area and we will not sit and watch as this evil spreads.'

Rumi was tipped off by his friend Shaheen, also an apprentice militant with the NSF, that his father's name has cropped up among the suspects whom they think collaborated with the army in the night-time raids on homes in Khanqah. Shaheen had asked him to stay away from the group for now, but Rumi, as headstrong as his sister, had decided to come to the meeting anyway. He simply does not believe all these whispers about his father.

As he sits listening to Panther's long address, invoking the holy Qur'ān and the need for justice, he goes over the last six months. The first day he met Shaheen by the river and how they decided not to go to Pakistan for training and instead join a smaller, locally trained group, so they didn't have to participate in any 'action' at the very start. They could observe for a few months, see how it went, get comfortable with the weapons, learn the lingo, as Shaheen had put it, then decide whether to join one of the proper, bigger groups. Rumi now wonders if this is all his group does, make rambling speeches, print posters that always have 'dire consequences' written on them, canvass for funds, raid restaurants to spot check if any male feet are in close proximity to female footwear. After one such inspection, Panther was slapped and kicked in the groin by a woman from Dalgate, who was having lunch with her son at Alka Salka after a morning's shopping. 'You little fart! Do you know where I'm from? If you have any guts, I dare you to go to that bunker and show them there. If you ever touch my son again, I'll crush your tiny balls with these,' she had announced on Residency Road, brandishing her newly acquired pencil heels from Rightway Shoes & Sandals.

Rumi smiles as Moulvi Panther finishes his long-winded statement, and decides they don't really have too much to worry about. However threatening, this man cannot be dangerous to anyone. He's just besotted with his own voice. Rumi suddenly misses his sister. She would have found it hilarious, the idea of our father being an informer for the army! The poor man doesn't even dare to smoke when Mummy's around. Roohi, he guesses, might even have a word or two with Commander Panther, make him tremble in his baggy khaki pants. They don't know my sister – if only she could be here now. People listen in silence when she speaks.

Sumit Kumar looks at the photograph of the man known as Panther and smiles. There is a three-page profile attached underneath. It has been written by HQ and advises 'extreme vigilance and caution regarding this unpredictable, eccentric character'. For God's sake, since when did militants become predictable in this place? God, these pie-chart hacks at HQ find it easier to create paper tigers sitting on their lazy backsides than venture out for some real work. He pushes the papers away and lights up. As nicotine courses through his blood, Kumar wonders if a cigarette is all he can look forward to in this nerve-shattering city. He has twice come close to making that phone call. Daddy can easily have him transferred to an unaffected hill station here or indeed outside but he doesn't want to come across as a wimp. That was the word his father had used, smiling, when Sumit had almost broken down while saying goodbye to his mother at the end of his first vacation from boarding school. But it's not as if I need to prove myself to him any more. I already have. A job had been going at HQ where there's a lot of open space, fields, gardens, even a whole mountainside they grabbed some years ago, and, of course, the officers' mess and club, but he had turned it down, thinking he would be miserable in a desk job. Now, sitting in Principal Shanta Koul's office, behind her desk, he wonders which is worse – a desk job or being holed up in a boarded-up, sandbagged girls' school. He picks up the Panther papers again and looks at the photo and description. He underlines 'May not pose any immediate or great threat to the personnel in the area but is capable of stirring up local trouble', even though he does not fully understand it. He's a joker, for God's sake. I know who he is. He makes all kinds of fantastic speeches, he even sent a warning to George Bush on a cottage-industry poster a couple of weeks ago.

He stands up and goes to check the special dinner waiting for him on Shanta Koul's desk. His local contact, the same man who had looked after the Zaal while it was in the area, had been insisting that Sir must taste the local cuisine and Kumar had finally given in, thinking it might make at least one evening different, if nothing else. There are three bowls on the small tray. (Shanta used it for visiting guests.) One contains rice, the second kebabs, small red meatballs alongside a huge intimidating white one, and the third bowl is filled with a scarlet, creamy and the most striking roghan josh he has ever seen. He closes his eyes momentarily. As he sits down to eat, he notices his hands aren't clean, that there is some dark grease on the edges of his palms. Standing up he looks at his trousers and finds there are black smudges near the pockets. He goes to the sink to wash his hands. He looks up at himself reflected in the mirror in the evening light, and breaks down, holding tightly to the rim of the sink. Gently, slowly, in barely audible sobs, he cries. Then he washes his face again, and again, and goes back to his meal: a sampler of wazwan, the cholesterol-infused but delicious feast, a version of which travelled here, some believe, from western Persia during a winter in the late fourteenth century when six hundred disciples had carried twenty-one sacks of condiments and recipes during a long and frozen trek through the high Karakoram passes.

Another dinner is under way not far from Kumar's solitary dining. Three floors below, in the sports store that was once the prized domain of the cricket-jumper loving Nazir Sir, are three boys, Shafeeq, Umar and Rayees (a.k.a. Seythhå, the Mirs' favourite auto-rickshaw-walla), Faiz's neighbours and teammates from a short-lived cricket team they had formed in 1983. Seythhå is halfway through his rice and dal, while the other two are picking at the food now and then. Any day now, they expect to be set free. No one, apart from Mahraazė, knows that the three are still here.

Kumar has had it conveyed to them that they are safe and will not be transferred anywhere. In return, they must not create any noise, and when they go back, they must keep an eye on the people Kumar's messenger called troublemakers. They are beginning to believe what they have been told, especially because there haven't been any beatings for a full week now, and their bruises and injuries from the last one are beginning to heal and hurt less. Seythhå wolfs down his food and eyes the spare breads lying nearby. Shafeeq nudges the newspaper holding them towards him. Seythhå doesn't want to go home looking emaciated, and has been trying to convince his cell mates that they, too, should eat all they are given. They try every day but somehow cannot finish their meals. The bread tastes bitter, as though it was made with stale flour, Umar says.

'Come on, do you think they make these especially for us? I'm sure they're from the same stock as their own food. Why would they cook separately for us? Do you think we're Hindustan's chief guests here, Umi?' Seythhå tries to cheer his friends up but they remain gloomy, in some pain from unhealed wounds, and terrified. Every approaching footstep could be the messenger of death, Shafeeq sometimes thinks aloud, to which Seythhå often says, 'The messenger of death is too busy roaming the streets, the border or proper prisons. Can't you see, it's a girls' school? My elder sister studied here. Even if they tried, they can't convert it into a death chamber, can they?'

Both Shafeeq and Umar look at Seythhá, and down at his fingernails, which are only now showing signs of growing back.

Here

Farhat runs from her doorstep to Roohi's in one breath. Off-balance, because her right hand is clasping the paper in her pocket, she nearly tumbles over at the door. In normal days, in ordinary times, she and, of course, Roohi and Faiz would have been more discreet. In fact, for Roohi and Faiz, discretion, muted, precautious footsteps, voices nearly always at a whisper, had gradually become their habit, relaxing only inside the basement of the shrine or during the occasional trip in Seythhå's curtained auto-rickshaw. Farhat, their aide in love, their constant co-conspirator and sometimes alibi, had perhaps become even more careful than the lovers themselves had. Now, she throws aside caution and takes a particular delight in her carelessness, even though she is aware of the circumstances that have emboldened her.

She knocks loudly at the door, and then, realizing she was perhaps too forceful, slows down. Must let my breathing settle first, she tells herself, and stops knocking. She reminds herself that she cannot, should not, spend too much time here as Roohi's brother makes her uncomfortable. It's the way he looks at her. What made them call him Rumi?

The door opens slowly and a hand pulls her in. The hallway is darker than before but Farhat walks on led by Roohi's firm hand. In the cool darkness, she relaxes and smiles to herself. As she climbs the many narrow steps to Roohi's private world, Farhat thinks about the future. Will this hallway still be so cool? Will she still be doing this, acting as go-between for her brother and Roohi? Will she be gone, far away for higher studies or married to someone she likes? What will Roohi be like? Will she really become Farhat's sister-in-law at some point? Will there come a time when Farhat will realize that she is never going to see her friend, her beautiful friend, ever again? That would make her brother very sad. Did he really have to go?

Farhat had been the least surprised when Faiz left. She was, in fact, surprised it had not happened earlier. Nearly every day at school she had heard of someone's brother, cousin or uncle who had left to fight, and a part of her might even have hoped that someone from her family would go, too, so she could join in the conversation in her class. She is not too sure now. She has seen the colour drain away from the face of the most beautiful girl in the world. Last week, she tied two votive threads, one in their own little shrine room on the top floor and the other at Roohi's shrine, sealing within the narrow folds of the silk kerchief she had used a promise for her brother's safe return. She will open it when he comes back and she will feed many poor people as a mark of gratitude. She is sure Abba will give her the money for it.

As she sits down in her favourite corner by the L-shaped bookshelf in Roohi's room, she puts the envelope on Roohi's desk. They both look at it.

There

My Dearest Faiz,

Assalamalaikum!

Hope my letter finds you in good health and spirits. It's nothing but the result of our prayers that I can write to you, and I have been assured that it will actually reach you. Khoda Saëb has rewarded me for my patience and I thank Him for that. There is so much to talk about that I don't know where to begin and what to keep for the last. I pray for you all the time. My hand trembles as I write this, and as I try to steady it, it trembles even more, so I will just let it be. I listened to the radio every night for two months in case you'd sent me a message or a song, but I now understand it's not possible for everyone to do so. We were so relieved and grateful when we found out you are safe. Oh, there is so much to tell. I don't know if I should go on about myself or what has happened here since your departure. I am fine, actually, apart from waiting every minute of the day to see your face. I sleep well at night except when Mahraazë is outside the shrine, lecturing the world and God. I cover my window with two sheets at night to muffle his sounds, but I can still hear him on certain nights. There are nights when he sounds furious and doesn't stop talking until its time for dawn namaz.

Farhat comes to see me when she can and tells me everything. She has forbidden me to tell you about your home but I think you should know. They all seem fine, going on about their life as everyone here is. But they also look scared. Who wouldn't after what happened to your brother and your friends? They are actually not very fine, Faiz. Your mother is a brave woman; she talks about you and smiles all the time, but Farhat says she doesn't sleep much, keeping an ear out for any sound around the house, at the door and by the windows, in the dark. Sometimes I think she's keeping

*a vigil for you. At other times, I feel she's constantly in dread of a raid.
I met your brother a few weeks ago, he seemed fine, healthy, but I doubt if
his hand will be normal any time soon. I feel terrible, and it is so sad that
it should have been his writing hand.*

*They have now even started arresting people from the newspapers and
printing presses, so maybe it's a good thing your brother cannot work on
books any more.*

*Something else happened. For some strange reason, Mummy hasn't
talked of my marriage for more than a month. That's a world record! But,
honestly, it's actually sad. She wants to keep me where she can see me all
the time. Rumours about girls being attacked are going around. 'You are
either insane or foolish,' Mummy said, 'if you want me to believe that the
bunker-wallas will protect you.' I had not said anything like that, but
I understand her anxiety. So I do not step out after twilight, don't even go
to the shrine for the evening prayers, which makes me sad. But I'm also
grateful that the marriage oppression is over for now.*

*I'm slightly worried about Papa. Did I tell you about his part-time job?
He had taken up this assignment for the DC's office, which he finished on
time and was happy about it, but then these raids happened, in nearly
every house in the neighbourhood, especially homes with young men. Now
he is worried someone may have used his report, copied it, you know . . .
I think that's a bit far-fetched, and I have tried to calm him down, but he's
suddenly started smoking a lot more. He does that when he's really tense.*

*It seems you left such a long, long time ago; too much has happened
here since. The main thing, however, is you are fine. I have a feeling you
are going to give me a lot more anxiety when you come back here.*

*I have decided, Faiza! When you come back, I will somehow talk to
Mummy and Papa so that we can be together as soon as possible. It's not
right keeping Mummy waiting. What do you think?*

*I don't think it will carry on for long – something is bound to happen
soon. I can feel it in the air. Lakhs of people are out every day. No one sits
at home. I want to join the crowds too but you know how it is. So I
sometimes just stand outside our front door with a jug of lemon squash.
I miss you even then. A boy came to drink water and I imagined he was*

you. His hair was long and messy, a bit like yours. In the procession, I saw one of your friends, Majeed the government employee. He smiled at me. At first, Mummy didn't approve. But when the freedom demos and chants refused to end, one day she herself came out with slices of watermelon for the people. We stood there until the last man had left our street. Some people stayed back for prayers at the shrine and a few sat by your chinar. They were not from around Downtown. One of them smoked the way you do, with the cigarette hand too close to his head. I wanted to tell him to keep it away lest he burn his hair, as you did when we went to Chashm-e-Shahi. Do you remember? I remember the emerald light on the lake and your hair in it. The smell of bathing soap on you. You actually fell asleep on the boat and dropped your head on my shoulder. I pretended to be asleep. You even started snoring at one point and the poor boatman began to row furiously, trying to drown out the noise, splashing water all over! I burst out laughing and that's when you woke up and smiled.

I think of you all the time, Faiz, all day, even when I'm praying, which is not good, not good at all. But Khoda Saéb will forgive me. He knows everything. You know what I miss the most? The waiting. There's nothing to look forward to, Faiz. Thursdays are like any other day. I do try to remember you have gone to fight in a war and, like everyone else, I must wait for it to be over and take pride in what you're doing, but . . . it's not the same, is it? You're not fighting yet. Then I think I will feel it when you come back and actually fight, but that fills me with a brutal fear. Scores of boys are martyred every day, some without even fighting. I know, I know, I should take pride no matter what, but I don't want to lose you before even . . . I hope you understand.

I am not angry with you, Faizá. You did what you felt you had to do. I miss you. When you come back to me, I will tell you everything.

Yours only,
Roohi

Country With a Post Office

The entry to Neel Gali is always dimly lit, as if to warn visitors that they are entering a world that exists outside the commerce and hustle-bustle of downtown Kathmandu. A visitor trying to escape from the noise and talk and the raucous music of automobile horns may find herself drawn to this sedate street just behind the tourist district.

At the mouth of the street, she may notice a row of discoloured wooden pylons, with numerous loops of electrical cable over them, that stretches into the twilight. In the middle of the lane, the houses on either side have large green balconies on the top floors. Tall flower-pots of narcissus line the balconies and wisteria droops from the low railings. Persian carpets hang from one of these houses. They are, in fact, not Persian.

The residents of the greenest of houses in Neel Gali include a silver-haired poet, who gave up verse twenty years ago to pen the constitution of what he believes will be a truly free country one day. There are whispers that the poet, who lives alone on the second floor, is at work on the fifth and final draft of the document, all written in longhand. On the large ground floor lives the Berlin-educated 'rebel princess', Rajkumari Sheena – disowned by the royal household for her views, she runs a small printing press in the house, publishing her quarterly journal *New Raj*. One day, she hopes to publish the very first copy of the poet's constitution, a promise she made to her friends in the Resistance who visit her every week. Their leader, the youngest of the group, who goes by her adopted name of Pratinidhi, spends a few hours at the reclusive princess's place and at the house of the Persian carpets on the top floor. Pratinidhi and Sheena have known each other from the time Sheena's father drove the little princess around in the royals' vintage Impala, while Pratinidhi sat in the back seat if no one was looking and followed on foot, singing imagined songs, if other royals were about.

On the top floor, you can sometimes see people seated on the balcony leaning against embroidered bolsters, and a samovar doing the rounds of a small gathering of men and women gently singing to each other, taking turns or all together. If you are an unhurried visitor, and happened to hang about in the area for a few weeks, you would see a middle-aged man appear in the street outside this particular house every Thursday morning and evening. A beautiful man, Ibteda Andrabi was once a teacher of literature. Now he lives by himself on the top floor of this house.

On first appearance, his room looks perfectly ordinary. It is large, with an en-suite bathroom at the back and a small bed near the balcony. The only thing that may set it apart from rooms in this or any other house are the pigeonholes on the walls. There are also stacks of packaging material under the bed, sheets of cardboard and bubble-wrap. Every week he packs a carton, writes the address of a handicrafts manufacturer in the back alleys of the lakeside locality of Rainawari in Kashmir. He also writes 'SAMPLES' in bold letters on the top of each carton. The cartons contain samples of papier-mâché articles wrapped in triple layers of thin brown paper and bubble-wrap. A jewellery box, a vase, a card-holder, a cutlery box, a cigarette case, a pencil box – all old pieces, crafted decades ago in Kashmir and now in the possession of Din Shah, the owner of the house and the handicrafts business he runs in Kathmandu. The samples go back to Kashmir via the Nepal Parcel Service, arrive at Peer Handicrafts of Rainawari and are given to select artisans, who hand-paint exact replicas by the hundred or thousand, as the orders demand. Carefully concealed under the glued velvet lining of the coaster set and cutlery boxes are tightly pressed envelopes that contain letters from Pakistan.

Ibteda picks up a bag of letters from a designated post office in one of the busy commercial streets we left behind a while ago, individually packs them into papier-mâché articles that he chooses, and takes the repackaged articles down to the main house. He retrieves the letters that arrive inside finished replicas from Kashmir and, in this final part of the cyclical work he has begun to love, posts them to Pakistan, bearing the Nepal postmark.

In the year and a half he has been doing this – in the service of country, family and love, he thinks – Ibteda has gradually begun to recognize handwriting, the way an envelope is sealed, the texture of the paper on which a letter is written and, most delightfully, if a dispatch simply bears family news or is a letter of longing. Letters from wives, husbands, girlfriends, fiancés, Ibteda has observed, are just a little heavier than the others, or so he thinks. Almost all the letters are written in Urdu. He waits for the day he can detect a letter in Kashmiri. It was a sore issue with him even then, when he taught modern literature at the university, that his land must be among the very few in the world where the teaching and learning of the mother tongue is frowned upon, even actively discouraged. A new generation had already appeared – when he hadn't yet gone into exile – that was proud of the broken, Anglicized, soap-opera accents in which they spoke the mother tongue.

But weightier matters are at hand, Ibteda tells himself. Messages to and from mothers are to be conveyed as efficiently and safely as possible. The stacks he retrieves are getting taller every week. Lately they have also started sending goods home for repair, not just samples. He is still waiting for a decision from Din Shah, his childhood friend, about changing the receiving address back home – why wait until it becomes suspicious? Din Shah, on the other hand, is not too worried – what will they find out if they confiscate the letters? Love, tears, waiting? Still, why endanger this lifeline? Don't be too sentimental, Ibtyá, let me think about it, I also have a business to run, Din had smiled, pressing his shoulder harder than usual.

Ibteda thinks of the letters as life-affirming talismans, bearers of hope and promise in these grim times. He has on occasion found himself pressing down a twisted edge or straightening a folded corner. Once, he even cleaned an unusually smudged envelope with cotton wool and white spirit. He remembers feeling enormously satisfied with the result. He also recalls the guilt he had felt when, giving in to temptation, he had opened a letter that had not been sealed firmly enough and whose envelope, he had guessed or liked to believe, was handmade. It was a long letter from a father to his son; an instruction that the son should continue to stay where he was and not attempt to come back home. In these letters, it seems the father would prefer an absent but alive child to a present and dead one. Did the father approve of his son's going in the first place? Ibteda wondered what the son had written in response. Did he insist on coming home? Did he write an essay explaining his motives? Did he stand by his decision and say that he would fight on, or did he agree with his father, strike a conciliatory note and continue to remain in that suspended reality? As Ibteda had already committed the sin of reading the father's letter he sometimes thinks he should have opened the next to discover what the son actually said. In any case, he had been struck by the father's letter, by his generation's somnolence, as he now looks back at his life.

It was only since his beloved wife Zulekha Syed had died – of cardiac arrest after having been touched by a soldier as she offered her namaz during a cordon-and-search operation – that he had felt such acute shame for not being *aware* from the beginning.

Two years ago, when he lived in Kashmir, he and all the men from the neighbourhood had been waiting to be ID'd in a field, like sheep colour-coded during a hygiene check before a visit to the slaughterhouse. The soldiers had searched their houses and one of them, finding himself alone in their kitchen, had decided to put his hands on Ibteda's wife's prostrate form. She had broken off her prayer and slapped him so hard on both cheeks that a few of his colleagues had heard him cry out and come running to find him. They had entered just as he was kicking her to the floor. The neighbours said something had come over Zulekha since that day and she often complained of a strange suffocation in her chest. Three weeks later, when the family had hoped that the worst was over, when the city's best heart specialist had declared her stable, her heart stopped as she was resting her head in Ibteda's lap. They had just had their afternoon tea.

For months, Ibteda had hardly moved from the kitchen where Zulekha had breathed her last. Apart from essential errands, mostly to do with wrapping up his professional life at the university, he would not leave the rug where she had last sat with him. It was only after his father's persistence – he had been heartbroken to see his son wear the departed wife's pheran – that the melancholic assistant professor of literature, Ibteda Andrabi, had agreed to leave Kashmir and fly to Kathmandu for a change of scenery. At least he wouldn't see so many people in uniform, his father had said, as he sent his son away. He had never dreamt, even though he was aware of the primeval tragedy of parents sending their children away so they might live, that he might not see his child before he died.

As Ibteda remembers Zulekha, tearfully but silently as always, he recalls new letters that had started arriving a few weeks ago. He knows they are between separated lovers. He always knows. The two from Srinagar have the faintest whiff of a female fragrance about them, he believes, while the three from Pakistan are tightly, almost too tightly, sealed, perhaps the desperation of a man who cannot believe his luck that his messages to his beloved will actually reach her.

All this, Ibteda tells himself, has come to him from the delicate weekly ritual of packaging and repackaging letters.

A Labour of Love

My dear Roohi,

I LOVE YOU.

I am sorry I left you. I did not have a choice. It was physically impossible for me to remain the way I was in those last days. I did not know that being unable to sleep could drive a person mad. Perhaps I was mad. I just couldn't forgive them for killing Faaté Baajé. How can I?

Being away from you has made one thing clear to me. I cannot be without you. It is, as you often say, actually simple. We were destined to meet and be together. Please forgive me for my handwriting and spelling mistakes. I am writing slowly and carefully. You will understand, it takes me a long time to write one sentence. I have never written a letter before.

I am fine here. This place is completely different from home. But I still don't know where it is. Some say it's an area called Ilaqa-e-Ghair but it doesn't make sense as there are quite a few people here. How can it be the forbidden land? My educated friend here (oh, I haven't told you about him) says this name was invented by white people during the British Raj. I don't know much about that. Some boys joke that, while we believe we are in a remote tribal area, we might in fact be just a few miles from Islamabad! I would like to visit the city some day, if they allow me to. They say it is the most beautiful Dar-ul-Khilafa in India and Pakistan. Anyhow, Engineer has been good to me and I like him. We have become close friends. I think he's the head of some high-level group or knows high-level people. It means, with the help of your and Mouj's prayers, I could soon come home. He can arrange everything. But I will not come until I am absolutely sure that it will be a safe transit. I don't mean to scare you, but a lot of us get killed on the way. Some don't get to see their home even once. I want to come back to you. I want to see Mouj, Farhat, Abba, everyone, before I can start, you know . . . I am at war, Roohi. I do not get enough time to work on my painting, but I have made some sketches and designs for it on pieces of paper. I hope they let me carry them when I leave.

I have learnt many things here. The big boss is a strange man, sometimes nice, sometimes very angry, ruthless . . . He once beat a boy who often came late to the morning drills so much that he passed out and had a frightening nosebleed. Next day, the boss brought a big bottle of Coca-Cola and a Nike cap for the boy.

I have gained some weight, probably because of the big meals, and we regularly eat beef here. It's nice, actually, beef. They have a dish called Kat-a-Kat here. It's very small pieces of beef or mutton fried in lots of spices. I like it a lot. It's the best thing I have eaten since leaving home. Unfortunately, these people don't like rice much, which means I don't get enough – only once a week. I will have a lot of rice when I come back.

After the daily classes, we play volleyball in the evenings. Everyone wants the Artist, which is what they call me here, on their side. All the practice against the college boys must have helped me, or the boys here are so bad that even I can be a champion volleyballer. You have never seen me play but I am sure the time will come.

It's the nights that are difficult here, Roohi. I do manage to sleep now but it takes time. Things go round and round in my head. I try to picture you but your face appears only briefly and then vanishes. Then I get restless and drink a lot of water. Engineer says drinking water always helps you to go to sleep. I see your hair suddenly, your hands, a glimpse of your neck, but I can't see your eyes. I try to tell myself I shouldn't try too hard but it never works. I am dying to see you. The silliest thing I have ever done is not carry a photo of you.

Anyhow, how are your parents? I just hope they don't talk too often about me. I will come and have a long conversation with them. I'm sure they will understand. And everyone must know about us by now, surely.

I wanted to ask you if I can ask my friend to write letters for me. Is it all right with you? I don't want to, but it takes me so long and there isn't enough time. It's just that I want to keep pace with your letters. I really do. We must be grateful for this opportunity. It really is miraculous that I can receive your letters in this place. I don't understand how Engineer manages it.

I think it's just a question of a few weeks now, two months or so at most, before we can meet. We will go to the Royal Spring Gardens and Pari Mahal and stay there till sunset.

Yours only,
Faiz

Her Father's Tears

When Kabir Ahmed Khan presented his updated census report to the new commissioner, complete and on time, he thought the only thing left to do was to wait for a handsome – by his standards – remuneration. He was pleased to see the commissioner's efficient secretary beaming with pride at the expedience with which he had drafted the report.

He had spent an afternoon and evening imagining what he might do with this unexpected extra income. A portable TV for Roohi would be such a surprise for her, especially since she had only asked for a new stereo, Khan had thought. New gold earrings for his wife would be perfect, given that in her efforts to accumulate an impressive dowry for her daughter's wedding, she has been wearing the same old ones for the last six years. The rare times of relative affluence in an honest government officer's life, if they arrive at all, are perhaps the few times he is in love with life, Khan has often thought recently.

If they manage to convince Rumi to sit the polytechnic test, the admission fees should not be a worry, Khan had concluded, during a satisfying smoke. He would also be able to clear the small debts he has gathered since his retirement. He hates having debts. More than that, however, he is pleased Roohi will not need to take circuitous routes any more, avoiding the main street, when she goes out. Roohi believes he doesn't know about this.

After everyone else had left the office for the day, the commissioner, on completion of his first major assignment for the Unified Grid Command, had promptly faxed Khan's 127-page report to someone at Command HQ.

Before the night-time raids on homes, a silence had descended on

Khanqah and its neighbourhood – Kabir Khan's ward of eight blocks and twenty-six neighbourhoods. This was the period after the Zaal swoops. The silence felt as though nothing had happened, as though those taken by the Zaal had returned and resumed their lives from the point at which they had been interrupted, as though no one had heard those haunting voices on Mahraazě's tape recorder, as though Mir Zafar Ali had never been dragged along the street and his spirit crushed. Some said it was exhaustion from grief, the fatigue of the forever teary-eyed. Others said, 'Well, people do have to make a living – open that shop, clean and oil that auto-rickshaw, slaughter the sheep that had begun to live a carefree life not seeing their friends disappear every day from the butcher's backroom, queue at the government ration depot by the Jhelum for the monthly supply of rice, flour and sugar.'

Now he feels a particular ache for Roohi, and for his wife. What will she do? How will they cope? Rumi might go further astray, or perhaps not. He loves them, after all. Khan Saěb rubs his eyes once, and double-wraps the shawl around his shoulders.

The Golden Canal

Until a few years ago, Professor Madan Koul would walk to the Golden Canal every morning. He would drop marigolds from his morning pooja into it, delighted to see the orange petals sail away rather than rot at the base of the wooden mini-temple in the centre of his study. He sometimes still does it but usually returns home dejected. Shanta looks after the temple and does not mind that the flowers are left to crumble at the feet of the deity. Koul feels wounded every time he sees the large foetid drain in place of the Golden Canal and yet, each time he returns to it, he expects some natural transformation to have taken place, some miracle, for the water from the mountains to heal it somehow. The canal once sent cool, fragrant breezes to Nagar, where the Kouls have always lived, and the localities around it. He refuses to admit it openly but knows that no one comes here now, except those dumping their daily refuse. The rich and the poor, Muslims and Hindus, the young and old, all do it. The hospital, the medical school, the sub-divisional police headquarters, and other institutions of excellence have all built man-size underground sewage pipes that pour their toxic effusions into the canal all day. If you take a boat trip on it, your boat might wobble over a carcass or you may find yourself rowing through sheets of shit; passing under a culvert you may be at the receiving end of the butcher's daily clearance. Madan once saw a bloated polythene bag burst on the concrete plinth of the pillars that support the culvert. The man who had thrown it down smiled at him and went away, as though he had graciously deposited a few gifts for the old professor. Intestines, guts, goats' ears and eyeballs flew into the air before landing on the dark water and sledging away like all the other scum that finds its way into this once golden arm of the Jhelum.

But Madan's angrier with the powerful men who run the city, who, he's been reliably told, have just spent five hundred million rupees on an imported golf course but said, 'No funds,' when the city's foremost young poet, Ayesha Azad, petitioned them to have the canal at least partially decontaminated. It will cost around a million rupees in all, she had said. He particularly misses the native roses that grew on its banks. Now there are only nettles. Professor Madan is a mild-mannered man, and he doesn't have many quarrels with the establishment, but even he wants to see all the politicians, administrators and visiting dignitaries from Delhi drowned in the slurry of the Golden Canal.

After his morning walk, he turns back home sadly. On the way, he will pick up his newspaper and milk from Ganjoo Bros., General Merchants, and bread from his old baker, Makhan Lal.

At home, Shanta prepares his tiffin box, expertly putting – same-old, same-old – white rice and lamb portions into finely delineated corners. Her father, who has had the same breakfast and lunch for more than forty years, complains if the rice is smudged with gravy; he likes to mix each morsel himself. Why not just get a new lunch box with at least two containers? Shanta has asked him in the past.

'You shouldn't be asking me that, Shannu. Neel Chacha – you remember him? – gave it to me.'

'I wasn't even three when Uncle died, Daadjee,' Shanta would always say, laughing. She waits for him most days so they can leave together, like the old days. Since her high-school days, she has always felt pride in walking with her father, to be recognized as the respected Madan Koul's daughter.

There was only that brief period, at most a year, during her master's when she did not want to go with him so that she could leave early and spend that precious morning hour before classes began with Afaq Bukhari, whom she had met during a seminar at the Department of Education. This was also when father and daughter had their only major disagreement, a quarrel, even. For all his educationist's progressiveness and humanism, Madan Koul had found it difficult, or had perhaps never recognized that he harboured such prejudices, to shrug off paternalistic ideas, especially when it came to his only daughter. He simply could not bring himself to be comfortable with the prospect that his daughter, even though he loved her more than anything in the world, wanted to marry a Muslim. That he would have a Muslim for a son-in-law. The idea, even to him, was radical, too much of a leap, as he had told himself then. And yet the professor himself had always been a bit of a heretic. Soon after his return from Government College, he had announced he was transferring some of his land in the country to the tiller family who, for generations, had ferried cart-loads of the harvest to the Koul home. Now in his slightly older years, he had been trying to appease his many siblings, aunts and elders, even family friends, when Shanta had revealed her own individualistic streak or simply her desire to be with the man with whom she wanted to spend her life. But Madan feared loneliness in old age and death – that many of his own would not be there for his last rites. It was, of course, irrational, especially since he wasn't old at the time.

When Shanta, expecting understanding from her great father, had told him that she wanted to introduce someone she had met at the university and that he was a Muslim from a respectable family – his name was Afaq Bukhari – he had looked at her with hurt and disapproval and had walked off without saying a word. She had waited and waited, her smile receding every day, but he simply refused to respond. Many evenings, as she put out dinner for them, she thought he might be about to speak on the subject, that the moment had at last arrived as they once again ate in silence, but afterwards he would wash his hands and retire to his study. Shanta's sadness came gradually, hope leaving her slowly, cruelly, as her faith in her father's wisdom and kindness gave way to despair. It was then that she decided to play his game and started leaving the house five minutes before he did. She did this for nearly six months, a long sulk, as he saw it, and a stand-off, as she knew it. She stood her ground, he his.

Evenings from then on were fraught, the father stealing glances from behind a book, the daughter busy preparing for the next day. Shanta did not mention her mother, Sharda Koul, even once during this strange and difficult time with her father, although she missed her more than ever before. She might have been the person to get Madan Koul to change his mind.

Afaq Bukhari, unable to see Shanta in this state of tight-lipped fortitude against her father's equally glum disapproval, one day took the matter into his own hands and sent a long letter to the principal's office, seeking a meeting. And Professor Madan, a man of letters and learning, impressed with Afaq's immaculate handwriting and stylish, albeit slightly dense prose, wrote back a short note, deliberately choosing official stationery for the purpose, inviting him to tea at the college. In the note, he gently forbade the young in-training academic to mention it to his daughter: 'Perhaps, it may not be a good idea to upset Shanta any further. I am certain a man of your ability and wisdom understands that.'

One Saturday afternoon in that fateful year, 1974, Afaq entered Principal Madan Koul's office dressed in his best clothes, which included the coat his father had worn for his MA, Urdu convocation at Government College, Lahore, in 1945. On that cool day in September, the college had shut at lunchtime so there were no students and therefore no noise in Koul's kingdom. For the next half an hour, Afaq heard the professor speak in crisp and clear words, a lecture delivered without a single pause.

The next day, Afaq, while sipping his daily tea with Shanta on the cypress-lined front lawns of the university campus, told her, as quickly as he could, that honouring his sick mother's wishes, he had decided to marry his maternal cousin. He could not do anything about it. His mother was very unwell.

Some heartbreaks, Shanta has come to believe, are a slow ruin-ation of the promise of love. At first, you don't give up just because the world says no. You never give up. She still remembers the maroon light created by the autumn leaves in the back gardens of the Naseem Bagh campus. It was a beautiful moment under the high chinars when Shanta first knew what true sadness felt like. For a long time, however, out of an unshakeable belief in her affection, Shanta believed that Afaq had only made his decision under pres-sure from home. She saw virtue in patience and waiting. She waited and waited – for the two men in her life to come to their senses. There are a thousand quiet heartbreaks amid the loud ones that we hear about, she sometimes thinks. Some carry on, quietly, over a lifetime.

She didn't mean to remember all this now, looking at her father's silent body. It just came rushing in and she couldn't stop it. 'Yes, it is my father, Professor Madan Koul,' she says to the sub-inspector who had come with the news and taken her to the Maharaj Bazar police station. As she leaves, she remembers Afaq's words again. Both of the men she had so loved, and briefly hated, are no more. When there is nothing to love or hate, what do you do? What is left to do? When Afaq was killed two and a half years ago, she had mourned properly, fully, for days and weeks and months. Then she had emerged from it, having fleshed out every moment she had spent with him in the university gardens, and her time with him at the school – twelve years spent in their love of teaching and of each other. She held to the memory of it all, as her most prized life experience, especially given that she had lost him once and found him again.

A few years after his marriage to his cousin, he had inexplicably been transferred to the renowned girls' school in the inner city. In spite of his education, which was higher than that of either the pro-fessor or his daughter – double MA and a PhD in philosophy – he had not protested at the school posting. Somewhat hesitant at first, he had soon found himself completely taken by the girls he taught. And there was Shanta, always present somewhere, always beautiful. In her principal's seat at the morning assembly, in her quick visits to the classrooms, smiling as she chatted with groups of girls in the courtyard. Afaq considered it a message from God, a just turn of destiny, that he had found Shanta again. He would look for opportunities to be near her, just to take home the fragrance from her saris every day. She would subtly make it easy for him to be close to her – but that was the extent of their proximity. Twelve years of this second chance at love. She was happy, he full of new life. Then they had killed him.

Garden of Whispers

Professor Madan used to walk by Dinanath's door every morning and sometimes he would pause to take in the smell of the rhododendrons and geraniums that Bimla nurses to blossom every spring. The flowers are in full bloom now, so large that Dinanath fears the stalks might break under their weight.

Dinanath is at the window, looking at the flowers nodding in the breeze, and assures himself that he will take care of the garden when his daughters adopt new homes after marriage. He looks at the doorway and its earthen roof where tulips grow by themselves every year, also the blackened iron chain-lock that has been there from the time of his grandfather. He doesn't want to change it, in spite of persistent demands from his daughters. 'My wrist hurts from having to lift this contraption from Patal Bhairavi every day,' Kamla had said last year. 'It's like a lock to keep the djinns away at night, and I'm sure they don't want to come into our house.' He knows they are right. The chain is quite heavy, nearly two kilos, but once in place there isn't a more secure lock in the city.

Dinanath turns to the birdhouse on the mulberry tree. There are four mynahs, four nightingales and two old fat wild pigeons in its three sections. He tries to work out from the movements inside which of the residents are at home at this hour.

If Professor Madan were to pass the house today and stop to look at Dinanath in that window, it is likely that he would notice another figure in the background. Masterji's wife Usha is observing his movements from behind. As Dinanath is lost in gazing at his garden, where they often have evening tea together, his wife comes closer and puts her hands on his shoulders. She stays in the background.

If Madan were to base his reading of Dina's wife on this scene, he might perhaps make an error of judgement. For Usha Parimoo only appears to be in the background, especially when she sees her husband vexed for this reason or that, often to do with their daughters' ever-changing career plans. Some days they want to leave and go to far-off places and on others, they seem perfectly happy where they are. Yes, the daughters will leave one day, but that has not happened yet. Dilli-Shilli, he has made clear to them, are for moneyed, connected people. Besides, it gets very hot out there. Kamla has hinted at scholarships, which fund higher studies outside, but he has always pretended not to hear her or muttered something vague in response. The truth is, if you asked the sisters their hearts' desire, what would they ideally like to do, they would probably say that they want never to leave.

But there is another, less mundane matter that makes Dinanath a troubled father these days. The old professor was admired by everyone, the young and the old; he was 'a respected member of the community', a phrase Dinanath often heard. Why him? It's the most disturbing news Dinanath has heard all his life – and it's beyond his grasp. He must discuss the matter with his school, and perhaps his best friend A. C. P. Javed Sheikh, or his wise neighbour, Mir Zafar Ali. Although he has been to see Mir Zafar twice in the last few weeks, which he hasn't done for years, with the intention of raising the issue, when he saw the patriarch fiddle with his near-dead hand, he changed his mind. Also, the subject is rather fraught, what with Mir Zafar's own brother having joined the ranks of militant boys. God knows what he's up to, these days. He finds it hard to believe that the little Mir boy in knickers, who was very good at art from an early age, has gone to Pakistan to become a fighter. He wonders if he might have understood things better if there had been more contact between the neighbours, if he had taken more interest in the Musalmaan family next door. He has avoided a conversation about Faiz ever since he went away. It has nothing to do with him, with them, he has repeatedly told himself. His daughters and wife, on the other hand, have talked to the Mir girls about it, often in loud voices between the windows. They remember Faiz's lacquered wares drying in the shade of their stone house. Mouj had once even asked Usha to pray for her son. 'I just want him to be safe wherever he is, whatever he does, and if he has to die he should die an honourable death,' she had said, standing by her door as Usha stood at hers.

Usha leads Dinanath away from the window. He feels the smooth skin of his wife's hands and feels somewhat reassured. Twenty-three years of marriage, a life shared together mostly indoors with their daughters, they have valued domestic bliss over everything else.

'Would you like a cigarette?'

'Yes.'

'All right, but spare a few drags for me.' As she savours the sharp taste of Dinanath's bonus cigarette – he is allowed only three a day – she turns his face towards her. 'Look, I am not saying nothing serious has happened, but let's just wait a little longer. Some people always panic. Yes, many have left but we have no reason to. Has anyone ever said anything to you, your daughters, me? No. So let's just wait and see.'

'If something happens to me, I can't imagine how you will cope. That is all I'm slightly worried about.'

'Slightly? Anyhow, why would anything happen to you? You have nothing to do with anything, Masterji!'

'And do you think Madan Koul had done something to deserve it?'

'No. That's not what I am saying. I know what happened with Principal Koul. Some militants killed him to make a newspaper splash, didn't they? Animals! I heard someone used him as target practice. I just can't believe it. Is that true? What a kind and magnificent man. Everything is happening too quickly, really, I just can't keep up. Every day, there's something new. And so many already dead, killed, even children . . . I don't really understand politics, certainly not what these people want, but they *are* being slaughtered in their hundreds . . . It's not right.'

'That's the problem, Usha, no one really knows what's happening. And that's what's bothering me. I wanted to talk with Mir Zafar but with the state he's in . . .'

'I'm sure he won't mind. If you don't want to, I will. There is absolutely no harm in talking about it. And, for God's sake, at least call Javed Saéb, he can give us all the information – he is in the police, after all.'

'And what if Faiz comes when I'm there? And how do we know the Mirs aren't involved in all this?'

'Are you scared of meeting that little boy? For God's sake, I've known him since he was two or three, since the time he would walk around in his underwear. What is wrong with you? Do you really think he'll come all the way back from Pakistan, or wherever he is, just as you go to see his brother across the wall?'

'I was speaking theoretically.'

'In that case you need to throw away some of your theories. You're beginning to frighten me.'

'Oho, that's not what I meant. Don't worry about it.'

'I'm not worrying. You are.'

'I've been thinking. What if . . . you know . . . Maybe we should . . .'

'No, I don't know. Now, relax and let's eat. The girls are waiting downstairs.'

The Ghostwriter

'Are you absolutely certain you want me to do it?'

'Yes, there's no one else.'

'Oh, is that your reason?'

'I was joking. My jokes are always badly timed. Sorry. Look, I trust you more than I trust anyone, and you're my friend. So, yes, please.'

'And you're certain you won't feel embarrassed later?'

'I won't ask you to write anything embarrassing, sir.'

They are seated on their narrow single beds in the room they have shared for six months now. There is no privacy here when you need it most. Not a single room where the boys sleep has a lock. You have to be ready to move at short notice, perhaps even run at night.

It is late at night for anyone to come suddenly into their room, and Faiz is sure he will hear footsteps if someone does approach, so he has kept his bag close to his feet under the bed. He smiles at the things he has come to do in this place, or at all the things he has had to do since leaving home. And it does not all have to do with his grasp of the simple but fine operation of a Kalashnikov, or with the meticulous way in which he can dress a bomb case, or with his reasonably high scores in marksmanship. He feels brave. Bold. He had serious doubts about his ability to go through with a decision that he took at a time of insufferable anger and pain. However, he now feels he has shown equal, if not more, courage amid the group of boys from home.

Most boys at places such as Camp Nadir Shah experience a slow, creeping, hardening of the gaze, a different way of looking at the world. Faiz is among those who in the end will qualify as 'men of the middle stage' – neither too hardened, nor too raw – men who have retained something of their old selves. In Kamal Mustafa's world, such men are known as 'safe'; they will be useful with small things for a long time but will never front big operations.

As Faiz begins to think about what he will write to Roohi, his heart comes alive. The two men sit on the edge of their beds thinking, one with his memories and heartache, the other with a pen in hand and a plan in his mind. Engineer smiles, full of affection for his peculiar artist friend, and determined to protect him at all costs.

Night on the River

Roohi wraps the black dupatta around her head, shutting her curls in. She turns on all the lights in the room, including the reading lamp that sits by the mirror. Angling its bright beam towards her, she studies this face. She sees a certain symmetry, a smooth, perfect alignment of the features, thrown into relief by the arch of the hijab she has fashioned. This is the face her mother, most certainly some of their neighbours, would be happy to see every day. Roohi turns by a few degrees and looks at it again. Her forehead is sliced horizontally in the middle, the brim of the dupatta gently digging into the flesh. There is a tightening of the eyebrows, and her chin, hemmed in by the double fold of the dupatta looks as though it belongs to someone else. Her hair has vanished.

Apart from prayer times when hair must be covered, Roohi hasn't done this for a long time, not since the Qur'ān lessons at the local Moulvi Saêb's; he never said anything on the subject and most certainly would never have prescribed any kind of head covering for small girls. It was understood. Girls simply had to cover their heads when they entered the Darsgah. Roohi remembers wondering why boys, apart from the few who wore tiny skullcaps, never had to cover their heads. Even during prayers now, she simply drapes her dupatta over her head, without using hairclips to fasten it. At the shrine, in the screened women's quarters on both sides of the main hall, most women have traditional headscarves draped around them. Colourful silk, crêpe, chiffon or polyester, most bought from the dyers' lane a couple of streets from the shrine. Outside, no one really bothers, and very few girls or women, in her neighbourhood, or out in the city, do the full hijab. 'We are already sufficiently covered,' many insist. Her mother, and perhaps more importantly, Naseem Aunty, have never done it, their long dupattas enough to cover the head and chest.

In any case, she hardly goes out these days, the rare strolls in the shrine courtyard or by the ghat with Farhat having become rarer still. The letters take too long in their journey from that side of the Karakoram to the high Himalayas, then back here. She waits every day for that image – of Farhat running to her door, panting, her hand holding the sacred object in her pocket. At times, she wonders if this tenderness, the enduring sweetness of heartache, is all she will ever have, and if waiting, for letters, for him, is to be her destiny, but then she shakes her head – it is not her purpose in life to pine. Hers is not the kind of love that rests on sacrifice, submission. Oh, why do the letters take so long? Can't he post one every day? Come on, Faizâ! She doesn't know anything about the circuitous journey the letter takes from the handlers in Camp NS to the lonely postmaster in the Neel Gali in Kathmandu. Or how crushing the ritual of writing letters is for Faiz, in spite of all the love he wants to put into them.

What is the point of this exercise, the close examination of her appearance now? Why is Roohi going through this ritual with the headscarf? She abhors the idea that one day she might have to do the full purdah because some vigilante boy says so. No one tells Roohi how to follow her faith, she has told her cousins. 'I know my faith and my relationship with the Almighty better than any of those unlettered men do,' she had thundered at a family wedding a few years ago, to cheers from assorted cousins and distant female relatives, although even then Roohi knew she had to do better than that. Her words, even to her, had rung a bit hollow. At the time, she had told herself she needed to read more if she wanted to engage in serious debate about the new-style hijab. Now, three years older, she thinks it doesn't really matter. Why should it matter? People can adopt any kind of veil they like, as long as she is free to do what she wants. And she doesn't need to be well read to defend her choice.

She doesn't need to defend her choice at all. It's not as though she would like to roam the streets in a swimsuit.

Although she does, however, want a swimsuit at this moment, a self-styled one at least, as she's been pining for the river again after many years. Having seen many photos of female swimmers in their svelte swimsuits, some head to toe, some rather spare affairs, in *Sports Star* magazine, she wants to create one for herself. Most certainly a waterproof headpiece, if nothing else, to protect her hair from the sometimes-polluted waters of the river. She will stitch a shower cap with polythene bags from Fancy Fabrics and put it under her improvised headpiece. Even so, she can't swim in the river during the day – only boys can – and will have to wait for the night, for a moonless night, in fact, so that she doesn't have to worry about being seen.

In her childhood – she must have been seven or so – she used to jump in with the boys near the ghat and splash about in the shallow water at the bathing steps. She would look at groups of boys attempting to cross the pushy river, marvel at the few who would wave to her from the opposite bank, many, even at that early age, hoping one of the prettiest girls in the neighbourhood might be impressed by their triumphs. There was one boy, a solitary swimmer, she would notice standing a few feet from the jubilant group. Later, when she was forbidden to go into the water, the sight of girls diving into small whirlpools by their boathouses on the river would fill her with envy. No one ever said anything to the nimble daughters of the boat people.

When she was ten, she felt again an intense desire to dip into the waters of the Jhelum. To jump into the river like the boys, to splash through its brown charge and emerge at the opposite bank – just like that calm solitary swimmer – to be able to go under water, open her eyes and witness the cities that lay beneath. Her father, putting his hands on her shoulders, had gently explained it was not meant for girls, that it was quite dangerous as the river was deceptively strong and swift in its city run, and only strong boys could hold out against it. He had ever so sweetly suggested she should do something else instead, learn knitting, for instance, from her marvellously skilled Naseem Aunty, or perhaps join the handball team at school. Roohi remembers the heartbreak this denial caused, but she had obeyed her kind father then, suppressing her desire with long bouts of self-pity and loathing for a society that denied her this basic delight. Her rebellion had resurfaced immediately when Papa had casually mentioned 'my ruby's naïve wishes' during morning tea the next day, and her mother had launched into a long speech – 'Why do you want to bring shame to us?' – during which she both scolded and embraced her daughter. 'You are *my* daughter. I didn't even play hopscotch with the boys when I was your age. Understand this, my dear, swimming in the river with all kinds of men around brings shame.'

One evening a year or so later, Roohi had decided to try again and asked Papa why she couldn't do what the girls from the houseboats did every day. 'They are different people, Roohi. They can do as they like and no one will talk, but if you behave like them, I wouldn't be able to show my face in the street,' he had said.

Roohi remembers his silent but resolute face when she had said, 'But why, Papa?' He never answered that question and Roohi never raised the matter again. Her silence, she has reminded herself ever since, does not mean acceptance of this strange order, and if she cannot go among those girls who swim with such freedom and joy, she will do it solo, when the world of men has gone to sleep, when all the fathers, uncles and brothers, those mean custodians of that order, are snoring in their smug beds.

It has been many years since. Now the thought of swimming with the boys – although very few venture into the water these days, as the river, too, is watched, even raided sometimes – is outrageous. She still longs to return to it in the darkness, though, at night. But now there are the people of the area to think about, her own family, the immediate neighbours, and Papa's friends, who sort of watch for her when she's out and about. And, crucially, who knows what kind of creatures are out at night nowadays? There's already been too much talk in the area about her. Perhaps it would be prudent to lie low until Faiz comes back when they can talk to her parents and Mir Zafar Ali and elders from both communities. Does she not feel her parents already have enough to contend with, that it would be kind not to distress them any more? But Roohi's answer to these thoughts is this: 'How low do I have to lie? Do I have to become completely invisible just because I'm a woman in love?'

The idea of flowing downstream with the river, which goes all the way to Pakistan, had come to her after her evening namaz on a moonless evening two weeks earlier. She had finished her prayers when she saw a fading star. She prayed for it not to vanish altogether, for it to stay in her sight. She held out her hands in supplication, trying to arrest the star's descent, but it went down into the Jhelum beyond the seventh bridge and sank.

She has waited fourteen days for the moon to disappear, and to go down to the river.

Papa and Mummy are fast asleep – she knows the exact timbre of their breathing when they're in deep sleep and, of course, her father's rhythmic snoring. Rumi, returned late yet again, has crashed out too, although deep down Roohi knows she can handle him if he were to catch her. Roohi has no idea what he has been up to, and feels a pang of guilt for not having thought of her brother for days.

Climbing down the steps of the ghat where she used to play with the river's loam in her childhood, creating entire cities and countries with her fingers, Roohi first dips her toes into the dark water, then walks in inch by inch, and soon finds herself immersed up to her chest. Safe in her dark cloak, whose inner waterproof lining makes her float, she sees the city glide past her. Tall houses with gables and balconies become smaller and smaller, the river somehow diminishing the city as she hurries downstream. Many of the half-brick half-timber buildings, mosques with roofs, turrets and spires that echo lands to the north, are new sights even to Roohi, for hidden behind the congestion of the old town, away from the daily toils of the city's poor, separated from the dust and decay and corruptions of this ancient city, are the spacious, hallowed seats of the city's oldest residents. These are people who have always lived by the river and slept with its ancient music; these are people who never sold up. Many of the houses have secret histories buried in their many wooden vaults. A new city seems to have come into being, where there are old wooden mosques with verandas for the muezzins, and gold-topped temples that throw glints into the river.

As she approaches Treng, the great marshland of the ancient past where green herons and red-crowned sparrows used to sing with nightingales, and deer thrived undisturbed on the chain of islands that could take them all the way to the high meadows of Nargismarg, Roohi sees endless dark-grey castles of cloud. Tall grasses on either side of the river show their tips. She sees the stars rise up. Suddenly the world outside is invisible except for the dark sky that has no moon but this multitude of stars. Nothing can be seen beyond the bright massifs of cloud that have descended to the grasses and hide everything on the other side.

It is the mountains beyond her gaze, beyond the castle of clouds, on the other side of the net of stars, which she thinks will take her to the Neelum Valley where Faiz must be. The Emerald Valley, where he must be thinking of her, too. Her heart trembles at the thought. For Roohi has never gone beyond her blessed and blighted land. She has hardly ever travelled alone, except the daily twenty-five-minute minibus ride to university. She knows she has covered only a small part of the journey, has reached only the point where the river is no longer hemmed in by ghats and people. There is an entire world after this. The river will slow down, spread out a bit, breathe over vast fields and marshes, fall in love with washermen and -women, and yield its bounty to them and the collectors of loam and sand. But the brightness of the cloud cover fills her with hope – that life on the other side will begin anew, that she can leave all this behind and be for ever with him. In time, they can come home and be embraced by their people. They can stay in that part of their divided country, see their lost kin, perhaps even locate a lost cousin or aunt, and build a life together. She can help Faiz in his mission while they are there – no, she'll do her own thing – and come back to a free land when it's all over, when the soldiers have handed back the keys and left. That way – she knows it is selfish of her – there will be no danger of losing him. As she holds on to the timber of a broken old bridge, she knows the impossibility of her fantasy, but even so, a small part protests, saying it can be possible, it is possible, all of it, and if not all of it, some of it, the last part surely, how can it not? There is, after all, only one conclusion to the story. A reunion, and freedom from all fear.

Roohi still has the river, the swim, and the long journey home on her mind, as she writes another letter to Faiz. She'd been foolish not to think of the journey back to the ghat. You need to be a jinn to swim upstream over such a long distance. She laughs now. She had waited for the pre-dawn hour when fishermen haul their dinghies upstream with the help of long poles, making the boat walk on the bed of the river. The two boatmen who brought her home had insisted she share their tea.

PART FOUR

'A Terrible Beauty is Born'

The End of Winter

Faiz likes the spring here. The air is alive again and the mornings carry the life-affirming scent of newborn buds. He has spent the winter months in near solitary sadness, going about the routine at the camp in quiet reflection. The winter here is often cruel and dark and it has been more so this year. It gets dark early and the hills cast morose shadows. Winters without water, Faiz has come to believe, are more hostile than the big freeze at home, where the snow creates a new order, a world of new colour, for a few months every year, yielding to explosions of almond and cherry blossom in the spring. There is no snow here and therefore there are no proper winter rituals. Nearly every day during the airless cold, he's missed his companion at home, the kangri, the warm, affectionate wicker brazier that everyone carries almost all the time. He would have given anything to have one imported from home.

The spring with its promise of things to come has filled him with renewed hope and, increasingly, his thoughts centre on Roohi. These last few months, the letters have become less frequent, sending Faiz into a depression that had Engineer occasionally worried for his sanity, primarily because he did not want Faiz to incur the wrath of Kamal Sir who will not tolerate disinterest or the appearance of it. But nothing his friend said would alter Faiz's attitude. It was as though the arid winter had taken room in his heart.

These last few months, reading Roohi's few letters, he's felt she may be getting tired of waiting, that she may be on the verge of breaking. He does not doubt her but has begun to feel that his own actions haven't exactly spelled devotion. The letters that did arrive didn't bear good news. He could sense her desperation. Or, perhaps, upon reading her account of life at home, his own quiet waiting could no longer stay quiet.

In one letter, she said her father had become despondent, constantly worrying for his own and his family's safety. *I don't recognize the man in our kitchen sometimes, Faiz, he looks at me in the strangest way, as though he is trying to remember my face*, she had written. He wanted to write back, 'At least you can see your father every day, Roohi. I haven't seen Abba in eight months now,' but in the end he chose not to. In the same letter, she said that Principal Koul, 'whom you have known, is no more. His body was found by a canal not far from his house.' Faiz could not comprehend the news of the professor's death. Pushed on by his anger, his inability to do anything about it, he went back to teaching himself to read and write. To start with, he read and reread Roohi's letters, copying the sentences he most loved; then with Engineer's help, he procured an Urdu book, *The First Book of Urdu*, from the older chef Reyaz who had a small personal library in the pantry, assuming it was a primer. He copied pages from it, too, read it aloud to his friend, wrote them down from memory until his friend certified that his writing had now become better, faster, even polished, compared to what it had been when he first arrived. Faiz has since tried to read the first few chapters from a big Urdu novel called *The Weary Generations*, again borrowed from Reyaz, who, as it happens, hails from the district of Bagh in the mountains of Kashmir.

Now, he's bored of the same routine, day in and day out, the cleaning of the Kalashnikovs, disengaging of the magazine in one motion, the rolling on the dusty-prickly ground with gun and grenade in hand, the shooting with one hand, the pretend hand-to-hand combat with his colleagues.

As he nears his room, there is the fresh scent of thistles in the air and, he thinks, of daffodils too. Back home every season is enunciated; even the condensation on his workshop window assumes a new intensity as frost gives way to bloom. Alone on his cot, he knows it now. Roohi is part of everything, even this. In one of the six letters that arrived during the winter, she had said her mother had changed too, her strict mode of communication with her daughter giving way to a certain tenderness. *She doesn't even talk of marriage now, Faiz. Do you understand what that means? Do you?* He curses himself, for the thousandth time, for not having brought a photo of her with him. *If only I could see her once, look her in the eye, hear the faint rustle of her hair brushing against her dupatta.* He must talk to Engineer about this. He must come to the point straight away and ask if he can arrange for his trip home as soon as possible.

As the daytime azan booms – and Faiz likes it a lot for this muezzin has a soft, intimate way of calling the faithful to prayer – swallows, mynahs and grey-headed pigeons from the kitchen compound rise and scatter towards the few trees spread around the camp. They talk as they fly, Faiz thinks.

Dear Faiz

Faiz,

My winter has been harsh, too. It snowed and snowed, so much so that broken electrical cables fell like dead birds across the city. The electricity still disappears for days and we live by kerosene stoves, lamps and candles. It is very dark here now. I didn't tell you in my last letter that the snow had one good effect at least. There were fewer gun battles and explosions in the days we were snowed in. Even the daredevils were stalled for a few days by the freeze. And the soldiers shivered in their pickets. You know, many of them have never even seen snow before, let alone lived through a long snowy winter. Sometimes, I feel sorry for them. They shouldn't be here.

But it's picked up. People are dying again. People are being killed like flies. I mean, these are actual people killed on the streets every day. I don't know if you've heard but they read out the toll on the evening news as if they were talking about the amount of rainfall during the day. I feel frightened, Faizà. It seems the angel of death is taking away our people. At the shrine, everyone weeps. As I offer namaz on Thursdays, I often hear sobs behind me. I dread turning around. The shrine itself feels like a melancholy place. Do you remember Mahraazé, who recorded those voices? He has disappeared or gone into hiding. There are rumours he may be in some jail, or dead, or in the Paradise Hotel. You know what that is, don't you? Now that he is gone, I miss his night-time screaming, even his swearing. I sometimes feel scared for Rumi, who refuses to stay indoors, but then I tell myself, actually it's nothing compared to where you are. How will I cope, what will I do, when you come back? Papa hardly goes out, unless he has to. Even then, he comes back quickly. His durbars at the shops have ended and he's lonely now. Actually, he's been feeling more and more scared since Principal Koul's murder. The only good thing I can tell you is that Mummy has changed. She is no longer burdened by thoughts of my wedding.

If you asked me what my heart's truest desire is I would say I want you to come back, but then I cannot be sure, when I think about it, that it would be a wise thing to do. Then I think you have to come back some day, so why not now? After all, you did go there to come back home, didn't you? Then I think about what will happen when you do, and I don't know, Faiz, it's a strange thing within me, and it's painful. Sometimes I wish I could talk to you on the telephone. You know, discuss it, and listen to you.

You haven't changed, Faizâ, have you? I wonder if you think about me at all. You must have bigger things on your mind now, and new friends. When I think of that I decide I do not want to get in the way. After all, you did not ask me when you decided to do this, but I do not blame you. Perhaps you had no choice. Perhaps you did. And I'm not the only woman whose . . .

If you asked me my heart's desire, I would tell you I want you to come back now. I would tell you I want to join in your fight. My blood boils, too, you know. Some days, I imagine blowing myself up near a bunker or one of those monster trucks, but then I think it would be no use in the end. There are so many of them here! Maybe I am more useful alive. I would be very sad if I died without seeing you, meeting you. The city is a lightless prison now. No one can stir without the permission of the soldiers. I sometimes imagine we are in a vast coop with thousands of them circling around it, and they hit out at my hand if I try to get some air. I can feel it, actually, the choking inside me. But that's not all. Crammed together in this cage, some have started lashing out at others. We jostle for breathing space and push at those around us. There is suspicion and, of course, death, all around. While the soldiers kill every day, the boys have started killing some of our own. Some of the boys are particularly hard on the girls and I just don't understand why. You, of course, are not like that. A few of them have actually killed for sport, to make the next day's headlines.

The soldiers ensure there is a blood-soaked headline in the papers every day. Two weeks ago, they killed seventeen boys across the Zainê Kadal

Bridge, shot them all dead after trapping them in a lane. Zaitun, my friend from college who lives near the bridge, said that the soldiers were so blind with rage that they wouldn't stop firing even after the boys were all dead, mown down next to filthy drains. They continued shooting until no one was left standing and the bullets started hitting the soldiers at the other end of the lane. Zaitun's little brother Uzair, who had been playing cricket in the lane earlier, was shot in the face. The machine-gun bullets wiped it off. Zaitun slept for three nights by his grave in the Martyrs' Graveyard, I found out later. She didn't mention her brother. It is so, so mad here. That's what scares me most and then I think maybe you shouldn't come back. Lately, some of the boys have started fighting among themselves. They actually form pickets to shoot at each other. As if we didn't have enough pickets! Some areas in the city are now considered dangerous for one group or the other. And a few particularly strange men – some say they are from Pakistan; others say no, some of them are our own – have killed our neighbours, Muslim and Hindu. I just don't understand why.

People say pandits have been leaving their homes at night. Leaving their homes for good, Faizâ. Isn't that so, so sad? You must have heard about Professor Koul. Oh, I already told you about him, didn't I? He was such a noble man. I don't understand why. Please, please, don't misunderstand me. I am all for fighting the enemy, and we will drive them out one day, Inshallah, but what kind of madness is this, hurting our very own?

Anyhow, when you come back you will see things for yourself. Promise me one thing: you will never harm an innocent man. Oh, what am I saying? Why would you? It's all so overwhelming. People are too busy counting their dead to make sense of anything, to stop those who are leaving. Or they are so torn by grief, so desperate waiting for their dear ones to come home to notice their neighbour's loss. I don't know! Those who haven't suffered themselves are racked by guilt. I read somewhere it's called survivor's guilt but I don't think it's actually that simple. It's a darkness, a heavy cover of the most wretched darkness I have ever seen, which has enveloped everything. The city is like an ancient ghost town. I see ash in the sky. Did you know that after the Zaal days people in the mohalla started to change the way they walked, sticking close to the walls, creeping close to houses, shop fronts, as though walking under some imaginary protective shade? No one walks on the road any more, lest the Zaal appear again and swoop them away.

A few weeks ago, I saw a woman and a man walking down the street in single file. There were children, perhaps their own children or nephews et cetera, in the middle. I watched from my window as they crossed the street. A couple of hawkers near the shrine gates laughed. Even though the area close to the shrine is safe enough, I understood why this family walked like that. The hawkers should not have made fun of them.

This is what I have thought, then. Since our mohalla is relatively safe because of the shrine, as the soldiers wouldn't dare to come close, this is where you should live until we decide what to do. What do you think? I think it's a good idea. You could take Mahraazé's place in the mosque by the shrine. Do you remember it? Akbar Shah, the caretaker, knows me. I have known him since I was a little girl. I'm sure he will understand and let you sleep in his quarters. That way I can see you every day and, God willing, I can also arrange for your meals. All you need to do is convince your family that it is for the best. I will take care of my parents. I think you won't need to do a lot of convincing. You won't be able to live at home in any case. No one who returns from the other side does, Faizā. I'm sure you know. Sorry.

I have to close this letter now. It is very late, just a couple of hours until daybreak, and I should get some sleep. Mummy still gets a bit upset if I wake up too late. She thinks I read into the night, which is not true. I don't read much now. I just can't get much sleep but that's normal. The weather is so, so beautiful now. The kind of weather that must bring down angels to the gardens. Pari Mahal must be full of laughter and music, I think. The soldiers can't stop them entering, you know. Oh, you may not have heard this, the Palace of the Fairies and the Royal Spring, the Shankaracharya Temple and Takht-e-Sulaiman are all barred to us. Rumi says soldiers live there too, and only government officials, army officers, VIPs from Delhi and their families can visit.

I want to go to the Badam-Wari like the old days and drink tea under

*the umbrellas of almond blossom, but we cannot. Some day it will be open
again, and you can't stop flowers blooming. Soon, we will be free to go
there together. It is very late. I can see the lone light burning away in the
shrine. It's on its last breath, I think. The old caretaker lights it every day.
It reminds me of you. Do you know why? The first time you saw me, I saw
the same light glowing in the upper hall. I will never forget that evening.
Please come back, Faiz, please.*

Yours for ever
Roohi

Prayer to the Moon

'I want to go home.'

'Calm down, calm down, sir, and then talk to me.' Something about Engineer actually helps Faiz calm down.

There are days when all he can do is dream about his masterpiece, drawing rivulets, sunlight, flowers and angels. On other days, he goes about his tasks in the workshop with his mouth shut, his fingers moving around detonators, fuses, wires, glue and pellets blindly, as though he were finishing papier-mâché pencil boxes for Mustafa Peer. On some evenings, Faiz speaks, in the hapless manner of a besotted teenager, to the moon, imagining Roohi must look at the same silver face from her seat opposite the shrine.

In a not too distant future people will say that Faiz had not given enough thought to practical matters – for instance, what he planned to do with his new life as a man with a gun, as a freedom-fighter. They will cast doubts on him. That he hadn't fully committed to this new life, or to his old. Some would go as far as saying he hadn't committed completely to Roohi either.

But Faiz, as we speak, even though he's overwhelmed sometimes, knows that his beliefs remain steady: to oppose, whichever way possible and available to him, the siege of his city, of his land; to be with Roohi; to avenge his godmother's killing; to complete his grand work, *Falaknuma*, one day and show it to Roohi. During the melancholic winter at Camp NS, he often found himself pondering his actions over the last year or so and nearly every time he found himself saying, 'I wouldn't change a thing.' He also had an argument, the only one, with Engineer when, in what seemed a rare moment of hubris to Faiz, the latter suggested that some of the uneducated or semi-educated boys crossing to Pakistan might not really know what they were doing. 'I'm surprised someone as educated and wise as you thinks that only a man with a piece of paper from a university can be educated. Is that how all educated people think? I expected better, Engineer Saèb. I mean, do you really think hundreds of these boys have come here just like that, as if it was a fair? Do you really believe that it takes a degree to understand that the murder of hundreds of men, children, women is murder? Do you have to be a college student to feel angry about it? Does it take an MA, BE, PhD to understand the meaning of countless soldiers appearing like a plague in our gardens, Engineer Saèb? Well, I also have a PhD, a PhD in naqashi. You see, even at home some people, especially those who come from Hindustan, and some of our own rich folk or officials or politicians or column writers, tell me that people without jobs, money, are the ones who decide to fight. One, it's simply not true. Two, I used to make more money every month than my government-employee friends. I was even a bit famous, sir. I was happy, in case you want to know. So, please . . .' Faiz had retorted without stopping, although calmly, unsure whether his friend's remark was meant to provoke him, test him, or if he genuinely felt so. In any case, his response made Engineer speechless for a full evening.

As he leans on his cot today, with his hands behind his head, Engineer tugs at his leg.

'I'm still here, you know. So what were you saying?'

'I want to go home.'

'Now?'

'Yes.'

'Hang on, hang on! This isn't a picnic at Nishat–Shalimar.'

'I know, but I want to go now. I can't stay any longer. I have learnt everything I can. I can even handle two AKs at the same time.'

'Keep it down, Faizā. You really don't want the boss to hear any of this. Words travel here faster than you think.'

'Look, all I want is to go home. Can you help?' Faiz whispers, sitting up. Outside, the calm of the night is interrupted now and then by the thud of bullets piercing the hard earth of the hills surrounding the training ground. Some senior boys, it's been rumoured in the camp, have been given night-vision goggles. Faiz is not allowed to witness these sessions.

'I can try, but it will take time. You must understand it's not easy. I have to talk to people, bring up the subject as naturally as possible, convince them, you know, make up an elaborate ruse . . . Have you thought about what you will do once you get home?'

'I will do what everyone else does, sir. Drive the bastards out! What I'm asked to do, what I want to do. If I get home, that is. Not everyone makes it, I know.'

'You're telling me? That's why I asked! If you can wait for a bit, I can, hmm, try to arrange for you to go by air.'

'What?'

'Yes. Some people, important people, take that route. It's not so surprising.'

'And you think I'm important? Ha-ha.'

'Look, my friend, do you want to go home or not?'

'How long will I have to wait?'

'A few months, maybe three, four at most. Think about it, there's no hurry. It's completely safe, and you will go on an international flight. Nepal Airlines.'

'It's all the same to me.'

'If you want to be absolutely certain that you will make it home, see Roohi, that's the way to do it.'

'And how soon can I go the way we came?'

'That, too, depends, brother. A month, two months. One, you can't go by yourself, and that's a given. We have to wait for a group that is scheduled to go. God, have you learnt nothing about how this thing works? Two, I have to talk to some people about it. I'm positive it can be arranged but you and I aren't free to come and go when we please, my friend. The bosses decide when a batch is ready and only then can you go. You have to have permission, brother.'

'You keep talking about these important people. I'd like to see them some day. How come only you know them?'

'You're seeing one now.'

'What?'

'Do you want to go home or not?'

'Yes, yes, sorry. Do it, please. I can't wait for your special plane for special people. Nepal will have to wait. My time is up. I have decided.'

'More like you've been summoned, huh? I'll try my best but can't promise anything at the moment. How is everyone back home?'

'As if you don't know.'

'I meant your family. Roohi.'

'Things are bad for everyone. You know that.'

As they fall silent, Faiz wonders if perhaps he should consider going via Nepal, taking the same route home as his letters. It will be safer. He certainly doesn't think of frostbite as a great trophy to show at home, although summer is on the way and the weather may not be as harsh as it was when they came. Yes, yes, he should just go at the first opportunity. But what if he's killed on the border? He'll never see Roohi again, or Mouj and Abba and Farhat and Shahida and Feroza. Never eat Mouji's red beans and rice again. He will never see his painting again.

He has heard of boys spending two, three, four weeks in the dark forests above Kalaroos, surviving on biscuits, dried and wild fruit, hiding in caves or under cliffs for days, walking only at night, moving inch by inch towards home where they may or may not live another day. He has heard of boys sleeping, lying low in the high meadows of Tos-e-Maidan, not far from a notorious mine-infested firing range, by accident discovering the ravishing beauty of what was once a secret place. He has heard of men fighting bravely, taking it on the chest, as Kamal Sir says, and sacrificing their lives for their friends, their bodies forgotten for ever in some dark valley. He has heard of boys with dead meat for toes, the frost having entered their very bones. He has heard of boys holed up for days in dark hideouts across the border, sometimes keeping entire battalions at bay so their seniors, more important comrades, can escape. He has also heard of boys who have turned back, again and again, and are now so bereft of the will to cross that they have set up home in the mountains here, in the Emerald Valley, looking at the mountains on the other side. He wonders if he might turn out to be like them, forever wanting to return, looking every day at the high peaks beyond which lies home. He is not like them; he will never become like them. He did not come here to stay. He came to learn how to fight.

He thinks of the basement in the shrine and the first time they hugged. His arms ache.

He thinks of Faatĕ, her golden pheran and the red chinar on it.

It has been a week since their conversation about home. Engineer comes with news. The moon is full tonight and the camp looks like the placid desert he has seen in movies, specifically in *Laila Majnu*, when Majnu, separated from Laila, sings songs under an open sky, imploring God, the stars and the moon to convey his heart's intent to her. In happiness, and fear, Faiz embraces his friend.

Rumi's World

Panther smiles at Rumi as he sits down in a corner. Since last week, when he was summoned to discuss an important matter concerning their area, Rumi has been rehearsing what he will say to the chief. He nearly went up to Roohi's room to seek advice, to tell her there's been talk in the group about their father, that he wants to do something about it, but then changed his mind. It would mean telling her everything, about himself, his group and the other boys. Besides, it would worry her unnecessarily. He is more than capable of handling the situation, he told himself; the confusion over his father's role in the raids would end soon, the moment he tells Panther everything.

Panther is spread out on a massive bolster. A calendar from the local bank hangs on the wall behind him. A majestic pink vista of the Almond Garden illustrates April, with the stern Hari Parbat Fort in the background.

'Look, what's your name? Oh, yes – Rumi. We just need you to talk to your father, if you can, that is. If not, you will need to keep an eye on him, tell us where he goes, whom he meets . . . If I were you, I'd check his things, his pockets, wallet, everything. What do you think?'

Quite suddenly, Rumi feels he might choke. His voice and courage seem to have deserted him. Only thoughts of Papa remain. He wonders again whether he should have told Roohi everything. She would definitely know how to deal with this.

'We will have to do something about it, Rumi, but we don't want to keep you in the dark. You are one of us, after all.'

'I don't know how I can help. He's my father. I know him! It's just not possible that he has anything to do with all this.'

'And that's what we want to ascertain.'

'Sir, there is nothing to ascertain.'

'So he should have nothing to worry about, then.'

'Yes, I know, but . . . he's my father. He's afraid!'

'We know, and that's why it's all the more important to get to the bottom of this.'

'There's nothing to find out. I'm telling you, he's a noble man. He hardly leaves the house these days. Please try to understand.'

'And what if you're wrong? What if we find out he is involved? What if we find proof?'

'That's impossible.'

'What if it's true?'

'Then I'll be the first to say we should . . . er, er . . . punish him. It won't matter that he's my father.'

'That's exactly what I wanted to hear. Good boy.'

Rumi feels an ache in his stomach. He wants to go home and smoke.

'Don't look so worried. You know me. We will be fair and only go on facts, but we have to make a decision soon. We cannot allow these things to go unnoticed. We cannot let people get away with it. Do you understand?'

'Yes. Can I go now?'

'Yes, yes. One last thing, don't speak to anyone about this. Not even your sister. Is it true she was, you know, sort of . . . with that artist? He went across, too, I'm sure you know. That's all good. He's one of us now.'

'I don't know anything about it, sir. People spread all kinds of rumours. My sister is a highly educated girl.'

'Yes, everyone knows that. That's why it was a bit of a surprise when I first heard she's with him, you know . . .'

'Can I go now?'

'Remember, keep your lips sealed.'

Rumi runs home, takes two cigarettes from the squashed pack that he keeps under the doormat outside his room and locks himself in the bathroom. Life, suddenly, seems unbearable. The days of trying out an AK47 against the lifeless concrete of the high-school walls are over. This is serious. It has not just arrived at their doorstep but entered his life, his father's life. As he smokes, squatting on the low toilet seat, he decides to tell Roohi everything, including his involvement, even if it's embarrassing. He knows she won't take his group seriously. But he must tell her that by being a part of the New Salvation Front he is privy to secret information, that he can intervene on behalf of Papa, that it is actually a good thing he has come to know Papa is being discussed in some high-level meetings. This aspect of his life, he thinks, will not find disapproval from the big sister, as her own boyfriend – at this he still flinches – is part of the movement too, and has now been across the border for many months. That's serious stuff. He may even have gone to Afghanistan. Rumi envies Faiz.

He can hear Roohi upstairs. The stereo hums. It must be one of those melancholy ghazals she listens to all the time. He cannot understand even half the Urdu terms from his sister's favourite music. He shakes his head. How does he begin? Once he's started, it'll be fine. He can then tell her everything in one go. She must take him seriously. Rumi pushes open the door without knocking and enters Roohi's sacred world. He is not used to spending time here. She is leaning against her low desk, elbow resting on it. In front of her are spread what look like two, three letters. His eyes narrow in disbelief. She looks at him and smiles without changing her position.

'Did the sun rise from the west today?'

'Maybe.'

'Has someone's pocket money run out?'

'As a matter of fact, no.'

'Oh, then the sun did actually rise from the west. Sorry, I didn't check this morning.'

'Didi, this is not a time for . . . jokes, I want to tell you something.'

'Oh, so the little brother doesn't have time for my jokes.'

'I mean it! It's very serious.'

'I'm sure. When did I say it wasn't? Everything is serious. Have you not looked around? The city is a slaughterhouse.'

'I don't mean generally! There's something I want to tell you about myself, about us, about . . . Papa, but promise me you won't tell anyone.'

'Okay, Rumi, tell me.' Roohi switches off the stereo and sits up. Two storeys down, on the ground floor, they can hear their mother washing the dishes. The sound of water from the main tap in the kitchen, an old brass contraption, does not evoke a happy mood in Rumi. In his childhood, it signalled the end of the day, when there was nothing else to do, to look forward to, after dinner. Outside, a lone travelling saleswoman from West Bengal is screaming about thermos cases, hot cases, as they're known here, lunch boxes, aluminium pans and stainless-steel plates. She is pushing her pots and pans in a cart meant for carrying gravel and bricks to building sites. She's hired it for two and a half rupees per hour. She has yet to earn the rent, unaware that no one will come out at this hour.

Roohi looks through the window and waves at her, asking her to stop. The saleswoman, bent over the handle of the cart, pushing it slowly, doesn't glance up. Roohi shouts to her: 'I want a hot case. Stop right there – yes, yes, by the door.'

She runs down, enters the kitchen, takes out their old, slightly rusty large thermos case from the cupboard under the gas stove, asks Mummy for three hundred rupees and runs outside.

Rumi waits upstairs, made speechless by his sister's strange ways. He finds himself praying for her. May God grant all her wishes, even that one, perhaps . . . He is surprised at himself, but also vaguely aware that this is the new state in which he finds himself.

As Roohi returns and sits down again near her desk, he says, 'Your good deed for the day?'

'Don't be silly. We needed a new hot case and that woman was selling one, end of story, but, yes, I suppose it was better to give my money to a woman who has travelled from God knows where to make a bit of money. So, tell me.'

'The thing is . . . Roohi Didi . . . First promise me you won't tell anyone?'

'I promise.'

'You know how it is. Everything has changed. The city has changed, the countryside has changed. It will never be the same again, but we will win in the end . . .'

'And?'

'So, everyone is involved, and I think everyone should be.'

'Spit it out, Rumya. I know what's happening around me. Everyone knows.'

'The thing is, I've joined too. It's a small group, local, but we do important work, keeping an eye on things, who's new in the area, what they're up to, relaying information to the bigger groups, helping them when needed, et cetera, et cetera. I can even handle a – you know . . .'

'Yes, I know.'

'What? What do you mean? How?'

'Because I'm your elder sister and I'm not blind. I've known for ages.'

'I didn't know. You never said anything?'

'I didn't think you stayed out late to watch films at the Firdous Cinema, because, guess what, it isn't a cinema any more. And you definitely don't play cricket in the dark. Have you noticed how you walk and behave, these days? You should look at yourself in the mirror more often, little brother. But, don't worry, Papa and Mummy have no clue. They think you're just being your good old irresponsible spoilt self, wasting your time with other wasters. They don't know you're a big boy now, hanging out with *the boys*. But don't start getting ideas that I'm going to be scared of you now!'

Rumi fiddles with a cassette on the floor, deep in thought.

'Oh, I also know you smoke. No matter how many clouds of that Brut cologne you make in the bathroom, I can always tell. Papa never smokes in the bathroom – he doesn't need to. But, again, don't worry, I don't think they know.'

Rumi blushes, his ears burning. He puts the cassette back into its cover. It says *Faiz by Farida Khanum* on the front, with a black-and-white photo of the Pakistani poet spread across as background. He thinks of the other Faiz, Roohi's Faiz, and wonders what he will make of his own attempt to be properly involved with the movement, to be like him. And it should be stated for the record that Rumi's been serious about what he's been doing. He's unsure if he joined NSF or if Faiz went across to Pakistan first. He would certainly like the former to be the case.

'Is that all you wanted to say? Oho, I said don't look so worried. It's fine, but you've got to be careful.'

'No. That's not all, Didi.'

'Are you now going to tell me you're in love too? That someone has actually fallen for your new heroics?'

'You can't –? Forget it. I need to talk to you about Papa.'

'Oh.'

'I think he's in a bit of trouble with the boys. In fact, with the same group as –'

'What? How dare they?'

'Oho, listen to me first, for God's sake!'

Roohi sits up, glaring down at her brother. The evening was supposed to be one of memories and thoughts of the future, her private hour. Faiz's short letter, written nearly three weeks ago, bore good news. Her prayers haven't been futile and her long wait may be over soon. *Trust him to spoil my happiness.* Roohi bites her lip as she looks at Rumi. 'Are you going to tell me anything or not?'

'Yes, but please don't shout at me. I'm already stressed out. You see, we have a leader, the chief of the group. His name is Hyder Khan, also known as Panther. He sent for me and I met him today. He said things about Papa. Please, please, trust me, I didn't believe a single word he said. I told him he should forget about it there and then. I was firm. But . . .'

'But what, Rumi?'

'He wouldn't listen. He said they want to get to the bottom of the matter.'

'What? Nothing is the matter with Papa. Oh, God, Rumi, what have you done? What kind of group is this? I mean, are they real militants, proper ones? What is it called?'

'NSF. New Salvation Front. We put up all the posters in this area.'

'And you think it's a legitimate group?'

'What else can it be? Otherwise why would someone form a militant group knowing the consequences? Of course, it's proper. It's got to be.'

'And these morons think Papa has done something wrong?'

'Yes.'

'Idiots. Have they even seen him? Didn't you tell them?'

'I did, trust me, but they want me to talk to Papa, keep, you know, an eye on him. How can I? I don't know what to do.'

'Spy on your own father? Are they completely insane? I'm sure this is a dodgy group, Rumi, or they wouldn't say such stupid things . . . I've heard that there are many agencies at work now. Did you know that the government has launched its own groups?'

'I know!'

'Was this the only group you could find? For God's sake, Rumi, the man calls himself Panther. Paper panther! Why didn't you tell me?'

'It was the only local group. It's . . . not my fault.'

'Yes, I know, I'm just angry with your friends. Isn't he the man who raided a few tuition centres, breaking up joint groups of girls and boys? Wasn't he scolded by his own younger sister at Khateeb Sir's, when she refused to sit separately with the girls? Is it the same man?'

'Yes, but that's not all he does. He's always in touch with the bigger groups, chief commanders, senior people . . .'

'Yes, yes. I know the type. The real ones cross mountains, leave their families and dear ones behind, risk their lives. This rascal just harasses little boys and girls.'

The big sister and the little brother, perhaps because each senses the beginning of panic in the other, perhaps because there is nothing left to say, or perhaps simply because they come together in filial solidarity, simultaneously arrive at the easiest solution. Roohi speaks first.

'Maybe Papa should go somewhere for a few days.'

'I was thinking the same thing. But where?'

'Naseem Aunty's, I think.'

'But wouldn't they ask why he's suddenly come to stay at theirs? He hardly ever goes there.'

'Well, Mummy can surely confide in her sister. If she can't, I will. I can talk to Naseem Aunty.'

'Okay. And I'll talk to Commander Panther again.'

As he stands up, Roohi raises her hand and offers it to him. He holds it firmly and pulls her to her feet. She hasn't done this in years, he thinks.

'Listen, don't worry, it will all be fine. I'll talk to Papa.' They go down the stairs together, Roohi's hands on his shoulders.

The Corridor

The view is that of an endless, hazy tunnel. Close up, the walls are thick, brimming with leaves. Ferns, creepers, red and purple berries and thousands of flowers surround him. Beyond rise enormous pine trees. The ground is millions of blades of grass, and the newly sprouted wild mushrooms look as if they'd break if you breathed too close to them. The many worms and insects that are born, and die, in spring, lend the space the buzz of life. The wet grass is up to his knees and Faiz thanks Engineer for giving him the long boots before he set off. Faiz thinks about his new friend's extraordinary kindness. He must tell Roohi about him, take him to meet her one day, and home to meet Abba, have him for supper, ask him to spend a night or two at their house.

Every now and then, a window opens in the foliage around them and he can see the Emerald Valley below. It is truly emerald, a shining green carpet rolling down the terraced hills, with the Neelum river sliding away in the deep middle. He sees the corridor clearly now, a neighbourhood of trees, and swarms of leaves hanging from age-old creepers and their newer, younger siblings. It almost seems as if a gardener, a keeper of forests, with an eye for detail and artistic composition, has put it all together. Where has he seen it before? It looks like one of those scenes that depict the Road to Heaven he has seen on religious calendars. Something about this memory disturbs him.

He memorizes the landscape. This is the way he has painted all his life, the repeated mental note coming to full life on the canvas, sometimes faithfully, sometimes with new character and colour. It's something he's always felt proud of.

Engineer is behind him, the third last boy in the convoy headed home. The important people his friend often mentions are some-where in the middle. Faiz has been forbidden to talk to them. 'You will have many opportunities to speak with them when we get home,' Engineer had said, when briefing him about the trip. Unknown to Faiz, he is on the route favoured by some senior com-manders and sometimes even Pakistani intelligence agents. All his friend had said was, 'This is the next best way after going by air – and you turned that down.'

As they proceed through the green corridor, slowly approaching the end of the track where they must turn right and descend into a gorge, which is almost fully shuttered by mountains on both sides, Engineer looks left, right, and smiles. Somewhere in the dense for-ests are the checkposts of the two countries, manned by figures armed with sniper rifles and telescopes.

At the last checkpost on this side, Kamal Mustafa sits in a spa-cious bunker behind a man operating the heavy US-made electronic telescope. The movement of the boys can be clearly monitored from here, such is the strength of these new looking-glasses. But Kamal Sir is not interested in the boys' progress. He wants to be alerted of any unusual movement in the checkpost on the other side, of equal or perhaps larger size, we cannot be precise, which, too, is full of the weaponry and gadgets in vogue now. The men and officers in this post, where a small tricolour flag droops above a makeshift desk, are watching with the help of an identical monitor-ing device, bearing the same trademark.

Today, the soldiers and their officers will just watch. No one will shout orders. No finger will touch a trigger. No magazines will drop empty on the floor. The wet somnolent mood brought on by the gentle spring rain will remain undisturbed. As the drizzle creates a rhythm in the jungle around him, the sniper on the other side of the border listens to Anuradha Paudwal and Kumar Sanu songs from *Aashiqui*, and once again thinks of Anu Agarwal's large breasts.

Only Engineer and Kamal Sir know that a large amount of money has changed hands to make this cosy arrangement possible.

Ten million rupees, if we want to be precise. This is not the norm. As Kamal had said to Engineer, it's only for the eminent ones, but Engineer had insisted on the Artist. The other boys, the common boys, have no clue of this. They will wait for another few weeks, perhaps months, and cross the border the usual way, slithering at night, knowing very well that some of them may never walk or be heard of again.

Faiz begins to enjoy the trek through this watercolour and starts thinking how he might replicate what he sees. He could somehow imbue his river with the raucous momentum of the Neelum river he once heard Shahida talk of but has only seen, with his own eyes, now. Only a few years ago, he had thought it inconceivable that he would see the river on the other side, in the forbidden other half of his country. He could use his silver pigment to create the foam. He could use rough gold to emboss rocks and boulders . . .

Suddenly he remembers the journey when he came to the camp. It was a long and terrifying walk, a journey he completed with sheer grit, stubbornly keeping thoughts of death and family at bay by constantly walking. Ahead, ahead, he had told himself. Even when they had stopped for a couple of hours to rest, he had continued to pace. When the frost had finally begun to seep into his flesh, on the third and last day of the hike, a part of him had welcomed it. He had even refused to take the special salt that the guide had given the boys to ward off frostbite.

This, in comparison to when they crossed into Azad Kashmir last year, is like a day trip. He smiles, and tries to imagine how he will describe the journey to Roohi. He looks forward to sitting with her in the basement of the shrine and telling her everything. It will be evening and they will light a few of the old candles. He will hold her hand, she his, and he will insist she stays longer. She will, of course, agree and remain until the minute she knows her parents will start looking for her or send Rumi, her annoying brother, to find her. Not that Rumi would dare to mess with him, Faiz thinks. But he knows he shouldn't use his new status in his personal life. He could perhaps let him see the butt of his Kalashnikov, or nonchalantly lift his shirt to reveal the outline of the pistol in his pocket, as though accidentally. No, no. That would be wrong, he doesn't want a bad reputation like a few of the boys he knows gained soon after their return. But they die, too, you see, even the bad ones, he tells himself, and decides to leave the matter for now.

Soon, he sees the boys at the front of the convoy disappear one by one into the green haze, as if someone were swallowing them whole. He is alert now, slightly unnerved by what's unfolding ahead of him. For a tiny moment, he wonders whether they are dying one by one at the front, being killed without a sound.

The image of the Road to Heaven he'd earlier remembered from calendars comes to him again. It had reminded him of death. That he, too, will perish one day. What if that day is today? He would be a dissatisfied, restless martyr if he died today of all days, when he is heading home at last. He doesn't want to be a martyr, not without having done anything, not without having fought or having lived the life to earn him that title, without having gone back to his people, his brother and mother, without meeting Roohi. Without having explained the case to himself fully. As he speaks these words to himself, he realizes he has picked up pace, rushing to check the scene ahead.

He gets closer and sees the men in front of him put their arms around a tree, then disappear round a sharp bend to the right. It is his turn now. His mind begins to calm and he sees that the world has not ended. He puts his weight against the tree. Then there are steep, rough steps, rock and earth and grass, descending into a deep grey world.

Dark Days

Meanwhile, Sumit Kumar has decided to become serious about work. It is unfortunate that the school is shut now, he thinks. Hardly anyone comes, apart from Nazir Sir, who is there every day, dressed, as he often is, in his cricket sweater and jeans. He is friendly with the soldiers but keeps his distance from the head of the camp, who remains torn in spite of his new resolve to focus on the task at hand. He doesn't want too many missives from the signal man, who is somehow always aware of what is going on, not just in the area but also inside the school. He remembers the communiqué that hissed out from the machine last week. He was advised, and that was the word used, to spend more time in the area, out in the open, visible among the people, and not stay holed up in the school. He knows he should have been doing daily rounds from the very beginning, establishing 'Area Domination', as the phrase in the message put it, and not have needed a directive from the top. And yet he laughs at the thought of roaming the streets in some desperate attempt to stamp his authority on the mad people of this mad city.

Shanta Madam, forced into a profound silence by the crumbling of her life's work, by the inexplicable killing of her father, and by the steep, and rising, death toll that she reads of in the newspapers, spends most of her time in the wing for little girls, some of whom still come for classes that may or may not take place. She sits by the window that looks directly onto the hedges at the back and corrects homework that they bring to her. She has not said a word to Major Sumit Kumar since their last conversation. There is no point, she has told herself a hundred times, and avoids his path when she is here, in his camp. The major avoids her too.

Her biggest worry is about the matriculation exam, which, she has been told, may now go ahead in the spring in spite of the situation in the city.

As she sits in the absent primary teacher's chair today, she works out a plan for the students. She'd visit each of the senior girls, distribute test papers from previous years, assign revision exercises, help those who have difficulty in the subjects she can teach and ask other teachers to do the same. It would be such an injustice if the school could not maintain its 100 per cent record. Then, she sighs, she may leave, too, like most of her friends and relatives who have abandoned their homes for the merciless heat of the plains. She is not entirely sure of this last thought. Can she really leave home, her father's house, her books, her kitchen and her favourite reading chair? Can she do it? Will she do it? She hadn't even noticed when months ago many of her friends disappeared overnight to live their lives elsewhere. It was only after they found her father's body, *like that*, that she began to think about her own well-being. Previously, the thought had never crossed her mind and, even now, she would rather defer the decision at least until the examination is over. There is something not quite right about leaving, she thinks.

Home

Engineer marvels at the door to the Artist's family home. He touches the raised curves of the verses of the Qur'ān carved into the wood, bows his head and enters. Faiz, quiet, still, taking deep breaths, follows.

Engineer had explained to Faiz that he should enter first, talk to Faiz's brother, lay down the rules of arrival, as he put it, and only then should Faiz show his face. 'We can't have the whole neighbourhood knowing you've come home. The sooner you and they get to know the terms of your new life, the better, my friend. Trust me.'

Faiz, drained by the enormous weight of anticipation, by the thoughts that oppressed him during the journey home, as ceaseless as the hard terrain they had to navigate after the relatively gentle, paid-for passage from the Neelum Valley, had shown his agreement with the plan by putting his arm around his benefactor's shoulders.

It is a Thursday evening, cold and smoky. Mir Zafar Ali, made gaunt by an anxious mind, wonders once more whether he should pull himself together and start going to the mosque again. It's been many months, ever since his escape from that metal beast. It wouldn't be too hard for him to pray in a group. In spite of his impaired hand, he should be able to rise and prostrate in sync with the rows of namazis, but so far he has been unable to put his thoughts into action. He thinks it was a bad decision to hide his reduced hand under the sleeve of his kurta while at work and under a shawl while at home. It was not out of a sense of shame that he had started doing it – certainly not – it was more to do with the unease his withered pale hand might induce in others and the fact that he didn't want to talk any more about his physical state. But a creeping sense of humiliation, mostly to do with the memory of that day, has stayed in a recess somewhere, causing him to feel more of the shame he tries to deny. The only thing that has kept his heart from sinking completely is the hope that his brother will return to him soon. Often, he has thanked Allahta'ala and prayed for the long life of the grandfather of the young man presently waiting for him to finish his evening namaz.

Farhat, sensing the arrival of an extraordinary moment, stands behind the visitor, waiting, like him, for her brother to fold his prayer mat.

There is something sacred about this moment, Engineer feels, about the prostrate form of this grey-bearded man, about the barely audible prayer on his lips, about the silver visible from beneath the edge of his skullcap, and about the considered motions of his namaz. Oh, but he must hurry. He turns to look at Faiz's sister with a slight nod, for he doesn't want anyone to spot Faiz standing by the wall of the lane that leads to the door of the Mir house. Farhat reassures him with a nod in return.

Mir Zafar Ali doesn't wait for the young man to say salam. 'Salam alaikum, please come in.'

Engineer colours, sits down near the door, and refuses a more comfortable position, in spite of Mir Zafar and Farhat's protestations. 'I'm fine here. Please don't worry.' They, of course, do not understand why he insists on sitting near the door with his feet on the doormat. He hasn't taken off his shoes either, an odd gesture that Mir Zafar tries to ignore. Engineer looks at Faiz's brother, then at Farhat who, although knowing she's being asked to leave, doesn't budge. 'Farree, go and get us some tea.'

'Yes – what news have you brought, sir?'

'Sir, I have brought good news, but can I please ask you to listen to me patiently, not rush out or anything like that and, most importantly, get all your family here quietly and repeat to them what I have to say.'

Mir Zafar closes his eyes and offers a prayer in his mind. Only a suppressed indecipherable syllable escapes his lips.

'I have brought your brother home, Mir Zafar Saėb. As directed by my grandfather, I have brought him home safely and in some comfort. He is waiting outside and, you will understand, he's a bit nervous, so I thought I should come in first and explain the situation. Oh, no, no, no, please don't thank me. My grandfather never asks for anything that isn't important. He told me Faiz would be among the most important men I will ever bring home.'

Mir Zafar cannot speak. He simply shifts closer to the young man, takes his hand in his and kisses it. 'May the Almighty always keep you safe and bestow great glory on you. You are an angel.'

The curtain rises and Farhat emerges. Mir Zafar can tell from her face and manner that she's heard the news. 'Sit down, Farree. No, forget the tea and listen to me. Our hero is home.'

'What? Where? Where is he?'

'Now, this is exactly what I don't want you to do. Stay calm, Hakeem Saėb's grandson has just told me Faiz is here, but we don't want any noise, definitely no tears. Do you understand me?' Mir Zafar lifts his fingers to the corner of his eye and pretends to scratch an itch. Engineer looks down.

Farhat stares at both men quietly, then runs out, her dupatta sliding off her head, leaving a trail of blue in her wake. She knows where to go and slows down only when she sees a grey shadow against the crumbling rock wall.

He turns and takes her in his arms. She hides her face in the cleft between his arm and chest. He is stronger than she remembers. She tries to feel if he has a gun on him.

'We're not supposed to carry it home, Farree. Can I go inside now? Bring Mouj to the drawing room. I don't want to unsettle her by walking straight into the kitchen.'

The Thursday-evening recitation of post-namaz prayers from their mosque booms in the near distance; a few dogs bark and then go quiet. Faiz smiles and imagines Roohi chanting along with the recitations from the shrine. He remembers their evenings on the balcony or down in the candle-lit basement. Suddenly he wants to run to her, take her to the shrine, and live there for ever, just her and him.

Mir Zafar Ali stands up to greet his brother, despite Faiz's protestation. The two men embrace and it is unclear who's refusing to let go. Everyone watches quietly. Then there are sobs and unchecked laughter, gasps, hands on mouths. Engineer shakes his head, looks down, and decides to wait a little longer. He must leave soon, though, his grandfather must be looking at his watch.

It is a revelation to Faiz that his toughest sister and night-time smoking partner, Feroza, cries the most. She balks at the sight of the man her brother has become. He appears to her a more serious, rougher version of the young artist she last saw in the flare of a matchstick as he lit her cigarette nearly a year ago. She never used to take anything he did seriously – perhaps owing to what she thought was his vagrancy at school – envisaging a wasted life for him, wasted slowly by bending his back over countless cheap papier-mâché bowls and cups. Now she is aware, perhaps more than the others in the room, that her little brother is only a temporary guest in his own home, and that he, like many young men of the city, may not live long. It is only after Mouj – having settled her shaking hands by putting them under her legs while she sits in a corner – stands up and says, 'Faizả, will you keep your mother waiting?' that Feroza extricates herself.

The mother makes the son sit down, takes his stubbly face in her hands and slowly brings it to her chest. He breathes loudly; she breaks into a tearful smile. Mir Zafar Ali draws closer and puts his strong hand on her knee. Farhat follows suit and sits by Faiz on the other side. Shahida moves close too and rests her head on Faiz's knees. Feroza walks over once more and completes the circle. Mir Zafar's sons, Faiz's old nephews, now both lowly government employees, watch from behind the curtain, unable to decide whether or not to enter and join the family. Finally, their father calls to them. They come in and sit near him. Faiz looks at them quietly.

Engineer shuts the door and watches this moment in the bright yellow light of the high-voltage lamp. He cannot put a name to it, this repeated rubbing of arms, the leaning of heads on shoulders, the mother now and then cupping the son's face, the elder brother patting everyone's shoulders, the older sisters holding hands, and the returned brother and son taking it all in, with such overwhelming feeling, that he cannot speak.

'Son,' Mouj looks up at Engineer, 'if I had known I would have cooked something special today, his favourites at least. Why didn't you send us a message? What is your name?'

Engineer looks at Faiz, then at Farhat, and, for all his ready wit, cannot quite figure out what to say to her. 'Please forgive me. It wasn't possible and you see –'

'Some families do get messages, I know. I have talked to some of the other mothers. Don't think I don't know . . . Anyhow, let's forget about it. Shabbir Saëba, can you go and check if Ali Clay is open, if he has any meat left?'

Everyone is surprised by her unusual frankness. Mouj had discreetly sent Farhat to the house of a boy they knew was across the border too, then to another house across the bridge near the shrine.

Mir Zafar Ali is not angry. Nothing happens in this household without his knowledge and, more often than not, he makes his disapproval known to erring members of his family, including his mother, but at this moment he's struck by her courage.

'You must stay and eat with us today, son.'

'I will.'

Faiz whispers in Farhat's ear. He wants a bath but also something else. Farhat leaves.

Not very far from Mir Manzil, under the dim roof of the temple across the putrid pond of Namchabal, Pandit Bishambarnath Zadoo lights three lamps by Shivjee's feet. Although it's not winter the old caretaker is yet to put away his long woollen pheran. Somehow, the smells accumulated in its weft and warp and its heavy drape make him feel safe. The rumours, and some proof of them, of the flight of his people have reached his solitary island seat. It's been months since he last saw devotees come and make offerings at the altar. His own meagre income has further diminished. The donations have dried up and there's been no sign of the money order that the committee president promised when they last met. 'There is absolutely no need to worry. I'm only going for a week or so, and Jammu is not Timbuktu. Besides, we can always send you a money order.'

'But I'm not worried. I'm just an old man who lives in a temple.'

Clearly, Zadoo thinks, the president isn't back and perhaps may not come back for a while. At least until the situation – that's what they call it on the radio – improves here. What will I do with a money order? He laughs. If someone were to try to send him a postal order, it would never get to him for there are no post offices in this country any more. Some are turned into pickets for the soldiers, some burnt, some locked, and others left wide open with heaps of letters inside but no one to look at the addresses.

In the long poem *Kalhana's Kismet*, the last piece of work Mir Zafar Ali was assigned to compose for the typesetter, there was mention of post offices where birds have made nests under hills of unsent envelopes. Also of women who visit them every week in case a letter has magically arrived from the husband working away in Delhi or Calcutta, or if a jailer has allowed an envelope to fly from prison.

Zadoo doesn't know of this, or much of the outside world, apart from the occasional bit of news he gets from the radio when he forces himself to listen to it. He has never liked radio or TV. Apart from his lone visitor and friend, he hasn't seen or talked to anyone in more than two months now. Sameer Manto, Bashir the milkman's son, comes every week to deliver potatoes, pulses, milk and the dried rusk from Meerut that Zadoo likes to have with tea. He loves the boy and calls him Dr Saéb even though it's only Sameer's third year at the medical college. Every Saturday, Sameer comes on a ragged boat, sits on the steps to the temple, hands the old man his supplies and refuses to take money. They both know it's a game; they both know they must play it every time. A ritual from history, an occasion when people insist on love, on belonging. The young man knows everything – he lives in the thick of it all. The old man knows some things, has noticed the fissures in his universe, has seen it go asunder since the dark winter, and sometimes senses danger too, but only sometimes. His decision not to join the others, at the time of the exodus, hadn't required long deliberation. In any case, no one had really asked him. He hadn't known about it until most people had already fled, leaving their age-old nests for the open skies beyond the mountains, in Hindustan. In any case, where would he go? For him, it is nowhere but here. This is home. There is no other. If he dies here, like this, bereft of the company of his kin, he is sure someone, in all probability the young Muslim doctor in training, will light his pyre. He has made sure his half-page will is easily found when he breathes his last. 'Please do not call anyone. There is no one to call. You will find enough willow at the back of the temple. Just make sure my sacred thread is tied properly around me. I have lived as a Pandit and I want to die a Pandit.'

Rain has started to fall. Farhat, unburdened today by the presence of a precious envelope in her pocket, walks calmly. She likes the drizzle on her face. The high wall of poplars that lines the fence they share with the rich neighbours on this side, away from Master Dinanath's house, sways in the wind. Each gust through the trees creates a music that rises and fades, as though a lyre is singing to itself. In her childhood, the poplars seemed so tall she had thought that if she could climb up the highest one she would be able to jump onto a helicopter passing by, during one of the city's long curfews, and fly away. She was four then. These days, the drone of any traffic in the air makes her shrink in fear. Often, she shuts the windows, draws curtains and checks latches if she hears anything in the sky.

Farhat knows her nephew Shabbir is out too, on his way to the butcher as Mouj asked. She doesn't want to see him as she knows he disapproves of her connection with that Sunni girl. A month or so after Faiz's departure, Abba had scolded him for saying he was glad the girl wouldn't be coming to the house any more. 'Teaching Farree *trigonometry* was just an excuse, Abba. She came to meet Faiz, who is foolish enough to think we'd accept a Sunni in the family.'

'Is that all you can think of, Shabbya? How about offering a namaz for once and praying for him? He is your uncle, *my younger brother*, for God's sake, and it's my decision in any case,' Mir Zafar Ali had thundered.

Farhat remembers this as she rushes to Roohi's house and takes the back route to avoid the possibility of bumping into her bigoted old nephew.

Roohi emerges from her hour-long bath, her hair wet, a glossy chadar. She pauses to look at the water drops that have dropped by her feet – they have a faint red colour to them. 'Ah, so they mix cheap paint even with henna now, very nice, my dears,' she mutters, rubbing off the moisture with her heel. As she begins to climb the stairs to her room, where she plans to spend the rest of the evening reading Parveen Shakir's posthumous collection of poetry – she's been looking forward to it – she bumps into a smiling Farhat.

There is magic in the way these girls communicate with each other. A shine in the younger one's eyes, the slow spread of a smile on the face of the older girl. A quick tight hug. A patting of the back. A kiss on the forehead. Another on the back of a hand. The only words exchanged relate to practical matters: when, what time, shall I come or will he? One more thing, what does he look like? Has he changed?

'I'm not telling. You will have to see for yourself.'

'I'll tell him how you've been teasing me all these months. Not helpful at all.'

'Please don't. I'll try to be better in future, sister-in-law!'

'Okay, now that you promise, I won't. Come here, you little angel.'

Hand in hand, the young one's head resting on the other's shoulder, they go up to Roohi's room.

Of Love and Letters

Roohi paces on the riverside balcony. The gladioli grown tall by the tombstones in the old graveyard behind her send their fragrance her way. It is late, quite late, but she simply couldn't stay indoors, and under the pretext of accompanying Farhat, her favourite pupil, home, she rushed here as soon as they had reached the end of her street. At the curve where it joins the main road, she did not walk back towards the main gates of the shrine. Instead, she took the short-cut that leads to the small side door of the compound. Just before the balcony, another stone-paved platform is covered partly by the tree that rises from the ghat below, the same tree that has a little temple under its arms but where the camphor hasn't burnt for a while now.

Roohi looks at everything – the white verses on top of the arch of the door that had once hypnotized Faiz; the papier-mâché and lapis panels built into the outer walls of the first floor; the thousands of votive threads, each a prayer, a promise, spreading across the grilled window like a cobweb; the stained-glass panels on the second floor, which, at this time of night, reflect soliloquies of the river below – and, turning back to the ghat, is reassured that her world is intact once more. The sky's cleared now. A blue canopy lit with stars presides over the scene. The washed ghat below her, and the one on the opposite bank, the brightly lit houses on either side, the shrine's still skyward posture, its spire and those earrings glittering amid the stars, are all part of her galaxy tonight. It's a good sign, Faiz, it's a good sign. No matter what, they will meet here, on the balcony, in the same spot they met the first time. It is impulsive, perhaps even foolish, she thinks, to risk being noticed, *him* being noticed, so soon after his return, in his new life, but it will be dark and few people come to the ghat now.

Predictably, Faiz cannot sleep. He remembers his nightly torment when he was last at home. He remembers the Corex bottles. He remembers Fatima. He remembers the dread of the Zaal. Today, even though it's a different room, the big hall on the top floor, he remembers the crushing weight on his eyelids that kept him awake for more than a month. This room is vast, the same size as the hall of mourning on the opposite side. Mouj uses it as a store for most of the year. Spare bedding in one corner, a couple of old trunks containing Farhat's books from her primary-school days, which she refuses to part with, in another; and blocking one of the many large windows, two tall copper jars – glorious remnants from the Mirs' years of prosperity – filled with rice for the next three months, including the big feast on the tenth day of Muharram, which is now only weeks away. On Mouj's insistence, Shahida and Feroza have spread Faiz's bed behind the jars, in the narrow space between them and the window. Mouj has put two amulets in each, buried deep in the rice, for his protection. Abba had started to protest that acquiring the amulets would alert Faiz's presence to Abbas Pir, the famous dispenser of amulets and other spiritual cures, although his real reason was his lifelong aversion to such superstitions. Mouj had silenced him with a single tap of an index finger on her lips. Faiz can smell the welcome scent of native rice. He remembers his meals at Camp NS, as he turns to look out of the window.

The gnarled old branches of the giant mulberry tree hang low over the back of the house. The architecture of the tree, reflected against the blue of the night, takes his mind to *Falaknuma* now lying unfinished behind the large Muharram banner in the next room. It gives him a lump in the throat. He could resume work on it but for that he has to stay at home, a prospect categorically ruled out by his friend. It might be possible to take it to wherever he spends his days and nights in the future. There is so much to do on it.

The mulberry tree stands in the back garden of their oldest neighbours, the Shahmiris, whose large house is the only one that is older than Mir Manzil. There is no interaction between the families these days, as hardly anyone lives in the grand house any more, just the caretaker and his wife and three children. The two Shahmiri children, both physicians, live abroad, in Sussex, England, and a few years ago, they took their mother, some say against her will, so she could live in comfort with one of the daughters. Every few Eids, the Shahmiris come home en masse and celebrate with their neighbours, including the Mirs, especially the Mirs. In the past, it is said, that the Shahmiris and the Mirs were close, one, like twin families – until the former fled the Valley after years of persecution by a king.

'If you hear anything, mark my words, *anything*, you will not wait. Just turn off the lights and slowly climb down the tree. I'm sure you will find your own way out of the house,' were Engineer's last words before he left. He had also whispered his real name to Faiz's mother just as she had patted his back thrice at the door – 'May you prosper in life, may God bless you.'

'I'm Maqbool, Mouji, Maqbool,' he had said.

Faiz peers at the expansive tree. He thinks he can make out some nests in its clustered branches, even some crows perhaps, and prays there are no raids tonight. He dreads the thought of disrupting this sense of night-time rest. He turns on his side again to face the copper jars and feels safe, cosy even, hidden behind the enormous vases of rice. He wants to wake his mother and hold her again.

At last, the night spreads its dark cover over his bed, and he begins to slip into darkness too. In this world, there is no worry, no dread of boots, no fear of the end. His last thoughts are of tomorrow, of Roohi. Nothing, no one else. 'It's good to be home,' he says, as he wraps himself in the familiar smells of his quilt, tucking it firmly over his head.

*

Roohi leaves, reluctant, happy. The stars have come down into the river. As she quietly locks the front door, she sees a shadow slip away in the corridor. For a moment, she thinks it might be Faiz, unable to wait for the morning, then recognizes the smell of her mother's hair oil. She checks the latches on the back door, a ritual each member of this family and every other in the city performs at different moments of the evening or night. Papa usually does the last check, unlocking and locking the latches again.

The Meeting

He is there early and, without much thought, walks towards his chinar and sits down under it.

She looks at him from her window, unable to move. She wants to own every moment.

He wants to look at everything before looking at her. During the day he received an envelope, possibly, he believes, from Engineer, with a single chit inside bearing an address near the Nigeen Lake where he must spend the next few nights. Until further instructions, it adds. He has it in his pocket now and will go to the hideout directly from the shrine. He wishes he could take Roohi with him.

Roohi climbs down the stone steps slowly, each moment measured. She doesn't want to trip. Faiz stands up, stubbing out his cigarette against the bark of the maple. She doesn't walk towards him but straight on, towards the main door of the shrine, then past it, turning left, only once looking at him. He follows. At the cold dark pavement that goes towards the back, she slows down, waiting. He catches up, his fingers plucking at his lower lip.

She curls her toes on the dusty floor of the balcony. He looks at her and forces himself not to break into tears. She sees through him as if through glass.

Come here.

Come here.

At this moment, Roohi feels she is married to him. All they need now is a home of their own, a simple life together – that is not too much to ask for, is it? she wonders.

He has a home they could go to today, but he cannot bring himself to say it to her. Speech seems difficult but they are happy with wordlessness for now. As they sit shoulder to shoulder, hand in hand, her hair touching his stubble, his arm tight around hers, her palm listening to his heartbeat, it gets pitch dark. He strikes a match, raising it high so that the orange light shines on them both. She smiles. He lights another, then another. Then she takes the matchbox from him and does the same. He watches each matchstick burn in her fingers. Then they stop burning matches and sit in the dark.

'Are you well, Faizâ?'

'Yes, I'm fine now.'

'In spite of what you have been through?'

'I had to do it. I'm not frightened any more. How are you, Roohi? I'm sorry.'

'I'm better now . . . Will you, too, take part in, hmm . . . action?'

'Of course I will, even if no one asks me. I haven't forgotten anything. I won't forget anything. Have you seen my brother? But don't worry, I'll be careful. Besides, I don't think I'll start immediately. I have to meet people from the group, decide on what area and all that. And I've been told to lie low for a few days. I think Engineer may also have some ideas. He's a brilliant man. I trust him.'

'I want to see you when you talk. Come.'

'Where?'

'To another universe, an underground one.'

He can sense her smile. She finds her way to the basement quite easily. Faiz only has to burn three matchsticks. It is the same as they had left it, although someone has neatly folded the white sheet, and the bags of muslin and the rolled-up carpets form huge cushions at the back. She spreads the sheet and they lie back against the improvised bolsters. He finds three candles and lights them all, placing them near their feet. They think they hear distant footsteps and stay still for a few moments.

Roohi is worried. She has some idea who it might be. Some nights, when she's alone in the women's hall, she sees four women come and pray quietly in a corner. She knows them. She has seen them before. They are the mothers of the boys yet to return from prison. She looks at Faiz and keeps looking.

Faiz rubs her shoulder, then cups her face. His hands are strong. In that small moment described by the space between her face and his eyes, in that short moment where he considers her full face and the unquestionable sadness in her eyes, in that moment of knowing, feeling, understanding, he realizes he may have got her into trouble. He *must* make sure she remains untouched by all this, by his new life and the world he inhabits now. He does not yet know how he will make sure of that.

'When do you have to go?'

'Now.'

'What? Why?'

'You know how it is.'

'Yes, that's the problem. I know. Here, take this, you'll need it.'

'What is it?'

'Open it and see for yourself. Not now, maybe later. It's up to you. Whenever.'

Faiz holds the blue pouch in his hands. It's heavy, tightly closed by a silver string at the top. He uncoils it slowly, looking at her, smiling, also contemplating another smoke. He takes out a large silver case and at once knows there is an amulet inside. 'From the greatest Sunni pir. You wouldn't have heard of him – he lives behind Makhdoom Saéb's,' she says. Next, he takes out two audio cassettes, put together by Roohi, selections of Pakistani ghazals mostly. 'For Faiz', the handwritten label says in Urdu. 'I thought since you have been there now, you may like some of them.' She laughs.

Last, and at this Faiz turns to her in some pain, he takes out a wad of hundred-rupee notes, folded and pressed cleanly into a small book. 'I don't think you're going to have an income any time soon. Do not give a single rupee to anyone else!'

'You never know, I may finish the painting and sell it for a lot of money. It will be my best work, Roohi, my best ever. I know exactly what to do with it now, to the last detail, I think. It just needs a month or two of work.'

'Yes, you should, but settle down first. Things have changed a lot here, Faizå, don't you know? It's not the same. On some days, I can smell fresh blood in the air, sometimes even in my food, especially at sunset. The sky across the river turns scarlet and I can smell it, trust me, and then I feel terrified and think of you, and everyone else, my father and brother and my poor sad mother, and Farhat – oh, she's such an angel, isn't she? All these months she's been my sole friend and supporter and soul-mate. Poor thing, she can't even go to school any more – they have turned it into a barracks! Can you believe that, my school an army camp now? They've done some terrible things there since you left. I was glad you weren't here. My God will never forgive them.'

Faiz is stunned. She, too, has changed, he thinks. Oh, what can I do to make you feel better, safer, happier? 'But I'm here now, with you, to be always with you.' He pulls her towards him, hiding her face between his chest and his arm. Roohi, happy to bury herself, secretly wipes her tears and wishes she could go with him. She wants to go with him now. Wherever he goes she will too, what he does she will do too, what he eats she will eat too. They could even do this thing together – she may not want to use a gun, or perhaps she does want to, but she could certainly do other things, work with his group, help those left behind by the martyrs, their children, perhaps even write things for the movement. They could surely do with some editing, she thinks. Some of those posters are so tedious and lengthy that by the time you get to the end, if you manage to, you forget what was said at the beginning. She could do all this, yes. It's better to do something than to suffer every day, spend every night dreading the midnight knock on the door or military boots creaking outside the window.

He thinks, too, going over what he's just said to her. Is it really possible? He's sure there are others like him, with families, wives, children even.

'Where did you get all this money from, Roohi?'

'What do you mean – I can't have money? Some of it is from your brother. I am Farhat's tutor, remember?'

'What if I refuse to take it? You've worked hard for it.'

'You will do no such thing, mister. I saved it for you.'

'I think I will get a monthly stipend from my tanzeem, so I don't think –'

'Stop it. If you can't spend it, return it to me. I don't want to hear any more about this.'

'Okay, madam, as you say. In fact, I'm going to hire an auto-rickshaw right now to go to my hideout. It's near Nigeen Lake, probably in one of the island localities. You remember the boat ride, how embarrassed that boy was on seeing you sleep on my shoulder?'

'Huh, I did no such thing! You were the one who fell asleep in the shikara.'

'No, I did not. Okay, I may have dozed off for a bit but you were definitely sleeping when I woke up.'

'I was wide awake, mister, wide awake.'

'You want to come with me? I may also have to take a boat to get to this address.' He shows her the chit.

Roohi does not say anything. She's glad he's still the same but wishes he didn't say such things and make her heart jump. As they slip out of the basement and Roohi shuts the door behind her, he turns back abruptly and kisses her.

The Itinerant

It is not entirely without delight that Faiz criss-crosses the many villages and small towns of his land. He has never seen most of these places or even known that this world existed. Every now and then, the painter is arrested by new moments of beauty; he wants to capture everything, casting his glance near and far, over everything, his eyes gliding across mysterious curtains of willow or towards the brush-tipped pinnacles of poplar trees around vegetable gardens in the middle of shining green paddies, alongside a highway that carries endless chains of olive-green trucks – with countless soldiers in them, pouring in to spread out far and wide.

One week, he finds himself in a vast apple orchard, resting a night or two in the gardener's hut, eating the most delicious meal of his life, chicken cooked with spinach in the open air, and the next he is sprinting off at dawn to avoid being caught in a cordon-and-search operation that has besieged the countryside overnight. There are forlorn houses hidden away in valleys and on precipices, on the banks of raging streams, and there are family homes where he finds a welcome meal and a bed in an attic. There are also frightful nights that he spends alone, under the open sky, surrounded by thick trees, shadows lurking behind them, and moments of panic when he hears approaching or receding gunfire in the near or far distance.

He is so consumed by the art of survival, the constant need to escape, to move on, that he hardly has any time to think of home, although pangs of guilt and heartbreak that he didn't see Roohi again, as he had promised, cast shadows over everything he does. He would give anything to close his eyes and be transported to their favourite meeting place, never to part again. But this has got to be done. He chose to do it, he reminds himself.

He remembers the rush, the release, he had felt when he first pulled the trigger on his polished Kalashnikov. (He keeps a small grade-one tin of Nerolac wood varnish in his backpack.) He remembers walking on his toes, often among the first in his group as they engaged the army in the mountains – like his friend he prefers to fight in the mountains, he has decided – and in charged moments coming out in the open with his gun to break the stalemate as both sides played the waiting game. He remembers a strange satisfaction coming over him upon seeing the fallen, both his comrades and the enemy's. He remembers these as moments of absolute clarity, when he truly felt like a warrior, fighting for honour, for his people, waging war against zulm, against oppression, occupation. There is no other way, he tells himself. They have left me no other way.

On his return to the city, he is possessed by a quiet, singeing rage. It's a city in ruin and in perennial mourning. In some houses and streets the dead outnumber the living. Even during the day he feels a darkness.

The sight of his home choking under the weight of concertina fortresses at every alley fills him with a sense of insult he has never felt before. He feels humiliation, as he smells the exhaust from the green trucks. He feels affronted when pedestrians, cyclists, cars, school buses, his favourites the Kebab Matadors, auto-rickshaws and ambulances give way to tinted army or VVIP cars. If there were hundreds of soldiers and policemen roaming the city when he had left for Pakistan, now there are thousands. It is as if their boots were marching across his chest.

He watches everything in silence, keeping it all inside, the massacres, the rapes, the mutilations, the sieges, the murders, the abductions, the starvations, the insults. In his mind, he tries to revise *Falaknuma* again and again but, overwhelmed by the relentless assault on his senses, he gives up. His capacity for memorizing and note-taking enrages him further. Fearing he may do something drastic, against Engineer's strict instructions – and he is tempted, more than a few times, to barge into the army camp that was once his sister's school and use all his ammo – he leaves town again, crossing through the torched and razed Downtown neighbourhood of Kawdora, its ash turned into grave-like mounds of grey mud, where a few bedraggled old women and men can still be seen searching for belongings, then on to the marshlands behind the far shores of Anchar Lake. He hides here for two nights, sleeping in the open amid man-size weeds on a small floating garden, and it is here he dreams of children.

Hundreds, perhaps thousands, of children in school uniforms, circling something, hand in hand, in a walled garden. There are no adults. There is no school. In the dream, he tries to look, to find out what is at the centre of these rings of children but he cannot see beyond their hands. There are too many hands, no faces.

Back in the city, on the streets of his childhood, people seem to know more about Faiz than he does himself. Perhaps they see him as someone else. Someone out of the ordinary, a saviour returned home to herald a new dawn. Someone capable of great deeds, a man who can work miracles, who can turn dust into a weapon. He is embarrassed at the aura of importance he is supposed to exude. Then he resolves he will try to live up to their expectations, rise above his own concerns. The personal and the collective have, in fact, become one, haven't they? If only he could talk to Engineer, tell him everything, ask if it's all right that his thoughts still wander to the basement in the shrine, the balcony by the river. He's certain his friend can put everything in perspective, but he hasn't seen him since that first day of his return home. All he's heard from him are terse messages written on hastily clipped chits: stay where you are, do not come out, you need to leave immediately, don't be a daredevil, you don't need to prove your loyalty any more than any of us does, do not turn on the lights on the upper floor, run. Run.

That's what Faiz does now and he's become quite good at it. Everything is a part of him as he runs from town to country, country to town, from house to boat, from lake to river, from rich man's guest bedroom in the posh part of town to a fisherwoman's mouldy one-room boathouse downstream on the Jhelum, near the riverside neighbourhood Roohi once saw during her wild swim down the river. Nothing tires him.

It means, he thinks, as he looks out into the river from a starburst hole in the brown-paper-covered window of the fisherwoman's houseboat, that the centre of his universe is still his own area, which, as it happens, is around half an hour's boat ride upstream from where he is. He could find a boat and do just that, disembark at the ghat by the shrine, climb the steps he used to sit on in childhood, have a smoke on the balcony where he used to dry himself and, best of all, where he first met Roohi – what would she be doing right now, at this exact moment? – then somehow slip into her room and quietly sleep by her side. In the morning, she will be thrilled to see him in her bed – *no, no,* he needs to be apart from her as she won't be comfortable with such closeness and he wouldn't want to regret anything, do anything that caused her the slightest discomfort. Just to touch her hair would be heavenly. All he would want.

Compared to the homes that have been arranged for him these last two weeks, it's cooler sleeping on the river, and peaceful as he can hear only the whispers of the water. The boat creaks when the current is strong enough to rock it. He likes it all. He trusts water more than land.

These people, the fisherwoman's family, husband and three children, have been kind to him without making any fuss, apart from the boy's direct questions about the power of a Kalashnikov. 'Is it true that its bullets can even destroy a tank?' He seemed disappointed with Faiz's vague answers, and more so with the absence of one on him. He's been allowed to carry only a palm-sized Chinese-made pistol, which he hides under his vest. The family have vacated their bedroom on the boat for him, choosing to sleep in the kitchen with a plywood partition between them. In the morning, the husband will row across to the opposite bank to bring back bread from the baker, spending an extra five rupees on muslin-thin lavase bread for their secret guest. He looks forward to it.

Faiz now hears the drone of soldiers' trucks driving over some bridge nearby. He can feel the vibration, which has transferred to the water beneath him. The soldiers don't even stop at night. Curse them. He turns away from the noise, as if looking the other way will drown the sound. Yet he hears it more clearly now. It's not a truck on a road but something on the water. There is a patrol on the river. A boat rushing down the Jhelum, or pushing up, he can't tell. He does not know that they have recently brought naval boats to the river. It crosses the city in just over an hour, going down from the civil lines, through all of Downtown, and then all the way to the barrage just outside the city, where people have recently started collecting the withered corpses dumped by the soldiers, which get tangled in the metal barricade put up last year to prevent boats escaping the city. The bodies often look like large pink dolls without any clothes on them. He waits, breathing slowly. The boat speeds past his houseboat, a low red flare washing his paper window. The waves from the boat's rotors hit the houseboat, making it rock to a quick rhythm. One of the girls in the kitchen wakes and he can hear the mother telling her, 'It's nothing, just some dogs in the water, go back to sleep.' He cannot resist peering through the hole again and sees a dark animal tearing through the river, nothing visible except the black snout of a heavy machine-gun.

Inside the boat, Major Sumit Kumar sits behind the machine-gunner with two of his closest aides. An Uzi lies reclined against a safety float, its graphite grey stark against the fluorescent orange. There is silence inside the boat. He glances at his weapon and stands to lean closer to the tinted side window. This is such an enchanting city at night, he thinks, and there is hardly any disturbance on the river. Since the last communiqué from Signal Central, Kumar has been making an effort to go out more often, have officer's boots on the ground, and this nocturnal vigil by speedboat is a godsend. He is grateful to the navy for providing these small patrol boats. He feels lucky he doesn't have to share his with anyone. There are four for the big lake, two for that desiccated mess, Anchar Lake, two for the inland waterways, and two for the river, one for the upper city and one for Downtown. It's much better than endlessly tossing and turning in his narrow bed in that grave-like storeroom. Although unfortunately, he sighs, he has yet to make a big arrest, or kill, since the Zaal swoop last year. What happened to those boys after they were moved? he wonders. I couldn't have kept them with me for ever, could I? They couldn't have been innocent, could they? I suppose everyone here must be involved in one way or another. Opening a slat in the window, he lights a cigarette. There is nothing better than a satisfying smoke at night on the river.

Faiz slumps down in his bed and closes his eyes, pressing on his legs, which won't stop shaking. He puts one hand on the pistol, gently unlocking its safety catch, and the shaking stops.

Heart to Heart

'You are the truest human being I know, Farree. Do you understand? You speak purely, from the heart. You probably even believed the soldiers at your school, our school, when they said they were here to protect you, didn't you? I love you almost as much as I love your silly brother.'

Farhat squats in front of Roohi like a dutiful pupil, even though there are no lessons now.

There's been no word from Faiz and no news of him for a month. He's been unreachable since their last meeting. Then he had said he'd be back soon, in a day or two, and they would 'discuss the future' as he might have a clearer picture of his new role, but he hasn't come back. Neither home, nor to Roohi. And the two women, mortally afraid of their own thoughts, resist voicing their worst fears.

At home every evening, Abba, with Mouj's aid, manages to calm, sometimes even cheer, everyone before they go to bed. He has fabricated an alternative universe, in which he is in regular touch with the kind Hakeem Saéb of Rainawari and his impressive grandson, both of whom have assured him that the Artist – yes, that's what the old man and his protégé call Faiz, Mir Zafar Ali announces proudly – is in safe hands and will visit home soon. He sends his salams and love to everyone. Don't worry. Now go to sleep. When he is alone he prays into the night, offering Nafl just before daybreak, then reciting the Qur'ān until his eyes begin to water.

Farhat senses that not all of what her brother reports may be true; it seems inconceivable to her that while Faiz is able to send news of his safety he would choose not to get in touch with Roohi, but she carries word to Roohi nonetheless, knowing it will settle her nerves, even if just a bit.

Roohi likes to hear anything from her young friend. This waiting is so different from the long wait when he was out there, across the mountains, in Pakistan. That meant waiting for the day when he would come home or at least write to her of a time when he would do so. This, on the other hand, is waiting to see whether he is alive or dead, and her mind sometimes veers towards funereal thoughts at night.

Today she wants to tell Farhat everything, empty her heart, as she puts it, spell it all out, even if she comes across as someone on the edge of madness.

'You see, I have never told anyone this before, not even Faiz – not all of what I'm about to tell you. Not even Naseem Aunty, who knows everything about me.'

'Roohi Di, what is it? Is all well at home, you know, with your parents, with Rumi?'

'Yes, they have been fine. They know everything. They didn't say a word when I met Faiz on his return. Even though I stayed out late, they didn't say anything. Mummy, I'm sure, must have been very worried but she didn't say a word.'

'What is it, then?'

'I'll tell you. Can you get me some water first?'

Farhat runs down to the kitchen and brings back a jug of water and a glass. They are sitting in Faiz's room. It's afternoon. Mouj, Feroza and Shahida are asleep, the daytime nap a short respite. No one remembers, or perhaps everyone, except Shabbir, has chosen to forget, the pretext of trigonometry lessons. Mir Zafar Ali's cold glares have foreclosed any discussion on the topic of Faiz's Sunni girlfriend visiting the house sometimes, and her presence has been made easier to ignore in the absence of Faiz.

Roohi takes a long sip of water, then sighs. 'Farree, I have known your brother longer than anyone thinks. I used to see him when we were children, when I was a little girl and he was a skinny boy. I used to watch him at the shrine actually, you know. I remember it all now. Even then he was different from the rest of the boys. Even then he – please don't mind me saying this, oh, I know you won't – he seemed lonely. When we were very small we may even have played hide-and-seek together. I mean in a group of children. I would see him swim in the river, racing quietly to the opposite bank, alone. He was very quick. He would sit at the opposite ghat and gaze at the river. He looked deep in thought. I would stare at him, willing him somehow to come closer so I could see his face properly and try to read his thoughts. Then he disappeared, and as I grew older, Papa forbade me to play with the boys. As if I would have wanted to marry any of them.

'When I saw Faiz again after all these years it all came back and I believed more than ever that it was destined. Something must have happened then, something must have drawn me to him, and him to me – when we were young, when he was a small boy, and I a small girl. You see, I think he knows it, too, but he hasn't talked about it. But he does remember his early days at the shrine, he told me. I didn't say much about it – I'm a girl, and I didn't want him, or anyone who might find out, to think I was . . . you know, desperate. Some of my friends ask why him, why a Shia boy, and a militant at that, when there are so many good Sunni boys around? I say to them, "I didn't have a choice, did I? I think it was written before we were born." I know, it probably seems a bit sentimental, like something out of a film, but this is exactly how I feel. I always knew.

'And when he saw me first, it was the most magical thing ever, the evening like no other evening. A wind blew and turned his eyes towards me. It was a moment of destiny. I recognized him instantly but told myself maybe my mind was playing tricks, that I was daydreaming. But later, he told me, although not in so many words, that he remembered a girl with long plaits from near the river. That was me, Farree. That was me! Now he's gone again. What am I to do? Sometimes I feel I'm already grieving. And that isn't fair. I want a life with him. I know this is selfish of me, but I don't want a life of waiting, or mourning, or just . . . nothing! I have waited enough for him, perhaps all my life, and now he makes me wait again.'

Of Departures

Even in his impaired state, with his hand invisible to visitors, Mir Zafar Ali is still a figure of seriousness, of great dignity, and Master Dinanath, himself a man of decorum, is conscious not to show any signs of a change in attitude towards him. But things need to be said, hearts needs to be laid bare, a chapter needs to be closed. They have been neighbours for at least half a century, but Dinanath, walking into the Mir Manzil, feels as though his feet are made of lead. If it wasn't for Usha's insistence, he would perhaps just turn and run, and write to Mir Zafar Ali later. They haven't exactly been friends but, it must be said, good neighbours, and, most importantly, the daughters from the two families, having spent many days together as children, are friends, although the families, owing to codes of piety, strict Shia and fastidious Brahmin, haven't shared any meals. Yes, free-for-all vegetarian fare on the tenth day of Muharram each year, when everyone from the neighbourhood and beyond, Sunni, Shia, Pandit, friend, stranger, poor and rich, eats from the Mir hearth, but no joint meals. Dinanath regrets that now. Mir Zafar has thought of it often, too, and he suspects it may have been different in their fathers' time but he isn't sure.

'I must abandon ship, Zafar Saéb, if I want to save my family,' the Master blurts out, as he sits by the bay window facing his own house. He can see the aged green-stone plinth from here, a relic from a time when building material was brought into the heart of the city on large boats from those old versions of the city turned into quarries and kilns in the last century. Mir Mohammed Ali, Faiz's father, had once contracted stone merchants to bring in boatloads of their goods to the ghat by the shrine. It had taken forty days to ship the rocks he had procured.

'But why? There is no need. No one will harm you, Dinanath, I swear upon my life. I can't see why anyone would want to trouble you or your family.'

'People have not been harmed, Zafar Saèb, they have been killed. Surely you don't want me to wait until it happens.'

'Must you punish us all for the sins of a few? Must you?'

'I must protect what I can while I can. No one wants to leave their home, you know that, but I have to.'

'I understand, but don't you think it's a bit drastic? You could move in with us until you feel better. How about that? Or I can ask the Shahmiris to let you use their house. They were your neighbours even before us. Or the Sheikhs? You've been friends with them since childhood, haven't you? Javed Saèb is one of your best friends, Dinanath! Come on, please don't leave. This is your home. I can't believe I have to say that to you.'

'It will break Usha's heart looking at her house from your windows every day. I came to tell you myself because I didn't want you to hear from others. I have just said goodbye to the Sheikhs as well, and I spoke with Javed on the phone. Look, it's probably only for a few weeks. We will be back, I promise.'

'You don't have to promise me anything, Masterjee. Just don't do it. This is your home. Where will you go? And do you really think Usha Jee and your daughters will be happy anywhere else? I'm sure this is temporary. Everyone's suffering. You know what happened to me, my . . . And the boys. Four are yet to return – we don't even know where they are or if they are alive. It will all pass. They can't kill us all. The soldiers, I'm absolutely certain, will leave one day.'

'It's not the soldiers I fear, Zafar. I don't think you quite understand.'

'I understand fully. I know what's happening around me. All I'm saying is that there are some rotten apples, as they say, and you shouldn't let them determine your choices.'

'I don't have a *choice* any more, Zafar. They killed Professor Koul. He is – was seventy years old!'

'Yes. I was shocked too, I still am . . . Please don't punish us for the sins of a few. You see, whoever kills an innocent will be punished, if not in this life certainly in the afterlife. Allahta'ala watches everything, Dinanath, everything. Do you remember the kindergarten children massacred by the army near Fateh Kadal? Apart from their parents, no one remembers their names now. And do you know where those soldiers are now? Still on duty, at the same bunker. Can you believe that? But one day things will change. Tyranny and cruelty are their own downfall, remember that.' Mir Zafar's mind wanders to his brother's painting, which he had found hidden behind a banner in the hall of mourning on the top floor. As Faiz was away in the countryside waging battle against the Indian Army, he had found it hard to resist and gone looking for *Falaknuma*. There it was, with the faint smell of fresh paint and bearing signs of erasure here and there. He had been struck and moved by its quiet power and the strange fusion of light and darkness. At the centre, around the lake Faiz had first sketched, he had looked wide-eyed at a boat full of figures resembling children who, it seemed to him, had no faces, just outlines. Unknown to him, or to anyone, Faiz had taken out his old paints and brushes and made changes to his masterpiece. At the two ends of the boat, Mir Zafar Ali had recognized the male and female figures, the woman at the front and the man at the back.

He's woken by Dinanath's voice. 'It's too late for me. You think I want to do this? It feels like I'm taking an axe to my chest and ripping my heart out. But I have a family, Zafar Saéb, I have daughters. God knows how I will feel when I shut the door, only God knows. Sorry . . . You see, many have already left. And today the government will help us, take us somewhere. Who knows if they will do that tomorrow? Here, keep these.' Master Dinanath takes out a bunch of keys from his pocket and dangles it in the air, waiting for Mir Zafar to raise his hand. 'I am leaving my home, my life's work, in your care. I have left another set with the Sheiks.'

Mir Zafar cannot move. He looks up towards the sky, determined

that his eyes will not well up. Through the window, he sees a familiar sight. Usha looking out of her window towards him, where she
knows her husband must be. He thinks she has caught his eye too.
Dinanath knows she is watching. The sun goes down behind the
houses, and the labyrinth of many others near them, and a blanket
of evening shade unfurls abruptly in the backyard separating the
two houses, hiding her form in the window.

Seated across from each other, they drink their tea silently, both
dipping pieces of fresh buns into their cups. 'Zafar Saéb, don't look
so glum. We have to leave. It's nothing personal and, as I said, we'll
be back soon. Pray for us.'

'I will. I will.'

The Vases

The sheets draped over the giant pots of rice make them look like veiled statues. Faiz remembers not to open the window during the day, in case the smoke from his cigarettes is seen from outside. Although it's just good old Masterjee and Usha Jee who can see his window, you never know, these days. It is, of course, unimaginable, he tells himself again, that they would spy on him, but better to be cautious. He lights a cigarette and crouches in the window, in his new cubicle-sized hideout on the top floor, of which only his mother and sisters are aware. In his mind he's never been clearer about what he wants to do, where he wants to stay, although he's somewhat uncomfortable about keeping his big brother, and the other men of the house, in the dark, but Farhat had insisted, contending that Mir Zafar would lose sleep again if he knew. 'He is very sad about Masterjee leaving home, Faizå, even angry. They are all leaving, Bimla and Kamla too – did you know? So, let's not worry him any more.' Faiz had looked at her in surprise, then at the house opposite theirs, and said nothing.

Shahida and Feroza take turns by the window in their room below. The moment they see a stranger, *anyone*, enter from the outer gate, they will run to him, so he can escape via the Shahmiris' giant mulberry tree. He remembers Engineer now and feels a little guilty for not doing exactly as he had said. 'Do what the chits say, nothing else, and you will be fine.' But he had started to miss his sisters and mother beyond bearing, he remembers now; fear of the future, longing for home and its affections, the familiar feel of the walls and, perhaps most importantly, the prospect of proximity to Roohi, leaving little doubt in his mind that he must go home, hide there, for a few days before embarking on new 'duty', as one of the latest paper missives had termed it. Roohi does not know yet. He wants to surprise her, an idea endorsed by his little sister.

Tonight is his third night at home and he's surprised at the apparent ease of it all, at the uneventfulness of it all. He hears every sound from the rooms below and plays little guessing games about who is talking to whom. He is saddened there is no sound of his big brother's roar: Mir Zafar no longer shouts. He longs to join the family at supper, to watch late-night TV with Sajad and Farhat. But he is grateful. Having crossed the length and breadth of his country in the last few weeks, he's happy to be home, although fearful that it may end soon. Strangely, he sleeps well at night, not thinking much of the body-snatching night-time raids taking place across the city as he sleeps. He has hidden his pistol inside one of the vases, buried in the rice. It's all he will need.

Tomorrow or the day after, on Friday, he will see Roohi and tell her of his plans. He is certain she will agree. The thought came to him last night. The seeming distance between his two selves does not cause him unease. He may have willed himself, some surmise, into believing that he can have both, live two lives. It is not as though every militant has to give up his family, he thinks.

He must remember, he tells himself, as he waits for his mother to come up with his dinner, to *ask* Roohi, ask for her permission.

Roohi has never known herself to be so anxious. 'Stay calm, stay calm,' she says, under her breath, as she paces back and forth in the hallway, just as her father does when her mother is late. Every two or three minutes, she opens the front door, cranes her head through the curtain, looks out in both directions, then at the shrine, and shuts it again. She's been waiting for nearly two hours. He may have gone to the mosque for evening prayers and stayed back for a chat. But it seems the last prayer of the day is over: the congregation has disappeared and the street in front of the mosque is still. There are no old men lingering by the door. She looks at her watch. Prayer time ended half an hour ago.

'Why is Rumi never here when we need him most? You've spoilt him rotten,' she says to her mother, who appears to be taking it out on a ladle she is using to stir the chicken stew that's been simmering for ever, it seems to Roohi.

'Yes, yes, blame it all on me. Everything is Mummy's fault. *Everything*. Why don't you say something to him if you're so bothered? You're his elder sister, after all.'

'I did, Mummy, and he promised he'd come home early from now on,' Roohi lies. She longs for Rumi to come home so she can ask him to go with her in search of Papa.

Earlier in the day, Papa said he had to meet the commissioner's secretary, who had sent for him. 'He mentioned some arrears that have accrued to him, money that the DC's office owes him, so I told him to go. It's all my fault. But how was I to know he would scare us like this? All these years we've been together, he's the one who's given me grey hair. You just want an opportunity to criticize me.'

Roohi wants to hold her mother. 'I wish he had listened and had gone to Naseem Aunty's house for a few days . . . Let's not worry too much, okay? He'll be home soon. It's official work anyhow. Oh, but, no –'

'What – what is it?'

'Nothing, nothing, Mummy. I was just thinking it must take ages to get into the DC's office, these days – you have to pass through so many checks before they let you in. Maybe that's why he's late.'

'I know. I'll sit down now. The stew must be done. Can you check if it's got enough salt?'

Khan Saéb does not return home that night. The two women wait in Roohi's bedroom, a long, mostly silent vigil behind a curtained window under the muted light of Roohi's night lamp. At some point, they hear the door creak open, but from the familiar and slightly irritating attempt at a discreet entry, they know it's Rumi. 'He should just stop pretending.' Roohi shakes her head, standing up to go down, but Mummy grabs her hand, asking her to stop. No point telling him now. We don't want him to go out at this hour. Roohi agrees.

This, then, is how they spend the night, in quiet, mostly unspoken understanding, the mother and daughter considering each other now and then. Mummy rests her head against the desk, her eyes fixed on her daughter's face. From time to time, Roohi creates a small slit in the double curtains and looks out. The street is a dead, still world, not even the night insects are visible. The municipal lamps, whose halogen glow has lit the night outside her bedroom for most of her life, are gone. In the distance, both near and far, vehicles growl. She wishes Faiz was with her.

'Sleep for an hour so, my dear – your eyes are red. Oh, be careful, be careful! Don't bring the curtain rod down on your head.' Mummy rises from her seat and rubs her daughter's shoulder, then rests her head on it. Roohi looks up at her.

On the floor below, Rumi is awake in his small room, smoking in bed. He, too, cannot sleep.

The Other Mission

People he doesn't recognize raise their hands to their foreheads to say salam. People he remembers only vaguely approach to shake his hand and press their hand to their chest. (This is a new form of greeting, made popular by the boys returned from 'across'.) People who didn't want much to do with a naqash, with a lowly papier-mâché artist, suddenly want to be seen with him. He steps lightly through the main street, fearless, people assume, because of his new status as a freedom-fighter, and finds himself imitating Engineer's mildly condescending manner. And yet, as he turns the first corner near the milkman's shop, he suddenly remembers Professor Koul's benign presence, and feels more than a tinge of guilt. He slows down, suddenly contemplative. This is another thing, he has told himself, he will raise with the chief, a man who goes by the *nom de guerre* of Maqbool and whom no one has seen. Why was the professor killed, and who was responsible? Shouldn't he, as a senior figure of the movement, get to the heart of the matter? There is so much to do, he thinks, as the memory of Professor Koul strolling in the street, his pale turban and ornamental walking stick welded to the consciousness of those who grew up watching him, lingers. He takes the short-cut Roohi showed him last week so that he can be at the shrine by himself for a short while before embarking on this important mission. He sits by the tree. There are no beggars on the stone platforms today, or crowds of pigeons pecking at the surfaces, seeking out scatterings of rice grains and roasted corn. The crows are still here, at least, perched above the outer cornices, treetops and verandas. He hopes he might recognize one of them.

*

Faiz leans back against the bolsters in Roohi's sitting room and considers the walls, the carpet, the wooden grandfather clock with the golden pendulum swaying inside as though nodding to him. He tries to find himself in its distorted reflection of the room. Roohi's mother – who else could it be, unless her aunt is visiting? – not knowing how to make conversation with him, left the room as soon as he sat down. She's upstairs now, telling Roohi Faiz is here, yes, *him*, downstairs in the sitting room. I couldn't turn him away, could I? He is, after all . . . and he is here to see you. I couldn't lie, could I? There's no point, is there, in denying it now? He is here, you are here, we are all here. Go, go, please, go now, while I make the tea. What kind does he like, salt tea or Lipton, or would he prefer lemon squash? We have some, or maybe lassi – I can put mint in it? Oh, just sit by the door, Roohi, in case, you know. I mean, what if someone comes suddenly?

Roohi, speechless, unnerved by her mother's manner, takes her time to go down the three flights of stairs, giving each step thought, her heart feeling a sudden tightness as she gets closer to the sitting-room door. What puzzles her is that there was no word from Farhat about this. Faiz, her Faiz, has not only managed to come to see her at her home but has already met her mother. Her mother. Months ago, when he hadn't gone abroad, the thought of him openly visiting her was quite simply illegal in the eyes of many, and the idea that he would one day be seated in her sitting room, waiting for her to come down, simply inconceivable. Her breathing slow, her heart heavy, she is at the door now, making the curtain rustle.

He settles his posture for the tenth time, making sure there is no visible sign of the pistol at his waist. But a part of him also wants her to see it.

'Would you like some water?'

'No, I'm fine. Yes, okay, then.'

She looks sad, tired, he thinks. Is she not happy to see him? She must just be unsettled to see him here.

She comes back, carrying a round copper tray with a copper tumbler on it. She spreads a tablecloth on the floor in front of him. He drinks it all in one go. The water is sweet.

'Oh, Faizå, why have you chosen today of all days to come? Papa is missing – we haven't seen him all night. Mummy nearly fainted this morning.'

Faiz stands up, looks at her and leans against the wall. 'I didn't know. How would I? Sorry. But, Roohi, I'm sure he's fine . . . I'm sure there'll be a reason for his delay – when did he leave, where did he go? Don't worry, he'll be back soon. I had to come. I just couldn't wait any longer.'

'He went to the cursed DC's office yesterday. Mummy says they sent for him. I wish he hadn't gone.'

'Okay, that's fine, then. It's some office work, right, so he'll be back soon? You know what it's like in the city. It might have been late last evening, so he must have decided to finish all his work, then come home. So relax, don't stress too much.'

'I know, I know. I'm sure it's just something to do with that office, but these days I worry . . . Faizå, I had no clue you'd turn up like this . . .'

'Roohi, let's get married. Can we get married? I want to. I mean, can we, please? There's nothing we can gain by waiting. I can't. I've thought about it all. What do you think? I mean, I'm asking, I'm asking your permission. I'm sorry, I don't know how to say it. It's up to you – it's up to you – but there is nothing more I want than to be with . . . you. I've thought about it all. What do – what do you . . . think?'

His hands shake, his voice is hoarse. But he also feels light, relieved. He looks at the pendulum, which, it appears to him, is swinging faster now.

Roohi sits there, knees bent, at the edge of the tablecloth, trying hard to say something, looking at him, his eyes and the lines on his forehead. Naseem Aunty had once told her that three deep furrows on a man's forehead mean he is good.

'Do not, even for a minute, think I have forgiven you for disappearing like that, not sending me even a single message. Do you have any idea what it is like to wait for your news day after day, night after night? You won't, because you never have to wait like I do. If you do it again – And today! Today of all days, Faizå!'

'You don't have to say anything right now.' Faiz deliberately raises his voice a bit. 'Think about it, take your time. I'm not, I'm –'

'We will. Of course we will.' Roohi shakes her head. 'But I can't say anything right now, can I, Faizå? Papa must come back . . . I'm so worried. Today of all days, Faizå!'

Khan Saéb looks drained, with the face of someone who's been up, smoking, all night. 'There was absolutely nothing I could do. They offered to drop me home in an official jeep but I'm not stupid. What do they think, hnnh? And I didn't want to walk home alone at night – you can surely understand that – so I slept in the secretary's office. But he didn't give me the keys so I couldn't leave early in the morning. Even the damn telephone there has a lock, a padlock, can you believe it? I couldn't call. Now, for God's sake, please tell me, how is it my fault, just how? You should all be glad I've returned home. Anyhow, the lesson is I should never go in the afternoon. They make you wait for ever, as if retired people don't have a life, as if we have nothing to do.'

'Okay, okay, stop it, I understand. You've said enough. Take this – I've put some glucose in it. Drink it. I'm just relieved you're back. And now there is something else you, I mean we, have to deal with.'

'Did you not hear anything I said? I'm dying for some sleep! Please ask your son to do whatever it is you want done. Have mercy on me, for God's sake.'

'Sssh . . . Someone is here to meet you. Listen to me, will you, and don't raise your voice. Calm down! I made him wait, not Roohi. I welcomed him in, not Roohi. I even made tea for him.'

'Who? What? What is the matter? What is wrong with the two of you? Can't I even rest in my own house now? Roohi dear, what is the matter?'

'It's someone who has come for Roohi dear. Keep it down! Shall I make you swear upon the Holy Prophet?'

'Oh, oh – him? Why is he here? Oh, God, will yesterday never end? You had to send him today of all the days, Khoda Saéb. Thank you for your kind and precise timing! Oh, God. Where is he? Why is he here? What does he want? Can I at least wash my face first? He is not carrying any . . . is he?' He addresses Roohi directly. It is a moment that, Roohi will think later, in spite of its immediate awkwardness, breaks the ice on the matter between father and daughter.

'No, Papa, he is not. Are you disappointed?'

'Roohi!'

'Sorry, bad joke.'

'This is no time for jokes. I spent a whole night in an office chair, and it was smelly too, and I come home to –'

'You promised to keep calm, didn't you? I have put out a fresh towel for you. The water is hot, now go and wash. But come back quickly. Don't spend all day in the bathroom.'

Roohi marvels at her mother, her calm and decisive manner, and is touched by a fleeting sadness that she may have to leave her soon. It is possible, she thinks, and hugs her.

Mummy goes to her own bedroom, unlocks a trunk that's been under her bed for years, covered with a heavy crewelwork cloth, and takes out a large sealed plastic bag of almonds, then another, of colourfully wrapped sweets, and gazes at them. Tomorrow, if he is to become my son-in-law, and it is quite possible, he and his mother should not think Roohi's mother forgot her basic manners. Is this it, then? She pauses in the middle of the room. Is this really the man Roohi will marry? Do we have a choice? Actually, it doesn't matter what he does or doesn't do for a living. Roohi has chosen. She feels decisive and hesitates again briefly as she leaves the room with the puffed-up bags. Perhaps she should check with Roohi. What is the point in hiding anything from her now, now that it's all happening, now that it has happened, now that it's out in the open, now that he is here, in our house, and her father may already have given his consent? But maybe she will feel shy. Don't let me embarrass her. I am the mother. I am the mother. I must do my duty, no matter what.

Mummy enters the sitting room with a tray – tea, cakes, pastries, the plastic bags – and sees two silent men seated across from each other with their heads down. She is not very pleased with her husband. She rips open one of the bags and, in the manner of all good and dutiful would-be mothers-in-law, showers a handful of almonds over Faiz's head, then a clutch of the sweets, which make a plastic noise as they brush against his thick hair and drop into his lap.

He fidgets a little, but only minutely, making sure he doesn't move too much and in the process reveal the weapon on him.

Some almonds roll away and reach Khan Saèb who glares at them. Then he picks one up, tries to crack it open with his hand, with his teeth, then with his heel, fails and gives up, and throws it back onto the carpet.

Faiz crushes a couple on his knee with a single blow of his fist, and quietly offers his outstretched palm to Khan Saèb. He feels a delayed sting in his kneecap but doesn't show it.

Behind the curtain, Roohi smiles.

'Please have a piece of the cake, for my sake,' Roohi's mummy, in the manner of all mothers who serve tea, insists and literally blocks Faiz's view, and mouth, with a colossal slice of the fruit cake from the legendary Foxy Bakers of Downtown. He has no option but to take it.

Roohi giggles.

'Mir Manzil? Oh, yes, yes, I may have visited your house in the past, son. God bless you, what's your name? I was a census director once.' Kabir Ahmed Khan, the former section assistant who rose to be assistant director over thirty-eight years of service, makes up a new designation for his previous life, and looks at his wife. 'I may even have written your name down with my own hand. Fate, I have learnt in my life, son, has strange ways. I have indeed heard about your noble brother and your late father, may he prosper in Heaven.' Roohi, an unmoving shadow outside, suppresses another giggle. 'Oh, please, please, finish your cake first . . . Now, I would obviously like to meet your elder brother, I mean as well, so please do convey my salams.' Oh, Papa, Papa, he hasn't said anything, let him say it, for God's sake. Let him say it first. I *want* him to say it.

'Would you like another cup of tea?' Mummy eyes her husband. 'Or would you prefer me to reheat it first?'

'Yes, another cup – for him, too. For you, too?'

Faiz nods.

Roohi's mother stands up with the teapot, trying to balance the tray with the biscuits and cake in her other hand, although she doesn't need to take it away. 'Will you help me carry this to the kitchen?'

Roohi doesn't run. She just shifts to one side, hugging the wall. Mummy launches into Papa as he follows her obediently into the kitchen with the tray. 'Just ask him to send his brother here, say you would like to meet him. That is how it's done. What's wrong with you?'

'What do you mean? Why should I? Shouldn't he offer it himself? Why should I have to ask for anything? She is my daughter –'

'Precisely! She is your daughter. He came here to see Roohi, not you or me, but it's clear why he is here. He should know that, if he is serious about it, he must have his family approach us in the right manner. It doesn't matter that he is a mujahid. We are the girl's family, after all, we can't be asking for a match.'

'Are we?'

'What else, Mr Khan? I mean, we won't ask for it. He, they, should. Why do you think he is here? Have you seen your daughter lately? When was the last time you talked to her or thought about her? Do you have any idea? I have seen her sit by that window of hers for hours without moving an inch. I have seen her cry at the mere whisper of tension in the city. I have seen her panic and turn pale at the sound of gunfire these days. I have heard her pace for hours in her room at night. I have seen her slip out of the house to pray at the shrine and have waited until dawn to see her return. She looks strange then, as though a jinn has possessed her. Some days, I worry she may go mad like this. She's lost so much weight. She hardly ever smiles now. Roohi, my Roohi of all people, doesn't smile any more. Are you blind?'

'Oho, don't be so dramatic. All mothers think their children are weak and losing weight. She seems perfectly all right to me. What is wrong with you? She reads at night, always has, that's what you must have heard. It is your son I'm worried about, madam. I hardly see him these days, where does he go? You must know!'

'Keep your voice down, and don't fight! What will he think if he hears you shout? He's just behind this wall.'

'But I'm not screaming.'

'Yes, you are. Anyhow, listen, listen. I know my daughter, and she definitely doesn't walk while she reads. I know her better than any of you do. She will not be happy, ever, with anyone else, in any other family, even if you find a prince for her. I know this. Know it in my heart. Do you understand what I'm saying? Did you know she once fell asleep in – forget it, forget it, you'll never understand. Just do as I say. Just this once, for the sake of God, listen to me. Talk to him nicely and subtly convey he should send his elders to meet us. This is not the way.'

Khan, who, contrary to his wife's belief, has always known of Roohi's world, decides to employ his assistant director's manner with Faiz. 'Okay, madam, I will talk to this boy. That's what he is, a boy, isn't he? So what if he's a Milton now?' Khan deliberately uses the Downtown mispronunciation, and does so quite loudly, perhaps

276

to remind his wife, perhaps to address his own fears, or simply to sound brave in front of the militant recently returned from Pakistan who's waiting in his sitting room.

'Let's say a nice gentleman came to a house, or sent his elders, his parents, uncles, grandparents and aunts, to ask for the daughter's hand.' Khan starts as soon as he enters the sitting room again. 'Now, let's assume I was the father or uncle or grandfather of this girl. Assume this gentleman was, you know . . . one of the boys. You understand? Of course, you understand. What am I saying? And what if this man belonged to a different, hmm . . . religious school, what if he was Sunni and the girl a Shia? Do you understand? What would you say to this boy, I mean, man?' He tries to look out into the hallway through a narrow gap between the curtain and the doorframe.

Faiz gazes at the bent reflections in the glass face of the clock, then tries to figure out if Roohi's still behind the curtain, blushes, and bows his head completely to hide his smile.

'I am aware these are hardly the times to think of such things, you know, Sunni, Shia et cetera, but, you will understand, this man has just returned from there and – how do I say this? – if it were a trad-itional marriage proposal, as a father I would ask, ask the matchmaker, for instance, wouldn't I, what does the boy do, how old is he, does he have a regular income, is their house nice, will she be very far from us, you know what I mean?'

Faiz manages to produce the slightest of nods, without lifting his head.

'So, in that case, I suggest we wait. Please do not think I'm being difficult, because I'm not, but she is my daughter, after all, and while I will do anything for her happiness, I have to consider this carefully. I'm sure you understand. You are also from a good family, after all.'

Papa, defying the ban on indoor smoking his wife had imposed five years ago, smokes two cigarettes, one after the other. It gives

Faiz a strange taste in the mouth, which makes him swallow and lick his lips, a gesture that almost makes Roohi giggle but, by poking the curtain with her toe, she signals to him he should not appear desperate for a cigarette in front of her father. This makes him more nervous.

As her mother waits for her, Roohi feels there is something of an anticlimax to the proceedings. First, Faiz's unexpected act of courage, however lovely and life-changing, has ended their secret world. And, what's more, when the time came for the big revelation she expected some fireworks both inside her house and outside, not that she had desired them, and had therefore prepared a forceful defence of her choice, ending the argument with the case of Hazrat Khadija's marriage to the Prophet Muhammad. It isn't every day, after all, that Sunni girls marry Shia boys or, as we have briefly noted with regard to Faiz's niece Mehbooba and his sister Shahida, that Shia girls marry Sunni boys. Roohi realizes there is an unspoken understanding at work here, namely that very few people want strife between the two communities in these times, when the smallest matter can get out of hand. She also acknowledges, not without some sense of disdain, that Faiz's newfound status as a militant may have killed off any remaining grain of opposition in her parents, or nipped in the bud any possible opposition in the area, therefore emboldening them. She doesn't know, however, what Faiz had to do to convince his own family. She's been aware of the vehement disapproval that some members of the Mir family, mostly the men, harbour towards her.

'Roohi!' Mummy waits by the door to her daughter's room. The last few minutes she, too, has been lost, thinking of the man who left a while ago.

'Oh, yes, Mummy, actually, we haven't thought about it. You and Papa can decide everything with them, also where I will live until he . . . you know. I'm sure something will work out. His brother is such a good man, Mummy, and has been like a father to him.'

'Yes, we will decide that later. Roohi, you know I'd do anything for your happiness, but are you really sure? Absolutely sure? If you change your mind, if you have the slightest doubt, we won't say a thing.'

'I love you too, Mummy. Yes, I am sure. You know that. I've told you all, remember?'

'Yes.'

'I wish every girl had a mother like you.'

'Oh, stop it now. No need to flatter me. Every mother is like me.'

They come down together from Roohi's room, happy comrades and co-architects of an unusual and unconventional wedding, the first of its kind in either family. They keep thoughts of the future at bay for now.

Threads

Soon after breakfast the next day, Roohi hurries out of the kitchen, then out of the house, without saying a word to her parents, and finds herself in the main hall of the shrine, in the men's hall where she is not allowed, never has been, but today the thought doesn't even cross her mind. It is her shrine before anyone else's, she remembers saying to her friends once. She heads straight towards the front, towards the central niche to whose side is the main, the all-important silver-and-glass reliquary. Slowly, hesitantly, she inches towards it. There are two rows of men seated behind her, just a few feet away, who, waiting for the next man to do or say something, stay in some kind of spiritual paralysis at the sight of this girl, this stunningly beautiful and, as some would later say, angelic woman and, in the end, just watch in complete silence. They let her do her thing and do not feel defied or affronted. That is the effect that her trance-like manner, although she is only doing what she'd promised herself long, long ago, has on these middle-aged and old men, who often come to find solitude and succour here but disapprove of women who long to see the inside of the sanctum proper. She caresses the blue thread she had tied to the tassels of the green and orange flag that has been in the same place, the same glass casing beside the reliquary, for hundreds of years, but does not untie it. While he is returned to her, he is not wholly hers yet, even though he has, in his nervy manner, proposed marriage and met her at her home. Instead she ties a fresh one, a sliver torn from her black dupatta, for her dear papa, who, she thanks Allah, is back home after going missing. Papa has said yes, hasn't he? And Mummy had never said no, she knows, but Papa has to be there all the time. I will forbid him to leave home ever again. I will ask Rumi to run all his errands for him, and if he doesn't I will. She keeps looking at the empty niche in the wall and walks backwards, a movement that forecloses any potential discussion amid backward glances from the assembled men, for they cannot bear to look at what they will later call her radiant face, a face flushed with the most dazzling, mystery-filled noor while she is looking at them.

She comes home and hugs Mummy and Papa.

At night, they meet at their old haunt, the balcony, and try to talk about the future. They are both a bit stunned at the relative ease with which their families have agreed to the wedding but they do not speak of it, telling themselves that talking about it too much may attract the evil eye.

'The present is the future, Roohi,' Faiz says, turning towards the river. 'We will just take each day as it comes. I want to promise the world and more to you. I want to devote my life to you, build a house for us in a village, but I cannot.'

'Faizā, what's happened to you? Are you saying our lives are separate? I'm with you even when you aren't with me. Don't you understand that, you fool?'

'Don't call me a fool. I'm respected in the world. Look at this.'

Roohi looks at the sleek MP5 submachine-gun Faiz has taken out from inside his sports jacket. It is a short, compact metal and plastic piece, with a short barrel, thick stock and almost no butt. It does not say Heckler & Koch on it as it is a replica made by a small private arms manufacturer operating out of the basement of a garment exporter in Korangi, Karachi. 'Can I touch it?'

'You may.'

'It's so heavy, Faizā! How do you . . . ?'

'I did spend some time abroad, if you remember, madam?'

'But this doesn't look like a Kalashnikov?'

'That's because it isn't one, Roohi. Everyone has seen a Kalashnikov, so I thought, why not show you something different? This is an MP5. Do you know what that means?'

'I'm listening, Commander Faiz.'

'Machine Pistol Model Five, do you understand?'

'Yes, sir.'

'And I'm no commander, Roohi – I'm not sure I want to be one. You see, everyone wants to be a commander, and I think that's not right.'

'What do you want to be, then?'

'Your husband.'

'You're making me blush, mister, stop it.' Roohi turns away in mock embarrassment to hide her face. Her heart slows down.

'I'm sorry. I want to remain a fighter, and when this is over, I'll go back to my art. In fact, I haven't really left it. I sometimes think of my painting even when I'm in action, even when I'm . . . I'll tell you about it later, when we have more time. I must go.'

'Don't be sorry. Just stay a little longer. I hardly see you, Faizå. I understand everything and I'm with you, but it's still hard.'

'I know. I'm sorry.'

'Why? Why are you sorry? I'm proud of you, don't you get it?'

'Because . . . Forget it.'

'Yes, forget it and go. There is a patrol in half an hour. Better leave now rather than run later.'

'I'm used to running. Let me stay for five more minutes. I hardly see you.'

'Okay, you can stay a little longer.'

A Quiet Affair

Mir Zafar Ali and Mouj come to the Khan house on an auspicious Friday, a date he has chosen carefully after looking up the latest edition of the Islamic almanac from Lucknow. Kabir Ahmed Khan and his wife wait until they're inside the house to greet them. On the vast floor cloth of the sitting room lies a feast. Mummy and Roohi, known as superb cooks in the extended family, have made all their favourites, apart from the kebabs and meatballs, both red and white, which they've bought from Shaal Wazas, the sixth-generation family of chefs who have cooked for hundreds of weddings and funerals. Roohi comes in to wash their hands, bent with the enormous weight of the tall copper flask and bowl, but Mir Zafar refuses.

Faiz's mother has never been inside a Sunni home and is amazed that it is exactly like any other, like her own, in fact. Mir Zafar cannot stop saying thank you to Roohi's mummy and papa for agreeing to marry their daughter to his brother. He does not realize that, like him, they had no choice.

As he looks at Roohi, resplendent in her moment of happiness, he thinks of the time he saw her first, when she had appeared frightened. Now, finding himself seated here, in her house, in the presence of her father and mother, he thinks a part of him perhaps knew even then, at that moment in the sunlight by his door, that it was destined to be, that even in that fleeting moment, he knew there was no other fate than this. She had, he thinks, conveyed her truest desire even as she had merely come to ask for news of Faiz. A sense of inviolate piety about her had conveyed to him that she was special. Now he understands it and, in doing so, he also feels shades of guilt cross his heart, for he remembers – how can he forget? – that he had calmly stamped on the idea of his own daughter being in love with, let alone married to, a Sunni boy. The unspoken tyranny of the provider. Never before, however, has he felt self-loathing as now, its edge made sharp by the happy moment he has come here to make possible. He also wonders – as Roohi's mother burns a pinch of rue to ward off the evil eye – whether he is doing this, making sure the union of Roohi and Faiz is sealed, to assuage some of his own guilt. But he cannot be sure since this is so real and urgent, and, he thinks, even if that were the case, on balance it is better to do this than have another pair added to the wake of broken hearts strewn all around him.

'You are blessed and God will bless you with everlasting peace and happiness. Those who care not to break hearts will never have their own hearts broken.' He raises his hands a bit, the lifeless hand in a glove, and mutters a prayer in Roohi's sitting room. Her father, not in the habit of offering personal prayers every day, and suddenly reminded by the glove of the Zaal, sits in silence in the presence of the silver-bearded man in front of him.

Everything is agreed rather quickly. Both parties soon learn it is to be the simplest of weddings. Neither Kabir Khan nor Mir Zafar want to invite too much notice; besides, these are hardly the times to have an extravagant celebration, although, in spite of everything – the daily killings, the rapes that are only whispered about, the arson and the plunder that hardly moves anyone any more for there is too much of it everywhere, the incarceration of thousands, the flight of the innocents, the murder and decay of this once magnificent city and, most of all, the frightened withdrawal of many from their own lives and the stunned faces of a grief-stricken people – some still host extravagant feasts amid curfews and funerals.

Roohi will go quietly to the Mir House as a bride. She will not wear all the gold jewellery, the necklaces, the tiered bangles and traditional earrings her mother has spent a lifetime collecting. She will put on the simplest of the three necklaces and the teeka she adores, its sun-like pendant on her forehead.

She will spend a few days with Faiz, then return home until Faiz knows where he is to be in the near future.

Then she will wait for him once more.

There will be two clerics, one Sunni, one Shia, at the nikah. 'I could read the rows myself, if you allow it,' Mir Zafar offers, but Kabir Ahmed Khan says, 'No, we must have proper moulvis, sir, witnesses, you never know in these times.' Mir Zafar quietly admires Khan Saëb's practical wisdom and attributes it to his superior education: an MCom, to his own FA.

'It will be just the immediate family who will come to your house,' says Zafar Saëb.

'We will have only my sisters here,' says Roohi's mother.

'Not many people should know the date,' says Khan Saëb.

'Agreed, I understand. The times are too tense, aren't they?' says Mir Zafar. 'I understand. Did you hear that, Mouji?'

'We don't want anything from you.'

'We don't want anything from you.'

'You have taken a brave leap, Khan Saëb.' Mir Zafar feels he must be unambiguous in his appreciation of Roohi's father. Somewhere in a narrow, deep, dark corner of his heart, he feels that guilt again, and some envy for the man.

'Sir, you should be a proud father – I mean elder brother, too, sorry. Your brother has dedicated himself to two great causes now.'

'I will pray he lives to serve both well.' When he arrives home, Mir Zafar regrets saying that.

The Meadow

It is quieter than anywhere else Roohi has seen. There are flowers everywhere, in front of the hut, in the pots on the veranda, some sprouting from its thatched roof as well, and many, many more, on the long slope that goes down to the stream, visible only as a silver rope. She takes out her ink-black silk salwar-kameez and admires it in the sunlight pouring in from the windows.

He covers the small pit in the kitchenette with a flowerpot, then removes it to check how quickly he can take out the pistol from the shallow crater. He is certain he will not need it, but rules are rules. He remembers his chat with Engineer. 'Look, it's a sentimental and terrible idea, this honeymoon of yours. No one is happy about it. But since you insist, you must carry a little something on you. The rule is simple: first, you try to run, save yourself. If that doesn't look possible, then you take down some of them with you. I would've insisted you have the big piece with you but we don't want to scare the bride. Terrible idea. One should never trust an artist.'

'You are just jealous, ha-ha.'

'Well, she is something, isn't she, your Roohi?'

'Yes, she is. Now stop – what if you have an evil eye?'

'Even if it was true, it won't harm her. I'm your friend.'

'Yes, you are. Thanks for doing this.'

'Remember to get off the bus before you see the big mountain. In fact, you should get off in the town centre. Then walk to the hut. Here are the keys. Please make sure you bring them back. Ask Roohi to remind you.'

'I will, sir.'

'The chief asked when you will give us a treat.'

'Oh, yes, I must invite you all for dinner once I'm back.'

'So that the entire group is arrested while eating some meat and rice? Don't be silly. He was only joking – he doesn't eat anywhere, says it's not right that people feel they must make an effort, spend money, to make special meals for us. I agree with him.'

'As if he would really come. Anyhow, you must come soon. One last thing . . . Please don't tell everyone I've gone on a honeymoon.'

Roohi straightens the few wrinkles in the shirt by spreading it on the bed and running her palm over it. Slowly and quietly, the evening is creeping up on them, as the shadow of the mountain across the ravine begins to cross to this side. Tonight, and at least for tomorrow's lunch, they won't have to cook, as she's packed enough rice and lamb prepared in yogurt. Oh, he's left the tiffin box on the balcony. 'Faiz – Faizå, why did you leave our food outside in the sun? Are you trying to heat it up?'

'What? Where is it?'

'Where you left it.'

'Sorry, I forgot about it, Mrs Mir.'

'Listen, mister, I'm not changing my name, in case you have any such ideas. I've known a girl named Roohi all my life. Don't think she'll become someone else because she loves you or because she has come to live in your house.'

'I was only joking, madam. Does it really matter?'

'It does to me. But forget it. I still love you.'

'Okay, Roohi Madam. I love you too. Where is our food? I'm beginning to feel hungry. You?'

'I can eat a bit early too, but first you have to find it.'

'I saw a few dogs earlier, Roohi. They were the size of lions. Let's pray they haven't walked off with our dinner.'

'Just the honeymoon I wanted! Who needs dinner in this place? Just look around you.'

'Yes, it's too, too beautiful, and so quiet. Okay, we don't have to eat, we can just lie in bed and watch the night get dark.'

'Oh, Faizå, Faizå, what am I to do with you? I was joking actually. It is, of course, all gorgeous but I still want to eat. Find me the tiffin!'

'Okay, okay. Here it is. I was joking about the dogs.' Faiz enters with the tiffin, which smells of roghan josh, and puts his arms around her, locking her in. She uses all her strength to turn, to touch his face and look at him closely. Outside, the mountain descends on the vast ravine with all its darkness, over the rope-like river in the depths below, then rising abruptly to cover the steep meadow that flattens into corn and walnut orchards in this part of the valley. As the shadow spreads over the lawn in front of the hut, Roohi and Faiz sit quietly on the floor, eating their first meal together. A half-moon appears from behind the mountain, and spreads a lucid cool light over their solitary dwelling. He brings in the kettle from the kitchenette to wash her hands. She says, no, no, what are you doing? He says I want to. He is standing up, pouring a thin jet of water from the flask; she keeps her hand still, relishing the flow of water over it, aware of his gaze upon her. His mind leaps into a workshop from the past where he is thinking of the Khayyám painting and its meaning. He touches her hair. Inevitably then, his thoughts turn to *Falaknuma*, and he thinks of painting this scene, the hut in the wild with the half-moon above. He considers her curls from above, their wayward drape over her ears and shoulders, revealing only slivers of her flesh.

Roohi changes into her black silk salwar-kameez. Faiz opens all the windows of the room. The soft light from the moon takes a while to spread in the room.

'You look like an angel.'

'Oh, do I?'

The clear air and light of the meadow, so unlike the city, so free of dust and the world's ways, Roohi thinks, is best for people in love. He is so free here, she so carefree. She picks overripe tomatoes from the flower beds in the lawn and presses them to check if they are good. She also presses one to her cheek. They feel firm, meaty, although she doesn't like the rugged skins of some. The bag Mouj insisted they carry with them contains onions, potatoes and red beans. Tomatoes and onions will make the beans tastier, she decides. Faiz, unschooled in the art of cooking, and ashamed that he can't be of much help, will rinse the dishes, clean the floor and wash the few dirty clothes down in the stream.

'I think this is where we should live. Think about it, how wonderful would it be? We don't have to go home. I mean, where is it written that we must live in the city? Just look around you. Isn't it a small Heaven, Faizå? It's like Pari Mahal without the soldiers and the smelly sandbag dens. And it's still home, nicer, more beautiful, without the whole neighbourhood knowing what we will eat for dinner today.'

'Yes, it is, but a Heaven with no shops. I will run out of cigarettes soon. I understand what you're saying. I like it here, too, lying on the grass with you, with no one to see us, no one to answer to, but we have to buy things, eat, run this place. And I have more serious duties, madam. You've probably forgotten.'

'No. I haven't. Please. My blood boils, too, and you know I want to do something too, but Mummy wouldn't be able to handle it. You seem so desperate to go back.'

'Not desperate, but I must. My friend is planning a major operation and wants me to be part of it. There is a new military camp in Lolab. We want to lay siege to it. A siege for a siege. He is the best. Oh, he said the posters and press releases read much better now, thanks to you. "Professional" was the word he used, so don't think you aren't doing your bit.'

'Don't patronize me, Faizå!'

'Sorry, but I wasn't.'

For these hours, as Roohi sees morning turn to noon and then to a still evening, they are mostly together, as though joined at the hip. He begins to understand what it means to be truly blissful. He watches her every step, every droop of the eyes, every gaze into the distance. A part of her wants to keep him here. A part of him wants to take her far away. She remembers Parveen Shakir and sings:

> Hame chahiye thha milna
> Kissi ahd-e-mehrbaan mein
> Kissi khwaab ke yaqeen mein
> Kissi aur aasman par
> Kissi aur sarzameen mein
> Hame chahiye thha milna
>
> We ought to have met
> In another, kinder time
> In pursuit of attainable dreams
> Below a different sky
> Upon a different earth
> We ought to have met there

'But we have each other,' Faiz says.

'Yes, we do . . . we do.'

At night, they go down to the river and find its water much colder than they had anticipated. Roohi wants to take a dip with him but the current is too fast. Faiz settles for a quick splash. Then they sit under a boulder and watch the foam dance over the stones of the riverbed. On the other side, the mountain is vast and unyielding. Roohi sees lights twinkle high on its slopes and imagines living there, in that house, in that cottage, tent . . . We will be forest people. Faiz turns to look up in the other direction, to gauge how far down they are from their hut. As he spots the blurry amber of the lamp he had left on and begins to trace the shape of the hut, he knows, at that instant, that Roohi is right. He looks at her, his heart broken.

Tomorrow will be their last night at Little Pari Mahal, Roohi's name for the hut in memory of her favourite haunt overlooking the

Dal Lake, the real Pari Mahal, barricaded and visitor-less now, except for the uniformed ones, before they head back to the city, to a life of uncertainty and waiting, a life of everyday dislocation, but a life together nonetheless, as wife and husband. 'We have each other.' She repeats Faiz's words.

As night falls they look at themselves in the mirror, each trying to commit to memory this picture of them. Faiz looks at her. My wife, he tells himself, then says it aloud once more.

She remembers his downcast appearance by the tree last year. 'My husband,' she says once and rests her head on his chest.

In the City

'You just need to convey our message to him, nothing else. Ask him to come out, meet us for ten, fifteen minutes, and then he can go home. What do you say?'

'I will say the same thing again. He has nothing to do with anything and we are wasting our time.'

'All right, let us waste fifteen minutes of our time. Just do it.'

'What if he doesn't agree? He's my father! I can't force him to meet you.'

'Tell him the DC's secretary wants to see him. He'll come.'

'The DC's secretary? How did you know?'

'I know everything. Remember what I told you once. We have little birds everywhere. We call them sparrows.'

'So what do I tell Papa?'

'I just told you, Rumi! Tell him you saw the DC's secretary and he wanted to know if Khan Saëb could meet him outside. At the back of the shrine should be fine. Isn't it near your house? Yes, yes, say that.'

'And what will you ask him? Don't you already know everything? I gave you all his papers. You have seen for yourself it was just some old report on the population in Downtown.'

'Yes, I and the others have seen all the papers. Now just do as we say. Enough.'

'Okay, I will. But I'll be somewhere around. He's my father, not yours.'

'Listen, we only want to ask him a few questions – there's no need for drama. You can make tea for him while he's out.'

'Panther Saëb, he's my father – please.'

'I was joking, son, don't worry. I'll tell the boss you have been very helpful, all right? We may have a few big sticks to distribute. I can't promise but I'll make sure you're on the list.'

'Oh, thanks, sir, thank you, thank you. When do I have to do this – I mean, tell Papa? Why can't the secretary come to our home? I'm just wondering.'

'I have to explain everything to kids, these days. It's because your father will come out to meet the DC's man. He wouldn't come for me, not even you maybe, ha-ha. Leave it to me. Do it on Thursday.'

Rumi is relieved he doesn't have to do anything today. Thursday is two days away and he can think through everything before then. He would give anything to have his sister at home but she's away with the man she's married; if it was up to him he would never have agreed to it. Even though he finds nothing particularly objection-able about Faiz, the fact that he is Shia, he thinks, means complications for his family, for himself, so why get into it? If she were here, at home, he would tell her everything he's been hearing, what he's been told to do, and ask her what she would do in a situation such as this. Did she really have to marry him?

On his mother's insistence, and on receipt of a hefty bribe of a thousand rupees so he could buy new clothes and sports shoes, he had done everything that was expected of him as the bride's younger brother at the wedding. He was the one who chaperoned her from her room to the side room next to the drawing room downstairs where all the women sat. Roohi, her friend Zaitun from across the bridge, Mummy, Mouj, Naseem Aunty, Farhat, Shahida, Feroza and the aloof, possibly sneering and disapproving younger aunt. In that order. Mir Zafar's son Shabbir had refused to have anything to do with what he called a Shia-Sunni tamasha, so he hadn't come, but Rumi didn't know this. He held Roohi's hand. He put the extra bol-ster behind her so that her hair didn't touch the wall and pick up flakes of paint, a prospect that might have made her furious on her wedding day. He put food on her plate and then went to the men's

293

gathering in the drawing room, shaking hands with Mir Zafar Ali, Faiz and his own father, who, he thought, looked ridiculous in a high Karakul cap. He even washed their hands, carrying the heavy copper flask full of water from person to person. Khaalu, Naseem Aunty's husband, had patted him on the back and said, 'Someone's become a big boy now, heh, well done, Rumi. Now go and bring in the food.'

After serving the men, he'd gone back to the women and cut a kebab and rista for Roohi, so her freshly hennaed hands would not smell of, or be stained by, the fearsome fat-infused wazwan. Through all of this, he felt sorry for his parents, as their dreams of a big feast, cooked by a large team of chefs at home, couldn't be realized. After all this, he was almost moved to tears when Roohi fed him a piece from the meatball he had cut for her.

As they bade a tearful farewell to Roohi during the Friday prayer time, as most people would be in mosques – Khan Saèb had insisted they should leave at this hour – Rumi quietly hugged her, then Faiz, but only after his mother had poked him in the back. He did not shed any tears. He held the hem of her long red embroidered shar-ara so that it didn't gather dust or get crumpled under her feet as she walked to the car, in which she sat next to the groom, fully hooded under her dupatta as is the custom in these weddings. He had even joked with his mother about the pointlessness of the car as the bride and groom could easily have walked to Faiz's house, to which his mother said, 'So you know where they live? What is their house like?'

'Of course. I checked everything, long before Papa had even said yes to them. The house is huge. Old but grand. And they don't have a telephone.'

'A good brother, you are, then,' she had said, pulling him towards her.

Now Roohi is gone. In a way, Faiz has taken her from him, from them. Rumi scratches his head. If Faiz hadn't existed she would still be here. And he could talk to her, whether he should do as Panther says or just ignore it, even perhaps leave the group, since all they seem to be doing these days is worrying about his father. Go and hit a bunker somewhere! 'Why are they after good old retired Papa?' he would have said, in utter frustration, to Roohi.

'Take me to this Panther chap,' she would have said, 'so I can teach him a few things. Who does he think he is? Has he even seen the border? Has he ever seen a soldier?' Or she might say he should go back and ask this make-believe commander for a detailed explanation as to what exactly he wanted from Papa, and he, Moulvi Panther, should provide clear and convincing reasons why they should do as he says. 'If not,' she would have said, 'he should just shut up and never bother my little brother again.' Trust her to say that. And if Panther didn't behave well, she would have no option but to report him to a proper militant, a freedom-fighter, just returned from Pakistan, or Afghanistan, who knows? At this thought, Rumi feels slightly uncomfortable.

Farewell

At the school, without students for months now, Major Sumit Kumar watches as two of his men dismantle the shelves in the laboratory storeroom and his bedroom. They pull down the beakers, the test-tubes, funnels, flasks, piping, iodine bottles, femurs, a ribcage, crania, and Kumar's old foe, now covered in a shroud, the falcon-like Bell microscope. A heap grows near his feet, booty from his little war with memory. He moves away. 'Put these in the gables. They won't be needed anytime soon.'

He has put on quite a bit of weight, and is glad that no one from HQ has come to inspect the camp or him. His trousers feel tight and his shirt struggles to keep in the bulge at his front. His love handles are beginning to feel like cushions.

'Sir, Principal Madam is here. She wants to see you but I asked her to wait downstairs. Shall I bring her to you, sir?'

'Why did you make her wait? When did she come? Don't you know who she is?'

'Sir, you asked us not to allow her anywhere near you without permission.'

'I did? Okay, okay, now go and get her.'

'So, how are you, Sir Sumit?'

'Oh, Shanta Ma'am, please don't call me that.'

'Why not? You are an officer and the boss here, are you not?'

'Not sir or boss or anything like that for you, ma'am. For you, I am the same as I was on the first day. I will never treat you differently.'

'How kind of you.'

'Not at all, not at all, ma'am. What can I do for you?'

'Nothing.'

'Let me do something, you must let me know if there is anything.'

'There is nothing, really. I didn't come to ask for anything. How can I?'

'Of course you can. Anything for you –'

'Forget it, Sumit, you won't understand. I just came to say goodbye. I came to see the place for the last time. I have seen enough now.'

'Oh? Why? Where are you going? Please stay. After all, it's your –'

'There is nothing for me here now. I couldn't even see all the classrooms. There are men everywhere. Someone was changing in the little girls' washroom. He saw me from the window as I approached. He took off his vest as he looked out. I turned back. It's my fault, I shouldn't have come. Sometimes I forget the school is not here any more. Can you understand that?'

'No, ma'am, I can't. The school is very much here.'

'Do you sometimes just pretend to be naïve?'

'What?'

'How can you say these things with a straight face? The school is very much here! Is it?'

'Shanta Ma'am, you see, this is the difference between you and me. I am not sentimental about my work.'

'And your work and mine are the same?'

'You are being sentimental again.'

'I have no will or energy to argue, Sumit. You are an army officer, you will no doubt have a better understanding of this place, us, the world, me.'

'You're not being sarcastic, are you?'

'Not at all.'

'Shanta Ma'am, please don't mind my saying this, but I have noticed you seem to think you are the only one with problems. Everyone has problems. You think I'm living a life of luxury here?'

'Well, you're the boss.'

'Again, I'm no boss. What boss? Boss of what?'

'You are head of the camp, are you not?'

'Enough, Shanta Jee. Do you have any idea where we are, what we're dealing with?'

'You mean you, not we. I know exactly where I am. My school.'

'And you think I enjoy living in this hole? I'll tell you what you think. You think the school not running for a few months is tragic and you're suffering because of it. You think you're the only one who has suffered. Let me tell you, ma'am, I don't like staying here either, in *your* school. Damn it, I can't even go for a stroll in Zainė Kadal to buy underwear without half a battalion with me in the shop. They all know what colour underwear Sir prefers . . . Do you know? I like rivers, water, a lot, but I can't even look at the Jhelum. I have to go in a patrol boat if I want to be on the river, that too at night.'

'That is sad. Everyone should have the freedom to go on the river.'

'You feel sad for your little girls because they have left the school, but I ask you, who told them not to come here? There is nothing wrong here. We go about our work, you and your girls could easily have gone ahead with yours. Did I ever ask you to shut the school? Did I?'

'Do you have any idea where you are, Sumit?'

'Yes, I know very well. Please don't lecture me about my job. I know exactly where I am.'

'In my school.'

'Yes, and I don't like it. Do you know? Sometimes I wonder why I am here, among these people. Who are they anyway? They mean nothing to me and I'm sure I mean nothing to them.'

'No, they hate you and please don't expect me to explain why.'

'I hate them too. I hate them for doing this to me, for being the reason I'm here, in this . . . garrison in the middle of the city. I hate these people for not having done anything to me. I hate them for being who they are. Sometimes I want to punish them for it. And some day I may, I will. I am here because of them. I hate them for that.'

'And you were accusing me of being sentimental.'

'It's the truth. I don't know these people, they are not my people, not part of who I am, not part of my story.'

'Sumit, I just came to say goodbye. I'm sure you will get to go home soon.'

'I feel I live in a cell where I receive instructions from my master. Which way to lie down, where to piss and how to walk. You, of course, have no idea, weighed down as you are by a temporary interruption in your classes.'

'Interruption in my classes. Well said.'

'Yes, what else is it? A temporary thing. I told you in the beginning that it's just a matter of time.'

'That was a year ago.'

'So what? That is how these things work. When I came here, I'd thought it'd be over in a few weeks. That once they saw a few hundred army trucks they'd scamper away like rats. Do you have any idea what I have to deal with? Attacks on my men, my bunkers, rockets flying past the roof or piercing a window, men with Kalashnikovs slinking through the shitty narrow lanes, hundreds of thousands of these people marching through the city – what is wrong with them? Can't they see our men with machine-guns in front of them?'

'Sumit, I really have to –'

'Wait, wait, there's more. And there are boys coming in droves with arms from Pakistan. Can you believe that? Boys from this city – did you know that? Boys from this area – my area!'

'Your area. You're right.'

'Of course it's my area. It's my grid, ma'am.'

'You're right.'

'While you've been taxed over the provisional closure of your school, some of us have been protecting your country, ma'am. In case you haven't noticed.'

'My country, huh. Which is my country? I don't have a country. I have a home and it is here. All we have ever had is this land of ours. All I ever belonged to was this school.'

'You're just angry. You know exactly what I'm talking about. You are not one of these people. They are not your people.'

'And you think you are my people?'

'I think so. You say all this in spite of what has happened, what happened to your father. Huh.'

'You don't know what I feel, Sumit. And please don't even try to imagine. You won't be able to.'

'Then you're a hypocrite.'

'Sumit! Don't forget who you're talking to. My name is Shanta Madan Koul. I am the principal of this school and you're sitting in my chair.'

'I'm sorry, ma'am, I shouldn't have raised my voice. Can I smoke, please?'

'Go ahead. What does it matter now? It's five o'clock. Soon it will be curfew time.'

'There is no curfew for Shanta Ma'am. I will have a full convoy take you home.'

'No. Thanks.'

'Okay. Listen, what would you say if I told you our own men, our countrymen, are part of the . . . let's just call it the "border trade"? Yes, that would be an appropriate term.'

'What are you talking about?'

'Some time ago, a posse of senior militants crossed over from Pakistan. Many commanders, who had been there for more than a year, some for two years, crossed back without a hitch. Not a scratch on any of them. Guess how?'

'I'm terrible at guesswork, Sumit. Please hurry up.'

'Our own men, our officers, took a big bribe and let them pass. Simple. And here I am, living this . . . life . . . every day. That is what I'm talking about!'

'I'm not very surprised. As you said, these things happen in such times.'

'It's evil, ma'am, evil.'

'Yes, corruption is evil.'

'And guess what? A local boy also crossed over. Nice lad, I've been told. A papier-mâché artist, apparently. Don't know what he'll do with a gun. Idiot. And the daredevil stayed at home, just nearby, near the Namchabal waterway. I decided to let him be, not disturb his sleep while I stare into the darkness of your storeroom. The fool is apparently involved with a local girl. Let them play *Laila Majnu* for now, I said. He may prove useful later, but I'll deal with him at some point. With all of them!'

'I didn't ask you to use my store as your bedroom.'

'I know.'

'I must go now, Sumit. I don't think I'll come again. So goodbye and try to get back to your mother in one piece.'

'Oh, I will. I'm not dying in this mad place.'

'Spare the Laila, please. Also her Majnu, if you can.'

'Not up to me, ma'am, not up to me. As long as the signal doesn't arrive, he'll be safe.'

'What?'

'Nothing.'

Shanta is annoyed at herself for having argued with an army man. These days, she finds home her most loved companion. Even during Daadjee's last rites, she had wanted to rush home and lock herself inside to touch his things, books. She does not feel unsafe, or afraid of being alone. All she wants to do is stay in the house, inhabit every inch of the space her father has touched or breathed in, and live an indoor life.

Briefly, she contemplates seeking out her old student Roohi Khan of Khanqah and telling her what she heard from the man in charge of the army camp, which was her, their, school. She weighs it a few times, trying to come up with the right words in her mind, then lets it be. Is she frightened of what Sumit Kumar may do if he hears of it, or is she apprehensive about what the papier-mâché-artist turned militant might think of her? We do not know. What we do know is that she thinks it's futile either way. The army will do what it wants to do, and she has no power to stop it.

It is late night now and she retires to her father's armchair, patting its arms slowly as she sits down to read his journals from forty years ago. Transported briefly to a past full of hope and activity, as she is every night, she tells herself she will stay in, refuse to leave, go out only when absolutely essential, retire officially from her job and her life. In a rare moment of self-pity, she wonders if her lot now is reduced to visiting the small mausoleum of her father by the river in the upper city, and the grave of the only man she ever loved in the Martyrs' Graveyard in Downtown. But she knows, she tells herself, that there is more, there will be more, and she will wait as long as it takes. Until then, she decides, she will stay put.

The Last Evening

'If I continue to stay behind the vases, without anyone knowing, how will word get out? Think about it. It won't. Only Mouj, my sisters and you know I'm there. Imagine, if it stays like that, no one will ever know.'

'But that's not possible. It's not realistic. How can people in your home not know that someone is living upstairs? Won't they hear you? Won't you go to the bathroom? Will no one ever notice people taking food upstairs? Will no one ever go into that room?'

'Mother and Farhat will take care of that, and when you start living with us, you'll make sure too.'

'And do you intend to stay in there all the time? What about your group, your friend, your chief? What about them? What about your duties? Isn't that what you said yesterday? It's not a vocation, Faiz, it's a dream you're fighting for, isn't it?'

'I will do everything, Roohi. I haven't forgotten anything. Fatima, what they did to Abba, what they're doing to my city. I'm not running away from it or hiding. I just want to stay near you. You know, this life is not an easy one, I have learnt. Neither to live nor to understand. Some days, I feel as if I have passed into another world. When you carry a weapon, that is what happens to you, you begin to inhabit another world, a real one, Roohi, a very real one, where things are both unbelievable and believable. I think about what's happened since last year and I find it unbelievable. Then I look at myself, feel the pistol at my waist, and think it's all absolutely normal. Do you understand?'

'I was just asking, wondering aloud about the basics, Faizå. Let's say you're part of an operation and you have to run. Where will you go – home? And have a horde of soldiers sitting in your kitchen in no time? I can't believe I'm thinking about all this!'

'I'm sorry.'

'No, that's not what I mean. You have to think of practical things, Faizá.'

'Staying at home is not as impractical as people may think. I will go out with the boys at night. I can ask Engineer to talk to the chief for me . . .'

'Let's just stay here. I feel scared, actually scared. Can't they transfer you to this area? Why not talk to your friend? You say he's resourceful and influential and whatnot, can't he do that for you?'

'It's not like a government job.'

'People are assigned different areas from time to time. Even I know that. Why can't you be an area commander here?'

'There is no area here, just the jungle and the river. And this hut – oh, I can't keep secrets from you – is meant for seniors when they want to lie low, you know what I mean? We cannot stay here permanently.'

'Oh, it's all right for the seniors. Certainly more precious than you and me. But that doesn't mean we can't live in the area. I did see a couple of villages on the way. Please, Faizá. It's so quiet here. And there are no soldiers here. Do you know how heart-stopping it is when I pass soldiers in the street? Do you know the kind of things they say to me, or to any woman?'

'No.'

'Terrible, terrible, unspeakable things. So vile I want the earth to open up and swallow them. But here there is none of that. No soldiers.'

'They will come here too. Soon they'll be everywhere. It's just a matter of time.'

'Are you sure about this?'

'We have no choice. We have to go back.'

Roohi falls silent, curling a thick strand of her hair around her index finger, curling and uncurling it, thinking of a hundred possible lives and worlds, some of which include children, *their* children, three being the number that most appeals to her. A girl, a boy and another little one later will be perfect. Other lives have her write a book, teach, travel around her country. She wakes up.

'It is like Heaven here, Faiz,' Roohi says, as she sees the light go dim, the evening suddenly filling with dark ink.

The Secretary

Thursday seems endless. Rumi has remembered every moment of it since dawn.

Papa is whistling in the kitchen, and from time to time he commands Mummy to pass the cloves of garlic, cardamoms, cinnamon, and to chop the ginger finely. 'I don't like ginger toffees in the meat, as you know,' he says. Mummy puts up with the tuneless whistling and the pointless instructions because it means she gets a break from kitchen work, and the food he cooks is actually quite good. He insists on using fresh spices and whole condiments, not the 'packed plastic powders these modern people use'.

In any case, Mummy has more important things on her mind. Her daughter is to return home today after four days away, during which there was neither word from her nor, as was agreed, did any of the Khans visit the Mir House to check on her. Khan Saéb and Zafar Saéb had, without even mentioning it to the women, let alone consulting them, decided there would be no visits between the families initially, certainly not until they know of Faiz's situation and most definitely not until people have forgotten about the Sunni girl marrying a Shia boy. The two men, we must note briefly, have been wrong in this, in their disregard of the mohalla, of their age-old neighbours, their respective communities and, most of all, the elders. While there have been some shrill detractors on both sides, Roohi and Faiz's successful love story, a phrase used by Raajé, the failed lover and street poet, has gained something of a folk status, a word-of-mouth fame among the youth of the area, and is now beginning to spread in the wider city. While the elders, clerics and other arbiters on how to conduct the business of life and love do not openly champion such marriages, most people have fallen in love

306

with the true story of the poet girl and the artist-turned-militant boy defying the odds to be with each other, although in reality they haven't had a lot of defying to do. The stars just lined up favourably for them.

It is the bride's homecoming today, and Khan Saëb is cooking because Roohi must be on her way. 'She likes my meat better than yours,' he had announced at breakfast.

'Your meat smells of tobacco and smoke,' Mummy says now, as she watches her husband.

'No one appreciates my jokes in this house, except my daughter. The food I cook smells of a father's love for his children.'

'Yes, Mummy does not exist.'

'You are the soul of this home, Mrs Khan, the very soul. Now pass me seven stamens of saffron. Make sure you count them.'

'Here, just throw in a pinch from the pack – they're crushed anyway, I can't find *seven* stamens here.'

'Seven is a number dear to Allah. Come on, count them and give them to me. It's for your own dear daughter, remember?' He starts whistling again, at which Mummy turns up the volume on the kitchen radio, which at this hour broadcasts an adult-education programme for farmers.

Rumi's ears are tuned into the conversation. He is horizontal in the drawing room, door ajar, his feet resting on bolsters he has placed in the middle of the room. He must tell Papa soon after they have had lunch, as they must get back home before Roohi comes. He has missed her but has not said a word about it. Except for this small unwelcome task, he wants all days to be like this one, his parents happy, reliving some of their youth in the kitchen, and an air of eager anticipation in the house for the return of his precious sister. There are moments when he can't believe that Roohi not only convinced everyone that she would marry for love but that she would marry a Shia. It has occurred to him to wonder whether the Mirs would agree if he, when he's bigger, were to ask for Farhat's hand.

But she didn't look at him once on the wedding day. He sighs. I washed her hands, for God's sake, and even then she kept her eyes down.

'Rumyå – Rumyå! Let's eat. Come to the kitchen – that's where we are.'

'As if you need to tell me,' he mutters, and gets up, looking at the spot where Faiz had sat on the wedding day.

'Papa, are you going somewhere after lunch?'

'I was thinking I might make a tour of my kingdom, why?'

'Ha-ha-ha . . . Would your highness like a cavalcade behind him or would he prefer to see his subjects in secret?'

'In secret, prince, always in secret. Sit down and eat now. Why are you standing like a leafless poplar?'

Rumi eats in silence, working out what he will say to his father.

Papa is silent too, considering and reconsidering the secretary's words. 'They somehow know you prepared the report for us. Are you absolutely certain no one saw your papers?'

'Yes. They're in a safe place at home,' he had said.

'Just be careful about who you meet. Leave the rest to us.'

When they finish, Rumi waits for his father to have his cigarette. 'Papa, I think I saw the DC's secretary earlier. Isn't he very thin, with no hair at all? He asked if you can meet him behind the shrine at four. I asked him who he was and he said, "Tell your father it's the secretary."'

'Why didn't you ask him to come over, Rumi? He's an important man. He's the one who got me the part-time job, remember?'

'Yes, I do, but I don't know him. He just said, "Ask your father to come out at four and wait by the ghat."'

'Oh, okay, but I met him the week before last, didn't I? Anyhow, let's see.'

'Maybe he has more work for you. Maybe we can buy a motorbike for me then – even a second-hand Hero Honda would do.'

'You and your sister, always wanting things. You more than her. I hope she's fine over there. I hope she has everything. The man doesn't do anything, you see, but there was nothing I could – forget it, Allahta'ala will sort out everything, and it's what your crazy sister wanted.'

'Your crazy daughter . . . She could have waited, Papa.'

His father is taken by surprise and cannot really understand what his son means but he chooses not to talk about it further. Thoughts of the future, what might become of his beloved girl should her husband be arrested, or even . . . give him a queasy stomach. 'I'm going to lie down for a little while. Wake me up around a quarter to four if you find me sleeping. Not that I have to go far, but I'd like to wash my face and change before meeting him. Go now.'

Rumi goes up to his own room to lie down. He is relieved that it was easy to carry out Panther's instructions and now thinks he shouldn't have made such a fuss. It's only a meeting, after all, with a man Papa knows – and it's hardly surprising Panther knows about him. They know everything.

The DC's secretary is a slim wiry man, one of those people who would probably slip unnoticed wherever they went if they didn't smoke all the time. He is seated by the platform behind the shrine, under the tree that rises from the ghat below and which shelters the small ancient tree temple – the faithful believe it was Goddess Kali's seat in the distant past. He is also the kind of man who smokes his cigarettes by holding it in his fist. The cigarette dangles between the little and ring fingers as he drags through the funnel formed by his other clenched fingers and thumb. This smoking style is not in fashion now and only the old diehards continue with it.

As Kabir Khan approaches with a smile, he decides to smoke in the same way. The platform is cool at this time of day – even the families of pigeons appear drowsy. The baker in the narrow lane outside, not far from the side door, is busy churning out hundreds of sesame buns from his wood-burning oven. The smoke from his chimney is beginning to spread here, filling the old graveyard first, then collecting slowly under the roof of Roohi and Faiz's balcony.

'Salam alaikum, Secretary Saéb, how come you remembered this poor soul today?'

'I was missing you.'

'What?'

'The boss's instructions, Khan, a few small clarifications, that's all. Come, sit.'

'Lend me a cigarette, I left mine at home.'

As Roohi's father attempts to copy the secretary's style, testing if the funnel he has made with his hand is tight enough not to let any smoke escape through the fingers, the secretary lights another for himself, taking a massive drag as though kissing a hookah. He watches Kabir Ahmed Khan smoke, and then quietly, without a breath, takes out a silenced pistol and shoots him in the chest twice, then once more, as though making a point. Then the Intelligence Bureau agent takes away Khan's cigarette and puts it out.

Roohi insists on going inside the shrine. 'You stay in the graveyard. No one will see you behind the grass. I will go in and come out in a minute.'

They arrived in the city in a packed minibus at five thirty and slipped into the shrine compound by the side entrance. A group of crows has maintained an hour-long vigil around Khan Saéb, as Roohi enters the main hall from the front door. She sees them from the high window between the mihrab and the reliquary. Those creatures are faithful, always here, she thinks, and leaves. She slips back into the graveyard, where Faiz is smoking, reclining in the grass, his back resting against a tombstone.

'I must go now. Papa and Mummy must have waited all day. I'll see you tomorrow, at your home, and please, for God's sake, for my sake, think carefully about staying at home. If you don't, I'll find that friend of yours and ask him to sort you out.'

'Okay, madam, as you say. Now go – it's getting dark.'

'Ha-ha, I'm not afraid of the dark. I'm afraid of you, what you will do with us.'

'Come here.'

Roohi lies with him for two minutes, leaning her head against his on the tombstone. She leaves.

Faiz

Faiz smokes another cigarette after Roohi leaves, trying hard to make a decision, to shake himself out of a peculiar lethargy that has afflicted him since leaving the hut. He must make a decision. Roohi is right. It's not safe to stay in the house. He looks at the river, which has swelled recently. The ice on the mountain peaks he saw during his time in the south of the valley, as he and Engineer moved from operation to operation, from one location to another, must have melted, he thinks. The water, more green than brown, moves quickly as though eager to fill the world around it.

At the back of the shrine, where a tree looms darkly in the evenings, he sees a man bent over something, shaking. Slowly, feeling the pistol tied firmly with a string to the inside of his waistband, he walks towards the man and waits for him to straighten. He sees another man, the shadow of a man, lying on the platform. The bent man is perhaps trying to wake an old relative fallen asleep in the evening shade. But he must remain watchful, he tells himself. You never know. He changes tack then, deciding to walk past as if he were just passing, and in the process check what the man is trying to do. As he moves closer, Faiz pulls furiously on his cigarette and blows smoke towards the two men. The standing man turns, slowly, as if unable to move his head, and looks at Faiz.

'Rumi! Oh, Rumi, it's you – I didn't know you came here too. What are you doing? What's the matter? Who is he . . . ?'

'Papa – Papa . . . He's –' Rumi breaks down like a little boy, shudders and hugs Faiz.

'What happened, Rumi? Tell me! For the sake of Allahta'ala, tell

312

me. Is he sick? Why is he like this? Why is he here?' Rumi wouldn't let go of Faiz.

'I don't know – I don't know. He just came to meet – You check him. Please, check my father. Please – check Papa . . .'

Faiz sits down by Khan Saéb's legs and smells something cold and familiar. He taps on his father-in-law's knees. 'Khan Saéb, it's me, Faiz. Let's go home. It's getting dark.' There is no answer. A few pigeons from the balcony try to get closer. Faiz shoos them away, strikes a match and holds it to Khan Saéb's face. Then he looks down again and sees three tears in his clothes and the congealed dark pool around his still form. He stands up immediately. 'What happened, Rumi? What happened? Tell me!' Rumi keeps staring at his father. 'Go home now and get all your neighbours. Don't tell Roohi and Mummy. Remember, don't tell Roohi and Mummy . . .'

'I can't. I can't stand up. He's my father – he's my papa. He'd only come out to meet someone. I asked him to – he'd told me it's just a . . .'

Faiz runs, leaps, hurdling over the steps that go up to the main gates, and slows down only when he's outside on the main road. He looks at Roohi's window and prays to God to give her strength, to protect her, to keep her safe, to keep her with him. He looks back once, wishing it had been some kind of vision, a dark thought, some trick played on him by Rumi and his father, then runs his thumbs over his knuckles, rubbing them over and over. *Ho Khodaya, who did this? Why?* Then he is at the door, face to face with Mummy and Roohi.

'You didn't go home? Come in, we're waiting for Papa and Rumi. Papa had gone to meet someone. I don't know why it's taken him so long. Mummy sent Rumi to look for him. This is the second time Papa's done it. I'll have a word with him when he gets back.'

Faiz's chin trembles with the effort he's making to stay calm. He can't bear to look at Roohi's still-happy face. He sees Mummy studying his face and rushes into the house.

'So you couldn't stay away from me, not even for an hour?'

'Roohi . . . Mummy . . . Something has happened to Papa. We need to go. He's with Rumi at the shrine. I'll come with you.'

Roohi begins to say something but stops. Mummy stands up and leans on the wall, her hand on the doorframe, the other making sure her dupatta is fully draped over her head. Roohi holds Faiz's hand as she stands up. 'Is he hurt?' she whispers in his ear.

'Yes, he is.'

'How – how bad is it?'

'Can I drink some water quickly?' Before they can say anything, he runs to the kitchen and drinks straight from the tap, trying to form the words he will say to Roohi.

The Officer

The message, as always, is brief and clear. Kumar knows that nothing more, no addendum, no amendment, will arrive. He reads it again, trying different tones, changing emphases each time. It's a game he has played often to amuse himself but today he knows there will be no delay. He must leave immediately and make it quite clear, known, in the camp, lest the people he suspects are informing on him report him to the signal man, whose two-line missive he remembers by heart now.

'Developing situation in your area. A team must rush to the shrine and evacuate if necessary. Comply with immediate effect.'

He looks at the roghan josh and kebab dinner that Rahim Razor now insists on bringing nearly every day, and his face lights up with an idea. Rahim is local, a veteran. Why not check with him first, get a sense from him of what is happening at the damn shrine? What is it with these people? In fact, he could come along – yes, he must. He cuts a piece from the still-hot kebab and rings the bell for his assistant. The man appears in no time, like an apparition. 'Call Rahim, tell him Sir wants to see him immediately. Don't let him make any excuses. Go now.'

Razor has arrived by the time Kumar has eaten half his dinner and stands outside the open door with folded hands.

'So what is this we are hearing? Some trouble at the shrine?'

'Sir, it's nothing. People of the area are angry at Kabir Khan's killing and they're protesting. It's understandable, sir. He was a good, much-admired gentleman. I knew him once.'

'Who is this man, Rahim?'

'He was a government officer, sir, honest to the core, did something for the local administration that got him into trouble, sir.'

'Rahim, do I have to keep asking questions for you to tell me everything? We do look after you well, don't we?'

'Sir, do you remember the night-time raids? Kabir Khan was the man who gave you – I mean us – all the information. He didn't know what it was meant for. He thought it was a new census of the area.'

'And why didn't you tell me this before?'

'Sir, you never asked. I didn't think you'd be interested in such a small thing.'

'Next time, you'll let me decide when a matter is small or large, is that understood?'

'Sorry, sir. Sir, I think some people at the top were concerned Khan might reveal what he had been asked to do, and you know how it is. So he needed to be taken care of, sir, without getting the . . . er . . . uniforms involved.'

'What do you mean?'

'Sir, forgive me, but you don't need to worry about it, sir. I have learnt that a local boy, one of ours, a man named Panther, whom yours truly convinced to join, was asked to help to prove his loyalty and he did. Nothing to worry about, sir, it's all taken care of. People will be angry, of course, they'll protest for a few days, then forget about it. Your food must be getting cold, sir. Shall I get it heated up again?'

'No, it's all right. So, what now?'

Razor shuffles his Karakul hat, pulling it down a notch. 'Nothing, sir. They'll get tired of screaming and shouting and go home. Until the next time . . .'

'I have to go there and you'll come with me.'

'But, sir –'

'No buts, you'll be in my jeep.'

'Sir, I cannot be seen with you, you know that.'

'Yes, I know. You can stay in the jeep. It's dark in any case.'

'Sir, please forgive me, but we don't need to be there. Let the people vent their anger – let them cry at the shrine all night. What is it to you – I mean us?'

'You've become an important man, have you?'

'I'm sorry, sir, it was just a humble suggestion. I'm nobody, sir.'

'We're leaving in five minutes.'

'But, sir, I haven't told anyone at home –'

'Comply with immediate effect.'

The Window

Roohi has her arms locked around Papa. No one wants to disturb her, and if anyone begins to approach, Mummy, a picture of stunned silent grief, raises her hand high. People are filling the space between the back of the shrine and the ghat. It is the hour of the evening when the light is about to die, when people, looking at each other, recognize a face only with the aid of memory. The river is quiet. A small group of people on the opposite bank is looking at those on this side, in curiosity, in solidarity, in fear. Faiz is at the centre of the crowd, willing himself to stay where he is. Some people watch him. This is the place where he had once marvelled at the verses from the Qur'ān etched in white on the arch of the door. Breaking his fixed gaze on Roohi, he turns to look at the verses and finds them faint at this hour but he can still just about make out the swerve of the letters. He longs to throw away all caution, against the strict advice of Majeed and Showket, and run over to Roohi, hold her, touch her, tell her he will always be by her side, he will take care of everything. He will never leave.

Mummy watches him, too, with a look that seems to say, 'See what happened to us.' Even she knows that only Faiz can pull Roohi away from her father's body, which must be done soon, as he needs the last bath so he can be on his final journey. The dead should not be made to wait, it is an affront to God – Mummy remembers her father saying this at the time of a death in the family decades ago.

At the front of the shrine, on the two stone platforms and in the paths between them, a group of young men and women shout his name, reminding her at each moment that she's lost him for ever. Every one of them knows that the slain man was Roohi's father and Faiz's father-in-law; every one of them knows he was a good man;

and every one of them by now knows who killed him. All of Faiz's friends are here; so are Roohi's. Some young men who might once have dreamt of being with Roohi have also come, a few still nursing a cinder of unrequited love. Regulars at the shrine encircle the core of the protesters, as though to form a defensive ring. Khan Saéb's friends, Nabbé Galdar the grocer, Ali Clay the butcher and Bashir the milkman are here too, in the ring, shaken from their separate memories of the deceased, and from fearful contemplation of the future, by the thunder of the slogans. Occasionally, they echo the chants. But soon they go back to be near their friend and his daughter.

Women, Mummy's neighbourhood friends, Roohi's friends and acquaintances, mothers and sisters of the disappeared boys from Faiz's neighbourhood, recent widows, stand on a separate platform, the one with Faiz's chinar at the centre, and start a chant of their own. The men go mute briefly, then join in. Mummy, choking from the effort she is making to remain strong behind her children, comes to the front briefly but is brought to tears again on seeing the circles of love around her and her daughter.

As she moves near to Faiz, one woman's chant from the front pierces the creeping night. 'Whose blood is this?'

It inspires a thousand resounding answers. 'Mine. Mine. Mine.'

Hands, fists, fingers rise into the sky. Voices rising into the dark sound as though they are reaching for God, calls for mercy from the heavens. Such is the force of this grief that the few policemen have no choice but to watch quietly from outside, through the gaps in the fencing, away from the main gates. As the faithful finish their prayers in the adjacent mosque, many find it impossible not to go into the shrine. The caretaker of the mosque, Akbar Shah, walks obediently behind the recently released Mahraazé who, as the two men had prostrated in prayer, in sajdé, had whispered in the for-mer's ear, 'I will go and console the princess and bless her father's soul. You, my child, will follow. Allah-u-Akbar.'

As they enter the shrine, Mahraazé waits for Akbar to catch up with him. 'Khan Saėb gave me money often. He always said, "Don't tell anyone." Come now, let's see him . . . Let's see the noble man. Hindustan killed him, do you know?'

'You don't know that, Mahraazė, you don't know that.'

'You are a fool, Akbar the Great. I always know. Hindustan killed this man, those before him and after him too. And that other mad place, Pakistan, killed the rest. You should know, Akbar Saessyå, you came here with armies once, didn't you?'

'What are you talking about? And I'm not a cissy or a cuckold, I don't even have a wife, crazy man!'

'There are souls roving in the river. I see them at night. They are restless, angry souls, did you know?'

'No. Now stop it. Is this the time?'

'Because you have forgotten them, Akbara! You people just want your meat and rice. Come on now, read a prayer for those in the river first. Now!'

Akbar raises his hands and reads the fateha for the unknown dead, whose souls, according to his friend, are in the river a few feet from Kabir Khan's quiet face. Then they proceed to the back of the shrine, piercing through the increasingly dense throng, and stop only when they see Roohi trying to tidy her father's hair with her fingers. Faiz walks closer to Mahraazė and nods at him.

'Hello, Mr Mujahid, so you got your father-in-law killed, after all, huh?'

'Sssh . . . Don't say that. Do not say that. He is, was, like a father to me. What are you talking about?'

'Good answer. I was just testing you. You did not get him killed. I know who did.'

'Sssh. This is not the time, Pir Saėb, just not the time. Can you do something for me?'

'Order, sir, order away.'

'You know my wife over there?'

'Who doesn't know Princess Roohi, hero, the bravest woman in the world? I have known her from when she was a little girl

320

with – what do you call it? – a ponytail and green ribbons, then long, snake-like plaits when she was older. I have seen all her looks.'

'Yes, yes, you have. Now listen to me, Mahraazė Saėb. You need to go to her and gently ask her to move away, to come to me, no, to Mummy, actually. Tell her it's time for him to go.'

A pull, a gravitational force has descended, forcing people to leave their homes and head for the shrine. Everyone knows where everyone else is going. Mouj, having heard her son is back – and that he's at the shrine, near Roohi's slain father – puts on her burqa and soon arrives at the gates. She beholds a swaying and rising crowd through the latticed diamonds of her dark-blue veil. As she goes down the steps, people instantly make way for her. It is not every day, after all, that they see the *grande dame* of the Mirs in public. As if following the trail of her son's smell, she heads straight to the back, stopping only to embrace Roohi's mother, and quietly stands next to him. He grabs her hand.

People keep pouring in, keen to pay their last respects. Someone turns on all the lights of the shrine so that it resembles the festive zool of Urs days when every room, every balcony, every window burnt brightly. A memorial mood pervades. Faiz's friends Majeed and Showket manage to squeeze past a thousand shoulders and stand behind him, watchful. The families and friends, beginning to become somewhat impatient with Roohi's vigil over her father, whisper to each other. The whispers form a string, and it is soon agreed that she will not be allowed to stay like this any longer. It is not Islamic. It is not safe. It is not right. It is dangerous for the people who have gathered. She must think of those who came to see her father.

Some whispers are right. These days you can't assemble as you did in the old days, as free people. The soldiers don't like it. A collective, whether in celebration or grief, is often the scene of a bloodbath now, and almost always blamed on the victims in the end. A night curfew has been in place for nearly two years. People are expected to be dead at night, to rise again only when the curfew ends. But people have defied curfews before. In moments of anger, in moments of unbearable grief, or when it simply doesn't matter whether you live or not.

Some people start pouring in on boats from the other bank, bearing torches, water and cigarettes. Since there is no room for them in the compound, they stay on the ghat, forming a third, riverside, tier of protesters or of those simply gathered to bear witness to the last rites of Kabir Khan of Khanqah. A relay forms, taking water and cigarettes to anyone who asks for one or both. The men and women on the steps of the ghat begin their own slow chants, as if pleading with the river to grant them liberty. They seek freedom. The groups of people on the opposite bank answer their chants. The fisherwoman, her husband and children, having sailed upstream, appear on their little deck, looking towards the shrine and the people on the steps. They don't know that Faiz is among them.

As light falls on Papa, Roohi sees his wounds clearly for the first time. She lets out a scream, just one, a howl of pain. Mahraazĕ starts towards her.

'He is already in Heaven, princess, trust me, I know. Do you see the river down there? I know people whose souls roam in it, but your father has gone straight to Heaven, don't worry. But we must bid him farewell, wash him, dress him in clean clothes. He is going back to his creator after all. So, let us take him now.'

Roohi turns towards him with eyes that flash fire but she doesn't say a word.

'This way, we are making him suffer. How about this? I will give him his last bath myself. What do you say? Time to go, my child, time to go and let him be on his way. I swear upon my Mighty Friend up there that I will take good care of him. I will say a special prayer for him, that's Mahraazĕ's promise.'

'Will you comb his hair? Do you know which side he parts it?'

'I know. I will do it.'

322

Faiz, unable to restrain himself any longer, leaps forward. He reaches out and places his hand on Roohi's back. She lets a few tears drop on her father's head.

'Roohi, we need to take Papa home so that Mummy can see him properly. She's been standing here for a long time. Besides, it's night now and you know –'

'Yes, it is night. It is night.'

'Mahraazė Saėb, what do you say? Shall we lift him?'

'No. We will take him properly. Ho, Akbar Padshah, where are you? Ask someone to get the bathing plank from the mosque. We will carry him on it and I will wash him over there. Then you can take him home. We will take him to the graveyard from there. Which is your graveyard?'

'We don't have one. I mean, I don't know . . .' Roohi mumbles, and breaks down for the first time since seeing her father.

Faiz goes to Mummy. 'Pir Saėb wants to know which is your – I mean, our – graveyard?'

'We don't have one. My father-in-law was buried in Malkhah, but that was many years ago. I don't think Roohi's papa . . . had designated a graveyard for himself yet. He didn't think . . .'

'It's all right, Mummy, it's all right. We can bury him right here, in this small graveyard. Would you mind that?'

'No. He can rest well here and I can see him every day.'

'I'll tell the committee people that I've decided to bury him here. I'm sure they're here somewhere.'

Roohi, up at last, her father's wallet and pocket comb in her hands, leans on her mother. She gives the wallet to her but keeps the comb, asking for permission with a bare nod. Mummy holds her tight, biting a length of her dupatta as she continues to look for Rumi. She decides once again not to tell Roohi or Faiz, or anyone else, that she hasn't seen her son for a while now. Roohi and Faiz have been looking as well, but they, too, decide not to tell anyone.

Roohi's eyes search for Faiz and, since she can't see him, she begins to panic. 'Where has he gone now? Where has Faiz gone, Mummy?'

'Oh, he had to talk to the people from the committee. We were thinking of burying Papa here.'

'Yes.'

Faiz and his friends come back with three middle-aged men, who sit by Khan Saeb's body to say their fateha.

'Why didn't you say so earlier? We would be finished by now,' the oldest of the group says to Mummy.

'We didn't know. What happened here? Who killed him? Do you know?' Mummy knows the man from her many years of Friday visits to the shrine.

'We were inside all evening, sister. Anyhow, we will need a few men to clear a space in the graveyard. You see, it hasn't been used in decades. Don't worry about grave-diggers – the mosque has its own and you deal with them directly.' He addresses this to Faiz.

'Yes. I'll take care of everything.'

Roohi and Faiz stand on either side of Mummy as she watches the committee men cover her husband with a large green blanket and transfer him to a palanquin-like wooden stretcher meant for bathing the deceased. It's grand, old, like a low four-poster bed. An instant quiet ensues near them, as people scamper to be among the first to lend their shoulder to the dead man. The slogans from the front rise and rise. The women sing a song of martyrdom and freedom. The men follow. The moon has stalled over the spire of the shrine, whose gold and bronze are aglow in the soft silver light.

There is a fever, a buzz, in the air, which makes anyone walking into this theatre of mourning tense.

Mir Zafar Ali arrives, carrying a black flagpole, draped with the banner his brother had painted in silver letters when he was sixteen. Since it is the first day of Muharram, a group of people from his Shia area is behind it. He simply had to do what he does every year and carry the first banner of Muharram himself, before passing the duty to others in the lead-up to the apogee of Muharram, the tenth day, when both Shias and Sunnis will commemorate the martyrdom of Imam Hussain at the battle of Karbala thirteen centuries ago. Shias will sing elegies, beat their chests and flagellate themselves with knives, and Sunnis will offer a more sober tribute with special prayers and sermons. They will also erect marquees on the streets, offering water, juice and fruit for the thirsty Shia mourners.

People inside the shrine area, as indeed those outside the gates, see a silver-bearded man approach with a tall black flag but soon recognize who and what this is. They part to make way for Faiz's brother as he solemnly marches on and parks himself on the last step on the stairs, raising the banner high in a declaration of intent, which some interpret as solidarity with his younger brother's wife in her moment of loss, and others as defiance that Muharram will go on no matter what. Some simply see it as a symbol of his anger at the killing of his relative. Only the few old men present are reminded of Mir Zafar Ali's Al-Fatah days when he and his friends, including Haqqani Saéb of Khanyar and the three sons of Hakeem Usman of Rainawari, had launched an underground freedom movement in the late sixties. He does not proceed any further, preferring to sit amid the large crowd at the front of the shrine where the main congregation is.

While some have joined in the protest because they felt the pull of it, for a feeling of community and togetherness, many know exactly what it might lead to. For them each moment is fraught. Some worry for their children, some for their brothers, some for their husbands and fathers. Some even for their homes. Yet they stay, in anger and in defiance of the soldiers.

As Mir Zafar Ali's stark flag rises from time to time, so do the cries of the protesters. When throats and arms begin to sag, Akbar Shah moves around with a large samovar of tea from his own little kitchen. While this spirited crowd are rising up, the rest of the city sleeps, as decreed by the strict curfew that has been the destiny of its dwellers for many months now. Zafar's group begins a sombre rendition of a Muharram elegy, encouraging their Sunni peers to join in, who, not knowing the words, first do so slowly and hesitantly but soon with force and passion, if not with full comprehension. People weep in age-old grief for the slain of Karbala but also in private grief for a missing or imprisoned brother, for a dead husband or father, in memory of a teenage son buried too soon at Eidgah.

When Kabir Khan's palanquin moves past the two platforms, Mir Zafar Ali paces through the crowd, putting a hand on a shoulder, accepting a quiet salam from an acquaintance. The palanquin bearers move slowly, as though under instructions to allow everyone a last glimpse of Khan Saéb who is now headed home after the bath at the mosque.

Some people swear he looked alive and fresh as the pallbearers approached the steps leading out of the shrine. Others report that a certain noor had descended on him and the whole scene was radiant. Some others suggest it was all too intense for anyone to notice anything, apart from the ghostlike appearance of his daughter, who walked behind her father with her mujahid husband and pale mother.

The slogans, the mourning songs and the crying grow as the slain Khan and his family approach. All those gathered are united in their unambiguous vision of a mohalla, a city, a country free of the soldiers from the plains. They sing and sing. The women around Faiz's chinar tree in particular sing farewell ballads. The men on the platform next to them match them with a crescendo of their own.

Major Sumit Kumar arrives with soldiers and quietly positions them by the gates. Rahim Razor advises him not to go inside – 'Just mark your presence here, sir.' Kumar listens to his local guide and informer, gets out of his military jeep, and climbs on top of the Zaal, asking one of his lieutenants to move aside and handling the LMG himself. Some people outside the gates scamper away, frightened instantly at the sight of the Zaal. Now it has a big gun attached to the top, they gasp. Some resist, in spite of the fear that has cast a pall all around. People inside the compound shout and scream even more, calling on each other to burn the thing. 'It's the devil himself,' someone says.

Kumar's lieutenant, a seven-foot man known in the area as Rathi, looms large with a megaphone. 'Go to your homes, vacate the shrine. We come in peace. You must evacuate the shrine.'

Mir Zafar Ali grabs Faiz's hand and takes him towards the main door of the building. 'Leave now, for the sake of God, for the sake of Roohi, for the sake of your old mother, for my sake.' Roohi comes running towards them, her mother in tremulous pursuit. 'He cannot go out at the front,' Mir Zafar says, to Roohi and Mummy.

'Yes, you must leave us now, son. Go, God will be with you. He loved you, you know.'

Faiz feels a peculiar freeze. Roohi feels a deep pain in her chest and a premonition that all is lost now. She clasps Faiz's hand and drags him towards the side lane that goes to the back, then turns left towards the exit that opens onto the short-cut they had used earlier. Mir Zafar and Mummy watch as the two vanish into the darkness.

On the main road, they run down towards Faiz's street but suddenly, as though a revelation has struck her, Roohi stops and peers into a narrow lane opposite the auto-rickshaw stand. Faiz knows, and soon he is leading the way, Roohi's arm in the cleft of his elbow. In five minutes of silent running, they are behind Roohi's house.

He brings her water. She drinks half from the tumbler and passes it to him. He drinks it all in one gulp and embraces her. They stay in that position until they hear someone in the house. Rumi appears at the kitchen door, a small boy with eyes the colour of blood, dirt and dried pools of blood on his clothes. He comes slowly and sits by them. 'Didi, I killed Papa. I killed him. Khoda Saéb will never forgive me.'

Roohi pulls him towards her, putting her arms around him. Faiz goes to fetch water for him. 'They must be bringing Papa home now. Let's go up, come.'

'You two go, Didi. I will wait here for Mummy and tell her everything. You go.'

Faiz sets off as soon as he hands Rumi a glass of water, and Roohi follows him. As they go up the stairs, Roohi says, 'What's he talking about?'

'Nothing. I'll tell you later. Majeed and Showket have told me everything. It's not Rumi's fault – he's a child.'

They are in her room. She takes off her dupatta and drapes a green stole around her head. He looks at her. Slowly, hesitantly, she opens the window and pulls apart the curtains, wide enough for them both to look out.

Sumit Kumar is seated on top of his vehicle, smoking, as the megaphone continues to warn the still-animate crowd inside the compound. People outside the gates, fearing for their lives, have left. Every time the megaphone man shouts, the protesters answer with a roar.

'Go back, go back! This is our shrine, this is our home.'

'Go back, go back, go back.'

Mir Zafar Ali, his dead hand in his pocket, is at the front of the protesters, raising his banner every time Kumar's man threatens action.

For a fraction of a second, Faiz thinks his brother might get shot, but then he throws off the thought with a shake of the head. Roohi looks at him, her chest in agony, and puts her head on his shoulder. 'Don't ever leave, Faizã, never.'

'I'm not going anywhere – never.'

Still an immense sense of foreboding won't leave her. Her father is waiting to come home, he has been out all day and still they won't let him come home, she thinks. Oh, Khodaya, let him come home now. My mother will die, too. Is that what you want?

'I'm scared, Faizå. Hold me.'

Suddenly, Faiz's brother is climbing the stairs, the pallbearers behind him, finding their feet on the steps. Oh, God, don't let him down, she thinks, don't abandon my father, Abba.

The megaphone booms again. Kumar throws away his cigarette. 'I have been patient for too long. These people must be taught a lesson, what do they take us for?' he says to Razor, who is seated inside the belly of the Zaal, safe and cosy, peering out at his people from behind a narrow tinted window. He looks up at Kumar but says nothing.

Kumar looks once more at the surging crowd and puts a hand on the safety of the machine-gun. Then he stops and nods at Rathi.

'Evacuate now and everyone can go home. There is a curfew in place. You must follow orders.'

Roohi and Faiz lean closer to discern what is happening at the gates. Their faces touch, cheek to cheek, their breath mingles. Faiz remembers an evening from last year. Roohi knows what he's thinking.

Mir Zafar Ali addresses his slow procession: 'I will go and talk to their officer. All we want is to be allowed to take Khan Saéb home with dignity. Do I have your permission?'

'Yes! Yes!' Hundreds of voices rise from the crowd.

As he slowly walks up with Mahraazė, Akbar, Kabir Khan's friends, and Mummy and Mouj at the back, to loud chants of freedom from the crowd, Kumar unlocks the safety and lets the LMG swivel on its tripod.

The chants resound with that one-word song, 'Azadi', over and over again.

Faiz stands up in the window, slowly chanting with the crowd. Roohi gets up too, singing, and crying, 'Khodaya, deliver us from this Hell.'

*

The megaphone voice is drowned out and can no longer be heard. Kumar grabs the trigger, then stops, looking through the fencing at the people inside. Mummy spots her daughter and son-in-law at the window and feels somewhat reassured. She looks down quickly so that no one will follow the direction of her gaze.

Roohi rests her head on his shoulder. He feels her hair on his cheek.

Kumar first raises the machine-gun skyward, etching a glistening arc with its steel in the moonlight as he rotates it. He has decided he will fire a few warning shots into the sky at first. And he turns away from the crowd, the shrine, towards the roofs of the houses opposite. He pulls the trigger just as he sees two shadows standing in a window a few hundred feet away.

The shadows shift, shake for a moment, but do not separate.

Acknowledgements

Musadiq Sanwal, who brought music and colour into our lives. I miss you every day.

My editor, Mary Mount, is the reason *The Collaborator* and *The Book of Gold Leaves* exist. Thank you, Mary.

Beatrice Monti and the Santa Maddalena Foundation, where I wrote the first section of the novel in 2011. There isn't a better sanctuary for a writer in distress. Thanks also to Arts Council England and Bill Swainson for help with the Fellowship.

Parvaiz Bukhari for his wisdom, many kindnesses and his friendship. The trip down the Jhelum wouldn't have been the same if he hadn't been on the boat.

Chiki Sarkar is a great champion of the kind of books I want to write.

Aijaz Hussain for his learning and for answering odd questions at odd times.

Suvir Kaul for his generosity and erudition.

Ambar Chatterjee for his patience and attention to detail.

David Godwin for his support over the years and the quickest email responses in the world.

Jasir Haqqani was ideal company during a couple of trips at home when I was pretending to research the novel.

Suhail Naqashbandi, who is always there. Thank you, Suhi.

Alex Starrit for being a friend in the wilderness.

Michael Jacobs, who departed too soon but left a lasting impression. He taught me how to look at art afresh. Tomaz Salamun for the delights of his poetry. The wonderful Alice Albinia for her company in the Tower.

Sanjay Kak for reading the manuscript at such a late stage and alleviating some of my neuroses.

Hazel Orme for her sharp editorial eye and making sure I do everything right.

Keith Taylor of Penguin Books for his meticulous care. Jillian Taylor for her great support.

All-weather mates Arif Shamim and Abdul Wahab Rafique.

The Authors Cricket Club of London kept me sane during the writing of this book. Badshahs of Banter, lads!

Downtown Srinagar, that place of magic and mystery, for life lessons. Akhtar Mohiuddin and Zareef Ahmad Zareef kept me company in the darkest hours. Naseem ul Haq and Waseem ul Haq for their songs.

Farooq Ahmad and Mohammad Iqbal of Verinag, where it all begins, for restoring my faith in humanity.

The Shah-e-Hamadan shrine and mosque, where this novel was born many years ago.

Mirza Mohammed Jaffer told me stories of the past when I was a child. They continue to ring true.

Mirza Fida Hussain, who went up to the attic and trusted me with a priceless family heirloom that is the cover of this book. Thank you, Abba.

Papa and Jaji for their love, understanding and being the kind of parents I hope to be one day.

My wife Mehvish for her love, intelligence and strength, and for making it possible for me to continue to write.

Above all, Shayan for giving structure to my writing life and making sure I write in the time he's away. As for the question 'What, another book, but you already have one, Daddy?', that may take a lifetime to answer.

Ehsanaat
Mirza Waheed

A

COVER

STORY

A faded photograph of my late grandfather and papier-mâché artist, Mirza Ghulam Mohammed, peers down at visitors from a glass cabinet on the wall of our family home in Kashmir. In the portrait Grandfather, or Touthh as we called him, is sitting in the workshop that used to look over the front lawn of our house. You can see a work trunk, a hookah and a clay fire-pot beside him. The pot served both as a heater for his bowls of paint and as a reservoir of embers for the hookah. I remember seeing him in that cabin throughout my childhood – he was always working and he stopped only as his eyesight dimmed a few years before his death. As he painted he lorded over everything and everyone from this perch, issuing instructions to anyone in earshot, and managing to keep an eye on us children trying to sneak out of the house. We weren't allowed to play with the 'street kids', but of course I had to – wasn't that the whole point of existence? To play with the cooler kids who were free to roam about the groves and orchards – apple, almond, pomegranate – near our house by the lake on the outskirts of Srinagar. The orchards are all gone now, replaced in less than twenty years by modern houses and shiny shops.

In the autumn of 2013, shortly after handing in the manuscript of my new novel, *The Book of Gold Leaves*, to my publisher, I had gone home to see my parents. I was in the living room and found myself looking at my grandfather's portrait, an image that encapsulates so much of my family history. That evening, over dinner I asked my father and my uncle what they remembered about *their* grandfather. After all, he was the man who taught his son everything about papier-mâché art. In those days art and craft was a family tradition, handed down from father to son . . .

I learnt that my great grandfather, Mirza Ali, was a much-admired but rather lazy artist, who did a piece or two every six months. He loved to go out in town and would be dressed to the nines, often wearing a fiercely starched white turban. A bit of a rake, it seemed, a bit of a ladies' man.

'I may have something by him,' my uncle nonchalantly remarked, 'it should be somewhere in the house. I'm not sure . . .'

The next afternoon, as I was packing up to return to my adopted home in London, my uncle appeared with a packet in his hands. It smelled of history. It felt fragile. It was some kind of a cardboard folder with faded but beautiful artwork in the centre of each panel. I held the jild (literally, 'a cover') in my hands, opened it slowly and was speechless. Inside the covers was a stunning pattern of flowers in gold and red, blue and green. The gold paint was fresh and alive over a hundred and twenty years after it had been painted – even though no effort had ever been made to preserve it. My uncle said it had retained its colours because in those days they used natural dyes and pigments which didn't fade. The details were exquisite, the effect extraordinary. My father said that back then artists and craftsmen would use brushes of just a single hair to paint the tiny, delicate images. My sisters and I looked at the shimmering piece in silence. For a moment I was upset that my uncle and father had never told us that this heirloom existed. I took many photographs of both the outside and inside covers. I amplified the high-resolution photographs to check for those single-hair strokes. And there they were. Immediately then, I emailed the photographs to my publisher in London.

During the trip back to England, I kept thinking about the rare specimen of a now-extinct genre of naqashi (papier-mâché art) that had stayed in my uncle's dusty trunk for decades, awaiting rediscovery. One of the two central characters in my novel was a papier-mâché artist, and he kept his most treasured letters in a book of the precious gold leaves which he used for his painting. A friend, upon reading my novel in manuscript, had asked whether I was trying to reflect on my family history. But I had finished the final draft of the novel, and had sort of settled on the title, before setting eyes on Mirza Ali's golden cover.

I'd been slightly doubtful about the title of my new novel at first. I had liked it but, as so often happens, I still felt slightly uncertain. When I saw my own great-grandfather's 'Book of Gold', I knew it could not be called anything else. It had created an extraordinary connection between past and present, what I had been writing about and my family's past. I brought the jild to my publisher's office in London. When she opened it and saw the painting inside, she knew she had found the cover for the book.

Over the next few months I would witness family history, art and modern publishing merge together to create the cover for *The Book of Gold Leaves*, which you now hold in your hands.

Mirza Waheed, London, October 2014

He just wanted a decent book to read ...

Not too much to ask, is it? It was in 1935 when Allen Lane, Managing Director of Bodley Head Publishers, stood on a platform at Exeter railway station looking for something good to read on his journey back to London. His choice was limited to popular magazines and poor-quality paperbacks – the same choice faced every day by the vast majority of readers, few of whom could afford hardbacks. Lane's disappointment and subsequent anger at the range of books generally available led him to found a company – and change the world.

'We believed in the existence in this country of a vast reading public for intelligent books at a low price, and staked everything on it'
Sir Allen Lane, 1902–1970, founder of Penguin Books

The quality paperback had arrived – and not just in bookshops. Lane was adamant that his Penguins should appear in chain stores and tobacconists, and should cost no more than a packet of cigarettes.

Reading habits (and cigarette prices) have changed since 1935, but Penguin still believes in publishing the best books for everybody to enjoy. We still believe that good design costs no more than bad design, and we still believe that quality books published passionately and responsibly make the world a better place.

So wherever you see the little bird – whether it's on a piece of prize-winning literary fiction or a celebrity autobiography, political tour de force or historical masterpiece, a serial-killer thriller, reference book, world classic or a piece of pure escapism – you can bet that it represents the very best that the genre has to offer.

Whatever you like to read – trust Penguin.